Ancient Secrets and
Biblical Prophecies
Lead One Man to Face
the Greatest Evil of All....
BABYLON RISING

I am more excited about *Babylon Rising* than *any* of my previous books.

My vision for *Babylon Rising* was to create a new fiction series of fast-paced action thrillers based on Biblical prophecies not covered in my Left Behind® stories.

*Babylon Rising* is set in one of the most dramatic periods of the history of the world—our present time. I have tried to make this a gripping, page-turning novel, a great big adventure filled with important revelations.

I hope you enjoy *Babylon Rising*.

# BABYLON

A DELL BOOK

# RISING

## TIM LAHAYE
### AND GREG DINALLO

BABYLON RISING
A Dell Book

PUBLISHING HISTORY
Bantam hardcover edition published October 2003
Dell mass market edition / August 2004

Published by Bantam Dell
A Division of Random House, Inc.
New York, New York

Library of Congress Catalog Card Number: 2003060842

ISBN 0-553-58606-8

Manufactured in the United States of America
Published simultaneously in Canada

OPM 10 9 8 7 6 5 4 3 2 1

# BOOKS BY TIM LAHAYE

**Tim LaHaye Prophecy Books—Nonfiction**
Are We Living in the End Times?
Charting the End Times
Charting the End Times (study guide)
End Times Controversy
Perhaps Today (90-day devotional)
Merciful God of Prophecy
Revelation Unveiled
The Rapture
These Will Not Be Left Behind
Tim LaHaye Prophecy Study Bible: NKJV & KJV
Understanding Bible Prophecy for Yourself
Understanding God's Plan for the Ages (chart)
Bible Prophecy: Quick Reference Guide (booklet)

**Tim LaHaye Fiction**
Left Behind ® (volume 1)
Tribulation Force (volume 2)
Nicolae (volume 3)
Soul Harvest (volume 4)
Apollyon (volume 5)
Assassins (volume 6)
The Indwelling (volume 7)
The Mark (volume 8)
Desecration (volume 9)
The Remnant (volume 10)
Armageddon (volume 11)
The Glorious Appearing (volume 12)

**Left Behind ®: The Kids—Youth Fiction Series
(volumes 1-40)**

**The Soul Survivor—Youth Fiction Series**
The Mind Siege Project
All the Rave
The Last Dance
Black Friday

**Additional Bestselling Books by Tim LaHaye**
Spirit-Controlled Temperament
How to Be Happy Though Married
The Act of Marriage
How to Win over Depression
Mind Siege
How to Study the Bible for Yourself

Dedicated to:

GENERAL LEW WALLACE, whose nineteenth-century classic *Ben-Hur,* subtitled *A Tale of the Christ,* taught me that fiction could be both thrilling and instructive at the same time and could appeal to both a secular and a Christian audience. With more than six million copies in print and a stage play seen by more than half a million people by the turn of the century, the book had an international audience and was made into three movies: first, for the silent screen; second, in black and white; and then in 1959, William Wyler's color classic, starring Charlton Heston, which elevated this story to one of the best-loved movies of all time.

JERRY B. JENKINS, my co-author and partner in writing the Left Behind® series, which has turned into a publishing phenomenon, who worked with me to bring to the printed page my vision of a fictional portrayal of Bible prophecy based on the book of Revelation. Together we proved that fiction with a message was still possible in the twentieth century.

GREG DINALLO, my co-author for this book, who has helped to shape my vision of a fast-paced action thriller for the twenty-first century that is based on Bible prophecies not covered in the Left Behind® books.

And to the HEBREW PROPHETS, who saw, under divine inspiration, forecasts of world events so necessary to know for those living in what they called "the time of the end," or what some modern historians call "the end of history," which could occur in the early part of the twenty-first century.

# A MESSAGE FROM TIM LAHAYE

Dear Reader:

Welcome to my new prophetic fiction series, Babylon Rising. I hope you will come to share my tremendous enthusiasm about this first novel, which bears the series name, whether you are one of the millions of readers who have read my Left Behind series (coauthored with Jerry B. Jenkins) or you are a first-time reader of my fiction writing.

I am more excited about *Babylon Rising* than any of my previous books. My prayer is that it will have the same effect on the lives of readers as have the Left Behind® books.

The fantastic popularity of the Left Behind series (54 million in print and growing) convinced me that fiction is a powerful way for me to share with readers some of what I find so completely fascinating about end times prophecies. Happily, readers were stimulated by the combination of great adventures and important revelations.

*Babylon Rising* is my newest attempt to create another uniquely satisfying combination of suspense and substance. I base this exciting story on the single most important prophecy in the Bible regarding international events, one that is having an incredible impact on our society today.

Bible prophecies and their interpretation are clear signs of what our present and future hold for this world, and they are a continuing basis for all of my writing. In the Babylon Rising series, you will find some truly fascinating and important material based on my continuing research on the prophecies of the Bible.

My hope is that you will not only find *Babylon Rising* a fascinating read, but that the series will help you understand that end times prophecy could be fulfilled in our lifetime, and that it will help you make sense of "the signs of the times" that we see being fulfilled internationally almost every time we watch events unfold on television or read a newspaper.

The setting for Left Behind, as you probably know, starts with the rapture of the church and then takes the world through the tribulation period, the millennial kingdom of Christ, and on into heaven. *Babylon Rising* starts in our present time and moves forward to the rapture, one of the most exciting periods in the history of the world.

To really make this a "grabber" of a novel, you will find *Babylon Rising* features a hero who faces many of the challenges of our day that are familiar to all of us. That hero, Michael Murphy, is one of the real appeals of this series for me. I like Murphy so much, I named him after my son-in-law. There are many wonders in our world, but many dangers as well, and I wanted to center this series on a hero who I think is very engaging yet very real, and someone who is up to the task of confronting a rising tide of danger throughout the books.

Murphy is a scholar in both archaeology and Biblical prophecy, but unlike other scholars, he is also a complete adventurer and risk-taker when he is on the trail of ancient artifacts that can help to further authenticate the truth of the Bible. Murphy is a man of action and a man of faith, a true hero for our times—which is a good thing, because as you will see right from the start of this series, Murphy will begin to confront a profound evil. An evil force he will soon discover has ensnared him in a countdown to what the Bible calls "the time of the end."

I thank you for your interest in my work. Starting with this volume, my hope is that you come to feel as I do that *Babylon Rising* is a real page-turning series that manages to be both a totally absorbing story and extremely relevant to our times.

Wishing you a great reading experience, I now give you *Babylon Rising!*

# ONE

EXACTLY THIRTY-THREE HOURS and forty-seven minutes after he had last been in church, Michael Murphy was hurtling through a terrible dark abyss. Prayer had never seemed more necessary to him than at that moment. In pitch blackness, with the only sound the *whoosh* of his body falling through the air, Murphy had no idea where he was heading.

Except down. Quickly. All six feet three inches of him.

Just a moment ago, Murphy had been standing on the rooftop of what appeared to be an abandoned warehouse on a desolate street in Raleigh, North Carolina. It was an unusual place for him to be on a Monday night during the university semester, when he normally would be preparing for his next day's lecture.

Yet it took only one word to make him drop all normal activities and race to this dank and deserted height.

Granted, that word was in Aramaic, one of the many ancient languages Michael Murphy could read with some fluency.

The Aramaic letters had been penned with elaborate style in a bright blue ink that had seeped deeply into a thick, expensive ivory-tinted paper stock that had been wrapped with great care and tied up by a translucent ribbon around a heavy stone.

A stone that came crashing through the lower window of Murphy's campus office late that afternoon.

Whoever threw the stone into his office had disappeared by the time Murphy got to the window. As he unwrapped the paper and translated the single word that appeared there, he first stared, then began to count.

Thirty seconds until his office phone rang. He knew what voice he would hear at the other end of the line, although he had never seen the face to go with that voice.

"Hello, Methuselah, you old scoundrel."

There was a high cackling laugh in answer, a sound Murphy would recognize anywhere. "Oh, Murphy, you never disappoint me. I take it I've piqued your interest."

"And cost me a replacement window." He looked down again at the single word on the paper. "Is this for real?"

"Murphy, have I ever let you down?"

"Nope. You've tried your weird best to kill me several times, but let me down, never. When and where?"

The cackling now was replaced by a tongue-clucking. "Now, don't rush me, Murphy. My rules. My time. My game. But trust me, this will be the best ever. For me, anyway."

"Then, I assume that, as before, no sane man would take you up on this challenge?"

"Only an eager lad like yourself. But as always, you have my word. You survive, you get what you came for. And trust me, you'll want to survive for this prize."

"I always want to survive, Methuselah. Unlike yourself, to me life is a precious thing."

The old man snorted. "Not so precious that you won't come sniffing like an eager dog after this bone I've just tossed you. But enough chatter. Tonight. Nine-seventeen. Be on the roof of the warehouse at Eighty-three Cutter Place in Raleigh. And take my advice, Murphy boy. If you do come, and I know you will, make the most of these last few hours."

With another cackle, the line went dead.

Murphy shook his head, put down the receiver, and picked up the paper. He double-checked his translation. This time, the name he read set his mind racing even faster than before.

For Michael Murphy, a scholar who could not confine himself to library stacks of dusty, ancient tomes, an archaeologist dedicated to hunting and rescuing artifacts that could authenticate events from the pages of the Bible, this was the name of the prophet who was guaranteed to intrigue him more than any other:

DANIEL

For the rest of the day, Murphy could think of little else besides speculating about his nighttime rendezvous with Methuselah. It had been approximately two years since Murphy had first been contacted by this eccentric figure. Each time, without warning, and without ever showing his face, Methuselah would get a message to Murphy, always a single word in an ancient language that would turn out to be the name of one of the books of the Bible.

This would be followed within a minute by cryptic directions, always to some deserted location, where Methuselah would watch from a secure hiding place and taunt him while Murphy would try to survive some very real, very deadly physical challenge.

The risk of death was very high and very real each time. Methuselah was seemingly as serious about his sadistic games as he was about the scholarship behind his finds. And apparently he had enough money not only to sponsor the acquiring of the artifacts but to indulge his wildest ideas to lure Murphy into the most elaborate death traps. Would he actually allow Murphy to die if it ever came to that? So far, each time Murphy had come extremely close to losing his life, and each time he had no doubt that Methuselah would have let him die.

Yet, despite two broken ribs, a fractured wrist, and too many scars to recall, Murphy had so far somehow managed to muster all of his considerable abilities to stay alive long enough to claim his prize.

And what prizes they had been. Three artifacts Murphy never would have seen in any other way. Each proven with laboratory tests to be genuine, yet Methuselah never uttered a word about his sources. There were lots of issues that plagued Murphy about these mad, whirlwind chases, but each time Murphy went public with the artifacts, no organization, government, or individual collector had come forward to claim they had been stolen.

So, however and from where Methuselah was getting his occasional treasures, they had proven to be just that.

Methuselah remained a complete mystery to Murphy. To say he was eccentric would not begin to explain his actions. The man was clearly a scholar of ancient artifacts, yet Murphy could find no trace of where he came from or how he found these artifacts that any archaeologist would drool for. It was especially mystifying why Methuselah did not keep these treasures for himself, or for a museum, or why he chose his really strange games to give Murphy a chance to claim them.

As a man of high integrity, Murphy believed he could overlook some potential gray areas regarding the source of these artifacts. Some wealthy, connected, but truly mad collector was as close as Murphy could come to an explanation of who Methuselah was. However, there was the troubling religious aspect.

Methuselah was clearly not a religious man. Quite the opposite. A good deal of the pleasure Methuselah seemed to get from these challenges was to taunt Murphy about his faith. So far, Murphy had been up to every challenge, and he had to admit that in addition to getting the artifacts, part of what drove him was the chance to defy Methuselah's nasty verbal insults about Murphy's faith.

Which was hardly a justification for his risking his life, Murphy realized. However, pride, temper, stubbornness were all high on the list of Michael Murphy's imperfections. Probably Murphy's greatest reservations about his Methuselah adventures were a result of his deep religious faith, which made it far more difficult to justify the extreme risk to his life and limb.

Justify the risk not merely to himself, but to his wife, Laura.

So far, his passion for the quest for artifacts had been a real test of Laura's passion for Murphy. It certainly helped his cause that she held a degree in ancient studies herself. However, there were many arguments after the fact, many pledges that he would try to resist the next Methuselah temptation, but Laura knew there would always be another insanely dangerous Methuselah trap. All he had to do was to dangle another artifact before her husband.

It was that understanding that caused Murphy to dash off a quick note to Laura before he left for Raleigh that evening. She was at a conference in Atlanta and would not be home for another night, and Murphy wrote down what little he knew about where he was going. He left the note on the mantel in their living room. Just in case.

Murphy kept a touch light on the accelerator all the way from Preston to Raleigh to make sure he did not get a speeding ticket. That was one risk he could definitely avoid for the night. The address Methuselah had barked at him was for an eight-story building on an empty street in a deserted neighborhood. When he got to the rooftop, Murphy looked for some sign for a next move.

Without warning, the very roof beneath his feet opened, and that was when he found himself dropping through the building.

Free-falling.

In the fleeting seconds after he started his descent, his multitasking mind flashed on how beautiful Laura had looked yesterday afternoon before she left for her plane, he offered up a quick prayer, and he forced himself to focus on his years of martial arts training, specifically on the best position for his body to be in when he finally landed.

Assuming he had to land eventually, it would not be pretty.

He settled on the combination he had come to call Cat's Last Gasp, his own poor interpretation of a Tibetan landing maneuver. He thought of it as the moves a cat in its ninth life would make to land safely. Murphy loosened every muscle, fighting the natural instinct to tense up in anticipation of what was bound to be one fearsome impact.

Instead, he bounced. In the pitch-black space his body hit what felt like a huge net, and Murphy bounced up and down, rapidly making him more disoriented than the falling had.

Feelings that were intensified by a blast of bright light that completely blinded Murphy.

"So good of you to drop in, Murphy."

Methuselah. Though Murphy still could not see, there was no mistaking the cackling laugh that filled the space. Murphy also knew that even if he could see clearly, Methuselah would be well hidden, as he always was.

"You're probably still getting your bearings, eh, Murphy, so you can't appreciate what a great old building this is. They built that chute to go through all the floors so they could drop things from the roof down to the main work floor here. I had my people set this up especially for you, but I took pity on you at the last minute and provided the net. I'm getting soft. Let's hope you're not."

Murphy finally stopped bouncing and rolled himself to the edge of the net. His sight was beginning to normalize, but there did not seem to be much to see inside this building. There were white walls enclosing one giant floor space. The ceiling, if there was one, must have been several stories high, but the combination of gloomy darkness and now the piercing glow from spotlights mounted on the walls made it impossible to be certain.

The netting was strung up at one end of the floor space. It was made of thick rope in a crosshatched pattern. The net had been stretched between four heavy wooden poles that were bolted to the floor and stabilized by heavy bags of what Murphy guessed was sand. At the opposite end of the vast room, what looked like a sliding door of shiny silver corrugated metal stood closed.

Surrounding the floor was a raised work area that was protected by heavy glass. That was where Methuselah must be, Murphy thought, but he could not make out any specific figure up there. His head was clearing and his breathing was starting to normalize.

"That was certainly worth the trip from home, Methuselah. Now, may I claim my prize and get back there?"

"You call that earning your keep, Murphy? That was just my special way to get you inside the tent. Get ready for the real show. Right now."

For the first time, Murphy heard an ominous sound, a low rumble that filled the empty space, but he was not sure what he was hearing. "Aaah, I see, Professor Murphy, by your perked-up ears, that you are ready to meet your match."

Murphy sighed. *So, now it really begins,* he thought. Then came a second, much more ominous sound. Something crashed against the metal door from the other side. Something that Murphy suddenly realized was about to come shooting out that metal door, heading directly for him. "Say, um, Methuselah, aren't you going to tease me first with a look at your latest artifact? So I at least know what it is that will make you try so hard to kill me."

"Yes, you do know I love to have my sport with you, Murphy. I actually wish you could live to get this one. It's hot stuff. Tell me, what made you so excited about seeing the word 'Daniel' from me today?"

Before Murphy could answer, there was another, even louder banging against the door. Murphy could not help but flinch where he stood and looked anxiously at the rattling metal.

"Up to now you've put into play some amazing artifacts from Biblical times, Methuselah. I don't know how you got them, but I never would have found them on my own. And Daniel, well, you know he was the most important prophet of all. I have studied him for years. Let me at least get a good close look at whatever Daniel artifact you've gotten your hands on."

"No. Enough talk, Murphy. You're about to get a closer look than you'll want. Because tonight you're not going to *study* Daniel, you are going to *be* Daniel."

With a metallic clang, the sliding door at the other end of the room was raised.

A full-grown lion stood roaring in the doorway. Murphy could not help but marvel at the tawny color, the tensile muscles along its flanks, its full mane, and the way the bright floodlights from the walls made the claws practically sparkle.

The lion, however, was wasting no time admiring Murphy. With a roar that echoed from every wall, and a propulsive spring of all four powerful legs, the lion bore down on Murphy as if he were an easy meal for the taking.

On pure instinct, Murphy threw himself to the floor, landing with a jarring thud just to the left of where he had been standing but close enough to smell the full hot blast of foul breath from the lion's mouth.

"Come on, Murphy, don't run. Make a fight of it, be a man."

The lion's claws braked on the wooden floor as its roaring head swept from side to side. Angry flecks of saliva pelted Murphy. After the first landed on his face, Murphy was already moving again, rolling twice and scrambling to his feet. Without stopping, he reached one of the wooden poles of the netting and swung himself back up into the net. The lion was in close pursuit and swiped its front paw within an inch of Murphy's leg.

Having missed once, the lion swung the razor claws again without resting, and again just missed. The third swipe ripped Murphy's left sleeve to shreds.

Before he could get raked again, Murphy bounced up from the net. He landed a few feet away, back on the ropes, and without stopping, he bounced up again. The lion swatted at the rope again and again, but looked frustrated and confused by this bouncing prey.

Between the wooden floor, which was slippery to its back claws, and the netting, which was tangling his front claws, the lion writhed and roared in frustration. Murphy kept bouncing as far from the lion as he could get each time because he knew that the moment the lion connected with him, even with a glancing blow, it could be his last moment on earth.

"Murphy, stop playing popcorn and come down and give the pussycat a chance to really play with you."

*I'll come down*, Murphy thought, *but not the way you're thinking*. He reached into his pocket and pulled out his army knife. He did not wish to intentionally take another creature's life, even though the beast had four paws full of blades to his one. Instead, as the lion clawed and tried to jump up toward him, Murphy stumbled to one of the poles in four bounds. There he slashed the rope holding the netting to the pole.

"Murphy, that's not fair," Methuselah screamed.

"Don't talk to me about fair, you maniac."

Murphy was bounding to the next pole. The lion swung furiously but seemed to be tiring, much like a heavyweight boxer in a middle round. Or maybe that was just wishful thinking, Murphy realized, but the lion definitely looked confused by Murphy's rapid movements.

As the second side of the netting fell away from Murphy's knife, the lion realized too late that he should have moved out from under it. Its two front paws were now hopelessly tangled in the heavy rope. Murphy slid more than jumped to the floor, careful to stay out of range of the lion's claws.

Or so he thought, until an intense pain seared his left shoulder when a back claw struck him as it jerked free from the ropes. Murphy forced himself to run toward one of the two remaining ropes holding the netting, able to run faster on the floor. Best case, he had maybe another ten seconds before the lion pulled himself free of the ropes that had already fallen around him.

The pain in his shoulder told him he would have to lift himself back up with only his right arm, and he was grateful for the hundreds of pull-ups he forced himself to do in the gym each week. He raised himself up and swung around, then bounced again to grab the pole and slashed the third thong just as the lion was twisting away from the heap of ropes it had torn away from its body.

Now with this new batch of netting entrapping him, the lion momentarily collapsed on the floor. It roared through ragged, heaving breaths, still trying to slash free with its claws. Murphy rolled to the floor but made sure to stay completely out of the range of the lion.

"Aw, Murphy, you spoiled everything." Methuselah was fairly sputtering. "But you got fight in you, boy. For a useless Bible teacher, you got moxie, I'll give you that."

Murphy was breathing almost as rapidly as the lion. He managed to gasp, "How about giving me my artifact instead?"

"Well, you earned it, I guess. Only it's not going to be what you think."

Murphy straightened and looked up at the platform. "What are you trying to pull here, Methuselah?"

"Shut up and listen. It's right there in front of you. You just have to grab it."

"Grab what? Where?" Murphy was getting a bad feeling.

"Oh, your body's still prime, Murphy, but I swear all those digs have turned your brain to dust. Look at the lion's neck." Sure enough, Murphy noticed for the first time that there was a thin leather strip tied around the lion's neck. Attached to the strip was a red tube approximately the size and shape of a very large cigar holder.

"Oh, no, Methuselah. You think I'm going to fight this lion again just to get at that thing around his neck? That's too crazy even by your standards." Murphy paused, sensing his opportunity slipping away. "Besides, what's in the tube?"

Methuselah started his cackling laugh again. "Oh, Murphy, I've put the fever in you good tonight. You can't resist. I know you too well. You'll go back at him; you can't stop yourself. And this time ... heh-heh-heh, your curiosity's going to get the cat to kill *you* for sure."

Murphy looked at the knife in his hand and was tempted, but he folded it back and pocketed it.

"Ooh, ever the good Boy Scout, Murphy. Going to make it a fair fight."

Murphy shook his head as he walked over to the pole nearest the downed lion. "No, Methuselah, not exactly fair, but I can live with it. I'd never kill that lion any more than I'd kill you tonight, and Lord knows you've given me more pause for thought than he has. But that won't stop me from taking advantage of him when I get the chance."

He picked up the heavy bag that was weighting down the nearest pole. He needed both arms to hoist it, but his bleeding shoulder made him shout with pain, and he almost dropped the bag on his foot. Instead, he dragged the bag over to where the lion was still tearing at the rope netting that hopelessly tangled his paws.

"This is definitely going to hurt you more than it hurts me," Murphy grunted, and he dropped the heavy bag right on the lion's head. The lion dropped in an unconscious heap.

Murphy watched the stilled beast take several shallow breaths before he reached slowly for the leather cord that held the red tube to its neck. He held his own breath and yanked the tube free of the lion's mane.

He grasped his prize. It was so light, he feared it was empty. "What gives here, Methuselah? This better be something besides a cigar."

At first, Methuselah did not say anything in response. Then the metal door rolled up. "You won, Murphy, now get out. Enjoy your spoils of this war on your own time. However, I will tell you these three things, because a warrior in victory does deserve some respect. First, like I told you, this one is hot, really hot."

"Hot as in stolen?"

"Never mind how I got it. Like the others I've given

you, there's no angry owner going to come hunting you. But there is somebody who will want to come after you once they know you have it. I don't know who they are or why they're so interested, but I cover my tracks very well, as you know, and I've picked up several hints that somebody is desperate to get this, and will stop at nothing—and I mean nothing—to get it."

"But get what? What's in here?"

"That's the second thing. The tube doesn't have the artifact. The tube has the key to finding the artifact. And what the key is and what the artifact is you'll have to figure out for yourself. But I think you're maybe one of a handful of people alive who can figure it out. And I also know that if you do figure it out, it will get you the find of your life. If you live."

"But Daniel, it's got something to do with Daniel?" Murphy was getting exasperated now.

"That's number three, and then that's all I'll say. The connection's not going to be obvious to you, but I swear to you, I'm certain it's the real thing, and it will make you the reigning king of your precious Bible circle. I guarantee it. Now get out."

"Come on, Methuselah, you can't leave me hanging like this. What is it?"

"Can and will, Murphy. Get out. I'm a sore loser and you know it."

Wincing with one last painful look over his wounded shoulder at the lion, Murphy walked toward the door, clutching the tube tightly. "Good-bye, then, you crazy coot. And thank you, I guess."

Just before Murphy was through the doorway, Methuselah growled, "Murphy, don't get overconfident with your Bible-boy heroics. I'm telling you to be careful with this one. If somebody's going to kill you, I want it to be me in one of our little contests."

Murphy looked up at the platform. "Ever the sentimentalist, Methuselah. Thanks for the warning, but so far, the way I'm scoring, it's Christians one, lions zero."

# TWO

THE SCREAM PIERCED the Babylonian night like the howl of a great beast in mortal pain. It rang through the stone corridors and could be heard even beyond the palace walls, in the moonlit market square, in the mazelike alleys where the beggars slept. Even the waterfowl at the edge of the great river squawked in disturbed response to the cries, then burst into flight over the mighty banks upon which the city was built.

The scream was followed by a silence that was, if anything, even more chilling.

Then the thrashing, the writhing, the uncontrolled rolling of eyes that were shedding real tears over the most horrible of dreams. Unearthly surroundings, swirling chaos, images and noises from a realm between wakefulness and sleep.

The ruler of the greatest power on earth was powerless to resist this relentless assault from within his own mind.

A dozen of his elite royal guards, strong men whose powerful *legs were pounding the great stone flags, shouted orders back and forth. The light from hastily lit flaming torches illuminated helmeted faces constricted in fear as they raced to confront whatever dire threat they had failed to foresee.*

*Short swords drawn, the guards poured into the king's bedchamber, eyes frantically searching the flickering shadows for the gleam of an assassin's dagger. The bedchamber shadows revealed no threatening figure, but there was no sense of relief, for each of the guards would rather have faced an assassin than turn his terrified gaze upon the body of the king.*

*Nebuchadnezzar, ruler of the Babylonian empire, conqueror of the Egyptian army at Carchemish, destroyer of Jerusalem twice in a decade, whose name struck fear into the hardest of hearts, now sat bolt-upright on the great ebony bed, eyes wide, mouth trembling, the skin of his torso a ghostly pale. The royal pillows were soaked with sweat.*

*"My lord." Arioch, commander of the royal guard, took a step closer, knowing that to approach too near the king's person was to invite death. But he had to be sure. The king's body appeared unmarked, and surely there had been no time for an assassin to make his escape. Had he been poisoned, then? The king's breathing came in ragged gasps, a hand fluttering at his heart. Though stunned, he didn't seem to be in pain. If it had been poison, he would be clutching his belly in agony by now.*

*Steadying himself, knowing he had to calm his panicking men by example, the captain waited.*

*"A dream."*

*The king's voice was a whisper. The usual thunder reduced to a breath of wind.*

*"A dream, my lord?" The captain's eyes narrowed. This could still be dangerous. Sent by a sorcerer with true knowledge of the black arts, a dream could kill as surely as a blade.*

"Forgive me, sire. What manner of dream was this?" The king whirled to face him. "For surely it was most terrible," he added quickly.

The king closed his eyes in thought as if trying to recall a forgotten name or bring the face of a long-dead friend to mind.

"No," he said finally, grimacing in anger. His voice rose to something approaching its normal timbre as he grasped the earthenware wine jug beside the bed and dashed it to the floor. "I cannot tell. I remember nothing!"

"Speak!" The king gripped the arms of his golden throne, his fingers kneading the elaborately carved lions' heads as he surveyed the men standing before him.

They were a strange sight. Two Chaldeans with shaved heads and hooded eyes, naked except for linen loincloths and the sacred amulets hanging around their necks. A black-skinned Nubian with a cheetah's pelt around his thin shoulders. An Egyptian, whose simple cotton shift was offset by a startling ring of black kohl around his eyes. And a Babylonian, a priest of Marduk himself, bringer of plagues.

"Bring me the best of the sorcerers this day" had been his decree. "Gather them from the four corners of Babylon, for my spirit is anxious. I must know the meaning of my dream."

They stood in a half circle below the king's throne, faces gleaming with the sweat of fear as the king bellowed once more.

"Speak, you dogs, or I promise your worthless carcasses will be food for jackals before the sun sets."

They had no reason to doubt his words. Since his dream, the king had thought of nothing else. His nights were an agony of sleepless agitation and his days were spent in a fruitless quest to recall the smallest fragment of the vision.

Now it was up to the soothsayers to recall it for him. If they could not, the stiff line of soldiers ranged behind the king's throne, short spears held at the ready, made it clear what the consequences would be.

As the silence stretched on agonizingly, Amukkani, leader of the Chaldean sorcerers, cleared his throat and attempted an ingratiating smile.

"Perhaps my lord has been granted a vision from Kishar himself—a vision only you are worthy of. Perhaps the god has taken away your memory so that you may not tell it to ordinary men."

He bowed low as Nebuchadnezzar fixed the Chaldean with his piercing black eyes. "What is the sense in that, you fool? To give me a vision and then to take it away. If it is meant only for me, then I must know what it is!"

The king fingered the oiled ringlets of his beard and turned to Arioch. "Be sure your spears have sharp points. These so-called wise men are as slippery as eels."

The commander of the guard grinned. Like most Babylonians, he feared the power of sorcerers almost as much as demons. It would be good to see them skewered on the end of a spear. Sensing that time was fast running out, the Egyptian gasped theatrically, as if a sudden thought had come to him. "My lord! I see it! My mind is filled with light, as if a thousand torches burned. And there in the midst of the flames is a river of fire, and upon the river—"

"Silence!" the king's voice boomed. "Do you think to trick me? Do you think I am one of the foolish old women who pay you to tell their futures? When someone tells me my dream, I shall know it. And I shall know when some mangy cur pretends to know it. Enough! A bellyful of iron will put an end to your lies!"

He raised a hand, signaling the spearmen to prepare.

"Wait! I beseech you, lord." The second Chaldean had stepped forward, as if in his terror he were about to lay hands on the king. "Spare us and I swear you shall know your dream."

Nebuchadnezzar let his hand drop. He regarded the speaker with an amused smile. "None of you has told me anything except lies and evasions. If I spare you, what will that profit me?"

The Chaldean swallowed, his mouth dry. "We cannot tell you your dream, lord. That is true. But I know of one who can."

The king leaped to his feet and the soothsayers cowered as one. "Who, then? Who is this man?"

"One of the Hebrews, lord," the Chaldean continued. "Brought from Jerusalem." He stood straighter now, half believing that he would live to see another sunrise.

"This Hebrew, he is named Daniel."

# THREE

SHANE BARRINGTON WAS a man who had never known fear. As a kid growing up on the dog-eat-dog streets of Detroit, he had quickly learned that survival meant never showing weakness, never letting your opponent know that you were afraid, no matter how much bigger and tougher he was.

And the lessons of the streets had served him just as well in the boardrooms of corporate America. Barrington Communications was now one of the biggest media and technology giants on the planet, and its success was built as much on Barrington's merciless destruction of his competitors as on his near-genius ability to manipulate numbers.

Now, as his private Gulfstream IV neared the Scottish coast, he stared out into the icy darkness and felt a chill that went right to the bone. For the first time in his life, Shane Barrington was afraid.

For the hundredth time, his eyes scanned the printout, now crumpled and stained with sweat. For the hundredth time, he read the columns of figures, the little rows of numbers that could spell the end of everything he had worked and schemed and lied for. Little rows of numbers that could destroy him just as surely as a bullet in the brain.

He had already given up trying to figure out how the evidence of Barrington Communications's creative accounting practices had leaked out. Custom-made, state-of-the-art data encryption systems, combined with the threat of dire consequences for anyone who dared to cross him, had kept his secrets safe for twenty years. Surely none of his employees was smart enough—or dumb enough—to betray him. One of his former business rivals, then? A gallery of names and faces presented themselves, but he dismissed them all. One was now a burned-out alcoholic; another had hanged himself in his garage. All of them had been thoroughly broken in one way or another.

So who had sent him the e-mail?

He would find out soon enough. As the first glow of dawn became visible on the horizon, he checked his Rolex and calculated the jet's arrival time in Zurich. A little before his blackmailer had demanded. Just a few more hours and they would be face-to-face. And he would discover just what the price of survival would be.

By the time the Gulfstream had taxied to a halt on an outlying runway near Zurich, Barrington had showered, shaved, and changed into a dark blue suit tailored to perfection to hint at the athletic frame beneath. Surveying himself in the bathroom mirror, he saw a face too hard to be genuinely handsome, thin lips, and severe cheekbones lit by flint-gray eyes still burning with the intensity of youthful ambition. The softening touches of gray at his temples, he knew, were what saved him from looking like the coldhearted corporate warrior he was.

He had used the last hours to compose himself, drawing deeply from the well of self-belief at his inner core to concentrate his energies. As he stepped down onto the tarmac, he felt focused, alert, like a warrior about to do battle. One thing was certain, he wouldn't go down without a fight.

A gleaming black Mercedes was parked next to the plane. Beside it, a uniformed driver with sallow skin and blank eyes stood at attention in the frigid morning air, opening the rear door as Barrington approached, and wordlessly motioned him inside.

"So, where are we going?" Barrington asked as the Mercedes eased onto a twisting mountain road that seemed headed directly into the clouds. In the rearview mirror he saw only a tight-lipped smile from his driver.

"I asked you a question. And I expect an answer. I *demand* an answer." The icy threat in his voice was unmistakable, but the driver didn't flinch. He held Barrington's gaze for a moment with those blank eyes before turning his attention back to the road as it wound ever upward.

In an instant the rage Barrington had held in check

for the last twenty-four hours burst to the surface. He leaned forward and gripped the driver's shoulder as he snarled, "Speak to me now, or I swear to God you'll live to regret it."

The driver smoothly brought the car to a halt in the middle of a hairpin bend that hugged the mountain. Slowly, he turned his face until he was looking directly into Barrington's eyes. He reached for the car's overhead light, flicking it on. Then he opened his mouth to reveal that he had no tongue.

As Barrington slumped back in his seat, his own mouth open in shock, the car accelerated once more, the only sounds the steady purr of its engine and the relentless thumping of his heart.

The castle seemed to grow out of the mountainside like a malevolent gargoyle clinging to a church steeple. Its massive granite walls, topped with spiked turrets, reached into the cloud-laden sky as if embracing the darkness, while a handful of ancient leaded windows emitted a flickering, sickly light.

It was nearly midday by Barrington's watch, but as the sky opened and the rain drummed on the car roof, it seemed like night. And in the gloom ahead of them, the castle seemed like something out of a nightmare.

While Barrington was still trying to adjust to this medieval apparition of rain-blackened towers, the driver was already opening the rear door, holding a large old-fashioned umbrella and beckoning him toward the castle's massive iron entry.

Taking a deep breath and silently telling himself that it was still day, that he was in a modern, civilized country in the twenty-first century—whatever his senses were telling him to the contrary—Barrington followed.

He was hardly surprised when the heavy door folded silently inward and he was ushered into a cavernous hall stretching into the shadows beyond. What startled him was the sudden shaft of light illuminating a section of wall to his left that appeared to be gleaming steel. Was this where he was supposed to go? He turned toward the driver, but the gloom had swallowed him. Barrington was alone, and despite the unearthly chill, he felt a trickle of sweat run down his spine.

Willing himself forward, he walked toward the steel door, which opened at his approach with a gentle hiss. As he stepped into the elevator and the door whispered shut behind him, he came as close as he had ever been to uttering a prayer.

By the time the elevator disgorged him, Barrington felt as if he had sunk into the very bowels of the mountain, and the unearthly silence engendered a moment of breathless panic, as if he had been entombed alive.

The booming voice brought him to his senses.

"Welcome, Mr. Barrington. We're so glad that you could make it. Please be seated."

Stumbling like a zombie, Barrington felt his way through the shadows toward the ornately carved wooden chair to his right. Easing himself gently into it, as if it were an electric chair that would take his life, he raised his head, hoping to lock eyes with his tormentor at last.

Instead, he saw the stark silhouettes of seven people seated at a massive obsidian table that seemed to draw the remaining light out of the chamber.

Illuminated from behind, each figure remained black and two-dimensional, like the moon during a solar eclipse, betraying no features he could discern.

The voice spoke again. It seemed to come from the figure seated in the middle of the seven. It no longer boomed, but beneath the smoothly articulated vowels was a grating harshness that made Barrington think of fingernails scraped down a chalkboard.

"Your presence here indicates that you understand the gravity of your position, Mr. Barrington. There is hope for you, then. But only if you do exactly as we command from this moment on."

Barrington felt light-headed, like a frog mesmerized by a viper, but this was too much.

" *'Command'?* I don't know who you people are—I'm not even sure where I am anymore—but one thing I do know: Nobody *commands* Shane Barrington."

His words echoed in the darkness, and for a moment he wondered if he had scored a victory, altered the balance of power a little. *Okay, let's go on the offensive,* he thought.

Then the laughter started. Softly at first, then gaining momentum until it cascaded through the chamber like a tumbling brook. It was a woman's laughter, and it came from the last figure seated on the left.

"Oh, Mr. Barrington. We knew you had no morals. But we did think you had brains. Don't you understand? You belong to *us* now. Lock, *stock,* and barrel. And we would use the barrel to carry off your soul as well—if you had one."

She was clearly enjoying herself as she paused to let her words sink in. "The information we have about

Barrington Communications's business practices over the past two decades would be enough to send you to jail for the rest of your life—if it were all to be made public."

Again, she paused for effect. "That is, if your angry shareholders, whom you have cheated so thoroughly, did not storm your corporate offices and beat you to a bloody pulp first."

A new voice rang out of the shadows, a voice with deep tone and a distinct British accent. "Make no mistake, Mr. Barrington, our invitation to you was brief by necessity, only the very tip of a massive accumulation of your business transgressions. Like an iceberg, an iceberg of financial wrongs, sir, which could sink you so horribly, it would make the *Titanic* look like a tub toy."

Barrington rose out of his chair, mustering the last shred of his arrogance. "Impossible. You bought off some people to get a little dirt, I can see that, but you could not possibly have more than a few embarrassing manipulations of funds that I can make—"

The British voice cut him short. "Do not take us for fools, Mr. Barrington. We have it all—the capital expenditures that have been listed as profits, the offshore companies set up to look like assets when they really concealed liabilities. Not to mention the threats to your competitors, the intimidation. Why, even in these impressive times of ill-gotten gains, you, sir, have been a Guinness Book-caliber corporate sinner."

*So this is it, at last,* Barrington thought. *Payback.* He'd always thought he was too smart, too ruthless, for any of his sins to catch up with him. Now, despite himself, the faces of people he had ruined on the way to becoming one of the world's richest and most powerful men began to flash into his mind. The grieving widow of a former business partner he had driven to suicide. The old folks whose pension funds he had decimated to cover his debts.

"So, you're going to turn me in?" Barrington croaked weakly.

A new voice answered. It was a male voice, Hispanic, with a sharp edge like the squawk of a bird of prey. "We did not summon you here to give you a Better Business Award from your chamber of commerce, Señor Barrington, but, no, we have no interest in exposing you to the authorities."

A gleam of understanding flashed in Barrington's eyes. "Oh, I get it. This is all about your getting a *taste* for yourselves."

His mouth snapped shut at the sound of a powerful hand clap, which was all the more startling when Barrington realized it had come from the woman. "Sit down, and stop your jabbering."

Barrington sank back down into the chair.

"A taste? This is no Mafia shakedown. Don't you get it yet? We *own* you, Barrington."

There was a throat-clearing cough, and then the British voice spoke again.

"Now that I see you understand your position, let me offer you an alternative to a life behind bars—short as that life would no doubt be."

Barrington could almost see the sneer on the darkened face. "We have chosen you, Mr. Barrington, because of what you can do for us. How you can help us in our . . . endeavors. We are prepared to inject a minimum of five billion dollars into Barrington Communications, enough to wipe out the debts you have so cunningly concealed, enough for you to continue to swallow up your remaining competitors.

"Enough to make you ... *numero uno* in the business of global communications. Except, of course, that you will be working for *us*. The Seven."

Barrington was suddenly dizzy. He felt like a condemned man who had been counting out the final seconds and then the governor had come through with a reprieve—*and* a check for billions of dollars. With a smile, he realized he'd do anything—*anything*—that was asked of him.

"Well, I think I'll go with option two," Shane Barrington said, his composure quickly restored as a hot buzz of adrenaline flooded his veins. "Just tell me what it is you want me to do."

Outside, the clouds seemed to embrace the castle walls even more tightly as a biting wind danced around the ramparts. Amid the keening of the elements, the castle lay cold and black and silent.

In the impenetrable silence of the subterranean vault, the thud of the castle's iron door as it clanged shut could not be heard. Nor could the Seven hear the subdued roar as the Mercedes began its journey back to the airport. But they knew Barrington was on his way, his mind afire with his new mission, their choice vindicated.

Soft lighting from hidden spotlights restored the Seven from their shadowed specters to a normal human appearance. However, even as they allowed themselves a measure of relaxation in their complete privacy, each of them exuded a fearsome aura. Third from the right, a round-faced man with a silvery mane of thinning hair adjusted his half-moon glasses and turned, smiling, to the man whose booming voice had first broken the silence.

"Well, John. I must offer my apologies. Barrington was indeed an excellent choice. I'm almost surprised he hadn't volunteered for the cause before now. He seems to positively relish his new duties." His lilting English cadences dwindled into a soft chuckle.

Unsmiling, without turning his gaze from the chair where Barrington had moments before been sitting, John Bartholomew spoke, and his tone remained chilling. "The time for self-congratulation lies far ahead of us, I think. Our great project is just beginning, and there is much yet to be done."

"But, John, John! Surely what we have started cannot now be stopped. Is it not written?" continued the Englishman. "I bow to your superior wisdom in the realms of finance. But as a man of the cloth, I think I can claim some special understanding of, let us say, the spiritual dimension. Think of Daniel, think of Nebuchadnezzar's dream. Think of what it means!" In his excitement he gripped Bartholomew's arm. "Surely with the plans of us Seven, the true power of Babylon—the dark power of Babylon—*will* rise again!"

# FOUR

MURPHY WASN'T SURE which was worse, the red-hot streaks of pain that crisscrossed his shoulder or the fiery blast of anger his wife was directing at him. At least the anger would burn itself out eventually. He hoped.

"So, Michael"—it was always *Michael* when he was in the doghouse—"tell me why I'm so special."

He grunted as she swabbed his shoulder with antiseptic. A little harder than was strictly necessary, he thought.

"Other wives come home unexpectedly in the early hours of the morning to find their husbands in bed with another woman, or betting the kids' college fund in a poker game, or just plain old dead drunk." She paused to shake out some more of the antiseptic liquid onto a fresh cotton pad. "But *me*, lucky old me, I come home to find my husband has been half killed by a *lion!*" She stopped working on his shoulder for a moment and smiled sweetly at him. "Please explain exactly what have I done to be so blessed."

Not for the first time, Murphy said a silent prayer of thanks that he'd managed to find such a wonderful woman, and that miraculously, or so it seemed to him, she had agreed to be his wife. He was taking a verbal beating from her now—and that wasn't a first either—but he knew that was only because she cared. And, as ever, it was well deserved.

It was also providential, to say the least, that she'd arrived home when she did. The last day of her conference on mapping lost cities had been canceled when the star of the show, Professor Delgado from the Mexican Archaeological Institute, was taken ill, and with a mix of disappointment at missing out on the great man's legendary stories and excitement at cutting short the time spent away from Murphy, she had hopped on the first plane out of Atlanta.

"I was hoping to surprise you," she'd said wryly. "But I guess I should have known. I'm the one who gets the surprises around here, right?"

She finished taping the sterile pads in place, and Murphy could see her in the bathroom mirror, nodding at her handiwork, before she helped him ease a clean T-shirt over his head. They both knew he couldn't have fixed himself up alone.

Downstairs she settled him in one of the rockers, then went into the small kitchen. She came back with two steaming mugs of tea.

"Okay, Professor Murphy, it seems you're not going

to die of your wounds. Your wonderful, long-suffering wife has therefore calmed down sufficiently to listen to whatever cockamamie nonsense you're about to tell her. So sit there and try not to go off your rocker for the second time tonight and let me hear your sorry story."

Murphy sighed. She wasn't going to like it.

"It was him. Methusaleh. I got a message while I was in my office. Very attention-getting."

"And you just dropped everything and went wherever this madman told you to go?" She rolled her eyes. "Oh, but I was forgetting, you're Michael Murphy, the world-famous archaeological adventurer. No assignment too dangerous. And the crazier the better."

She was just shaking her head. He waited until he was certain she was done. She finally took a sip of tea. The signal for him to go on.

"He said *Daniel*. The Book of Daniel. How could I not be interested?"

"Ah, hence the lion's den. I get it."

"Exactly." Murphy put down his mug on the little coffee table between the rockers and leaned toward her. "One of the most important books of the entire Bible. The mother lode of prophecy. It's all there, Nebuchadnezzar's dream, the statue, everything." In his excitement, the throbbing in his shoulder was forgotten. "Methusaleh was offering me an artifact that related to the Book of Daniel. Such hard evidence would certainly cause skeptics to think twice before dismissing Daniel as mere fiction. Imagine!"

Laura sat back in her rocker, out of reach. "And all you had to do to get it was to go three rounds with a man-eating lion." Her tone was icy.

"Now, sweetheart, it could have been worse," Murphy said with a grin. "If it had been the Book of Revelation, I could have been going head-to-head with the Beast himself."

The look she gave him was icier still. Not funny. Not funny at all.

Murphy tried a different tack. "Honey, the point is, Methusaleh may be crazier than a bucket of snakes, but he always plays by the rules—"

"*His* rules," Laura interrupted. "The rules of a crazy mystery man who has nothing better to do with his money than to lure you into risking your life. And you've fallen for it each time!"

"Yes, because his rules say," Murphy continued, unfazed, "that if I win his game, I get the prize. Look, we've talked this over before, Laura. I know this sounds insane, but it's true. I'm just not a half-measure kind of man. I love my work full tilt, I try to love God full tilt, and above all else, I love you full tilt. It's a package deal, sweetheart, even on nights like this, when you feel the prize package you're stuck with is the booby prize."

Laura frowned in defeat. She'd said her piece. She knew Murphy could no more resist the lure of Methusaleh's artifacts than decide not to breathe. And though she was not about to tell him, Murphy's fearless passion for bringing the truth of the Bible to light was a big part of why she loved him.

She dragged it out for ten more seconds and gave in, reaching around to hug him. "Michael Impossible Murphy," she whispered, calling him by the middle name she had given him several years earlier, "you know too well that the most impossible thing about you is still the fact that I can't stay angry with you for longer than it will take you to get into trouble the next time."

He nodded toward the table. They both looked down at the red tube as it lay innocently, like an unexploded bomb, between them. "Okay, then, Murphy." She smiled her sweetest smile, and he wondered what was coming as he saw her smile turn into a worried frown. "This bleeding is worse than I thought. That lion got deeper into your shoulder than it looked. I am driving you over to the hospital to get you stitches. No argument."

Though he had rejected her earlier insistence on getting him to the emergency room, now Murphy did not even offer the meekest resistance.

Laura softened again. "Hey," she said, wrapping her hands around Murphy's good shoulder, "since you went to all the trouble of getting this thing, tomorrow, after your lecture, how's about I come to your lab and help you look at what's in there?"

# FIVE

"SO, YOU PUT your life on the line every day?"

"That's right, my friend. One slip, and *splat*!"

The bartender, who stood just close enough to his only customers to hear their conversation, shook his head and kept flipping through the newspaper. Here on a slow Tuesday afternoon in this dingy neighborhood bar in Astoria, in the shadow of a not-too-distant Manhattan, he felt a million miles away from the excitement of the big city.

He had been listening to these two guys rattle on for twenty minutes and with only one beer between them. That was for Farley, the big hero, one of his regulars.

The other man was a stranger. He would have to be, to be talking to Farley this long. Every other regular knew that Farley was a bore who would talk on and on about how risky his job was. The guy was a window washer, not a combat marine! The bartender eyed the stranger again. He would have thought the man must be deaf to listen to Farley drone on, but the stranger was lapping it up. And he wasn't even drinking anything stronger than water.

When the stranger had asked for a water—not even sparkling water—the bartender had started to give him his standard rebuke about this being a bar, not a public drinking fountain, but there was something about the stranger's manner that stopped him. Not because he looked threatening. Farley was a drab-looking, doughy kind of figure, and if anything, this stranger was even plainer-looking—gray-haired, clunky glasses, a thick, pockmarked nose, a pronounced slouch to his stance. However, while Farley was a threat only to bore you to death, there was something about this meek stranger that made the bartender not want to challenge him.

"Hey," he heard the stranger ask, "you want to go get a burger?" Then, showing that he was a quick study, since everyone knew Farley was the cheapest man in all of Astoria, the stranger added, "I'm buying."

As the bartender watched the two men shuffle out of the bar, he knew better than to check to see if Farley had left him a tip, but raised an eyebrow when he saw a five-dollar bill sitting next to the stranger's empty water glass. *Man*, the bartender thought, *I hope I see him again soon.*

He had no way of knowing he would never see either man again.

———

Outside the bar, the stranger said, "Why don't we take my car? It's just around the corner."

Farley nodded and followed him. "Say, friend, tell me your name again."

"I didn't tell it to you the first time." He stopped in front of a dark green Jeep, and Farley paused, a puzzled look on his face.

"Hey, that's right. So, what *is* your name?" The stranger gave him no notice, darting his head from left to right to survey the deserted street. Then Farley saw the stranger make some quick movements around his head. "Huh?" Farley looked even more puzzled.

Only then did the stranger turn to look at Farley. But the face that Farley saw before him now was an entirely different one. Gone were the gray wig, the glasses, and the nose. "You'll never need to know it."

Almost too quickly to see, the stranger swept his right hand in front of Farley's throat. A thin line of blood appeared there before Farley could cry out. Now, as he tried to make a sound, nothing came out.

"You'll never need to know anything again." He reached over to grab Farley and threw his limp body into the car. "Now that I know the only things you knew that were worth knowing."

The stranger got behind the wheel. He wiped some blood off his right index finger on the shirt of the dead man beside him. Farley would not mind, he thought. He took out his cell phone and looked at the index finger in the greenish light from the phone panel as he dialed. The finger looked like a normal index finger until you looked more closely and saw that it was an artificial digit, carefully sculpted and tinted to look real. Except for the very tip, where the nail should be, which was honed to a deadly edge.

His call was answered with a single word. "Status."

The stranger replied in a cold, deadpan, accentless voice, quite a change from the hearty tone he had used with Farley. "I am ready to proceed at your order." He straightened in anticipation.

"Go," he was told. "And, Talon, do not fail—and do not fall."

The man known as Talon clicked shut his phone, taking a split second to make sure all of the blood had come off the digit that gave him the name he went by. He pushed Farley down below the car window sightline and headed for the spot where he would dump the body. A place where it would never be found.

He allowed himself a grim smile. Failure or falling were not options for him any more than breathing would ever again be an option for Mr. Farley.

# SIX

THE KING AND *the captive of Judah looked each other in the eye, and the king was intrigued to find that the slave held his gaze. True, there were no guards at his side to intimidate the man with their swords and murderous looks. But wasn't his royal presence alone, the majesty and power of Nebuchadnezzar, whose name made kings and princes quake, enough to terrorize a humble Jewish slave?*

*And yet the man seemed calmness itself as he waited patiently for the king to speak. It was strange indeed. These people had a reputation for cleverness. Yet this man seemed not to understand that his own life would be forfeited if he could not give the king an answer. An answer the wisest men in the kingdom had so far not been able to provide.*

*The king took in the simple woolen robe, the relaxed posture—neither arrogant nor submissive—and the blank, patient gaze, and wondered if this could really be the man to reveal his* dream. If he failed like all the others, then one thing was certain: Daniel would be only the first of many to feel his anger. The gutters of Babylon would be awash with blood before his wrath was spent.

The king shifted in his carved cedarwood chair and broke the silence. "Well, Daniel." His pronunciation of the slave's Hebrew name was mocking, as if he had alluded to some shameful secret. "No doubt I do not need to explain why you are here."

"I am here because you commanded it, my king."

Nebuchadnezzar scrutinized him for signs of impudence. His tone was as maddeningly neutral as his expression in the flickering torchlight.

"Indeed, Daniel. And I'm sure in your wisdom you understand why I commanded it. And what it is I would have you do."

Daniel bowed his head slightly. "You have been troubled by a dream, my king. An awesome dream that stirred your spirit, and yet when you awoke, not a fragment, not a shred of it, remained. Only an empty echo, like the sound of a word in a strange tongue."

Nebuchadnezzar found himself gripping the amulet of Anu he wore around his neck. By the gods, how did this man know his inner thoughts so well?

"Yes, yes, all of Babylonia knows of this. But can you tell me the dream, Daniel? Can you restore it to me?" He realized with alarm that his voice was breaking, his habitual tone of command replaced by the fretful whine of a child.

Daniel closed his eyes and took a deep, slow breath. The moment lengthened and Nebuchadnezzar felt his nerves stretch to their breaking point. At last Daniel opened his eyes, now bright with a new intensity, and spoke.

"The secrets which you have demanded cannot be declared to the king by soothsayers, magicians, astrologers, or sorcerers. Only the God of heaven can reveal such secrets." Daniel silenced his voice as he concentrated deeply.

"Yes, yes, do not stop now," Nebuchadnezzar shouted.

Daniel would not be rushed. Finally, he looked calmly at the king and spoke slowly and loudly so there would be no mistaking his message.

"The God of heaven, in this dream, has revealed to you, King Nebuchadnezzar, things which are to come in the Latter days."

# SEVEN

AS HE WALKED purposefully toward Memorial Lecture Hall B, Michael Murphy looked like an unlikely academic. Sure, he had the slightly ruffled look of someone who cared more about ideas than outward appearances—the tie slightly askew over a creased denim shirt, an old canvas jacket worn at the elbows, and a pair of sneakers that clearly had some serious mileage on them.

But if you looked a little harder, you could tell from his measured, economical stride, the callused hands, and faint scars that neatly highlighted his handsome features that this was no ivory-tower dweller. This was a man who was happier outdoors than in—and happiest of all when he was dealing with tough physical challenges.

For just a moment, Murphy found himself wishing that he would be suddenly called away to complete such a physical challenge. *Any* physical challenge would do. Usually not a man plagued by lack of confidence, all during his brisk stroll through the Preston University campus in the late-August heat, he had been getting ready for an embarrassingly low turnout.

Biblical Archaeology and Prophecy had been a late addition to the curriculum. Murphy's regular lectures drew an enthusiastic audience, but it was a small one. There just weren't that many students in a university like Preston who wanted to devote themselves to the study of the past—let alone the Biblical past. Then, at the end of last semester, some of the wealthy alumni had put pressure on the university president to have more Bible-based courses for the general student body.

*Bless them*, Murphy thought, although it could turn out to be a mixed blessing indeed. The two most troubling negatives were that he would have a lot of explaining to do to the donors if nobody showed up to take the course, and that Dean Fallworth of the Arts and Science faculty absolutely hated having another Biblical archaeology course.

Murphy tried not to be a vain man despite his growing notoriety for his discovery of Biblical artifacts. So far, he had starred in three cable television specials about his work, which had attracted some corporate funding for the department and some revenue-enhancing exhibits at the university museum.

All of that attention brought on the jealousy and anger of Dean Fallworth. There had been several veiled comments by the dean that struck Murphy as being antireligion, but Dean Fallworth was both direct and vocal when voicing his opinion that what Murphy studied and taught was neither worthy science nor credible history.

This from a man, Murphy had pointed out to Laura last week, whose most recent published scholarly paper had been "Button Materials of the Eighteenth-Century Georgia Plantations."

The positives of getting to teach the new Biblical Archaeology and Prophecy course were that Murphy loved teaching and these additional funds would allow him to wing it with a new course that he had described in his posted syllabus as "Studying the Past, Proving the Bible, and Reading the Signs of the Prophets."

Here for the first time was an opportunity for any student, no matter what their major, to take one of his classes. His plan was to liven things up by incorporating some of the background video that had not made it onto his television specials, and he figured he would also include viewings of some of his most recent finds.

Still, he had been leery about checking the enrollment before this first class. He had hoped for the best, but a nagging voice said, as it sometimes did when he allowed the real world to crowd in on his frequent thoughts about his studies of the ancients, *It's the twenty-first century, does anybody care about Hittites in a hip-hop world?*

"Well, I do," Murphy said out loud, not meaning to. "I'm going to have a great lecture even if it's just me and my slides who show up."

As the excited buzzing from within became audible, he took a breath and strode into the lecture hall. To his amazement, every seat was filled, several students had taken up position against the walls, and some were even squatting on the floor below the lectern.

Murphy clapped his hands and the chattering came to an abrupt halt. "Okay, people, let's get started. We're dealing with thousands of years of history here, and we've got only forty minutes, so there's no time to waste." He scanned the rows of faces and wondered what they were hoping for. What were they expecting? And would he be able to deliver it? Spotting Shari Nelson's bright eyes and eager smile in the first row brought a half-smile to his own lips. At least he had one friend in the audience. If they started to throw things, maybe Shari could calm them down.

"It's great to see so many of you here, so let me just check that you know what you're letting yourselves in for. This class is called Biblical Archaeology and Prophecy, and according to the prospectus it's the study of the Old and New Testaments with an emphasis on archaeological evidence that supports the historical accuracy and prophetic nature of the Bible. Anybody who just got lost on their way to the seminar The Matrix: Movie or Blueprint for Our Future, now's your chance to sneak back out."

A few snickers, but no one got up to go. Okay, they were still with him.

"So, what does *Biblical archaeology* mean? Well, let me ask you some questions: Did Noah really build an ark and fill it with two of everything?

"Did Moses really part the Red Sea with a wave of his staff?

"Did a man named Jesus really live and breathe and

walk around the Holy Land two thousand years ago, teaching and healing and performing miracles?

"How can we truly know any of this for sure?"

A slender hand went up at the back of the hall. It belonged to a blond girl with long, straight hair and big, round glasses he had seen once or twice in the university chapel.

"Because the Bible tells us," she said in a quiet but confident voice.

"And because Hollywood tells us," another voice interrupted. It belonged to a chunky, dark-haired student with his arms folded across his Preston sweatshirt and a smug smile on his face. "If Charlton Heston believes it, it's got to be true, right?" That got a few laughs, even a little ripple of applause.

Murphy smiled and waited for the students to calm down.

"You know, when I was your age I was a skeptic too. Maybe I still am. Christians are supposed to take the truth of the Bible on faith. But sometimes faith needs a helping hand. And that's where Biblical archaeology comes in."

He pointed to the still-smirking young man in the row just behind Shari. "What would I need to do to prove to you that Noah's Ark existed? What would convince you?"

The student looked thoughtful for a moment. "I guess I'd have to see solid proof, you know?"

Murphy seemed to chew that over. "Solid proof. Sounds about right. Well, let's see, when it comes to scientific research, you have to be willing to go wherever the evidence takes you. In just the last one hundred fifty years, there have been more than *thirty thousand* different archaeological digs that have unearthed evidence supporting the Old Testament portion of the Bible alone.

"For centuries, skeptics scoffed at the idea of there being a Hittite nation, as recorded in the Bible, until archaeological evidence unearthed irrefutable proof of the Hittites' existence. Likewise, the mere mention of the city of Nineveh used to bring laughter and ridicule to the lips of nonbelievers until the entire city was discovered near the Tigris River by the great archaeologist A. H. Layard.

"And yet, to date, *not one piece of evidence has been unearthed that disputes the Bible's authenticity.*"

"Whoa! That's impressive!" someone called out from the back. The student looking for solid proof still was not satisfied. "I'd still want to see, like, Noah's rudder if you want to sell me on the Ark being real."

Murphy smiled. "Well, no one has yet found the rudder of the Ark. But here's something you might find interesting."

Murphy clicked his first slide onto the large screen behind the lectern. It showed a box covered by a sheet. The next slide revealed a pale stone box with an overlapping lid beneath the sheet. About twenty-four inches long, fifteen inches wide, and ten inches deep, it still bore the marks of the primitive tools that had been used to carve it out of a solid block of limestone.

"Anyone know what this is?" Murphy asked.

"How about Fred Flintstone's lunch box," came a now-familiar voice.

Shari turned and gave the speaker a withering glance

before offering her own answer. "Is it a sarcophagus? A child's sarcophagus, maybe?"

"Good guess, Shari." Murphy gave her a warm smile. "It's a coffin all right—a bone coffin. What we call an *os-suary*. Thousands of years ago, it was a common practice in some parts of the world that after the flesh of the buried dead had decomposed, the bones were dug up, wrapped in muslin, and placed in one of these."

"So whose bone coffin are we looking at here?" came a voice from the back. "Russell Crowe's, maybe?"

Murphy ignored the laughter. "Well, let's take a look." The next slide was a close-up of the box's side panel showing its worn and faded inscription. "It says here, James—"

"Hey, Jimmy Hoffa, we was wondering where y'all got to!"

Seemingly lost in thought, Murphy didn't hear the comment or the sniggers that followed. He was somewhere else. Somewhere far away in time. He clicked to a greatly enlarged close-up of the ossuary panel and began to read from it.

"James . . . son of Joseph . . ."

A hush had descended on the hall.

"*. . . brother of Jesus.*"

He let the silence stretch, then turned back to his audience. "In this little box you see here—which I have actually touched—lay the bones of Jesus' brother.

"Normally, only the name of the father of the deceased would be inscribed on an ossuary *unless* the deceased had another relative who was extremely well known. And no one was more famous, or infamous, than Jesus in that part of the world during that period.

"What is significant here is that this ossuary not only confirms the historicity of Jesus—that is, that He truly was a real figure in history—but it confirms that He was of such notoriety that the family of James identified his dead brother with him. Once this ossuary is proven to be legitimate, it will prove that Jesus not only lived during this time period, but was a prominent person in His day. Just as He is presented in the Bible."

As he did every time he looked at pictures of this stone box, Murphy was experiencing a strange, disorienting feeling, as if the thousands of years separating him from this long-dead man had been swept aside, as if they were somehow present together in this timeless moment.

His mood was abruptly shattered by a voice from close to Shari.

"Maybe it says that on the box, but how do we know it isn't a fake? You know, like all those saints' relics that used to be churned out in the Middle Ages like cheap souvenirs. Like the Shroud of Turin. That's supposed to be a fake, isn't that right, Professor Murphy?"

Murphy looked intently at the questioner. He seemed to be a skeptic all right, but he seemed more serious, more thoughtful, and better informed than the class joker who'd been hogging the spotlight up to then. He noticed Shari had turned to give him a cool appraisal too.

"You have a good point there . . ."

"Paul," the student offered, then started to blush, clearly not seeking this much attention in the hall.

"Okay, Paul. Some experts have concluded that the Shroud of Turin probably is a medieval fake. I am not convinced. So, how can we tell the fakes from the real thing? What makes me think that this ossuary really contained the bones of Christ's brother?"

"Carbon dating?" The response was quick and confident.

"Thanks, Paul. Anytime you want to step up and take over the lecture, let me know. It seems you have all the answers," Murphy said with a smile.

Paul blushed again, and Murphy quickly realized he'd been too tough on him. This guy wasn't trying to give him a hard time, he was just that much sharper than the average student.

"Yes, carbon dating is how we can tell almost to the year when an artifact was made or when it was in use," Murphy continued. "Carbon-fourteen is a radioactive isotope found in all organic objects. Since it decays at a known rate, the amount of C-fourteen remaining in an object can tell us its age."

Paul looked more sheepish now. He clearly didn't relish being in the spotlight. But he couldn't keep his questions to himself either. "Um, Professor Murphy, wouldn't carbon dating just tell us when the original stone was formed, not when the box—the *ossuary*—was carved out of it?"

"You're absolutely right, Paul. But inside the box, embedded in minute cracks, we found bits of muslin and fragments of pollen that carbon date to just after the time of Christ—around A.D. sixty. And not only that, the inscription was written in a form of Aramaic unique to that time. And if you want *more* proof, microscopic examination of the patina that formed on the inscription proves it wasn't added at a later date."

Murphy paused and noted the attentive faces. Nobody having private little conversations at the back. No text messaging on handheld devices. Nobody goofing off. Even if they weren't convinced, at least he seemed to have gotten their attention. Now for the real test.

"All very well and good, ladies and gentlemen, but everything I just told you is a bucket of hogwash. This box is a complete fake."

The class erupted in cries of dismay and confusion. *So much for sedate old archaeology,* Murphy thought.

"Make up your mind, man."

"That's right, this ossuary is a fraud. That's what more than one body of scientists and scholars have said. I, however, have been impressed by both the carbon-fourteen testing, which we will examine in a later class, and by the writing in Aramaic that was limited to the first century. This is a relatively new find, so there will be lots more study and debate over this ossuary in years to come. I raise all this as we get started on the journey of this course for a reason."

Murphy paused. "I'm a scientist, the people who have challenged the authenticity of the ossuary are scientists. I'm very proud to be a serious, practicing, full-tilt, believing Christian as well. I suspect the scientists who are crying fake might be motivated to challenge this very important discovery because it could force them to change their preconceived doubts about Christ. Is my religion clouding my thinking; is their lack of religious belief distorting their judgment? Folks, these are just some of the interesting extra issues that an archaeologist searching for proof of the Bible faces. I look forward to exploring all of this and more with you in the coming weeks."

Just his luck. He noticed Dean Fallworth pacing the back of the hall. How long had he been back there? Murphy wondered. "Now, not to leave you in suspense, let me assure you that the question of whether Jesus of Nazareth was a bona fide person in history does not rest on the authenticity of this ossuary. We will study some of that body of evidence in this course. But when the ossuary is proven to be authentic, as I believe it will be, this will be further evidence for those who do believe in Jesus that He once walked among us."

Murphy checked his watch. "Now, let us go over the course reading list before I ramble us out of time."

"Hold it, Murphy!"

A bony hand grabbed Murphy by his backpack as he left the hall. "Dean Fallworth. What a fine example you set for the students by monitoring my lecture."

"Can it, Professor Murphy." Fallworth was as tall as Murphy but cursed with a library-stack pallor that would make some mummies look healthy by comparison. "You call that a lecture? I call it a disgrace. Why, the only thing separating you from a Sunday tent preacher is the fact that you didn't pass the plate for a collection."

"I will gratefully accept any donation you wish to make, Dean. Did you need a syllabus, by the way?"

"No, Mr. Murphy, I have everything I need to get the university board to begin accreditation hearings for this evangelical clambake you're calling a class."

"Temper," Murphy mumbled to himself. "Dean, if you feel my work is unprofessional in any way, then please help me to improve my teaching skills, but if you want to bash Christians, I don't have to stand here for that."

"Do you know what they're already calling this silly circus around the campus? Bible for Bubbleheads, Jesus for Jocks, and the Gut from Galilee."

Murphy couldn't help but laugh. "I like that last one. I'm intending this to be a quite intellectually stimulating course, Dean, but I confess I did not post an I.Q. requirement for taking it. The knowledge will be there, I promise you, but I will likely fall short of your apparent requirement that the only acceptable instructional method is to bore your students to an early ossuary."

"Mark my words, Murphy. Your hopes of this course surviving and your hopes of tenure at this university are as dead as whatever was in that bone box of yours."

"Ossuary, Dean. Ossuary. We're at a university, let's try to use multisyllabic words. If it doesn't turn out to be legitimate, maybe I can get it for you cheap and you can keep your buttons in it. Now, if you'll excuse me, I have a new artifact to begin work on."

# EIGHT

CLOSING THE LAB door behind him, Murphy breathed a sigh of relief. This was his inner sanctum, a place where bloated egos and petty academic infighting had no place. The only thing that mattered here was truth. Fittingly, the pristine space was painted pure white. Bathed in halogen light, the room was lined with high-tech lab benches and chrome-plated equipment racks, the only sound the quiet hum of computers and high-tech environmental control systems.

In the middle of the room was a table specially equipped for photographing artifacts, with two halogen strobes for shadowless and colorless lighting and scales for size reference. Perched on a tripod was a state-of-the-art digital camera. Shari Nelson, in a clean white lab coat, was hunched over it, loading a diskette.

"Hi, Shari," said Murphy. "Thank you for clearing

your schedule to help me this afternoon. Laura's going to try to get away, but let's get started, because I'm sure she has her office full of huddled masses of youths yearning to complain for free."

"Professor Murphy, sometimes I think you were never young."

"I wasn't. I have an ancient soul. Just ask my mummy."

"Ancient jokes, anyway." She looked up and gave him a radiant smile. "I've been here an hour, getting everything ready. I mean, it's so exciting!" She pointed to the metal tube clutched tightly in his hand. "Is that it?"

He placed it on the table in front of her. "I don't want you to be too disappointed if it turns out to be nothing, Shari. Until we look at it, I really have no idea what it is."

"But you think it could be something big, right? You said so. I mean, I could tell from your message how excited you were."

She was right. At three in the morning, half delirious with pain and exhaustion, Murphy had been convinced he was holding something of monumental importance, and his slightly manic e-mail message to Shari had reflected that. Now, in the cold light of day, doubts were creeping in, along with a throbbing pain in his shoulder.

"I hope it is, Shari. But you remember the first law of Biblical archaeology?"

"I know, I know," she chirped. "Always be prepared to be disappointed."

"Right. Don't let your hopes cloud your objectivity." She knew the drill, but it did not sound as if she had really taken it to heart. He hoped for both their sakes that the tube had more in it than a handful of ancient dust.

Before he and Laura had finally fallen into a fitful sleep, they'd examined the tube minutely, and discovered the almost invisible seam in the middle. It looked like the two halves screwed together precisely to form a perfect seal.

Shari seemed mesmerized as Murphy took the tube in both hands and prepared to unscrew it.

"Wait!" Shari shouted. "Isn't there something we need to do first?"

Murphy looked puzzled. "Oh, you mean X-ray it? Shari, you're a credit to your old professor. You're right, normally we'd want to get some idea of what's in there before we expose it to the air and potential damage. But I'll bet you lunch that what we have here is a papyrus scroll. It's the only thing that could be that small and light and still contain the clues that I was told were in this tube. And if it is papyrus that has survived for a couple of thousand years or so without rotting, that means it's pretty well dried out, which also means as soon as you've taken your photographs—"

"We have to rehydrate it!"

Murphy couldn't help smiling at Shari's enthusiasm. Even though she was still a student, she was probably the most levelheaded person he'd ever met. But the prospect of a genuine Biblical find had her bouncing on the balls of her feet like a hyperactive two-year-old. "Exactly. So, you all set? Okay, let's do it."

As Murphy tightened his grip and began to exert pressure on the seal, Shari slid a white plastic tray onto the table beneath his hands. The tray would catch any debris that came loose from the papyrus, fragments that could be used for carbon dating. The background hum of the machines seemed to increase in volume as they concentrated intently on the tube. With a pop the seal gave way. He was pretty sure that Methuselah must have already opened the tube to verify what was in there, but he had somehow sealed it up as perfectly as the original owner had. Now the two halves slid apart, revealing a faded papery scroll. Murphy tipped it gently onto the tray.

"Lunch is on me, I guess, Professor," said Shari breathlessly. "I'd say that was genuine papyrus." She hesitated. "Isn't it?"

Murphy didn't seem to hear her at first. He was leaning close, already trying to decipher the faint marks on the surface of the scroll. Ink? Or just spots of decay? Was that a man-made shape or just a stain? After a moment he grinned and patted her on the shoulder.

"I'll have my usual, please, Shari. Chili cheeseburger with extra pickles."

"And a root beer," she added happily.

They set to work, Shari alternately taking pictures and sucking dust and debris from the tray with a flashlight-sized vacuum, while Murphy scrutinized the scroll from every angle. When she was done, Murphy carried the tray over to what looked like an oversized microwave, complete with windowed door and electronic control panel on the side. He slid the tray inside the hyperbaric chamber, latched the door, and keyed in the settings for humidity and barometric pressure.

With luck, the scroll's ancient fibers would gradually absorb moisture until it was supple enough to be unrolled without disintegrating. If not, then the photographs Shari had just taken would be all they had to unlock its secrets.

Together they gazed through the opaque glass like new parents anxiously watching a baby in an incubator.

"And now," said Murphy, "we wait."

As Shari Nelson left Professor Murphy's lab, Paul Wallach had to quicken his step to catch up with her. He was at risk of losing her as she strode briskly through the mazelike corridors of the history building.

"Excuse me. Can I talk to you for a moment?"

Shari turned, and Paul was surprised to find her smiling at him. With her jet-black hair tied back in a short ponytail, and dark blue jogging pants and sweatshirt, she looked as if she didn't work on the way she looked. But the effect, especially with those sparkling green eyes, was captivating. Paul was suddenly at a loss for words.

"Look, I . . . I know you work with Professor Murphy, and I just wanted to apologize for what I said back at the lecture. I didn't want you to think I was trying to be a wise guy or anything."

She tilted her jaw as if she were weighing his words in the balance.

"You raised an important question. Isn't that what they keep telling us we're supposed to do here? Ask questions?"

"I guess. It's just that I noticed you were . . . you know." His eyes went to the simple silver cross at her throat.

She frowned and he felt himself blushing. She was being nice, and now he'd offended her. If he was so smart, how come she made him feel so dumb?

"Christians can ask questions, too, you know. So, here's one. Who are you?"

He blushed even deeper. "Paul Wallach. I just switched to Preston this semester."

Shari held out her hand. "Shari Nelson. Nice to meet you, Paul. And I didn't think you were being a jerk, not at all. Actually, when it comes to the really big questions, maybe it's the *atheists* who don't like to ask them." She laughed. "Sorry, I'm sure you didn't come to Preston to be lectured by *me*."

"Well, no, I mean, it's fine, you can . . ."

He took a deep breath to compose himself. *Come on, get a grip here.*

"I'd certainly like to ask you some stuff, if that's okay. If you have time. About the lecture and Professor Murphy. I've heard there are some doughnuts in the cafeteria that are in urgent need of carbon dating. What do you say?"

"So what's he like, Professor Murphy?" asked Paul. "He seems like a cool guy."

"For a Biblical archaeologist, you mean?"

Paul and Shari had been chatting for twenty minutes. One ancient-looking doughnut sat uneaten on a paper plate in front of them, alongside two now-empty mugs of coffee, and as far as he could tell, she wasn't getting bored with his company. But she still had this unnerving ability to make him feel like a total bumbler.

"No, I didn't mean that. Really. I meant cool for a professor."

She gave him a smile to show she believed him, or

maybe that she'd just been teasing him. Either way, his sigh of relief must have been audible.

"Murphy is cool. And he's the best at what he does. I've learned an awful lot from him."

"You said he lets you work in his lab sometimes, on his finds. Is that right?" Paul asked.

"That's the best. I'm so lucky. Sometimes I can't believe he trusts me not to drop these things—really important historical artifacts, you know?"

She looked at Paul with those green eyes that he now realized could be as intimidating as they were enticing. Maybe she'd told him more than she'd meant to.

"Okay, Paul, that's enough about me and enough about Professor Murphy." She looked him up and down. "You haven't told me a single thing about yourself yet. Hmmm." She put a finger to her chin. "Judging from the pressed slacks and shirt, neat haircut—not to mention those shiny loafers—I'd say you weren't exactly typical of Preston's student body. In fact," she continued in a lower tone, leaning over the table toward him, "I'm not sure you're a student at all."

He winced, choking on a reply, and Shari instantly realized she'd gone too far. She'd been enjoying herself at his expense, and that was wrong.

"Look, I didn't mean—"

"No, you're right," he said, his eyes fixed forlornly on their empty mugs. "I don't really fit around here. I'm not sure *where* I fit in anymore."

"Why do you say that? You must have had some reason for transferring to Preston this year."

Paul was deciding whether he should launch into his

story. He really liked Shari, so he did. "Well, you asked for it. I transferred here to Preston from Duke."

Shari was taken aback. "Wow, not a lot of students give up Duke to come here."

"No, and I didn't really do it the easy way. You see, my dad was pretty hard-driving. He never went to college; he built up the family business, a printing business, the hard-knocks, old-fashioned way. He drove away my mom when I was pretty young by working day and night, and pretty much all the time he ever had for me was to tell me how I had to go to college and learn business the 'fancy way,' as he called it. He made enough money so he could send me to boarding school, which is where I got in the habit of dressing up for school, plus there were always servants around our house who really raised me, and they were pretty strict. I went to Duke to study business because that's where my dad always dreamed of going. Then, last winter, my father died of a heart attack—bam!—no warning."

Now Shari instinctively reached across the table for Paul's hand. "Paul, I'm so sorry. That had to be rough."

Paul was trying hard to concentrate on talking and not on how nice it felt to have his hand touched by Shari. "You know, I never really knew my father much, so as lousy as it sounds, I didn't really miss him when he died. The rough part came when the accountants and attorneys started going over his business and discovered that he had been drowning in debt. I took a leave from Duke to try to help sort things out, but it was hopeless. By selling the business and our house at a fire sale, I could pay off the debt, but I couldn't afford to go back to Duke even if I wanted to. I liked the area, though, and

I realized it's as close to a home base as I have now, and I thought I could afford Preston. Or at least I will if I can get a job."

"And why did you register for business administration courses here if you hated them at Duke?"

"All those years of having it drummed into my head by my dad, it's still what seems like my destiny. I want to finish college, I'm trying hard not to just fall apart, and business is as close to a plan as I ever had. I did promise myself I would try to audit a few other courses just to try them out, and Professor Murphy's seemed interesting."

Shari smiled. "I know. I felt the same way. I certainly never dreamed about being an archaeologist."

Paul looked again, inadvertently, at the cross around her neck. "Well, you at least had some religious background. I don't even have that. Religion was on the long list of things my dad never had time—or use—for."

"Neither did my parents while they were alive, but the great thing about our church is, you can start anytime."

"I guess so. But first I think I'll worry about my business major. I feel like an athlete who's been training, then doesn't get to go to the Olympics. It's all my dad had me concentrate on, but I really hate it."

Shari looked at her watch. "I have to run to my next class, but I bet that being pretty new to campus, you could use a home-cooked meal. Why don't you come over for dinner one night this week and we can talk some more?"

Paul did not hesitate. "You don't have to ask me twice."

# NINE

UNLIKE SO MANY big-city high-rise luxury-apartment dwellers who pay a kingly fortune for a terrace but seldom take the time to go out to admire the view, Shane Barrington made a point each morning of studying the dazzling urban skyline that surrounded his penthouse. Much like the lords of the manors of old, Barrington felt that he would one day own everything in his sight.

Most mornings, Barrington was lost in his own plans for short-term and long-term business conquests and was left undistracted by any street noises from sixty-two stories below. On this particular morning, he was disturbed from his scheming by a repetitive sound that he could not place at first. It sounded as if something were being pumped.

As a shadow momentarily fell across the front of the

terrace wall, Barrington turned to see what was coming up behind him, which led to the surprising sight of a large peregrine falcon swooping out of the sky and landing not more than five feet from him on a wrought-iron table on the penthouse deck.

The bird was majestic and haughty in its bearing, much like Barrington himself. The two predatory beings eyed each other with a chilling respect.

Barrington's stare broke away first as he became aware of something in the forward claw of the falcon. He realized the bird was clutching a pair of very compact, ultrasophisticated-looking binoculars. Now, having noticed that the binoculars had registered with Barrington, the bird dropped them and they clattered lightly onto the table. Barrington waited until the falcon stirred its wings again and flew away over the rooftops before he reached over and picked up the binoculars.

As the falcon slowly began to soar majestically into the sky just above his head, Barrington was further surprised to see a small banner unfurl from the bird's other claw. Barrington quickly trained the binoculars on the cloth to read the words that were written there:

ENDICOTT ARMS 14TH FLOOR 12 MINUTES

Curious now, Barrington sought out the Endicott Arms apartment building diagonally across from his own building and counted up fourteen stories from the street, then put the binoculars to his eyes. The meticulously crafted lenses chipped but did not crack when Barrington dropped the binoculars, so shocked was he by what he saw through those lenses.

For through the windows on the fourteenth floor of the Endicott Arms was a face he instantly recognized. It was not exactly the face of an acquaintance he saw regularly; in fact, he had not seen the individual for some three years. But the face bore many similarities to a face Barrington had seen as recently as that very morning, and every morning of his life—his own.

There through the binoculars, Barrington stared at the face of his twenty-five-year-old son, Arthur. The only offspring of his short-lived marriage, the son had grown to be a good-looking, younger version of his father. Barrington had had little interest beyond child support and perfunctory holiday visits through most of Arthur's childhood, especially once his ex-wife moved to California with her new husband.

Barrington did have his secretaries keep tabs on both his ex-wife and Arthur over the years as a defense against their coming to him for financial support. So he was not surprised when Arthur was thrown out of his fourth art school and relocated to downtown Manhattan with every intention of having his wealthy father set him up as a sculptor.

The elder Barrington was therefore prepared when his son showed up in his office with purple hair, ripped leather pants, and a pierced tongue to demand money to open a sculpture gallery. Arthur Barrington got a one-minute-thirty-second angry lecture from his father about there being no money forthcoming for "a loser freak freeloader," and those were the last words that had passed between them as security guards hustled him from the offices of Barrington Communications.

Now Barrington was able to recognize his son

instantly through the binoculars, but his son could not see him from across the street and many floors below. However, his head was turned in Barrington's direction. He was held forcibly to face his father, by a figure standing next to him in the window.

That figure was clearly squeezing the young man's head very hard with one gloved hand, while the other gloved hand held a very long, very menacing knife blade to the young man's throat. The final image that registered with the elder Barrington before the binoculars slipped from his shocked hands and crashed to the deck was the handwritten sign hanging around his son's neck:

FATHER, YOU HAVE
11 MINUTES, 30 SECONDS
TO GET OVER HERE TO APT. 14C
OR THIS MAN WILL
KILL ME

"Are you people homicidal maniacs?" Shane Barrington was screaming with what breath he could muster after his race out of his penthouse and across Park Avenue to the fourteenth floor of the Endicott Arms, as instructed. It had taken him only eight minutes to arrive, and in just the three minutes since, his world was once again collapsing in on him, much as it had in the castle in Switzerland.

The Seven.

He was yelling at the man who had been holding the knife to his son's throat just minutes before. The knife was no longer in sight, but Arthur Barrington was now stretched out on a bed, seemingly unconscious, his face attached to a breathing mask which in turn was hooked to a rather complicated machine that was lit up and beeping.

"Mr. Barrington, I'm honored that you accepted my invitation. But no warm welcome for your long-lost son?" The man's voice seemed to have a hint of a South African accent, but there was no trace of human emotion in it.

"Who are you and what are you doing with Arthur?"

"I am the man the Seven told you would be contacting you, Mr. Barrington. I don't believe they mentioned my name, however. I go by many different identities, as my work requires, but you can call me what the Seven call me: Talon."

Barrington's anger, and now fear, would not subside. "Talon? What kind of name is that, a first name or a last name?"

"It makes no difference. I use it because it is a tribute to the one serious wound I have ever gotten in my life as a warrior. The first falcon I raised and trained as a boy in South Africa, the last thing I allowed myself to grow attached to, turned on me one day and ripped my index finger right out of my hand."

He removed the glove from his right hand, and it took a moment for Barrington to realize what he was being shown. At initial glance, Talon's hand looked perfectly normal, but he noted that the index finger had been replaced by some kind of hard flesh-colored material shaped to look like a finger, except where the fingertip should have a nail, the whole tip was honed to what was certain to be a deadly sharp point. "I killed the falcon, and carry this to remind me of what happens when you get soft or careless. And it comes in very handy in situations where a weapon is not convenient. Which, you can appreciate, being a man of the world, happens more often now that we live in such nervous-making times."

"So, am I to believe that the Seven want me taking orders from you?"

"Correct, Mr. Barrington."

"But what does my son have to do with any of this? I haven't seen him in years."

"Three years and two months, to be exact. He's just a little exercise we need to go through, to satisfy the Seven and to convince me that you are truly ready to do what will be asked of you. No matter what. So although you are not the picture-postcard family, I figure you must have some baseline feelings for him, even if it's just as one human being to another."

"Feelings for him in what way? What have you done to Arthur?"

"It's a little late for fatherly concern now, isn't it, Barrington? But actually, that's a reasonably convincing act. And I say that as one heartless man to another." Talon moved to the plastic tubing attached to the breathing mask covering Arthur Barrington's face.

"I don't get it. Why is he lying there unconscious? Is he sick? Did you do something to him?" In spite of himself, there was desperation in Barrington's voice.

Talon gripped the plastic tubing in his right hand. "You see, Barrington, I'm going to be giving you your marching orders for occasional, very specific actions the

Seven will need you to undertake. Some may be illegal, some may be unpleasant, all of them will come when I decide to give them to you directly, and you will act upon them instantly, without asking for explanation, without making excuses, and without fail."

"I know. I already agreed to all that in that castle in Switzerland."

Talon's eyes cut right through Barrington as sharply as his index finger now cut into the tubing, causing a sudden hiss of air to shoot out. The bedside machine started bleating a high-pitched alarm, and four different red lights flashed urgently. "Yes, it's easy to pay lip service to your pledge when there is nothing immediately at stake, Barrington. But show me you have what it really takes."

"Got what it takes for what? What's happening to my son?"

"Don't pretend some great sudden love for this kid. Granted, he's a life, but he's not much of a life. No real friends, no purpose, nobody will miss him when he's dead."

"Dead? What are you talking about? Why should he die?"

"Because I say so. Right here, right now. That's our test. It's completely arbitrary, senseless, brutal. Just like many things the Seven will make you do. That I will make you do. Things you will either do—or you will die."

Barrington lunged toward Talon. "Why, you're—" Talon grabbed his arm, stopping him instantly.

"Don't even think about it, Barrington. Not for one second. Oh, I'm not completely heartless. If you tell me to save your boy, I will." With his index finger he covered the spouting airhole cut into the tubing. The hissing stopped immediately; the alarms ceased. After a few seconds, he lifted his finger and the air shot out and the alarms restarted. "Yes, I will stop for a few seconds. Just long enough for me to slash *your* throat." He held up his razor-sharp finger just an inch from Barrington's eye. "Then I'll kill the boy."

Barrington collapsed on the bedroom floor but could not stop his eyes from moving from his son to Talon. After two minutes, the machine emitted a long, continuous beep and the graph on its monitor flatlined.

"Congratulations, Mr. Barrington. The Seven would be proud of you. I'm proud of you. You did the right thing when it counted. Now, just keep doing the right thing every time I contact you and you will be successful and powerful beyond even your wildest dreams." He threw a sheet of paper down at Barrington. "Here are your first instructions. Some information I need."

"What will happen to my son?"

"I assumed you wouldn't feel some belated familial tugging of your heartstrings to bury him in the family plot, so I will take care of disposing of him and no one will ever know. Actually, that's only partly true. People will actually know quite a bit about Arthur Barrington and his death. There is, as always, a plan. You do not have to know the next parts of the plan for now. That will all be revealed to you when I am ready. For now, just get that information. Show yourself out."

# TEN

LAURA MURPHY WATCHED the young man with the shaved head and the baggy jeans loping down the hallway, and shook her head, smiling. She remembered enough about her own student days to feel a rush of sympathy whenever a student turned up at her door with red eyes and chewed nails, looking as if they hadn't slept or eaten for a week, and while today's young men and women seemed to find it harder than her generation had adjusting to the big, bad world, she didn't judge them harshly.

Negotiating that tricky no-man's-land between childhood and adulthood had never been easy, and there were certainly more temptations and distractions nowadays for them to deal with. When you considered all the disturbing images and messages being pumped out daily on TV and in the music they listened to, she sometimes felt it was a wonder any of them turned out as well as they did.

Even if their taste in clothes was still occasionally beyond her.

And if she could play a small part in helping their transition to adulthood, she was more than happy. She had been the university's student counselor for two years now. While some people close to her—notably her father—had berated her for throwing away a potentially glittering career as a field archaeologist just so she could listen to some acned teenagers "whining about their grades," she had no regrets. She knew few professional triumphs that could match the sense of achievement she felt when a formerly suicidal English major she had helped was able to get a book of her poetry published and then start her own creative writing seminars, helping others channel their inner emotional turmoil into something positive.

Besides, Laura was still able to find time to work on her own book on lost cities. It might not hit the bestseller lists or spawn a hit movie, but when she proudly handed a copy to her dad, she would at least have created an archaeology artifact of sorts of her very own.

She also shared fully in her husband's work, not just acting as an unpaid diplomat in his frequent brushes with authority, but adding her considerable expertise to his in the quest to search out and authenticate Biblical artifacts.

Which, she realized with a keen shiver of anticipation, was what she was supposed to be doing just then. She had missed Murphy's day-after initial scroll investigation because of a typically jammed office of students, but now it was time to see if the rehydrated scroll was ready to reveal some wonderful secret about Daniel.

She closed her office door behind her, adjusted the sign that read I KNOW I SAID MY DOOR IS ALWAYS OPEN—BUT I'LL BE BACK SOON, I PROMISE! and walked briskly down the corridor and out of the building. After a few minutes, she arrived at Murphy's door, knocked smartly, and walked in.

Murphy was seated at a workbench, denim sleeves rolled up, hair awry, peering at something through a magnifying lens, and seemingly lost in thought. *That's the Murphy I think I like best,* she thought with a smile, *the so-absorbed-in-his-work-he-wouldn't-notice-the-building-is-on-fire Murphy.* The Murphy who had called her with such buzzing excitement a few minutes before to shout that the scroll was ready.

She gave his hand a squeeze, said hello to Shari, and turned her attention to the hyperbaric chamber. "So, you think the scroll's properly rehydrated?"

"I reckon it's as plump and juicy as one of your mother's Thanksgiving turkeys," Murphy declared. "Actually," he added, "it may even be slightly juicier."

"I know, I know, and probably tastes better," said Laura, rolling her eyes.

Murphy put on a pair of white cotton gloves, opened the door to the chamber, and carefully removed the scroll. "Let's see what we have baked," he said quietly.

Gently he began unrolling the papyrus over a plastic tray. Laura held her breath, amazed at the steadiness of his hands, considering he was holding something that had been made in the reign of Nebuchadnezzar, the time of Daniel. *Right now,* she thought, *in this room, we three living, breathing people are linked to the Biblical past through this impossibly fragile object that could crumble to dust at any minute.*

But the ancient papyrus didn't crumble. Like a butterfly emerging from a chrysalis, it slowly unfurled, intact and beautiful.

"Will you look at that," said Murphy as line after line of ancient cuneiform appeared. Solid triangles with linear tails, and V shapes like birds against the sky, crammed together in narrow columns. Fully unrolled, the sheet of papyrus measured about nine inches by fifteen. It was scarred by long creases across its tobacco-brown surface, the edges were tattered, and much of the surface had flaked away. But more of the lettering remained than Murphy had dared to hope.

"I'd say that was Chaldean."

Laura couldn't bear to look away from the strange geometrical symbols, in case they faded to nothing in front of her eyes. "That makes sense. In Nebuchadnezzar's day, half the priests and sorcerers in Babylon were Chaldean. Can you read it?"

Murphy tilted the scroll slightly to get a better angle. "Well, I'm not exactly fluent. I can order a salad or ask directions to the post office, but anything more complicated than that . . ."

Laura gripped his arm. "Be serious. I've seen you doodling in Chaldean. What does it say?"

"Well, that's the funny thing." Murphy squinted intently at the letters. "I can definitely make out the symbol for 'bronze,' and here"—he pointed to a barely legible smudge—"is the symbol for 'serpent.' And look, there they are again, with the symbol for 'the Israelites.' "

They were silent for a moment, and Shari watched as it seemed both Murphys' minds were racing to make sense of the images before them. "What does it all mean?" she asked.

"The Brazen Serpent," whispered Laura.

"Exactly," said Murphy. "Made by Moses thirty-five hundred years ago..."

"And broken into three pieces by King Hezekiah in seven fourteen B.C."

"But, ladies, this doesn't make any sense. Methuselah said this prize was an artifact that had to do with Daniel. He lived in the time of King Nebuchadnezzar—which was almost a hundred fifty years after the time of King Hezekiah."

Murphy pushed his chair back and started pacing. "It doesn't make sense. What would a Chaldean scribe be doing writing about the Brazen Serpent? And what's the connection to Daniel?"

Laura peered at the scroll to see if she could make out any more details. "Any chance of asking the crazy person who gave it to you?"

"*Gave* it to me?"

"You know what I mean."

Murphy shook his head. "Methusaleh likes me to figure things out for myself. That's part of the game." He snapped his fingers. "But there's no reason I can't ask for a little help. Come on, let's take some photographs. I know someone who practically speaks Chaldean in her sleep."

Laura folded her arms and gave him a stern look.

"Not," he added quickly, "that I know from personal experience. In fact, I've never even met her."

"Relax, Murphy. I know you love only me—and anything that's been lying in the ground for two thousand years. Who is this oracle?"

"You're not going to believe me, but her name," said Murphy, pronouncing each syllable carefully as if he were ordering an exotic bottle of wine in a fancy restaurant, "is Isis Proserpina McDonald."

# ELEVEN

THE PARCHMENTS OF Freedom Foundation was one of hundreds of private organizations headquartered within the very official-looking stone buildings in Washington, D.C., that many citizens automatically assumed must be government offices. The plaque on the door of the office on the second floor of the PFF building read simply DR. I. P. MCDONALD and only initiates would have known that behind the door was one of the smartest living experts on the subject of ancient cultures.

Nor would anyone passing by this office make the connection between the study of dusty, forgotten civilizations and the very loud, persistent commotion coming from behind the closed door.

The noise of books thudding to the floor one by one was followed by the gentler swish of cascading paper, then a crash as a heavy object (a lamp? a paperweight?) connected with something solid. It was lucky for the perpetrator of the chaos that few people ever did pass down this particular corridor.

The small, windowless office was lined with bookshelves on three sides, but many of the volumes—some irreplaceable, almost all of them rare or at the very least out of print—now lay in a sprawling heap on the faded brown institutional carpet. Standing in the middle of the carnage, a petite, lithe figure was scanning documents from a large pile on an antique rolltop desk and furiously tossing them aside.

"It must be here. It *must* be," rasped a voice as a tottering column of academic journals was heaved onto the floor. Now the desk's drawers were exposed and these were systematically rifled, but judging by the hiss of anger that accompanied the search, the desired object was not inside.

The figure stopped suddenly, head cocked toward the door. Footsteps. High heels tapping their way down the corridor. In the office all was still. The footsteps continued, coming nearer. Then stopped. A pause. Then a knock, soft, tentative. Then another, louder, more insistent.

"Dr. McDonald? Do you need any assistance?"

The prim young woman in the neat navy blue suit hesitated. Sometimes when Dr. McDonald didn't answer, she was simply concentrating so hard on a manuscript that she literally didn't hear you knocking, and woe betide you if you marched in without being invited. One thing she'd learned early on was that Dr. McDonald didn't take kindly to being interrupted in her work. It was a little like sleepwalkers, she thought to herself—if you woke them up, they could get terribly confused, violent even. Best to leave them well alone until they found their own way back to the land of the living.

But this was different. She'd distinctly heard several loud crashes as she turned the corner, and as she neared the door there was no doubt in her mind that someone was trashing Dr. McDonald's office.

Fiona Carter wasn't brave. The thought of any sort of physical violence made her nauseated with fear. But if there was one thing she feared more than a confrontation with a determined burglar, it was trying to explain to Dr. McDonald why she had allowed someone to decimate her precious library.

Her hand shook as she slowly turned the knob and pushed the door.

It swung open gently, revealing a slim female figure in a tweed skirt and a shapeless fisherman's sweater standing ankle-deep in tattered journals and manuscript pages, a few of which stirred briefly in the sudden draft. The figure glared at her.

"Dr. McDonald!" Fiona took a step forward and almost tripped over a hefty black volume. "Are you all right? I heard such a noise—I thought there was an intruder. I thought someone was—"

"I can't find the blasted poem of Charybdis! I was looking at it only yesterday, and now it's disappeared. Fiona, have you been interfering with my manuscripts again?"

Fiona stifled a nervous laugh. How could anybody,

however ill intentioned, make Dr. McDonald's office any more chaotic than it already was?

"The poem of Charybdis? Is it possible you were consulting Merton's *Early Coptic Literature* while you were reading it?"

Dr. McDonald looked dubious. "Possibly. I suppose."

"In which case perhaps you put the poem inside the book for safekeeping?" If she remembered correctly, *Early Coptic Literature* was bound in dark green cloth with red lettering on the spine. It wasn't in its usual place on the shelf against the far wall. Very little was. She looked down at the book-strewn floor.

"Is that it? Over there, next to Eliade's *The Sacred and the Profane*?"

Dr. McDonald turned in the direction Fiona was pointing and scooped up a fat green book. She riffled nimbly through its pages and a single sheaf of parchment fluttered to the floor. The poem of Charybdis.

Dr. McDonald turned back to Fiona, beaming. With her matronly clothes and permanently severe expression, it was easy to miss the fact that Isis Proserpina McDonald was a stunningly beautiful woman. It was only her rare smiles that gave it away. Not that you were likely to see her smile if you called her by her given name.

"Clever girl. How on earth do you put up with me?"

Before Fiona could frame an appropriate answer, they were both frozen in place by a sudden ringing. Turning instinctively to the empty desk, they then scanned the floor, trying to pinpoint where the sound was coming from. Fiona pushed back a pile of journals and picked up the phone.

"Hello, Dr. McDonald's office, Fiona speaking. Oh, good morning, Professor Murphy." She turned back to Dr. McDonald, who was still standing amid the rubble of her library, furiously shaking her head and mouthing *no*.

"No, she's not busy at all, Professor Murphy. I'm sure she'd love to speak with you." Fiona smiled sweetly and held out the phone.


Isis sat at her desk, arms folded, lips pursed, and waited for her computer to register an incoming e-mail. While she had been standing in the wreckage of her office, listening to Professor Murphy and his rather wild story about a Babylonian scroll, she had hardly noticed as Fiona began the laborious task of restoring order. Now almost everything was, if not in its place, then at least off the floor and in neat-looking rows and piles. She'd even done her best to rearrange Isis's collection of ancient pottery figures—her goddesses—in the correct chronological sequence on the top of her one filing cabinet.

As Isis's eye traveled over the dear, familiar forms, beginning with a bloated fertility goddess from the Neander valley in Germany and ending with a graceful Sumerian moon deity, she felt a tear welling up and quickly blinked it back. The little figures were a precious legacy from her father, another Dr. McDonald and one of the most eminent archaeologists of his day, the result of a lifetime's digging around the Mediterranean and Near East.

"For my own little goddess, worshiped and adored above all others," he'd said when he'd presented her with the big, square cardboard box done up with ribbons. To her thirteen-year-old eyes, the little figures, some missing an arm or a little hand, all grooved and pocked with the dirt and dust of civilizations long disappeared, were better than any Barbie doll. The gift marked the beginning of her own passionate commitment to the secrets of the past.

Unfortunately the goddesses were not the only legacies of his obsession that her father had passed on to her. There was also her name.

She supposed there were girls called Freya who had never been teased at school. She knew a Greek paleontologist called Aphrodite who didn't seem in the least self-conscious about it. And wasn't there that tennis player called Venus? No one gave her a hard time because she was named after the Roman goddess of love. But *Isis Proserpina* was a different matter. It was like being born with a circle of stars around your head. Or writhing snakes instead of hair. It made it rather hard to blend in.

At the little Highland school it had been *Issy* or *Posy*, both of which she loathed. Why couldn't she be a Mary, Kate, or Janet like the other girls? In the museum, in the haven of her office, at least she was able to insist on *Dr. McDonald*. But with friends it was a little trickier. Which was perhaps one reason, she supposed, she didn't really seem to have any.

She drummed her fingers—narrow, elegant, with nails bitten down to the quick—on the desk, impatient for the promised pictures of the scroll. A watched kettle and all that. She frowned.

Professor Michael Murphy had seemed something of an oddball. Very concerned with Biblical prophecies. Babbling on about the Book of Daniel. But the scroll did sound intriguing. Could be a forgery, of course, or just turn out to be something rather mundane—a three-thousand-year-old shopping list or a form for a hyena permit. God knows, those Babylonians could be a bureaucratic lot.

Over the years, as her reputation as a philologist had grown, the trickle of ancient enigmas in need of her language skills had become a steady stream. If you dug up a shard of pottery with a puzzling inscription or discovered a scrap of papyrus covered in a meaningless scrawl, eventually you would turn to Isis McDonald. And nine times out of ten, even if it took her six months and she nearly drove herself to distraction in the process, she would solve the riddle, crack the code, or unravel the linguistic knot that had had the rest of the experts stumped. It was her unique gift.

Her father, happily watching her career begin to bloom as his faded, had speculated that it was a matter of memory rather than expertise. Surely only someone who had been an Egyptian priestess in a previous existence could have such a facility with their sacred hieroglyphics. Ridiculous, of course. But it was the sort of silly thing he said toward the end. Probably just his funny archaeologist's way of saying how much he loved her.

She blinked the memory away as the screen began to fill with images of the scroll, and she turned with relief from the troubling world of emotion to the much more straightforward one of ancient Babylonia.

What she saw instantly got her attention. And kept her staring at the screen and scribbling furious notes for the next two hours.

He was jolted back into the present by the phone.

"Professor Murphy? Dr. McDonald. I've been reading your scroll."

He gently put the Bible aside. "Good to hear from you. And please, the name's Michael. Though most people make do with Murphy."

There was an awkward pause.

"Well, Mr. Murphy, it seems you were right. We're definitely dealing with the Biblical Brazen Serpent—"

"But the scroll dates from a period a hundred fifty years *after* the Serpent was destroyed." He could sense her frowning at his impatience. "I'm sorry. This thing has got me wound a little tight. Please go on."

"Well, the scroll appears to be a sort of diary written by a Chaldean priest named Dakkuri. As far as I can make out, the Serpent was indeed broken into three pieces, as in the Biblical account, but someone apparently forgot to put the pieces out with the trash. The pieces must have been stored in the Temple, and when the Babylonians came to sack Jerusalem, they found them somewhere in the Temple and obviously thought they were worth taking back home."

"And when the pieces got to Babylon, this priest, Dakkuri, put the pieces of the Brazen Serpent back together?"

"I think so, yes. But that was just the beginning. I

think Dakkuri believed this Serpent had far greater value than as a handsome bronze sculpture."

Murphy's mind was racing ahead. "So, what you're saying is that the Babylonians heard the stories in Jerusalem about the Serpent's healing powers when Moses first made it and they felt it was worth letting Dakkuri see if he could get it working again."

Isis was not pleased with Murphy's interruptions, and she realized she would have to be just as pushy if she was ever going to get through her piece. "Actually, Professor Murphy, my point is that I think Dakkuri tried to use the Serpent as part of a cult."

"You mean Dakkuri had his Babylonians worshiping the Serpent just like the Israelites in the time of Hezekiah?"

"Not many of them. The scroll seems to indicate that there was some kind of priestly inner circle led by Dakkuri that surrounds the lines of power that are drawn from the Serpent symbol."

"And then doesn't it look like the Serpent-worship turned out to be a big mistake for the Babylonians, as it did for the Israelites back with Hezekiah?"

"Well, there is some reference to trouble with the Serpent, but there's some damage to the scroll at a crucial point." Isis made it sound as if this were due to carelessness on Murphy's part.

He let it pass. "It looks like that trouble, as you call it, was big trouble. The king symbol is there, which could mean that Dakkuri's cult of the Serpent was banned by Nebuchadnezzar himself, right?"

"Yes, I'm sure you don't need me to teach you your Bible, Mr. Murphy," Isis said smugly. "According to the

Book of Daniel, Nebuchadnezzar built a great statue with a golden head, a likeness of the one in his famous dream. And all the princes from far and wide were ordered to bow down and worship it at certain times. When they heard the sound of the cornet, the flute, the harp—let me see, what else?"

"Sackbut, psaltery, and dulcimer," said Murphy without hesitation.

"Thank you. Yes, *psaltery* and *dulcimer*—how poetic the King James can be. Takes me right back to Sunday mornings in our little kirk in Scotland." The memory seemed to derail her for a moment, but she quickly got back on track. "Anyway, the long and the short of it was, God made the king mad as a March hare as a punishment for his arrogance, and when he finally regained his sanity, Nebuchadnezzar got the message that idol-worship was evil. So he banned it."

"Right, and, of course, the ban would have included the cult of the Serpent."

"So I would imagine."

Murphy tried to put it all together in his head. "So this priest—Dakkuri—gets the order to stop worshiping the Serpent, to get rid of it."

"But I'm beginning to think this Serpent is rather hard to get rid of. Nobody who possessed it ever wanted to just melt it down and recast it."

Murphy bolted out of his chair. "Yes! That's it! The reason for the scroll. Dakkuri isn't taking the trouble to write all this down just to let people know he's been a naughty Serpent-worshiper. No. He made it look as if he broke it again and got rid of it, as ordered by Nebuchadnezzar. He wasn't stupid. But he hid the three pieces, and that's what he's telling us in this scroll, isn't it, Dr. McDonald?"

"Better than that, Mr. Murphy. I believe what Dakkuri has written here is not just that he hid the pieces, but the beginnings of how to find them."

Murphy sank back in his chair as if he had been deflated by her last comment. "What do you mean, 'the beginnings of how to find them'?"

"The last part of the scroll is really in two parts. Part one continues Dakkuri's report of events. It looks like he picked three of his acolytes to scatter the Serpent pieces far and wide within the Babylonian empire."

"But does he tell us where they went to hide the pieces?"

Isis was getting good at talking past Murphy's interruptions. "That's the second part of the end of the scroll. It looks like Dakkuri was setting up a kind of high priest's scavenger hunt for the Serpent pieces, and the last lines are a key for where to find the first piece. Then it looks like he's indicating that once you find the first piece, that will lead to the rest of the Serpent."

Murphy stared at the blow-up of the scroll in front of him. "And based on this pattern here, the curve with the ridges at the bottom, this first piece must be the tail, right?"

"The tail of the Serpent gets my vote."

"Dakkuri sure went to a lot of effort to save this Serpent, yet made certain that it would be awfully hard for somebody to find the pieces."

Isis found talking to Murphy brought into full play her twin drives of scholarship and competitiveness with smart men. "Not hard for somebody smart enough to work out his clues."

Murphy felt every archaeologist's bone in his body starting to quiver with excitement. "This means that we can find the Brazen Serpent made by Moses! Better still, if we do find the Serpent based on this scroll, it proves that it was still in existence during Daniel's time!"

A particularly unladylike laugh escaped Isis's mouth before she could stop herself. "Forget this 'we' business, Mr. Murphy. I can barely find things in my own office. I don't go on expeditions. However, you are free to charge off in search of the first Serpent piece. Nothing could be simpler. So long as you know the location of the Horns of the Ox."

# TWELVE

*HORNS OF THE OX.*
   *Horns of the Ox.*

Murphy kept replaying the phrase in his mind and marveled at the seeming ease with which Isis McDonald had come up with that site from the symbols at the very end of the scroll. As hard as he had stared at those same symbols, he had not come close to making that connection.

Of course, now that she had given him her interpretation, it seemed crystal clear. With more than a bit of both his professional and male pride rebounding, Murphy did note that here was where his field experience could put Dr. McDonald's bookish linguistic skills into operation.

The Horns of the Ox would have to refer to a fairly prominent landmark reasonably close to the old

Babylon. Dakkuri probably would have chosen a natural landmark as opposed to a man-made one, because he could not have known how long it would be before this Serpent piece would be dug up.

For a few hours he pored over his map texts, but he realized that nobody knew the ancient landscapes better than his own wife. Her studies of ancient cities gave her an encyclopedic knowledge that he now needed.

Desperately.

Murphy finally tracked Laura down in the faculty lounge. "Honey, you've got to get out all your books and maps. I think I've found the location of the Serpent."

"Murphy, really, you figured out where the Serpent is?" Instantly, Laura shed her counselor's cloak and was one hundred percent archaeologist.

"Well, it was really Dr. McDonald. And it's only the clue to where the first piece of the Serpent is hiding. According to her, the scroll is a kind of Chaldean treasure map, with the Serpent piece as the treasure."

"How exciting!" Laura said. "But where is it?"

Murphy knelt down and showed Laura where he had written *The Horns of the Ox* and sketched out several rough pencil drawings of landscapes that could have inspired that nickname. They all had two high vertical points curved like horns, straddling a mound of land that could be seen as the ox's skull. "This is about as far as I got. The truth is, I need your ancient-map-reading skills. It's been a while since Dakkuri wrote down the directions, and I think the neighborhood's changed a little in the meantime."

Laura laughed. She took Murphy by the hand and they started off down the hall.

"I don't know, Murphy," she said, shaking her head. "Why is it men just can't read maps?"

As soon as he'd shown Laura the partial translation of the scroll, she had gone into overdrive. Within minutes their already cluttered living room had become a stormy sea of paper, as maps, reference books, and computer printouts had been laid out on the floor. Laura sat in the middle of the chaos, grabbing maps, throwing them aside, scribbling furious notes while she hummed a tuneless ditty to herself.

As she put it, it wasn't like looking for a needle in a haystack. It was like trying to reconstruct a two-thousand-year-old haystack, figuring out where each individual piece of hay had originally fit before being bumped around by a couple of millennia of winds, floods, and earthquakes—and then trying to find the needle.

Dakkuri's directions—assuming Murphy and Isis had correctly deciphered the scroll—to the final hiding place of the Serpent's tail had been pretty specific. Laura gave a more refined interpretation to Horns of the Ox than Murphy's crude sketches, saying it most likely referred to a particular geographical feature—probably a curved ridge ending in two sharp promontories. Maybe with a big hump of rock or a prominent hill lying behind it—the "body" of the ox. And the whole thing was likely to be visible from some distance, so the surrounding area might well have been relatively flat.

But the landscape Dakkuri had had in his mind's eye was ever-changing. Sea levels advanced and retreated, erosion moved hills around like pieces on a chessboard, the courses of rivers and waterways could be diverted, turning desert into pasture and vice versa. And on top of that, earthquakes could shake things up like a kaleidoscope, totally changing the picture from one year to the next.

To see things the way Dakkuri had, it was necessary to reverse the process. To somehow look at the modern landscape and see the ancient one beneath.

Such a task required an uncanny ability to read relief maps in three dimensions, a detailed knowledge of ancient geography, and an intuitive sense of geological transformation through time—not to mention a kind of sixth sense that you couldn't put a name to.

Luckily Laura was one of only a handful of people on the planet who had the full skill-set. As Murphy watched her pore over her papers, he marveled at these unique and powerful skills. Finding the tail of the Serpent at the Horns of the Ox was going to test those skills to the limit.

# THIRTEEN

IT WAS THE second punch that Murphy regretted. No one was fighting him; he was hitting a heavy bag in the Preston University gym. The first punch, a sharp right jab, felt good to him, so good that he quickly snapped his left hand with a pop against the bag that sent a jolt from the boxing glove straight up his shoulder. The shoulder he had momentarily forgotten was still throbbing from the clawing by the lion.

When Murphy dropped both arms to let the pain ricochet around his upper body, the burly figure next to him let out a gruff snarl. "Come on, Murphy, no coffee breaks. This isn't government work, it's supposed to be a workout." Levi Abrams pushed Murphy's shoulder to get him started again. His left shoulder.

Now Murphy had to double over to keep the pain

from shooting around his torso. "Levi! Didn't you hear me say I had to take it easy today with that shoulder?"

"Suck it up, Murphy. Intensity. Focus. Do you remember nothing of your army time? Train, train, train some more. That's the only way to keep yourself from decaying like one of your desert mummies."

Murphy had to laugh as he looked over at the six-foot-five Israeli who was always so serious about their training sessions. Actually, Levi Abrams was serious about everything he did, as far as Murphy could tell. He had been recruited to the United States by the high-tech companies in the Raleigh-Durham area as a very highly paid security expert. So highly paid that he could afford to take an early retirement from the Mossad and relocate his family to Raleigh.

However, Murphy was certain that Levi had not completely retired. He would never ask Levi directly, and Levi was far too serious and closemouthed to say anything, but he remained extremely well connected in the Mideast, in the Arab countries as well as in Israel. So much so that Levi had been able to help Murphy on a number of occasions with expediting papers to get himself and, more important, some objects out of the Mideast.

For his part, though you would never guess it from his always stern expressions and no-nonsense conversations, Levi seemed to respect Murphy. Like Murphy, in his way Levi was a natural instructor, though if Murphy worked his students the way Levi worked him, the university would have him brought up on abuse charges.

They had first met by eyeing each other before sunup on the running track two years earlier, when Levi was overseeing the security needs for a high-powered computer system being donated to the university by his current tech firm. Eventually, Levi offered to expand Murphy's martial arts skills, which led to high-intensity training sessions whenever they could fit them in. With Levi, Murphy always pushed himself way beyond the effort he put in on his own, and he normally pushed himself hard. Right now, getting so carried away had brought on the pain that kept him doubled over.

This morning Murphy would have skipped working out altogether to let his shoulder heal, but he had an urgent reason to get together with Levi. He decided to get to it while he was waiting for the pain to subside.

"Levi, my friend, I have a major favor to ask. I've gotten a lead on something really huge, an archaeological find that I need to jump on."

"Another of your dusty knickknacks?" Levi's respect for Murphy as a fighter did not exactly extend to Murphy's choice of profession. "Let me guess, you need, as my son has taken to saying, 'wheels'? Transportation to somewhere dicey in the Mideast?"

"You know me all too well, my friend. Levi, all I need is to get Laura and me into Samaria ASAP, try to find the hiding place for this piece we're looking for, and bring it back to Preston and have no hassles with officials or customs. Oh, and have it cost me no money."

Levi gave a long, low whistle. "What, you're not going to make time for a round of peace talks as long as you're in the neighborhood? Let me see what I can do. How soon can you get away?"

"We have most of next week off for independent study, and I've just about got all my students covered, so

I can leave immediately. Laura's getting her office hours covered as well. I really owe you, Levi."

"Let's see if I can deliver first. In the meantime"—Levi punched Murphy's shoulder—"your coffee break is over. Get back to the bag."

# FOURTEEN

"WE ARE TWO men, but we make an interesting couple, Professor Murphy, do we not?" Murphy nodded deferentially to his host, Sheikh Umar al-Khaliq, but he wondered where he was going with this conversational opening. They sat drinking strong Arabic coffee in al-Khaliq's beautiful home in Samaria, after a day of traveling, all arranged by Levi Abrams with amazing rapidity.

Laura had gone to their guest bedroom, saying that she was exhausted from her flight, but privately she pointed out to Murphy that she was sensing the sheikh was no believer in women as being worthy of inclusion in any serious discussion. "Typical," she said, "of so many Arab men of his generation. In fact"—she jabbed Murphy with her finger—"typical of so many men of every country."

"Hey, don't point that finger at me. It's loaded," Murphy said. "I'm clean."

"But you could help bring the sheikh into at least the nineteen hundreds."

Murphy sighed. "I agree, dear, but could we not offend the generous hand that has made this trip possible? At least until the trip is over. Then, I promise, I will leave you behind to enlighten him. You will be my very special gift for the Samarian host who seems to have everything else."

"Murphy, it's a good thing I have my maps to study. Because tomorrow, when we set out exploring, I'm going to pick out a really great place to leave *you* behind. Don't stay up too late with your manly man talk."

Actually, Murphy was pretty certain what the sheikh might want to talk about, thanks to Levi Abrams, who had connected him with the sheikh. After working his cell phone for fifteen minutes while Murphy finished his workout, Levi said, "I think I've made a perfect match for you, my friend. Sheikh Umar al-Khaliq."

"And he's perfect because . . . ?"

Levi sat Murphy down. "This may sound like the last thing you would expect me to know about the Mideast, Murphy, but did you know that there are more and more Arabs who are seeking out *your* God?"

"I had read a little bit about the Christianity movement among Muslims, but I honestly believed it had to be about as likely as their coming to your God. No offense."

"None taken. At any rate, al-Khaliq is wealthy beyond belief, still enjoys diplomatic status for his fleet of private airplanes, and somehow, I guess, it was not enough. I had heard that he was putting out some discreet feelers to some of the Christian missionary groups in the region. As you can imagine, such seeking is not a popular extracurricular habit in the Mideast, no matter how powerful you are. So I told him that you would be happy to counsel him in return for round-trip passage and supplies for a little digging."

"Levi, you are a genius. Can I trust him?"

"I helped the sheikh out years ago with a messy situation with some trigger-happy Bedouins who were making it a little awkward for him to fight back against them on his home turf. I would trust him."

"Thank you, Levi. I owe you big-time."

"You owe me nothing. Take care of that wonderful wife of yours. You, I would miss not so much. Her, I would miss. And, Murphy, trust the sheikh, don't necessarily trust anyone else who's working with him. But you know the drill, so to speak, about digging in strange lands."

Now, two days later, Murphy sat across from the sheikh, waiting for him to explain in his sometimes tortured English why the two of them made such an "interesting couple." The trip could not have gone more smoothly. The sheikh's main adviser, Saif Nahavi, had made all of the travel arrangements, and al-Khaliq's wealth and diplomatic status had eased all bureaucratic hurdles.

Of course, as Laura had pointed out, "Murphy, your

trips are always a lot like prison, a whole lot easier getting in than getting yourself out."

Certainly, Murphy had a lot to be thankful for due to the sheikh's generosity, and he wanted to live up to his part of Levi's bargain by counseling al-Khaliq about any and all aspects of his apparent interest in Christianity. However, his many trips to the Mideast had taught him that he must wait for the sheikh to bring up the discussion of such a sensitive topic in his own way. If he broached it at all.

"Professor Murphy, you are a Christian man who comes to my Muslim land in search of something that has been lost for centuries, something you feel is still vital today. I am a man who has every modern possession tenfold, but I feel I am seeking something even more ancient, more simple than you seek in your journey here."

"Sheikh, I respect your courage in your search. Are there questions you have?"

"So many questions, Murphy, but it is enough for me to meet you and help a man of your faith. In my position, as long as I stay here in the land of my ancestors, and despite all I can afford to do, I do not have the freedom that you enjoy, you who come here with your hat in hand."

Murphy had to suppress a laugh once again at the sheikh's unintentional knack for the embarrassing phrase.

"Let me just say, Sheikh, that I am at your service at any time of the night or day. I am indebted to you for your generosity toward my work and on such short notice. But after tonight, I realize that I am doubly blessed, because you have reminded me of how lucky I am to be an American and to be free to pursue any religion I wish."

"It is I who must be thanking you, Murphy. Someday perhaps we will be able to discuss many things in your land."

"Are you sure we must wait for that time, Sheikh? I'm sure we do not have time tonight for all of your questions, but how about giving me the two that are of greatest concern at this time?"

The sheikh smiled. "I see, Professor, that you are good at your digging. All right. Tell me, what do you see as the main difference between Allah and your God? Many people think they are the same."

Murphy sat forward. "There are several similarities. We believe our God is the creator of all things, and you agree. But we also believe in a triune God, one God made up of three divine personalities who have individual works. He is a merciful heavenly Father and sovereign sustainer of the universe who loved mankind so much, He gave His only Son to die on the cross for our sins so that we can have eternal life. He sends His Holy Spirit into our hearts to create a new spirit in us and lead us through life."

The sheikh sighed. "There is so much to try to understand. My second big question is, what would I have to do if I wanted to become a Christian?"

"According to the Bible, a person becomes a Christian by believing that Jesus Christ is not only the Son of God who died for the sins of the world, but that He rose again on the third day and will save all who call on Him by faith."

"That is all? It seems too easy, too simple."

Murphy nodded. "Yes, it does. That is one reason so many people miss it. But the truth is, it was not easy for Him to die one of the most excruciating deaths in history. As you know, Sheikh, those of your faith believe He was simply a good man, a teacher, or even a prophet. But Jesus was much more than that. The fact that He then rose from the dead shows that God the Father was pleased with His sacrifice and is willing to save all who call on Him by faith."

The sheikh looked tired. Murphy gently added, "Sheikh, what I have explained tonight is a matter of the heart. In the quiet of your own thoughts you can call out to the Father in the name of the Son, and the Holy Spirit will save you and give you eternal life."

"Thank you, Professor Murphy, for not squeezing me on this." Murphy winced again at the torturing of the language. "And thank you for your answers to my questions."

"You are welcome, Sheikh. I will pray that you make your decision soon. One thing I would ask: When you do, please drop me a note and inform me. Here is my card. You can reach me by phone or e-mail."

"Fine. Now you must get your rest, Professor. Tomorrow, my aide, Saif, will escort you through my land and see that you return to your land—with as little interference as possible."

An hour after the sheikh had retired and half an hour after Murphy had turned out his reading light in the guest quarters, the sheikh's right-hand man, Saif Nahavi, slipped unnoticed to the marketplace. It appeared that he was securing last-minute supplies for the Murphys' excursion the next morning.

As Nahavi passed an electronics store that was closed, a low voice called out, "Nahavi. Behzad. Do not turn around. Just look in the window."

Nahavi did as instructed. Behzad spoke from the darkness of the recessed doorway of the store. "Are you ready for tomorrow?"

"Yes. The regular driver has already taken ill. You, Behzad, will be our last-minute replacement driver. It will be just the Murphys and me. They are traveling light, to say the least."

"And what are they seeking?"

"I do not know what Murphy is hunting in our country. I have to believe that because he has been so secretive, it must be worth a lot of money."

"It had better be." Behzad's cold tone was not one to be dismissed lightly.

"Do not doubt me, Behzad. We have never worked together, despite all the times you have tried to convince me to use my position with the sheikh to steal things for you to sell on the black market. But I know value, and whatever the Murphys will find tomorrow will be worth a fortune. Plus, there is the not-insignificant matter of my gambling debts, which this month have finally gone beyond what I can free from the sheikh."

"You, with your mighty position with the sheikh, are always looking at me like dirt, Nahavi. I always figured you were a thief like me."

"You are the professional thief, Behzad, which is why we are doing business tomorrow. But remember, we do this my way. It must look like a robbery by strangers. I will not jeopardize my position with the sheikh."

"Yes, Nahavi, I will take care to protect your precious innocence in all this. As long as the money comes from the black market for what I take from the Murphys."

"The money will come, Behzad. Half for you, half for me, and just to be fair, if you do your part right, two full shares of death for the Murphys."

# FIFTEEN

MURPHY WIPED HIS sleeve across his forehead, squinted through the glare toward a distant line of dusty hills, and breathed in a deep lungful of hot desert air. It felt good to be home.

In fact, he had never before set foot in this particular region of Samaria, but as his sneakers crunched over the dry ground and a ragged herd of goats scuttled past him, leaving the clatter of bells and a sharp, musky scent on the air, he knew this was where he was meant to be. The first Christians might have walked here. Perhaps one of the apostles had rested awhile in the shade of that large boulder perched on the escarpment. For all Murphy knew, he might literally be following in the footsteps of Jesus.

He grinned at his own flight of fancy. Maybe that was a stretch. But there was no doubting that this was the stage where some of the key events of the Bible had unfolded. And he was convinced that this seemingly dead and empty landscape could tell a miraculous story, if you knew how to read it.

That, unfortunately, was the tricky part. The official cover for the Murphys' visit to Samaria was to shoot some test footage for an upcoming television special. So, while Laura continued her methodical searching of the landscape, Murphy kept raising and lowering his digital camera, pretending to be doing the main work.

Through his camera monitor Murphy watched as Laura paced slowly back and forth, scanning the low ridge to the south, checking it against a handful of maps stuffed into the pocket of her cargo pants, suddenly turning one hundred eighty degrees as if she'd suddenly remembered something—then turning back, frustrated, as if the memory had eluded her. Murphy knew better than to crowd Laura when she was in the zone.

The other members of their party, provided by the sheikh, were Saif Nahavi and a driver named Behzad. Both men remained down below with the Land Cruiser, watching for intruders but seeming to be paying no attention to either Murphy. They had told Nahavi nothing about what they were seeking other than the general vicinity to which they wished to be driven. Going beyond Levi's warning to him, Murphy did not tell even the sheikh about the Serpent's tail.

They were otherwise alone in their little corner of the desert, a natural semicircular amphitheater formed by the curving horns of the ridge. The goat bells had faded in the distance, and the only sound was the whisper of sand being gently blown up from the desert.

After her map study the previous night, then early that morning, Laura had been fairly dizzy with excitement and strong Arabic coffee. She was convinced that she had nailed it. After staring at the countless hills and gulleys, not allowing herself to be distracted, Laura had stabbed a finger at the map spread on the kitchen table. "That's it! I'm sure of it. Just north of the old riverbed, before you reach the wadi. There!" And Murphy had hoped she was right. After all, she was a natural.

Now, he could tell, that sense of certainty had disappeared, evaporating like the dew under a fierce desert sun. Laura had her head down, shoulders sagging like a defeated athlete as she picked her way through the boulders and little outcrops of rock toward him.

And then, in an instant, she was gone.

# SIXTEEN

MURPHY STOOD OPENMOUTHED for a moment, like a member of the audience at a magic act who could not figure out where the girl in the suddenly empty box had vanished to. Then he broke into a run.

Laura had been about fifty yards away, he figured, when she'd disappeared. Heart hammering, he felt the soft ground sucking at his feet as he pounded through the sand toward the plume of dust marking his last sight of her. It was like one of those dreams where you are running from a monster but your legs don't seem to work. He suddenly had an image of Dakkuri, dark eyes gleaming with malice, and whispered a silent prayer.

He stumbled, righted himself, and finally crested the shallow rise that had divided them. There, where Laura must have been, was a gaping hole some four feet wide, sand pouring into it like water down a drain. He threw himself down, leaning as far into the hole as he dared. He remembered rescuing a classmate who had fallen through the ice one winter, hoping the ice would take his weight as he inched closer. Did desert sand behave the same way?

He thought he heard something, a muffled cry that might have been Laura, and leaned farther over. Suddenly, the solid ground beneath him gave way and he was plunging like a kid down a park slide. He landed with a thump, and rolled onto his side, choking on a mouthful of sand. As he spat it out, the dust began to clear and the world came into focus again.

On three sides were rough-hewn walls of dark, uncut stone. The fourth was buried in the tidal wave of sand that had sucked him down with it. And there, seemingly oblivious of the chaos around her, was Laura. Murphy scrambled to his feet and reached out for her.

"Laura, are you okay? Are you hurt?"

Her cargo pants were shredded at the knees, a dark stain seeping through, and sand seemed to be falling off every inch of her. But as she shook a big swirl of sand from her hair, Murphy could see that she was smiling.

"You see—I was right! It was right under our feet the whole time. No wonder we couldn't see it."

Murphy wrapped her in a bear hug and laughed with relief. "I never doubted you for a second, sweetheart." He stood back to make sure she really was still in one piece, then followed her gaze to the far wall.

Their eyes were adjusting to the mix of light from the holes they'd fallen through from above with the shadowy, mostly stale-aired gloom of the underground sand cave in which they had landed. They saw that the sand actually started to give way fifty yards ahead to some stone. The stone formed steps, and the steps led to the entrance of what appeared to be the kind of natural stone cave they were used to seeing when hiking through North Carolina.

They stumbled through the sand to the steps, where they could move more swiftly to the entrance of the cave. Both Murphys took their flashlights from their pants now and swept the cave entrance in twin arcs.

"What are we looking for?" Laura asked.

"Probably an amphora."

Laura drew up her mental image of the ancient clay jars that were bulbous in shape with two handles that stuck out like ears from their narrow necks. Amphoras were used to store grains, dried fish, water, wine, and valuables. She spotted a piece of one that was lying in the sand and handed it to Murphy.

"Yes, this certainly looks like the 'vessels' the Bible speaks of, what we call *amphoras*, the kind the Babylonians took when they sacked Jerusalem. If I'm right, the tail of the Serpent is in one of these." Murphy turned the clay jar upside down. Something horrible and snakelike crawled out of it and slithered away. "But not this one."

Laura shuddered and jumped aside as the slimy thing skittered past her. She lost her balance, went stumbling backward against the cavern wall, and fell through a narrow vertical fissure.

Murphy heard her scream and whirled around with his flashlight, searching the darkness for her. But Laura was gone.

"Laura? Laura, where are you?" he called out, staggered by a surge of anxiety. "Laura?"

"Over here, Murph," Laura finally replied after what seemed like an eternity had passed. "Over here. I think I found it!"

Murphy was relieved to hear her voice but still couldn't see her. Tense moments passed before he saw the beam from her flashlight through the narrow fissure. He dashed toward it and slipped between the gap in the cavern's walls that had swallowed Laura.

Murphy found himself in another cavern, considerably smaller than the first. "Laura, you have got to stop trying to disappear on me."

Laura was standing there, sweeping the beam of her flashlight across what she had discovered. "Look, Murph!" Laura exclaimed in amazement. "Isn't that incredible?"

Murphy trained his flashlight beam alongside Laura's, and both of their mouths dropped open.

"Murph, do you see what I see?"

"After all this, it's almost too good to be true."

The neck of a large stone jar was sticking out of a mound of dirt and sand as if it were just waiting for them to open it.

They approached it together, like hunters stalking a buck they feared would bolt before they could get it in their sights. Silently, they knelt down and scooped the dirt and sand away from the jar. It was about eighteen inches high and the neck was just wide enough to get a hand through.

Murphy was bursting with anticipation, and he raced to pick it up. Trying not to think of scorpions, vipers, or other stinging creatures, he reached inside. Laura, being the more cautious of the couple, trained her flashlight beam on the floor of the cave between where she stood and the amphora, to make sure there was nothing crawling before she moved another step toward her husband. The path looked safe and she was about to join her gleefully shouting spouse when, just to be sure, she shined her flashlight against the far wall of the cave.

There was nothing crawling there either, but what she saw instead made her heart sink. "Um . . . Murph . . . we have a problem."

# SEVENTEEN

THE REST OF the cave was filled with amphoras. Hundreds upon hundreds of amphoras. Amphoras of all shapes and sizes.

Murphy put down the one he had been cradling, the one that only seconds before had seemed like the certain hiding place for the Serpent's tail.

The floor was flat and free of water, which was why the amphoras had likely been stored there many centuries before. Stored and forgotten. "Great," Murphy groaned. "This must be where amphoras came to die. I wasn't planning on spending the next six months down here."

"And I was doing so well."

"Yes, you were, sweetheart. You got us this close."

"Any idea how we know which one is hiding the Serpent's tail?"

"Hmm...I wonder if that sneaky high priest Dakkuri pulled a clever trick here. What if he instructed his minions not only to bury this piece of the Serpent but to go one step further and kind of bury it in plain sight?"

"Yeah, kind of like looking for the needle in a stack of other needles instead of a haystack."

"Maybe not as bad, Laura. You know this stuff better than I do from your research—how did they use these amphoras?"

Laura began sorting through her vast knowledge of ancient artifacts. "They usually sealed them with plugs made out of cork, clay, or wood, if they were sealed at all," Laura explained. "But something this important, we should be looking for one that was sealed with wax."

"If we find one full of pennies, we'll definitely know it's a fake."

Laura took one side of the cavern, Murphy the other, and they began examining amphoras by the dozen. Most were empty. Some held animal bones, others primitive household tools and personal items. Every one of these amphoras, let alone their contents, was an ancient artifact that under different circumstances would have had Murphy, or any archaeologist, doing cartwheels.

They searched amphora after amphora and were at their wits' end, when an idea struck Murphy. "Hold it," he said in that tone he used when he couldn't believe how blind he had been to something. "If you wanted to hide a piece of the Serpent, which is presumably long and thin and hard, you wouldn't put it in one of these fat ones so it could rattle around, calling attention to itself every time it moved. You'd wrap it in something soft and slip it into one of these, right?" He picked up a tall, narrow amphora that resembled a flower vase. "Find one like this that's sealed with wax and we've got it."

Most of the amphoras in the cavern were of the pot-bellied and bulbous variety. Murphy's moment of insight had eliminated every one of them. He and Laura quickly picked out the potential candidates, and just as quickly eliminated those not sealed with wax.

"How about this one?" Laura soon asked, showing Murphy one whose mouth was sealed so tightly, smoothly, and totally that the plug had to be made of wax.

Murphy began digging at it with a knife, first placing all of the wax he removed in a plastic bag for future study. The plug soon popped out with a dull *thwack*. His eyes were wide with anticipation as he reached inside and removed something wrapped in a coarsely woven cloth.

What he found when he unrolled it was a perfectly preserved piece of cast bronze about twelve inches long and two inches in diameter. It was tapered snakelike at one end and broken off at the other. Murphy had no doubt he was holding the tail of the Brazen Serpent in his hands.

# EIGHTEEN

"MURPHY, WE'VE FOUND it. Let me hold it."
Laura marveled at the weight of the bronze snake's tail
in her palm. "Imagine, Murphy, Moses made this!"

"Amazing. We are blessed today. Now let's try to get
out of here so we can live to tell about it tomorrow."

They retraced their steps but realized they would not
be able to climb back out of the holes they had fallen
into to get to the underground cave. There were two
passageways leading back in the opposite direction from
where the cave entrance was. Murphy chose the one
that was least sandy. After several hundred yards, the
sand was turning into dirt and the ground was even a
little damp, indicating that water would be nearby. A
few yards farther, and there were roots of trees and
shrubs showing through some of the soil, and Murphy
was able to hoist himself up on a combination of rock

and roots and poke his head aboveground. "Honey, I think we can squeeze through here."

"Murph, I'm stuck!"

Murphy whirled to see that Laura's foot was caught in the network of snarled roots. He crouched down and worked it free, having to break off a knotted clump in the process. He was about to discard it, when he noticed a small shoot growing out of it in the shape of an almost perfect cross. He snapped it off and handed it to Laura.

"For you, my amazing wife. A souvenir of your visit here to the Brazen Serpent attraction."

A thin shaft of daylight from above was passing right between them. The tiny cross was struck by the light. It gave off a sparkling aura that seemed providential. Murphy and Laura were speechless. She hugged the cross to her chest as Murphy wrapped his arms around her. They stood in the shaft of light, embracing, both forgetting where they were for the moment. But they were suddenly reminded of where they were when the first bullet slammed into the rock two inches from Laura's cheek.

The second bullet hit an overhanging branch just above the hole in the ground through which Murphy had poked his head. They were both peppered with pieces of bark.

Murphy threw his body in front of Laura's for protection, pushing them both back against the rock wall.

"Murphy, what's happening?"

"Bullets. Somebody isn't fooling around. Unless we

can backtrack in hope of finding an amphora full of guns and ammo, we've got to move. Now."

Laura had never been shot at before, but she quickly got the message. The third bullet, kicking up sand at Murphy's foot, helped to get her moving. They started running farther underground but hit a full wall of sheer rock. "We're going to have to risk coming up out of the hole. And whoever is shooting at us knows it. Come on."

Murphy led Laura back to the clumps of root in which she had gotten her foot tangled, since it afforded the best protection from the gunfire. It wasn't much, but at least they weren't out in the open. "Stay here and stay down."

"Murph, where are you going? Don't leave me!"

Murphy ran to the rocks just on the far side of the hole. "Shh. I've got an idea that might work, but it's going to get noisy." Whoever was firing was able to shoot down the hole but would not be able to establish much range unless he stuck his gun inside it. Which was what Murphy was counting on.

There was quiet for a moment as the gunman was reaching that conclusion on his own once he no longer saw the Murphys running underneath the ground hole. First, the tip of the barrel of an AK-47 showed itself in the hole, then the rest of the barrel. As it was being pushed through the hole, it was firing dozens of rounds of ammunition at the ground, making a deafening racket and breaking the ground into a furious cloud of dust, dirt, and sand.

Murphy hoped his timing was correct as he leaped for the gun barrel while it was still spitting out round after round and yanked it downward. With a horrible shout, the rifle and the man who held it came hurtling through the ground hole. Murphy straightened, positioning himself to pounce on the gunman once he hit the chewed-up ground into which he had been firing. Murphy figured he had, at most, a split second to take his only advantage, the momentary element of surprise.

In the end, the surprise was greater. For the gunman did not actually hit the ground for long. He fell right through and just kept falling. The bullets had torn up the ground to such an extent that they loosened centuries of sand, dirt, and stone that had provided only a relatively shallow covering—for a deep pit of sand way underneath the ground.

As Murphy looked on in wonder, the gunman finally stopped with a soft thud. Since the rifle was still in Murphy's hands, he assumed the gunman had nothing else to fire at him. Murphy peeked over the new, much-deeper hole. He need not have worried about the gunman. Or what was left of him.

As Murphy tried not to listen to the horrible, high-pitched scream, he could make out the body of the gunman being buried alive. Tons of sand that had not been touched by humans for centuries, if ever, rushed to cover his body within seconds of landing. Even if he had wanted to, there was nothing Murphy could have done to save the shooter. In fifteen more seconds, there was only a mound of sand where the head had been in the sunken chamber.

Before it disappeared completely, though, Murphy recognized the head as he shined his flashlight beam on it. Bezhad, the driver.

Gun still in his hands, Murphy whipped around, ready to fire, when he felt a hand on his shoulder. "Hey, Murph, take it easy. It's me."

"Oh, sorry, sweetheart. Let's get up that hole in case this whole floor collapses." Then to himself, so as not to scare Laura, he muttered, "And since that was our driver trying to kill us down here, I wonder what's waiting for us up there."

# NINETEEN

BLOOD OOZED OUT at them. Murphy and Laura had pulled themselves out of the ground hole after Murphy carefully surveyed the opening, rifle at the ready. It was blessedly quiet after the roar of gunfire underground. They had worked their way down the ridge to where the Land Cruiser was, calling for Saif.

When they reached the car, they realized why Saif had neither answered nor helped them. He was slumped in the front passenger seat with his head bleeding from what looked like a blow from a heavy object.

"Is he ... dead, Murphy?"

Just as she asked her question, Saif gave a weak groan and his body stirred. "My professional opinion is no, Laura, Mr. Saif is not dead." Laura glared at Murphy.

"Get out of the way, wise guy, and let me look at that

wound." She reached for the bottom of her shirt, which was as close to a clean cloth as she saw in the vicinity. "Mr. Saif, can you hear me? Somebody hit you. Probably Behzad, the driver, the goon who came after us. Did you see *anything* before you were knocked out?"

Saif opened one eye, then the other, and moaned. "Aaah, Mrs. Murphy, you are all right. Did you . . . are you . . . praise Allah, you are safe. I believe that substitute driver must have been a robber. He overpowered me and must have come after you. I am so sorry. The sheikh will be outraged. I am sorry the robber stole your object."

Murphy looked at Saif warily. "What do you mean, Saif? We were attacked by the same driver who knocked you out, but he didn't rob us. And he won't be robbing anybody ever again."

Saif tried to look relieved. "Then you got what you came for?"

"Yes, and a lot more—mostly bullets. Let's get to the airport now."

Two hours later, the Murphys were settled safely aboard the sheikh's jet, heading for home. "What a day, Murph!" Laura snuggled beside her husband, her eyes closing quickly despite her coursing adrenaline.

"The first piece of the Brazen Serpent."

"And my first time getting shot at. But I'm so impressed by the Serpent that I almost forgive you for nearly getting me shot to death."

"It may take a little longer for me to forgive myself." Murphy turned and put a hand to her cheek. "Sweetheart, if I'd had the slightest idea I was putting you in danger . . ."

Laura smiled and put her hand on his. "I know, you'd have left me at home to do the dishes and darn your socks. Now that it's all over, I can just savor the bragging rights I'll have next week in the faculty lounge."

"And I don't think I'll ever forgive or forget our friend Saif."

Laura shot Murphy a puzzled look. "What do you mean, Murph? The poor guy was practically killed himself."

"Yeah, 'practically' being the operative word. I'm no doctor, but have you ever seen a more perfect head wound? Nice amount of blood to get our attention, but nowhere deep enough to cause any head damage."

Laura bolted upright in her chair. "Oh, no! Murphy, I was too scared and deaf from the bullets to realize it at the time, but when he opened his eyes, there was no way he was coming out of unconsciousness. Those pupils were clear as the dunes."

"Yes, I noticed that. I think Saif was in on the whole thing and just trying to make it look like he was a victim, too, just in case we survived, but we were never supposed to get past the goon driver to see Saif's faked act."

"But how did he know we were looking for the Serpent?"

"He didn't. He couldn't. Nobody over here knew. I think he knew the sheikh was helping us find something of value. He didn't care what it was, he just wanted to steal it from us. I don't think the sheikh had anything to do with the scam. But once we land, I'll be letting him know just what a scheming skunk he has working for him."

"Now, Murphy, the sheikh was our host. Don't lose your famous temper with him on the phone."

"Not at all. I just believe he would like to know the truth. Speaking of the sheikh, what do you say we take a closer look at what we almost got killed for today?" He reached for the sheikh's diplomatic pouch and removed the cloth-covered metal piece.

No longer struggling with her exhaustion, Laura smiled. "What took you so long?"

Murphy began to loosen the knots, half expecting the tail of the Serpent to slither away between the seats with a hiss. He pulled back the cloth and held it up to the light. It had been forged thirty-five hundred years before, but the rich bronze surface seemed undamaged by the corrosive forces of man or nature.

The expertly cast texture of the Serpent's skin was intact. Each reptilian scale had been faithfully rendered, and Murphy recognized the unmistakable pattern of a venomous sand viper.

*"Moses made this,"* he whispered. *"Moses actually held this in his hands."*

Laura reached out and touched it with a finger. "In obedience to God, they put their trust in Him and were healed. It was a symbol of their faith."

Murphy could see there were goose bumps on her arm. "But after Moses was done with it, what did this Serpent become? That has been the question all these centuries since."

Murphy tilted the tail of the Serpent so the light

from the window raked its surface, making the scales glitter and dance. It almost seemed alive. "Hey, sweetheart. Did you see this?"

Laura leaned closer. "What do you mean? It's just the—" Then she saw it. Another set of markings. Barely visible, as if they had been crudely engraved, almost scratched into the bronze. But once she focused on them, they were strangely elegant—and instantly familiar. Triangles with linear tails and V shapes, like birds seen against the sky. "Chaldean cuneiforms," Laura gasped. "Just like the scroll."

"Yep. I'll bet this is Dakkuri's handwriting too." Murphy turned and pressed his face to the window. Thirty thousand feet below, the desert rippled toward the distant horizon.

"You know, whatever this high priest Dakkuri was up to, it looks like he made good on the promise in his scroll. He did leave something here on the first piece that looks like it can lead us to the rest of the Serpent."

# TWENTY

"SO, ANYBODY DO anything interesting last week? Me, I was in Samaria."

There was only a mild stir of interest among his students. *Tough crowd*, Murphy thought. He resisted getting their attention the easy way by adding, *Getting shot at by an Arab*.

Instead, he reached into his backpack beside the lectern. "And look what I found."

"A shower pipe?" someone called from the back of the hall.

"No, but the next wise guy is getting sent to the showers. This amazing foot or so of bronze, ladies and gentlemen, is a snake." Several of the heads in the front rows recoiled. "Relax, it was never alive, but it has had several lives, all of them more interesting than any real live snake ever had."

Murphy clicked his slide projector to life. "Now, these Biblical names and kingdoms are mouthfuls, I know, so I'm going to try to help you keep them straight by flashing them up on the screen. All of these gentlemen ruled way before they could be on the cover of *People*, so I don't have big, glossy color photos to help you remember them.

"Now, this slide shows a decrepit-looking document, an ancient papyrus scroll that came into my possession not too long ago. However, as is often the case for archaeologists, I had no real context for what I was looking at. It would be a lot easier if these artifacts already came with the background audiotape you get at the museum for the walking tour, but I haven't found one yet that does. So we have to discover all those facts ourselves."

The next slide was a close-up of the scroll. "Don't worry. Those of you who think you're hungover, that's not English up there. Not even close. It is a language known—or, these days, mostly unknown—as Chaldean, dating back to the time of Nebuchadnezzar, the greatest king of Babylon."

Murphy clicked the king's name up on the screen, followed by a map of Babylon. Then he forwarded to the figure on the scroll that he had interpreted as representing the king. "Again, this didn't come with an instructional video, so how did I know that this lovely artist's rendering is of King Nebuchadnezzar? By knowing the period of the writing and knowing my succession of kings, which is to say, folks, eat your vegetables, say your prayers at night, and study, study, study. There are no Hollywood shortcuts in this business.

"Now, here's why this scroll is so exciting. A lot of what archaeologists have found from Babylonian times are storage receipts and ordinary everyday records, because the Babylonians were the early-day versions of college administrators. They loved to write everything down."

He clicked on the next slide. "Now, that might look like an eyelash on the projector lens, but it is the cuneiform symbol for a snake. Combining that with this next symbol, which we believe to stand for what we call *bronze*, I began to get excited. And then when I pieced together enough of the rest of the scroll, I started to realize this was no Babylonian grocery list."

That was his last slide, so Murphy turned off the machine. "I'm going to come back to some greater detail about methods for interpreting ancient writing in a later lecture. For now, let me skip all the way ahead, past what I learned by reading the scroll, and how that led me to find my snake friend here." He pulled the bronze Serpent tail out of his bag once more. "Because the point I wanted to get to today is about having the courage to make some leaps of logic and knowledge, because it's oftentimes the wild, crazy, impossible notions that lead even boring old archaeologists like me to discover new truths.

"This bronze piece, I believe, once we test it out in the lab, will prove to be the tail of the Brazen Serpent, which in your Old Testament was made by Moses in fourteen fifty-eight B.C. The Israelites started complaining about wandering around in the desert for so long and began acts of 'unbelief' against God. As punishment for their rebellion, God sent down poisonous serpents to bite the offenders. That got everybody back on track and they prayed and asked Moses for help. He prayed to God, who took mercy on the Israelites and told Moses, 'Make a fiery Serpent, and set it on a pole; and it shall be that everyone who is bitten, when he looks at it, shall live.'

"Moses interpreted 'fiery' as bronze, because he made this Serpent figure and held it up before the afflicted, and those who repented were healed. All of this Serpent symbolism, of course, is a very potent direct line back to the Serpent tempting Eve in the Garden of Eden, which started the world down the road of sin and judgment. And one of these days I'd like to come back and talk about what healed the Israelites. Was it some magical dark power in the bronze snake, or was it the fact that the Israelites recommitted to their faith in God? But Dean Fallworth will start accusing me of being a tent-show preacher if I dare to wander off into issues of faith. Plus, I want to get to my real investigative point today.

"There are two places in history that are recorded in the Bible where this Brazen Serpent makes an appearance. The first is in fourteen fifty-eight B.C., when Moses forms the Serpent for the purpose of healing the Israelites. We then fast-forward to seven fourteen B.C., to the only other time it's mentioned in the Bible, in II Kings 18:1-5, where, contrary to the First Commandment, the Brazen Serpent becomes a special object of worship.

"The young King Hezekiah, who was one of the most devout kings of Judah, discovers that his people are beginning to adopt the practice of idolatry, which was common among the neighboring tribes. Evidently, this Brazen Serpent had been secretly preserved and used as an object of worship. Some people even attributed mysterious healing powers to the Serpent.

"When Hezekiah discovered the people of Judah bowing down before the Serpent in worship, worship that belonged to God alone, he was so enraged that he smashed it into three pieces.

"And that, as far as the Bible goes, is the last we see of the Brazen Serpent. Until this scroll set me on the trail of some connection to the Serpent's being around in the time of the greatest empire of Babylon, during the kingdom of Nebuchadnezzar. That's a long time and a long way from where the Bible leaves the Serpent lying in three pieces at Hezekiah's feet."

Murphy paused. "So, because archaeologists look for some way besides time machines to explain how artifacts may survive leaps of time and distance, I have a theory, and that theory helped me to find this piece of the Serpent last week. I believe that when Hezekiah ordered the Serpent destroyed in Judah, it was broken into three pieces and placed in the old Temple. Back then, even if the king told you to destroy an idol, you didn't just throw away a three-foot piece of perfectly good bronze. About one hundred forty years later, when the Babylonians stormed through Judah and sacked the Temple, they took back to Babylon anything that looked like it was worth something, and somebody eventually rescued the three pieces of the Serpent.

"Now, some of the writing is missing from this scroll I uncovered, so some greater speculation than usual is in order, but we have pieced together enough of the message to reveal that some high priest among those idol-worshiping Babylonians put the Serpent back together, probably believing that it had great powers.

"In my next lecture, I will begin to talk about prophecies, and how Nebuchadnezzar got his fear of the true God and ordered idols destroyed left and right—and there goes the Brazen Serpent on the chopping block again. Except the high priest who wrote this scroll wanted the Serpent saved again and split up the pieces with instructions on this scroll for finding them to put them back together. Which, if I have any luck reading what's written on the bottom of this tail here, I will endeavor to do. So, while I dash off to do that, class dismissed."

A student called out, "Professor Murphy? Nobody got healed when you held up the tail, but don't you think that if you do find the other two pieces and Lego them all together again that you will be able to heal people?"

"That is the big question, yes. Or just as possible, according to believers in the so-called dark arts, who have sought out the Serpent for centuries, if the pieces are ever connected, you could wield this Serpent for evil."

# TWENTY-ONE

SHANE BARRINGTON WAS forcing himself to not think of his son. Naturally, even for a master at turning the coldest of mental shoulders toward all the vicious acts and ruthless business sins he had perpetrated in his life, Talon's murder of Arthur while he had just stood by helpless was proving to be a difficult memory for Barrington to ignore completely. Especially with no idea as to what Talon had done with the body, despite his cryptic promise that he had some further plan.

Odd, he thought, how after cutting his son out of his life completely for so many years, now, in death, Arthur kept coming to mind. Not that Barrington was in any danger of suddenly becoming sentimental about family. Other than his ex-wife, who had been paid off more than two decades earlier, Arthur had been his only living relative. And he had no need of nor interest in something as pedestrian as a friend. Associates, staff, servants, yes; friends, no.

Nor did Barrington have a great attachment to places. There was nowhere he would really call home, though he owned luxurious houses on three continents. The place he came from certainly held no sentimental value for him. It was a place you escaped from if you were lucky, not one you dreamed of going back to. As for the attractions of magnificent architecture or priceless works of art, that was for weaker souls. The truth was, he was happiest when he was on his way somewhere, in a plane or a fast car. Moving, at speed, feeling the world shrink under his feet. And with the state-of-the-art systems Barrington Communications manufactured, he could make things happen wherever he found himself.

But if he had to choose one place where he felt most at ease, as if he were standing at the very center of the universe, it would be here, in his penthouse, watching the vast, jagged landscape of towering steel and glass come alive in the growing dawn. However, after that horrible moment of seeing Arthur tortured by Talon from his terrace, Barrington had not even looked out his window, let alone used the terrace.

Now, with four minutes before his guest would arrive, he told himself it was time for the great Barrington willpower to come to the fore. He forced himself to open the draperies and part the sliding glass doors to the terrace. He would not be like every weak creature he had conquered in the past. There was no room for guilt in the Barrington game plan. He strode toward the railing and looked down at the Endicott Arms. For a second, he shuddered, then he wiped his mind clean.

Immediately, he started to feel the return of total command, as if he were a barbarian king standing on the piled-up corpses of his vanquished foes. Barrington Communications had recently become billions of dollars richer and had never been stronger than it was now. The gaping holes in its financial structure had been shored up, leaving more than enough to bankroll further expansion, further conquests. Any business magnate foolish enough to think he could stand toe-to-toe with Shane Barrington was about to discover the error of his ways.

He put his hand to the glass and smiled. All this, and how little, really, they had demanded in return. Now to initiate his second assignment from the Seven. As with his first assignment, this task seemed odd, arbitrary, and unconnected to any big master plan, and had been delivered in terse fashion, with no supporting explanation. However, like obtaining the checklist of U.N.-related security information, it was something he could accomplish from his position of power with ease.

He checked his Rolex. The meeting had been scheduled for seven o'clock. Late enough to have forced her to cancel any plans she might have had for the evening. And he had made her wait a further ten minutes. Long enough for confidence to drain away and be replaced by fear. Cheap tricks, perhaps, and hardly necessary anymore. But the exercise of power, however petty, was what gave him pleasure, and if he could not indulge himself in that, life would surely be very dull indeed.

He turned away from his shadowy reflection and spoke into a microphone woven into the lining of his jacket. "Send her in."

Stephanie Kovacs, Barrington News Network's up-and-coming star reporter on the national beat, willed herself not to check her hair, her makeup, one more time as the cropped-blond receptionist behind the desk motioned her toward the door with a curt wave of her perfectly manicured hand. Here she was, Stephanie Kovacs, ace TV investigative journalist, fearless exposer of the crooked and corrupt, a woman who'd been shot at, slashed by a knife-wielding maniac, and threatened by slavering attack dogs—who had always stood her ground and kept her head while facing down men twice her size and ten times as aggressive—here she was, nervous as a kitten just because her network's CEO summoned her to a meeting.

What was the worst that could happen? Okay, he could fire her. That was the thought that had been racing around her brain for the last five minutes, forcing her to flip urgently through her mental Rolodex. *Who would I call first? Who was that executive who said at the awards dinner, "If you ever think of leaving the show..." Which network needs a new face to boost the ratings? Which news program is desperately seeking some credibility?*

But finding a new job in TV wasn't really the point. She was successful and respected enough in the business not to worry unduly on that score. What was eating away at her and making the butterflies in her stomach do loop-the-loops was the certain knowledge that when Shane Barrington fired you, he didn't just let you go. He made sure you were finished. Career over. If that was what he had in mind, she'd be lucky to be standing in front of a camera in a month's time and talking about the unseasonable June rainfall's effect on the soybean crop.

She paused at the door, patted a stray hair into place, and walked in, hoping he wouldn't see beneath her practiced veneer of confidence.

"You asked to see me, Mr. Barrington?"

Shane Barrington seemed taller than in photographs and the rare pieces of TV footage, but the harsh features and dark eyes were ominously familiar. Without a word or a change of expression, he gestured toward the dark leather couch against the far wall. He remained standing as she seated herself, forcing her to look up at him from below.

"Miss Kovacs," he began. "Stephanie. I'm so pleased you could spare me a few moments of your valuable time. I hope I haven't kept you away from an important investigation. I'd hate to think some wrongdoer got off the hook because I'd distracted you from your work."

She tried to laugh. "Well, there's always more fish in the sea. That's the great thing about this job—you never run out of worthwhile targets."

Barrington looked at her without smiling. "Sure. I know exactly what you mean." He turned and sat behind the long, smoked-glass desk in the center of the room. She couldn't help noticing the absence of a phone or a computer. In fact, there was nothing on the desk to mar its perfect crystalline surface.

"Sometimes I hear people say I don't really pay attention to this part of the corporation. That I'm not really interested in TV. Like it's old technology, a thing of the past. And Shane Barrington is always interested in the future, right?"

"Right," she found herself saying.

"But that's not true at all, Stephanie. I pay very close attention to what goes out on the news channel. And I've been paying particularly close attention to your reports. To your fearless investigations."

It seemed to her the word *fearless* was his way of mocking her. If anyone else had used that sneering tone, she would have gone for their throat instantly. No one trivialized her and got away with it. But to her own surprise she continued to smile meekly, as if she were a dog being stroked, not a lamb being lined up for the slaughter.

Barrington's eyes seemed to lighten a little, as if he were enjoying her discomfort. "You really know how to stick it to the bad guys. No mercy. No quarter. I like that."

He made her sound like a prizefighter, not a reporter, but if he liked her style, that was fine with her. She still wasn't sure where he was going with this, but her anxiety level was beginning to drop just a little. Maybe she wasn't going to get fired after all.

"People also say I'm a hands-off CEO. I don't tell the producers at the station what to do. As long as it gets the ratings, what do I care, right? Make a program about anything you like. Killer cockroaches, grandma serial killers. Whatever rings your bell."

Better and better. He liked her news judgment. He believed in editorial freedom. What was she worrying about?

Barrington leaned back in his chair and laid his hands flat on the desk. His eyes darkened again. "But sometimes people just can't be trusted to do their job.

Sometimes they need a little direction." He smiled humorlessly. "From above."

Okay, not so good. The conversation, if you could call it that, had just taken an ominous turn.

"I've decided that someone ought to do an investigation—a ruthless exposé, no holds barred—on a certain group of people who pose a major threat to this country—to the world. Someone needs to expose them for the dangerous fanatics they are."

He paused. *Uh-oh, here comes the punch line,* she thought.

"The group is evangelical Christians. And that someone is going to be you."

Whew, she had not seen this coming, not where she thought this conversation was heading at all, but Stephanie Kovacs had not risen past the other bright, desperately eager TV talent by being slow on the uptake. She recovered from her puzzlement quickly by flashing a humble smile. "I am honored by your confidence in me, Mr. Barrington. I will try not to let you down."

"See that you don't. I will be watching."

# TWENTY-TWO

THE MAN CALLED Talon paused in his labors, allowing himself a few seconds to take in the part of Manhattan that lay below him. In fact, there was only a narrow railing and some ropes keeping Talon from dropping down to the street.

He stood ten stories up on the window-washer platform descended from the top of one of the most recognizable structures in the world: the Secretariat Building of the United Nations.

Talon turned back to one of hundreds of windows that made the outside of the U.N.'s tallest building look like a towering wall of glass. There were thirty-nine floors, but Talon had done his calculations carefully and he was interested only in floors five through twelve. That would make enough of a statement for his purposes.

Shane Barrington had come through as instructed and managed to get Talon some of the security-defying access he needed to carry out his task. He had told Barrington what he wanted and left it up to Barrington, whose many subsidiaries designed communications, security, and utilities systems for thousands of businesses, to figure out how to get him what he required.

Talon had not needed too much because the very boring Mr. Farley had given him endless details about his window-washing routine. And Talon had lifted all of Farley's personal identification before disposing of his body. Which he did only after relieving Farley as well of the necessary body parts for the fingerprint and retinal scanning he would have to pass through to gain access to the U.N.

Now, in makeup that transformed him into the late Mr. Farley, and having padded his body to fill out his uniform, which said EXECUTIVE BUILDING MAINTENANCE, Talon consulted the paper in his hand. It was a meticulously rendered grid he had drawn for himself of every window of the Secretariat Building. If he could continue to raise and lower himself on the motorized window-cleaning platform at this swift pace, everything would be in place well before zero hour.

# TWENTY-THREE

MURPHY'S EGO AS a proud male and a proud professional archaeologist was taking quite a pummeling. "Shari, I have to admit, I'm stumped. For the life of me, I don't know what's written here on this tail."

Shari wished there were something more she could do to help. They had already performed as many dating tests as they were equipped to do in their lab, and she had taken careful digital photos from every angle. They were looking at the enlargements now. "I don't think I can blow them up any larger, Professor Murphy, or we won't be able to see anything besides smudges."

Murphy rubbed his hand through his hair in distracted frustration. "No, whatever tool Dakkuri used to etch this message into the tail, he made it last pretty much intact for all these years, and seeing it is not my problem. I just can't make head or your proverbial tail out of this. Because he didn't have a lot of room, he must have used some kind of ancient shorthand. And I suspect Dakkuri must have been trying to be more than somewhat cryptic beyond that, because he was giving directions for uncovering the next piece of what he believed was his most powerful icon."

Shari drew a deep breath before saying what had been on her mind for several minutes now. "Umm ... Professor Murphy ... have you thought about—"

"Don't even finish the sentence. I know when I'm beat. I've got to get Isis McDonald back on the phone."


"Wow, Professor Murphy, that's some whopper of a tale ... er ... story." Isis McDonald looked back over her hastily scrawled notes and shifted the phone receiver to her other ear just to give her neck a chance to uncramp. "But tempting as it is, I can't do what you ask."

"Why not? Look, I know we haven't met, but you've got to know I'm not a crackpot and I usually know my stuff. You backed me up on the scroll and it seems to have been proven right. This is the next step now. I'm closer than anybody has been in thousands of years, presumably, to finding the entire Brazen Serpent."

"Yes, yes, Professor Murphy. That's all very well and good, but I'm a philologist for the Parchments of Freedom Foundation, not a starry-eyed, glory-seeking archaeologist, and I've got a deskful of my own research I'm behind in. Actually"—she craned her neck to look around her—"it's more like an office full of things I should have finished months ago."

"Please, Isis. Believe me, I don't want to ask for your

help, but I can't wait on this—and I also hate to admit that I'm just not smart enough to figure this out and you are."

Isis sighed, but, to her surprise, her lips were forming a smile. "Oh, Professor Murphy, I can see how you bull your way to all these breakthroughs. You are skilled in the ancient art of flattery."

"I am a licensed professional. Will you help me, please?"

"Look, Murphy. Here's what I'm willing to do. I have to be here for foundation review meetings for the next few days, and you're a busy man as well. However, the good thing about the foundation is that resources are generally not in short supply. Which is why I need to be here for our review meetings, since you are not the only skilled practitioner of necessary flattery. But I will dispatch my very able, very trustworthy secretary, Fiona, on our foundation jet to pick up your Serpent's tail and bring it to me."

"Whoa! That's very extravagant, but I can't let this out of my hands. How can I be sure it would be safe?"

"Murphy, you're there in what I'm sure is a quaint, perfect-little-tiny-town school and I'm sitting here in the world's largest privately funded historical research center with state-of-the-art systems and security. Who are you kidding?"

Once again, Murphy knew when he was bested. "Point taken, Isis. Before I scurry off with my tail between my legs and lick my wounded small-town pride, let me just say thank you, the Serpent's tail is yours for as long as you need, and when can Fiona be here?"

Murphy surprised Laura in her office. He was holding a small box.

"Murph, what are you doing here? Did that mean old dean send you here for detention again?"

"Sweetheart, I was sitting and moping in my lab because I had to call Isis McDonald to take the Serpent's tail because I'm clearly not smart enough to figure it out. Then I realized I was still good for something, so I dug this out and fixed it up. I've been meaning to give it to you ever since we got back from Samaria."

He handed the box over to Laura. She looked as eager as a five-year-old on Christmas morning as she ripped the lid off. "Oh, Murph, it's the cross formed by those root branches in the cave. I was wondering where it went."

She held up the now-polished wood to admire it. It was approximately an inch and a half long and a half inch wide. Murphy had drilled a tiny hole through the top, then burnished the finish with a few drops of oil, which brought out the grain and enhanced the color of the wood. At the meeting point was a rounded burl from which the four tendrils of root that formed the cross had grown. It shone like a hardwood gemstone.

"I've strung it on my very best leather moccasin lace. No expense has been spared to keep you in jewelry befitting your status, m'lady." He bowed before her.

Laura bent down and hugged him hard. "Arise, you noble lad. Your queen has greater things in store for you. Come, take me home, let me show you why it is good to be the king."

# TWENTY-FOUR

PAUL WALLACH WATCHED as Shari dipped a spoon into the sauce. She took a quick catlike sip, gave a little nod as if to say *Not bad, if I do say so myself,* and went back to stirring the pasta. In the cramped kitchen, the steam made her look flushed, as if she'd been running and hadn't had time to change. To him the sheen of perspiration somehow made her look even more beautiful.

She turned and caught his abstracted gaze. "Hey." She frowned. "You're supposed to be watching closely. How long did I say the pasta had to cook?"

"Five minutes?" he offered. "No—fifteen."

Her frown stayed in place and her grip on the spoon tightened.

"Oh, I know," he said. "Trick question. Until it's, you know, whatever the word is—al dente."

She brushed a damp strand of dark hair from her forehead and turned back to the steaming pots. "Hmm. I don't think you've been listening to a word I've been saying, Paul Wallach. I mean, you're the one who said he lived on cans of tuna and takeout pizzas and wouldn't it be great to learn how to cook a meal once in a while that actually tasted of something. I know this isn't exactly duck à l'orange or anything, but you could show a little more appreciation."

He quickly put his glass of Coke down on the counter and adopted a sincere expression. "I do appreciate it, Shari, I really do. And it smells incredible. It's just that I find it hard to concentrate on things that don't really interest me—"

"You'll be interested enough in eating it, I bet," she interrupted.

"Sure, yes, you're right. What I mean is, I don't think I'll ever be any good at it. However hard I try, I don't think I'm ever going to be a great cook."

"Just like you're never going to be the next Bill Gates, right?" she said, glancing quickly over her shoulder to make sure she hadn't upset him.

He sighed. "Exactly. I feel like I've spent my whole life trying to be good at things I'm not. Pretending to be interested in stuff I couldn't give a . . . give a fig about. I mean, I wanted my dad to be proud of me and all. I didn't want him to think I was, like, a failure, or whatever. And it turned out he was the failure."

Shari had promised herself that she would let him talk without interrupting him, but she turned from the stove to face him. "Paul, you can't think of your father that way. He may have failed at business, but he provided a good life for you for a long time."

"Yeah, some *good life*. I'm not sure which he was a bigger failure at, business or being there for me."

"Paul Wallach, let me tell you something I discovered when my parents were killed in a car accident years ago. You can blame them for anything you feel is wrong in your life, you can feel guilty about things that went unresolved while they were alive, but at some point, good or bad, you have to live your own life, whether they've given you a good foundation or not, and stop making them an excuse."

Paul slouched in his chair. "Oh, I keep telling myself things like that. That's why I pushed myself to go back to college here at Preston, because I didn't want to just sit and mope about my tough luck. At least my dad gave me the example of working hard. But it's tough working hard at stuff when your heart's not in it."

Shari handed him two steaming plates of spaghetti and red clam sauce, and for a moment he was distracted by the rich, warm smell.

"Wow!" he said. "I mean, really. Wow! You must let me have the recipe sometime," he added, grinning.

"Ha-ha," she said, shooing him into the little living room, where she'd set the table. "Sit down and eat. And then you can tell me what it is exactly that your heart *is* in."

"Thanks," Paul said, handing Shari a mug of coffee. "And not just for a delicious meal. Thanks for listening to my problems like this. I feel bad taking up your time with this stuff when you could be, I don't know, doing more exciting things."

She smiled. "I like helping people, Paul. And I know from my own experience that someone just listening can be a big help."

He'd hoped she was going to say something else, something a little more personal. Something that indicated she was interested in him. He wanted to be more than just her good deed for the day. But maybe he was hoping for too much. Or maybe it was just too soon.

"So," she said, "the first thing you've got to do is be honest with yourself. You no longer have to live your life for how your dad feels. If you don't think you're cut out for high finance, then find something that does interest you."

"I think I've found a subject I want to study."

"Great." She beamed. "What is it?"

He hesitated. Would she think he was faking an interest just to impress her, to worm his way into her affections? He didn't want to blow everything.

"It's about as unbusinesslike as I can get. Biblical archaeology," he said, watching her expression.

She looked steadily at him for a while. Not smiling, but not quite frowning either. As if his sincerity were being weighed in the balance and the scales hadn't quite come down one way or the other. Finally she said, "I guess you know how *I* feel about it. I can't think of anything more fascinating, more worthwhile. And if you want to get into it, well, that's good. But are you sure you totally understand what it's all about? I mean, it's not just about digging up artifacts and finding out where they came from. That's what regular archaeologists do. It's about proving the truth of the Bible."

Paul started to frame an answer, then stopped himself. He did have an answer, at least he thought he did, but he wasn't sure he could put it into words. No, he couldn't claim to be a fully paid-up member of the Christian faith. He wasn't even sure what it was exactly he believed in. But when he'd seen Murphy's photos of the ossuary in the lecture hall, when he'd heard him read the inscription, he'd felt something deep inside that he'd never felt before. All he knew for sure was that he wanted more of it.

A loud buzzer broke the awkward silence. *Saved by the bell,* he thought.

"I don't know who that could be," Shari said with a trace of real annoyance as she got up from the table and went to the front door. She pulled the latch, there was a moment's silence, and her hand flew to her mouth. Standing in the doorway was a young man with an unruly mop of dirty-blond hair, a couple of days' stubble, and an unpleasant grin. He shouldered his way past Shari and planted himself in the middle of the room.

"I don't see balloons. I don't see ticker tape." He scanned the room, looking straight through Paul as if he weren't there. "I definitely don't see booze. I gotta say, you don't do a great homecoming party, sis."

*You just never know about families,* Paul thought. Here he had been unburdening to Shari about his turmoil over his father issues and his future, and she seemed like this peaceful, perfect, wise person who had it all figured out. Then—*boom*—that awful guy comes barging in and it turns out he's her brother who had been in prison for burglary and got released early and surprised her.

Some surprise. Chuck Nelson didn't stay long. Just changed his clothes and stormed back out. Shari seemed really upset, so Paul ended up staying for another whole hour, talking, only this time about her. Paul was even more impressed when he listened to her.

"My parents were killed instantaneously in the crash when Chuck and I were teenagers. They had never taken us to church, so I did not know Christ personally. However, I started going to a Bible-believing church with my friend's mother and it was there that something wonderful happened. I received Christ personally as my Lord and Savior and He changed my life. Salvation gave me something to hold on to when I needed it most. But Chuck went bad fast."

Paul shook his head. "He must have, to have ended up in prison."

"Chuck fell in with the worst elements from the surrounding area, committed crimes from stealing to drug dealing, and eventually got caught. He would never listen to anything I had to say and refused to put me on his list of visitors in prison, so I stopped going to see him. I've never stopped praying for him, though."

"What will you do now?"

"I don't know. You know as much as I do. You saw him storm in and out. I guess he thinks he's going to live with me here, and I would never throw him out, but I will not have him fall back into his wild life. I'll need some help here. I think Laura Murphy and Pastor

Bob at the church will be good to talk to. And you, Paul, you've been really great to listen."

Paul blushed. "Hey, you listened to me, I listened to you. That's what friends do. And, hey, I guess that means we're friends."

Shari gave him a friendly pat on his hand. "Well, friend, you'd better be getting home. But I tell you what, why don't you join us for church Wednesday night. The Murphys will be there, and I'd like you to meet Laura. She can help you too. And you should get right in the spirit by coming early and helping out in the basement, sorting clothes for the church clothing drive. Say, six-thirty Wednesday?"

*I think I'm going to like it here at Preston,* Paul thought as he whistled the whole way back to his apartment.

# TWENTY-FIVE

THE NEARLY TWO hundred flags of the members of the United Nations were flapping in a light evening breeze coming off the East River. At six P.M., as twilight was passing rapidly to full darkness across Manhattan, the U.N.'s brilliant night-lighting beams switched on.

There was an immediate burst and flash, thousands of lights turning the thirty-nine stories of the Secretariat Building into one of the jewels of the New York City night skyline.

Since it was not completely dark yet, the lights did not create their full dazzling effect. However, the explosion of attention was immediate.

Horns honked as passing cars screeched to a halt along First Avenue. Pedestrians gasped, shouted, and pointed up at the glass facade of the U.N. And by 6:02 P.M., the first of numerous phone calls sounded in the office of the head of United Nations Security in what was going to be a very long night.

For painted on half the windows from floor five up to floor twelve of the United Nations Secretariat Building, in a bright red that took on an otherwordly glow in the night lighting, all the world was now reading:


J 3 16


Within a half hour there were even more lights trained on the Secretariat Building.

The premises were cleared, as were the surrounding buildings and streets, except for dozens of official vehicles. The mobile units of what seemed like every television and radio station in the world were also now jammed as close to the U.N. as they could get.

It was a full-disaster reaction scene without any apparent disaster. Preliminary search and evaluation teams could find no victims and no damage to any of the U.N. buildings. Except for what appeared to be meticulously applied blood that had cascaded down eight floors' worth of windows on the Secretariat Building front. If the writing on the windows was some kind of warning about an impending explosion or attack, no further clue had been found, though it would take many hours to complete a thorough search.

Because the U.N. was technically on eighteen acres of international property, the United Nations security chief, Lars Nugent, was in charge of the operations that night, but the New York City police and FBI and other federal emergency teams were swarming all around, lending services and giving advice.

By nine-twenty, Nugent had gathered together Burton Welsh, senior FBI official on the scene, along with the police commissioner of New York and the undersecretary of state for the United States, who had flown up from Washington to try to coordinate the many government services that would be called upon if there was an attack on the United Nations. Despite its official international status, it would be both a danger and an embarrassment for the United States if the U.N. was in any imminent danger of an attack of any nature.

Nugent, a man who looked more distinguished than many of the diplomats he protected, said, "Let me summarize what we know. The message was painted on the outside of the windows on floors five through twelve. We need to do some real testing, but we've determined it is paint, not blood, as those TV reporters have been speculating. The paint that was used is some kind of chemical that goes on clear and takes on its color only when really bright light zaps it, some kind of super glow-in-the-light chemical."

The police commissioner interjected, "How did it get on there?"

"We assume it was done from the window-washing platform. It was up and running today on those floors, but so far everything checks out normal with the washer and all the security screenings. The police are trying to round up the regular window washer, a Joseph Farley, lives in Astoria. No luck yet, but he's been on the job for ten years and has nothing unusual on his record either here at work or with the police."

The undersecretary looked up from his notes. "It's almost one hundred percent certain that whoever painted this up there wanted to make a statement for the world to see. The U.N. is obviously *the* world organization. So far, though, we have no communication from any terrorist group taking credit."

Burton Welsh shook his head. He unzipped his FBI windbreaker before speaking. "We're not necessarily looking foreign on this."

The undersecretary raised his eyebrows. "You mean domestic terrorists? Like Oklahoma? What would be their beef with the U.N. that would make it worth trying to crack one of the tightest security systems in the world?"

Nugent waved his hand in disgust. "That security doesn't seem to have done squat today. What's the latest analysis of the markings?"

Welsh picked up the book in front of him. "Pretty crude, pretty basic." He opened the book. "We're assuming it refers to the Bible, New Testament, 'J' for Book of John, 'three' for Chapter Three, 'sixteen' for Verse Sixteen, and I quote: 'For God so loved the world that He gave His only begotten Son, that whoever believes in Him should not perish, but have everlasting life.' "

Nugent nodded. "Yes, it's maybe the most famous quote from the Bible, but why here, why now?"

Welsh reached for his cell phone. "We've got some th_____ ___ ___ ___all I'm expecting, we'll be

# TWENTY-SIX

MURPHY WAS STILL trying. The symbols were starting to wiggle in front of his eyes, he had been staring at the cuneiforms for so long. They seemed to be moving to a regular rhythmic beat, until Murphy realized it was his office phone that was ringing.

He shook his head to try to clear it as he reached for the receiver. It was Laura, from the house. "Murph, thank God you're still in the lab."

"A fine thing to be saying to your husband in the middle of the night."

"Murph. An FBI agent was just here looking for you."

"FBI? Wh

FBI agent Hank Baines sat in Murphy's office twenty minutes later, holding Murphy's extension phone against one ear while Murphy paced. Laura had told Murphy to turn on the TV in the department lounge and he had watched the BNN update live from the U.N. Murphy was completely dumbfounded, like the rest of America, by what he saw.

Agent Baines had been ordered by Washington to race from the Charlotte field office to Preston to wake up Professor Michael Murphy for questioning. The questioning, however, was not to be undertaken by Baines; he was merely ordered to get Murphy situated for a conference call with Burton Welsh, head of the New York office.

"Mr. Baines, this makes no sense. What does this have to do with me?"

"I do not believe it is about you, sir."

"It is now if you've sped down here to question me."

"Like I said, Professor, I am not going to question you."

"That makes even less sense. If all this is about is my getting a phone call, what are you doing here? Do you shoot me on the spot if I answer a question wrong?"

Baines spoke into the receiver. "Agent Baines in position, New York. I will put Professor Murphy on the phone directly." At Baines's nod, Murphy picked up his desk phone.

"Professor Murphy, I'm Burton Welsh, senior FBI agent on site here at the U.N. We have you on speakerphone with the U.N. security chief, Lars Nugent. Thank you for taking the time to talk to us."

Murphy frowned, then said into the receiver, "Gentlemen, I don't know what you think I can do for you."

"Mr. Murphy, I'm sorry to disturb you, but we've got a situation up here at the U.N."

"I've just seen the TV coverage. What do I have to do with any of this?"

"Sir, we're quite familiar with your expertise with all things having to do with the Bible."

"Hogwash, Agent Welsh. I've never dealt with you guys before, but I always figured the FBI would be straight shooters in every way. There are dozens of experts you could have called who know more about the Bible than I do, including lots right there in New York, so you wouldn't have had to roust Agent Baines here to babysit me."

"Sir, could I ask you to tell me what you make of this message, J three sixteen."

"Welsh, I'm an expert in ancient Biblical history, not modern graffiti."

"Take a whack at it anyway, Mr. Murphy, if you would."

Murphy took a deep breath before answering. "John Three: Sixteen, as I'm sure you know, is the verse many Christians believe is the most important verse in the entire Bible."

"Because?"

"Because it tells us that through faith in God's Son, Jesus Christ, we will receive the gift of eternal life."

"So, you think this is the work of some religious fanatic," Nugent interjected.

"Whoa, gentlemen! *Religious fanatic?* You mean because it refers to a Bible quotation? Look, *fanatic* would seem to be a fair conclusion, because somebody obviously went to a whole lot of trouble to paint it all the way up there on the U.N. But there're many millions of people, myself included, who think about that quotation every day of their lives and would take offense at being described as *religious fanatics*."

"Look, Murphy." Agent Welsh's official tone of moderation had disappeared. "I don't have the time to argue semantics with you. You've got to admit there are a lot of fringe evangelical Christians in this country."

"So, now I get it. You called me because I must be the only Bible expert who popped up on your computers as a known evangelical Christian. *Religious fanatic* is your definition for *evangelical Christian*, is that it? That's the kind of ugly cliché thinking I would have thought had no place in the FBI."

"Come on, Murphy, we've got files and files on fringe Christian groups that are ranting and raving about the U.N. Don't you agree this looks like one of them on the warpath here?"

Murphy looked over to Baines, who was listening in on the extension, but the agent was rubbing his eyes, perhaps to avoid Murphy's stare. Murphy's voice actually got much quieter as he waited an extra few seconds to try to regain his composure. "And I don't consider myself fringe, crackpot, reactionary, nuts, or any other code words you want to tar me with because of my faith. So I don't see how I can help you."

"Can't or *won't*?" Welsh fired back.

Before Murphy could answer, his office door opened and Laura came charging in. "Murph, what's going on?

What does the FBI want with you and this crazy U.N. business?"

"Sweetheart, for the life of me, I don't know. But it's beginning to smell like a smear that's bigger than what's covering those windows up there." Into the phone he said, "Welsh, my wife's joined me. She shares my faith as well. You'd better call in backup for Agent Baines here—the religious fanatics now outnumber him. I'll put you on speakerphone."

Laura looked first shocked, then puzzled by her husband's outburst.

"Professor Murphy, Mrs. Murphy, hello, I'm FBI agent Burton Welsh up in New York. Look, we just seem to have pushed each other's buttons—"

"I'm pushing the hang-up button, Welsh. I don't see how I can help with any of this, and I've got some writing that's a few thousand years old that I can do something useful with. So, unless you want Agent Baines here to arrest me and my wife, and then round up our entire church, I'm going to go."

Welsh bristled in his chair in New York. "You can go, Mr. Murphy. Just don't go far."

"What's that supposed to mean?"

Agent Baines reached over and disconnected the call before Murphy could get an answer. "I'm sorry, Professor Murphy. Things seemed to get a little out of hand here tonight." He paused, and Laura sensed an awkwardness behind his hesitation.

"Agent Baines, is there something else we should know?"

"No." He looked away from them both.

"Baines, you can talk to us. We're not monsters, no matter what New York thinks."

"No, ma'am, I know that. Agent Welsh is a fine man and a superior agent. I saw him in action at Quantico. But ... I'm from down here, and I know how funny some big-city folks get about religion. I just wanted you to know, we're not all like that at the FBI."

Murphy shook his hand. "Agent Baines, thank you. It takes a special man to stand up for both his God and his job sometimes. You seem to have figured that out, and I admire that. I could probably have used some of your balance tonight."

Laura put one arm around her husband and gave him a loving squeeze. "You, choosing balance over temper? If Agent Baines could teach you that, we'd give him tenure here at Preston. Agent Baines, it was good meeting you, even if the circumstances were bizarre."

"Hey, I'm just a messenger in all this, but I'm glad to be out of the frying pan, whatever is going on up there."

Laura put both her arms around Murphy. "That FBI man can't possibly think you had something to do with the U.N. thing, can he, Murph?"

"No, I think he's just desperate to make some sense out of why somebody would leave a big Bible quote on the U.N., and like a lot of people, he looks at all of us believers as some vast conspiracy opposed to individual thinkers. Still, he is right about one thing. Somebody went to a lot of trouble to paint that up there."

Murphy reflected, as he had for the last half hour, on the possible reasons why. The entire message of the Bible was condensed into this one tiny sentence by the Holy Spirit, who had inspired John to write it down.

The Scripture itself had crept into the mainstream a few years back when an individual started a habit of holding up a crude cardboard sign inscribed with a big black JOHN 3:16 at countless televised sporting events across the country, always in direct view of the cameras.

Sometime later, the Scripture survived the silliness of a pro wrestler's using a variation as part of his act. But now things were about to turn really ugly. Just based on tonight's hyped-up coverage, Murphy sensed that the media was poised to use the same Scripture, the most beautiful and poignant of all Scriptures, which had brought hope to countless millions down through the ages, as part of a smear campaign, a conditioning process against evangelical Christians. The irony was not lost on Murphy.

"John Three: Sixteen is a pretty good message to get out there," Laura said.

"Yes," Murphy agreed, "but something tells me it wasn't some Sunday-school teacher who put it up there."

# TWENTY-SEVEN

SHANE BARRINGTON WATCHED his own BNN network's live coverage of the U.N. events alone in his apartment after he had been alerted to tune in by the president of the news division, who had a standing order to call Barrington's personal hotline whenever there was important breaking news.

Of course, his network news head had no idea that Barrington had been peripherally involved. *How could he?* Barrington thought. *Even I'm not certain I was involved.* These people he was now working for, these *Seven*, along with their creepy thug, Talon, were a strange lot. He dared not ask them questions, and he had no way to contact them even if he had wanted to. They seemed to know everything about his business, however, and he assumed they would know about his personal life as well, if he had one.

Most nights, like this one, he would be poring over reports and figures by himself in his apartment. With the financial security assured by the Seven, Barrington was even further empowered in his greed, so he was driving every division to expand, to look for takeovers, to seek new ways to crush his competition.

The Seven's backing also allowed him to pay off the few trusted lieutenants within his organization so that he could be assured there would be no betrayals or sell-outs. Except for the moles who were obviously report-ing to the Seven, but he didn't mind about them now because he was not planning on trying to cross the Seven in any way in his business dealings. They knew what they were getting when they aligned with him: a ruthless, hard-driving, take-no-prisoners bottom-line business mogul.

He just wished he had some better idea of who these people were, these Seven. What was their goal? Other than making money and building an ever-larger and controlling communications systems and electronics empire, what was his role in their plan?

Take this U.N. stunt, for instance. He had gotten his specific instructions from Talon to find some ways to circumvent some of the U.N. security systems and he had been able to do so in a complex round of maneuvers that could never be connected or traced even under the tremendous focus that would now be brought to bear on the U.N.

However, once he transmitted the information him-self to Talon, he never heard another word about the U.N. until that night. He just assumed that somehow

Talon and the Seven were behind the deed, but to what end?

Barrington marveled, as he always did, at the quickness and cleverness of his network producers, who had already come up with one of their trademark alarmist names for this latest crisis: *U.N. VIOLATED*. However, this painting of the message on the front of the building looked more like a high-school prank than a world-shaking security threat.

His phone rang. Expecting his news president on the other end, he answered, "Jim, what's the latest?"

"You're not going to be getting the news tonight, Barrington, you're going to be making some." *Talon.* Despite himself, Barrington froze at the sound of his voice.

"You're going to give your lady news star, that Kovacs woman, the big scoop of the night."

"I am?"

"Just listen and write this down. It's a house at One Hundred Sixty-fourth Street and Seventy-sixth Avenue in Queens, a house rented by Joe Farley, one of the regular window washers at the U.N. It's not where he lived, it's a secret place he kept. So secret, in fact, he didn't even know he rented it, if you get my drift. Tell Kovacs that one of your big lawman buddies tipped you that the FBI is about to bust in on the place. The FBI doesn't even know that yet, so she's got a jump on the story."

"So what's the big deal? Is this guy Farley hiding out there?"

"The 'so what' is that this guy kept this other house, which is full of crazy rants and Bibles and all sorts of religious-nut papers—and plans to blow up the U.N."

"How do you know this? You couldn't have gotten this from the information I supplied you with."

"Let's just say that all this is information I supplied myself."

"You mean you've planted the evidence to frame this Farley? When the FBI finds him, won't it be clear that somebody set him up?"

"But the FBI will never find Farley. Nor will anyone. And trust me, *never* is sooner than anyone will find you if you ever ask me another question. Just get Kovacs on the phone, give her her scoop, and tell her to get over there with her cameraman and start broadcasting. She can make up some excuse later for breaking in. Then tomorrow tell her to redouble her efforts on her assignment to investigate these evangelical Christian crazies. Why, it's a disgrace what they could do to an international treasure like the U.N."

Barrington was unsure whether he should laugh, but the line went dead. As he punched in Kovacs's speed-dial phone number, he decided he would use those very words on her.

# TWENTY-EIGHT

"THIS IS STEPHANIE Kovacs, broadcasting a live world exclusive for BNN. I am now standing on a deceptively quiet street in Queens, New York City. Here in this seemingly ordinary two-story brick house you see behind me, the apparent mastermind behind tonight's shocking attack on the United Nations had his secret terror cell."

Talon watched from his hotel room and gave a grim chuckle. *This woman is good*, he thought. *She may have more ice water in her veins than her boss, Barrington, has.*

He would have to keep an eye on her for future use.

In U.N. Security headquarters, Burton Welsh broke in on Nugent and turned on the television.

"Look at this, will you? That BNN reporter Kovacs

is broadcasting from the window washer's secret hiding place."

Nugent swore. "How did she get there?"

Welsh shrugged. "My people say all she's said is 'street sources.' And we'll probably never be able to sweat it out of her. But look at what she's found there."

He turned up the volume on the set. "... Although there is no sign of the alleged renter, Joseph Farley, here at this house, BNN has confirmed that he was a regular window washer at the U.N. who would easily have been able to perpetrate tonight's shocking attack. And we have confirmed that he was new to this neighborhood, which is not his legal residence, but at least one neighbor told me she has seen him coming in and out of this house at strange hours."

The camera now panned away from Kovacs, and in the harsh brightness of the TV lights it zoomed in on piles of books and papers on the table in what looked like a dining room.

"Here is what BNN has found, as we are the first on the scene of the Farley-the-Fanatic house. Bibles that appear to be marked up with key passages about Christ and the resurrection. Floor plans of the United Nations also marked up for what I fear could be a terrorist attack."

Nugent swore again. "How long until the NYPD are over there and get her off the air?"

Welsh held his cell phone to one ear while cupping his other ear. "ETA a minute and a half. I'm getting myself patched through to her as soon as they arrive. This is turning into a night at the circus."

Talon did not want to take the time to wait until Kovacs interviewed the foolish old woman who lived next to the house he had rented in Farley's name. He knew Kovacs was too good a reporter to miss the half-blind but fully nosy Mrs. Sorcatini, who Talon had made sure would see him when he made his two late-night forays dressed as Farley to set up the house.

No, he had seen enough of BNN's very satisfying hyped-up news coverage. Apparently, so had his contact at the castle. By the second ring he had unlocked his security-scrambled phone. As expected, the voice was John Bartholomew, his main contact from the Seven.

"I tell you, Talon, if Christ had the miracle of twenty-four-hour satellite television, there would be no need for evangelicals. I suppose we could say that tonight you have actually begun to do the same thing, using that TV newswoman to begin destroying them."

"I don't know about that, sir," Talon replied. "This is just a flash in the pan. Nothing is going to stand up when the authorities investigate, and they will never be able to produce Farley to prove anything."

"Now, Talon, this is no time for false modesty. You've established a great worldwide media event. That's what news is these days. Nobody cares about the fine points, the correction, the follow-up—they'll be on to the next scandal by then. But people will remember that some Christian nut job, as they say on the talk shows, was going to blow up the U.N. I'd say that's a good night's work."

"If you're happy, I'm happy. Do you want me to step up the next wave?"

"No, Talon, just keep doing your prep work. My

colleagues and I must decide which paths to pursue and on what timetable. We want to do this right so that we can remain in control. Chaos is a noble pursuit if properly orchestrated. Otherwise, it is just that, chaos, unless you can manipulate it to your advantage. I will be in touch."

Stephanie Kovacs held her cell phone a foot from her ear as Burton Welsh screamed at her. The network had gone back to the anchor desk for the hourly update. "Mr. Welsh, you know I'm not going to reveal my street sources for how I beat the police—and the FBI—to the Farley house."

Welsh refused to lower his decibel level. "All the freedom of the press in the country is not going to save you from a breaking-and-entering charge, Miss Kovacs. You had no right to bust into that house tonight, and you know it."

Kovacs spoke in her most innocent voice. "Why, Agent Welsh, I was watching this house from my news van because of my tip, when we thought we saw smoke coming out. We were just doing our duty as citizens to save whoever was inside from the fire."

Welsh snorted. "Fire, my foot. There will be fire coming, I promise you, when I fry your fanny in court!"

Kovacs smiled. "Mr. Welsh, don't you feel that one psychopath threatening violence is enough for tonight? Any further questions you have can be referred to the BNN legal department. Good-bye, FBI."

# TWENTY-NINE

"OH, TALON, I swear it is enough to make one believe in a higher power." John Bartholomew's usually somber voice sounded almost jolly on the secure phone line. "The next phase of our plan has fallen into our laps. Pack your bags."

Talon, as usual, exhibited no emotion whatsoever. "Where am I heading?"

"You will be strengthening your inspiring new devotion to evangelical Christianity, young man."

"This time I hope I will actually get to follow through with something bigger than paint cans."

"I believe you will, but you will need to exercise some patience, Talon. We have somebody else doing the heavy lifting for us at the beginning of this next phase. Only he doesn't know it yet."

Talon sounded wary. "Who? Our agreement was that I was to be in complete control of any U.S. actions."

"And so you shall be, you suspicious boy. You are just going to monitor our unsuspecting helper while he rises to his challenges. He has a skill-set that even you cannot match."

"What skills are those?"

"Finding things. Old things. You're going to Preston, North Carolina, to keep tabs on Professor Michael Murphy."

"I hunt things, I kill things. Why do you want me watching a professor?"

"You are a man of few words, Talon, but such clear, colorful phrases. You see, one of our sources in the Mideast has alerted us that this Murphy has stumbled onto something we want very badly."

"Then let me just go take this thing you want."

"Oh, you will, but it's not that simple. We've had it checked out, and what we want is actually in pieces, pieces that probably no one else in the world could find."

"That's preposterous. You've demonstrated that you have power and money enough to do almost anything you want."

"Murphy cannot be bought. He's got morals, principles, things you wouldn't understand. And he tries to be a very good Christian, something you *certainly* wouldn't understand. And yet, surprisingly, he is also a risk-taker, much like yourself, a man of action, sometimes foolish action. Which is why I wish I could be there when you finally do battle with him, Talon, because that should be something to see."

"You're not frightening me."

"I'm not trying to. I am warning you that this is not some flabby window washer in Queens you're going to be tracking. He's smart, he's capable, and most of all he is the only person in the world who has such a unique combination of knowledge, courage, and drive to recognize the value of these pieces we want and to go find them."

"What are these pieces he's finding for you? He finds old Biblical junk, doesn't he?"

"So eloquently phrased, Talon. Yes, he finds ancient artifacts that have helped to validate events in the Bible as real historical events."

"Why is that of interest to you? I thought you all hate religion of any kind."

"No, we do not hate all religion. We will one day soon have a new religion, and only one religion. To help lead all of those millions of Christians toward our one religion, we want to lure them over with some of their own symbols from their own Bible. If we can show that we have been entrusted by their God with these symbols, it will make us seem that much more legitimate and will help to distract them as we wean them away from their old God to our new God."

"What do you need the real artifacts for? Why don't you just make your own?"

"Because there are people like Murphy in the world who would be able to spot a fake. Besides, this particular artifact he's hunting has been rumored for centuries to have some real power all its own. The Brazen Serpent of the Bible."

"You mean to tell me that you Seven have all the

power that money can buy and you still believe in some Bible souvenir?"

"Well, Talon, when Murphy finds the three pieces of the Serpent and puts them together, we'll just see. Whether it has a darker power or not, we will eventually use it as a centerpiece to rally believers to our religion. So, you are going to keep close tabs on Professor Murphy while he finds the other two pieces, and then take them all for us. Got it?"

"I'll need something besides babysitting to do down in North Carolina."

"Ah, great minds do think alike, Talon. You know how we have been considering what our next moves should be in our other goals, such as stirring up general fear and distrust in all of the world's organizations and institutions. Our focus has been on the urban centers, but we have decided to combine several of our goals for your next action. We're going to take the terror to a small town. And continue our drive against our dear evangelical brothers and sisters."

For the first time in their conversation, Talon sounded more energized than usual. "Let me guess. The small town is Preston, North Carolina. And the evangelical church is Murphy's."

"Very good, Talon. You go right to the head of the class. In fact, you're ready for the university."

# THIRTY

NEBUCHADNEZZAR COULD stand to wait no longer. Daniel seemed to be straining to hear an inner voice.

Finally he spoke again. "You saw a great image, O King. You dreamed of a statue—"

"A statue! Yes! I see it!" The king was on his feet, smiling from ear to ear like a blind man who had just had his sight miraculously restored.

Daniel continued, taking no heed of the king's excitement.

"The statue you saw in your dreams, its splendor was excellent in form, awesome. A mighty statue that towered fully ninety cubits above you.

"The head of the statue was of gold, wondrously bright, like molten fire, the chest and arms of shining silver like the moon when she is full." He paused as the king stepped forward and gripped his shoulders fiercely. It was as if the statue were standing before them under a great black veil and Daniel was pulling the veil away inch by inch with his words.

"The belly and thighs of the statue were of bronze, the legs of iron, the feet of clay and iron mixed." He paused, and the king became still, not daring to move or speak in case the vision was lost.

Nebuchadnezzar sat back on his cedarwood chair and drank deeply from a cup of wine. The exhilaration that came with remembering his dream was intoxicating but short-lived. Now he was filled with a gnawing hunger to discover what meaning might lie behind such an extraordinary vision.

He looked up, and Daniel seemed to sense his question before he asked it.

"The four portions of the statue represent four empires. First gold, then silver, then bronze. Each empire less mighty than the last. Until the final empire of iron, which will be the weakest, for its foundations, the feet of iron and clay mixed together, shall likewise be divided."

"Four empires," the king mused. "And only four?"

"Yes, there shall be only four world empires until the Latter times. This is how the people will know that only the God of heaven can accurately reveal history before it comes to pass. Then, in the Latter days, ten kingdoms of the world will join together in an attempt to rebuild a world kingdom similar to yours, O King. After that, the end shall come."

It was extraordinary. Nebuchadnezzar lived in a world where lies were common currency. Even those closest to him—perhaps especially they—could not be trusted. He had long ago concluded that only a man bound and chained and who sees the red-hot iron in the approaching torturer's hand could be relied upon to tell the truth.

Yet, he had no doubt, not the smallest shred, that every word

Daniel spoke would come to pass. For the first time in his life he, the ruler of countless nations, felt there was no solid ground beneath his feet.

Once again, the Hebrew slave anticipated his next thought.

"And what of Babylon, what of Nebuchadnezzar in all of this?" Daniel looked the king in the eye once more, and his deep, resonant voice seemed to fill the chamber.

"Here is the dream's interpretation. You have been chosen by God to be the ruler of all things and all men. The God of heaven has given you a kingdom, power, strength, and glory. Before the coming of the kingdom of God, yours shall be the greatest empire the world will ever know. You, my king, are the head of gold of the dream's statue. When the fourth kingdom arises, it shall be as strong as iron. That kingdom will break into pieces and crush all other kingdoms."

"Break into pieces?" the king shouted.

"That is the rest of your dream. You watched as a stone was formed without hands. The stone struck the image with great force and shattered the feet made of iron and clay. The image came crashing to the ground. Its iron, clay, bronze, silver, and gold were all crushed together and became like chaff from the threshing floor. Then the wind came up and blew them all away so that no trace could be found. And the stone that struck the image grew to the size of a mountain and enveloped the whole earth."

The king arose and began to pace with agitation.

"My king, the feet which you saw, made partly of clay and partly of iron, they indicate a divided kingdom, both strong and fragile. As you are aware, O King, iron cannot mix with clay. And in the days of this divided kingdom, the God of heaven will set up His own kingdom, which shall never be destroyed. It will not be ruled by ordinary men. It will consume all the other king-doms and stand forever."

Daniel then concluded, "The God of heaven has made these things known to you, O King. The dream and its interpretation are certain."

King Nebuchadnezzar then commanded his men to present an offering of gifts and incense to Daniel. He placed his hand on Daniel's shoulder.

"From this day forward, you shall be ruler over this entire province and chief administrator over all of the wise men of Babylon. For you, Daniel, serve a God which is greater than any other."

# THIRTY-ONE

CHUCK NELSON FISHED in the pocket of his jeans and pulled out a handful of crumpled bills. He looked at them sourly. Ten bucks, give or take. Enough for a burger, maybe some chili. He swept a hank of greasy blond hair out of his eyes and squinted at the bills, as if looking harder was going to change anything.

Nope. The same ten bucks he'd had in his pocket when the cops had pulled him over in the stolen Chevy. Just like he was wearing the same oil-stained jeans with the tears at both knees, the same stained green sweatshirt and muddy sneakers. At least they'd laundered his clothes. Didn't look like they'd done the same for his money.

His stomach began to rumble and he tried to remember when he'd last eaten a meal that was fit for a human being rather than a hog. A big bowl of chili would sure go down easy. And he needed a drink right now.

He'd need every cent, unless they'd passed a free-beer law while he'd been away, that is. It was only a couple miles into town. And hey, maybe somebody would pull over and give him a ride. But he doubted it. He knew he looked like what he was. Trouble. And the oh-so-good folks of Preston always liked to avoid trouble if they possibly could.

He pulled his old Preston High jacket closer as he felt the first spatters of rain, and started marching down the two-lane country road.

First get that beer. Then settle a few scores.

Two hours later Chuck was sitting at a table in Mooney's Tavern and shaking the last drops out of an empty pitcher. He had a little buzz going now, but his money was all spent and the barman, some new guy probably straight out of bartending school, had refused to run him a tab. He slammed the pitcher down and spat on the floor. How much money had he spent in this lousy dive over the years, drinking their lousy watered-down beer? Math wasn't his strong suit, but it had to be a lot. And now the barman was eyeing him like Chuck was something nasty he was fixing to scrape off his shoe. He could feel the rage mounting, that tingling feeling at the ends of his fingers as if a fuse had just been lit.

A screech followed by raucous laughter diverted his attention from the barman, and he swiveled to see a pretty blonde choking on a beer, while another girl thumped her on the back and the two guys sitting across the booth slapped the table, whooping.

He didn't need to see the words "Preston University" on their sweatshirts to know they were students. And probably underage too. He'd been getting drunk in this place when they were still wearing braces, and now he was the one the barman was giving the evil eye to.

He sauntered over and put his hands on the shoulders of the two guys. "Hey, boys, don't you have a class to go to? I think your little friend here could use a beer-drinking lesson." He grinned and gave them a friendly pat.

The blond girl wiped beer from her mouth with her sleeve and glared at him as the two guys shook off Chuck's hands and jumped to their feet. They were both an inch or two shorter than he was and looked out of shape. Too much time reading books and not enough working out, he guessed. He could see they didn't want to look bad in front of their girlfriends, but the worried look in their eyes told him they weren't going to give him any trouble.

"Tell you what. You boys buy me a pitcher of beer and I'll give you a free demonstration. Show you how it's done. What do you say?" He gave them his best good-time grin and winked at the girls. They were still glaring at him like wildcats. *Hey, it ain't my fault if your boyfriends are such wimps,* he thought.

He was about to press the point when he felt his jacket being yanked from behind. Off balance, he staggered backward and fell heavily against a table. Before he could regain his feet, someone pinned his arms behind him and started shoving him toward the door.

"Hey, get your hands off me." He managed to wrench himself out of the armlock and whirled around. The barman stood smirking, arms folded. Next to him was another man Chuck had never seen before, heavier set, unshaven, with faded tattoos on his forearms. *Must have come out of the kitchen*, he thought. The man stepped forward, getting right in Chuck's face.

"Get out. Now. Before we decide to get nasty. We don't want scum like you in here no more."

Chuck reckoned he could take the barman, no problem. But the kitchen guy looked like he meant business. No point getting all busted up for a pitcher of beer, no matter how thirsty he was. He brushed himself off and did not look back.


A few minutes later, the man known as Talon left an untouched beer on a corner table and walked out of the bar. He scanned the street. No sign of Chuck in either direction. No matter. It wasn't exactly hard to predict his next move. He sniffed the air, then turned right. Toward the river.

As he walked through the town, past the little corner drugstore, then the thrift shop with its display of teddy bears in the window, he wondered how long his work would keep him in Preston. Long enough to make a lasting contribution to the place, he felt sure. To make a few changes that would be remembered. He stopped at the Hey Preston! magic shop with its hand-painted sign depicting a rabbit peering over the brim of a top hat, and smiled. Oh, yes. He'd show them a few new tricks before he was done.

Another ten minutes and the cute little shops and family restaurants began to give way to boarded-up storefronts and vacant lots. Even Preston had its bad part of town, where the street lighting wasn't so good and the picket fences were missing a few slats and a coat of whitewash. He began to search for a likely spot.

He found it almost at once. An alley between a Chinese takeout place and a liquor store. A good short-cut if you weren't afraid of the shadows and anybody who might be lurking there. Somebody who might be badly in need of some cash and didn't care how they got it, for instance.

He peered into the gloom. There was a powerful stench of rotting vegetables. No doubt this was where the restaurant dumped its garbage. The scraping and scurrying sounds told him he was not the first to figure that out. He took a few steps into the alley and listened. Just in time. He walked another ten yards through the discarded boxes, then ducked behind a Dumpster and pulled out his cell phone.

Chuck kept the little man pinned to the wall with one hand while he tried to flip through his wallet with the other. The guy was so terrified, he probably could not have run, let alone fight back. But the lessons you learned in jail stayed with you. Never turn your back. Never let your guard down. And never assume your opponent is down for the count unless he's actually stopped breathing.

The other rule was to listen hard. You might not see trouble coming, but maybe you could hear it. And right now Chuck could hear a siren. Hard to tell how far away, but it seemed to be getting louder. Time to finish his business and get on his way.

Suddenly a flashlight swept across the alley, blinding him for a moment. Behind it stood a cop, nightstick at the ready. "Stop right there," he shouted. "Step away from the wall with your hands out front, where I can see them."

Chuck shoved the wallet into his jacket and let go of the little man, who crumpled against the wall and slumped to the ground. Now what? He didn't have a weapon and the cop was advancing steadily. He'd be on him in a second.

If he didn't think of something quick, he'd soon be back in Cell 486, and this time they'd throw away the key.

The cop found his target again with the flashlight, and now Chuck couldn't see a thing. Then suddenly there was a crack, a sharp cry of pain, and the light veered off into the shadows. As his eyes adjusted again to the gloom, he made out a dark shape—a tall man standing over the cop with what looked like a piece of two-by-four in his hand. The cop wasn't making a sound now.

The man turned toward Chuck and he saw his face. Bone-white features and blank eyes that made him shiver. He beckoned Chuck forward with a gloved hand.

"His friends will be here in a minute or two. Time to ship out, Chuck."

Chuck froze in place, uncertain what this ghoul had in mind. His brain had shut down.

The ghoul seemed to sense his fear. He flung the

two-by-four into a pile of boxes and held both arms out to the side. "You have nothing to fear from me, Chuck. Quite the opposite. In fact, you could say I'm your savior." He laughed, though Chuck couldn't see the joke. It was a harsh, animal sound, not really a laugh at all.

The sirens were loud now. Only a few blocks away.

"Come on, I have a place where you can get cleaned up. Money. I even have a job for you. Unless you'd rather go back to jail, of course."

Chuck's brain unscrambled itself enough to figure out he didn't really have any more choices.

"Okay, mister," he said. "You're the boss. I guess you better lead the way."

# THIRTY-TWO

STEPHANIE KOVACS FOUND herself gazing out the window for the third time in the last half hour, wondering how she had gotten stuck talking to one of the most boring men in the world while researching a story that to her great surprise was one of the hottest of her career. Since her worldwide exclusive at the home of Farley the Fanatic, the U.N. window washer who still had not turned up, Stephanie's media star was rising at BNN even faster than before.

Of course, it did not hurt that Shane Barrington himself seemed to be following this story with keener personal interest than he had exhibited about any prior news story. From the moment Stephanie had gotten the anonymous phone tip to rush to the Farley rental in Queens the night of the U.N. attack, she had wondered about the coincidence of Barrington's first meeting with her, essentially ordering her to investigate the evangelical Christian movement and this headline-making discovery. Considering she herself had barely picked up a Bible since she was twelve, religious talk was now filling her days.

The competitive reporter in her was more than a little envious about not getting to follow up some of the links resulting from the U.N. window painting. That seemed like hard news, or, more appropriately, hard lack-of-news, because no further evidence had been uncovered to connect Farley either to a known evangelical group or to any additional physical evidence of a U.N. bombing plot. But her revelations of that night still stuck in people's memories.

Now she was following a direct tip from Shane Barrington himself. When he called to congratulate her—first time ever—on her scoop, he let slip that high-level people in Washington had told him that the FBI had questioned none other than Professor Michael Murphy in connection with the U.N. attack. Stephanie had suggested that they were probably talking to Murphy as an expert on the Bible to get clues about the painted message, much like the networks all had talking-head experts for every crisis.

But Barrington suggested she should go to Preston University and snoop around about Murphy. After all, he was a TV personality, and TV people like nothing better than a whiff of scandal about another TV star, even if he was only the star of some dusty archaeology specials on cable.

Which was how she found herself listening to Dean Archer Fallworth drone on and on about the university grade-point average and student community service initiatives. She did not want to tip her hand about her interest in Murphy until she had gotten a sense of how he fit into university life, but now it was time to cut to the chase.

"Dean, how about the evangelical Christians? Are they active on campus?"

Fallworth's eyes narrowed. "Evangelicals? Well, yes, we do have some very"—he waved his hand, searching for the right word—"*energetic* members of that particular religious group at Preston. Only a handful, really, but they tend to make rather a lot of noise." He flashed a smile he wanted to appear to be conspiratorial. "What exactly is your interest?"

"Let's just say there's a lot of concern among ordinary citizens that these evangelical groups are getting too big, too scary. I want to find out how a fine liberal arts university like Preston is affected. Institutions like yours as the front line in the battle against bigotry. Our viewers would be interested in that."

Fallworth's smile became a Cheshire cat's grin. "I like to think we do our best. Fighting the good fight against ignorance and intolerance." He clasped his hands together and leaned forward over the desk. "But it isn't always easy. They're *very* well organized, you know. And some of their leaders are tremendously cunning."

*Here we go*, thought Stephanie. "Anyone in particular?"

Fallworth pursed his lips. "I don't want to speak ill of any faculty members, of course. . . ."

"Unless it's in the public interest."

"Quite so. Well, there is one professor here who

makes it his business to stir up trouble, filling impressionable young minds with the worst kinds of spiritualistic nonsense. His name's Murphy." He winced, as if Stephanie had forced an unpleasant confession out of him. "Professor Michael Murphy."

Bingo. That was the name Barrington had given her when he'd called two nights earlier. Just a little follow-up, he'd said. To focus the investigation. She had no idea why he was so keen to nail him, but there was no doubting the strength of his feelings. In his icy way, he was practically breathing fire into the phone. And Murphy seemed to be just as unpopular with Fallworth.

*He must be quite a character,* she thought.

"So, what does this Murphy teach?"

"Biblical archaeology, if you will. His mission is to authenticate the Bible by digging up artifacts that confirm Bible stories. The very opposite of science, in my opinion."

"And has he found any?"

"So he would claim."

"And his classes are well attended?"

"I'm afraid so. Students tend to find him . . . charismatic. He's something of a cult figure on campus, and I mean that in the worst sense. Perhaps it's because he's an outdoors type." *Unlike real scholars such as yourself,* thought Stephanie, noting Fallworth's paunch and pasty complexion. "Rock-climbing, archery, all very gung-ho."

Stephanie stood and gathered her briefcase. "How intriguing. If I'm going to go after these evangelicals, it looks like Murphy's the place to start. So, where can I find him?"

# THIRTY-THREE

THE MAN KNOWN as Talon entered the house and let the screen door shut in Chuck Nelson's face behind him.

As he scrambled to pull open the screen door to this place where Talon said he was living, Chuck was really puzzled. The guy had plenty of cash, whipping out a large roll of small bills at every store, yet he was living in this house Chuck figured was two grades below a dump. It was about twenty miles outside of Preston, so it was not even close to anything except back roads and forest. The porch was sunken to the point of near collapse, there was a leak in the roof over two of the bedrooms, and the bathroom sink had only one faucet knob, and it was crusted with a muddy mix of years of rust and dirt.

Chuck's reflexes were a little slow because he was tired from having driven Talon around for four hours.

There were stops in three different megastores—each in a different county, miles apart from one another. None of what they bought made sense to Chuck, and it especially did not make sense that they couldn't just buy it all in one place, but Talon made it clear early on that questions of any kind were not part of his routine.

"Start hauling the bags and boxes out of the car," Talon ordered.

"I'm beat. Can't it wait until morning?"

"Haul. Now. School's in session."

Chuck scowled. "What school?"

"Shut up and learn, genius. I'm going to teach you how to shake things up but good in this hick town of yours."

Within an hour, the card table in what once might have passed for a living room was spilling over with torn bags and ripped-open boxes. As Talon showed Chuck how he wanted the crude ingredients mixed, he surprised Chuck by being in a more talkative mood than before.

"That sister of yours, she got a thing for that Professor Murphy?"

"I told you, I haven't spoken to her pretty much since I was in the joint. I'm just living there because I can't afford to be on my own yet, and it's clean, a lot cleaner than this place. But I doubt it. She's just a goody-goody girl, always was."

"What do you know about Murphy, or his wife?"

"Don't make me laugh. You expect me to know something about a teacher and his stupid wife? My sister knew him from church, before she went to college, I know that much. Why are you so curious about Murphy?"

"A warrior always studies the enemy."

After Talon sent Chuck home for the night, letting him drive the rental car and telling him to be back in the morning to pick him up for a full day of errands, he grabbed his secure satellite-link phone and dialed a New York number.

It took a while for Shane Barrington to answer. "You're not a religious man, I know, Barrington, but get out your sackcloth and your funeral suit. In two days, you're going to announce the tragic death of your only son, Arthur."

Barrington had now come to dread Talon's calls. The only consolations were that they were brief and that the calls were better than visits. "You know you killed my son days ago. Whatever you did with the body, how can I just announce that he died?"

Talon pulled out his checklist, to make sure he did not forget any detail. "It's rather simple. First off, you're rich and powerful, which in this country means you can do whatever you want, pretty much. Why, a rich creep like you can even buy the sympathy of the American public. And that's exactly what you're going to do."

# THIRTY-FOUR

"DO WE NOW find ourselves in the best of times or the worst of times? Show of hands." Murphy stood in front of the lectern. "First, you doomsayers. Who thinks we are living in the worst of times?"

A few students' hands shot up right away, but most looked hesitant to commit. "Come on, folks, your answer will not count toward your final grade. At least not in this course. So, worst of times?" About half of the students raised their hands.

"Okay, now for you more optimistic folks. How many of you feel that you are alive during the best of times?" A little less than half of the students raised their hands. "I'm going to give the rest of you who didn't raise your hand the benefit of the doubt that you are not unsure about whether you're alive at all."

"So, what's the right answer?" a student in the last row shouted.

"Well, I'm not here to tell you my opinion, despite Dean Fallworth's fears, but I can tell you that going right back to Eve's fall from the Garden of Eden, many people in each generation have believed the human race's best times are in the past, that civilization as they know it, or perhaps as they nostalgically prefer to remember it, is declining, and that even darker times are coming."

A voice rang out, "The end is near!"

"Yes, many of you have probably seen the cliché cartoon figure, the madman storming through the streets carrying the sign REPENT! THE END IS NEAR.

"Well, lots of people consider such belief so extreme that it's to be laughed at.

"But in most societies throughout history, people sought out signs, gods, idols, superstitions, science—yes, science—to try to get some predictive leg up on exactly what the future held, especially about any dark times on the horizon. In most of those societies, the men and women who could convincingly make interpretations and predictions held a place of honor, at least until they were proven to be frauds or, sometimes, when their unpopular predictions came true.

"The more formal practitioners of this predictive knowledge are called prophets.

"You probably have never met any prophets, but you might be surprised to know that today, many of your family, friends, and neighbors, millions of people of all ages, in all walks of life, in all parts of the country, all believe in prophecy. These people especially believe that the end is near, and they believe that the end is near not because of reading the entrails of a goat they have sacrificed in their yard, nor by calling the Psychic Hotline, nor by how their bunions feel in the rain, or secret signals from little green Martians, but because of this book."

Murphy held up his Bible. "That's right, the Bible is not just a history of what happened back in ancient times and a compilation of lessons for how we should live our lives. The Bible also is filled with many prophecies that have *already* come true and many more prophecies that a huge number of people believe *will* come true. People who are not crackpots, I daresay. People like me.

"Now, one day, I hope that the university will allow me to teach a course in Biblical prophecy, because I believe it is both a fascinating and an important intellectual discipline, separate from the issue of belief in what the prophecies lay out for us. However, here in good old Biblical Archaeology, I am going to focus instead on showing you how one archaeological discovery, which I hope I am very close to digging up, could help to authenticate the historical facts behind the prophecy that many believe is the most important one in the Bible, the prophecy of Daniel based on the dream of King Nebuchadnezzar.

"Nebuchadnezzar was the greatest ruler in the great empire of Babylon and had at his beck and call the best prophets and high priests of his pagan world. None of them could interpret his dream of a statue, but one of the Hebrew slaves, Daniel, was able to tell him in no uncertain terms that his dream was a vision given him by the one true God.

"Daniel explained that the huge image in the dream was a statue of Nebuchadnezzar himself, built in four levels. Each of the four levels represented one of the only absolute world empires: first was the Golden Head, representing Babylon; next the silver chest and arms, representing the Medo-Persian empire, which consisted of the two countries that conquered Babylon; then came the belly of brass, which represented the Greeks; and they were followed by the iron legs of the Romans. The closer you get to the present, the weaker those empires became, as you can see by the declining quality of the materials used to render their portion of the statue.

"Prophecy, which is history written in advance, is one of God's ways of proving that He exists. For example, the fact that God twenty-five hundred years ago revealed to Nebuchadnezzar that there would be only four world empires until 'the time of the end' is a miracle in and of itself.

"For, as all students of history know, there have been only four world empires since the days of the Babylonian empire. The most amazing thing is that many ruthless leaders have tried to rule the world, such as Genghis Khan, Napoleon, Hitler, Stalin, Mao, and others. But they all failed. Why? Because the God of heaven said there would be only four world empires until the Latter days.

"Not a bad piece of prophecy, you have to admit, considering it was written five hundred years before Christ.

"And the real reason so many millions study Daniel's prophecy is that based on the accuracy of his account of the *past*, there is every reason to believe his account of what will happen in our *future*.

"Again, time and our course work will keep me from going into greater detail now, but feel free to stop by my office anytime and I will be happy to explain why this generation has more reason to believe that when you study Daniel's prophecies and others, there are more Biblical reasons to believe that Christ will return to set up His kingdom in our lifetime than in any generation before us.

"But back to where archaeology fits into all of this. I bet it's safe to assume there are some skeptics among you who figure Daniel never lived and his prophecies have no basis in fact. Well, remember in my last lecture I told you about the Brazen Serpent made by Moses at God's instruction, and I showed you a piece of the actual bronze Serpent as proof of its truth as the Bible told it? And remember, I went through the incredible journey of that Brazen Serpent over so many decades and so many different ancient societies, finally ending up, based on where and how I found it, to have been right there in Babylon, in the time of Daniel's prophecies for Nebuchadnezzar.

"Well, while I've called in a much smarter scientist than myself to try to interpret the next clues for me, which will lead to the finding of the rest of the Serpent, I hope, I went back to study the scroll that got me started on all of this, the new interpretation of the life and times of the Brazen Serpent. A much longer life and much more interesting time than we knew about that Serpent up to now."

Murphy brought a slide up onto the screen behind

him. "I'm sorry that once again, for you lazybones in the class, the underlying message here is not a religious one; it is: When in doubt about what you're doing, study, study, study, and study some more. I still could not figure out what the connection was between my source for this scroll telling me that it had something to do with Daniel and what we had known about the Brazen Serpent.

"Now that I have found the tail of the bronze Brazen Serpent, thanks to a scroll dated from the time of Daniel in Babylon, a scroll seemingly written by King Nebuchadnezzar's most trusted high priest, Dakkuri, I believe that we can place the Serpent in Daniel's time even though the Old Testament never mentions the Serpent after Hezekiah had it destroyed in the Second Book of Kings.

"However, even I would not claim that this is absolute proof of Daniel's historical existence or that it unequivocally helps to authenticate his prophecies.

"Then, as I pored over the scroll, it hit me. Actually, it was when I was taking a break in the lounge, when I passed the NO SMOKING sign I've passed a thousand times before, that it hit me. You know the international slash-through sign for taking all the joys out of everybody's life?

"Well, I thought this mark here over the symbol for the king—that would be Nebuchadnezzar—this line aiming at his head, was just a decay line or some dirt on the scroll. But I realized it was the writer of the scroll doing his version of a NO SMOKING symbol, except he was saying 'no king.' That wouldn't make sense though, for a high priest to be making a sign against his king. After all, what if the scroll fell into his enemies' hands? One look at the 'no king' line there and you can bet there would quickly be no high priest's head instead. Unless, I realized, King Nebuchadnezzar had said it was okay to do away with his own head."

"You mean King Nebuchadnezzar committed suicide?" someone asked.

"Not suicide as we know it, no, but he did have himself destroyed. Again in the Book of Daniel, we learn that Nebuchadnezzar let the news of his supreme empire, the Golden Head of his dream statue, go to his own head.

"Nebuchadnezzar had the dream statue built and then went mad worshiping himself. After seven whole years, he recovered from being crazy and made amends to God by having the statue destroyed, broken into pieces, much the way Hezekiah had the Brazen Serpent broken into three pieces.

"That's right, Nebuchadnezzar went on a tear—literally—when he stopped being a madman and was returned to power. He pledged his renewed loyalty to God by ordering all idols and graven images destroyed—including the Brazen Serpent, which he had broken into three pieces again—and his own giant statue of himself. What this symbol of the line coming down toward the king's head has to mean is that Nebuchadnezzar himself ordered the statue destroyed.

"And this is the amazingly exciting conclusion I have realized, ladies and gentlemen. Because I think there is a big fat clue here to a discovery that will absolutely prove that the events in Daniel really took place.

"What the scroll shows us, and what my finding of the tail of the Serpent by following the scroll seems to prove, is that whoever wrote this scroll had secretly gone against King Nebuchadnezzar's orders. He had somehow *rescued* the pieces of the Brazen Serpent from the royal trash heap.

"And why would Nebuchadnezzar's high priest, Dakkuri, save the pieces of the Brazen Serpent? So that one day they could be rediscovered by some worthy person who would put the Serpent back whole, just as Dakkuri did after Hezekiah had destroyed it.

"And because the high priest Dakkuri was going against the direct orders of his king, who had just renewed his faith in God, it seems most likely that Dakkuri did not believe in the God of heaven. He was holding on to some idol. Or I think it's possible that he felt he was getting some special powers, most likely some dark powers, from the Brazen Serpent.

"And I think he's telling us right in the scroll that whoever finds the Serpent pieces and puts them together will be able to plug into the very same powers that Dakkuri believed in and that Nebuchadnezzar wanted destroyed.

"But that's not all. He's showing us something else here in the scroll. That in addition to the special powers of the Serpent, you get an even bigger prize, according to the high priest Dakkuri, a bigger prize that Nebuchadnezzar was trying to keep from the world. Somehow, the whole Serpent put back together will lead you to the *other* object that this Dakkuri saved and hid away against Nebuchadnezzar's wishes.

"I think he's promising a prize the Bible tells us is gigantic in size. I think he wants someone to use the Serpent to find and dig up the Golden Head of the statue of Nebuchadnezzar."

# THIRTY-FIVE

LAURA SAT ON the bench at the top of the little hill overlooking the campus. It was a beautiful day, a warm breeze blowing leaves across the grass while starlings chattered in the little stand of birch trees behind her. The kind of day when you'd catch yourself smiling for no reason. She was meeting Shari after Murph's class to go for a quick lunch.

The tranquillity was shattered by a car she did not recognize screeching to a loud and sudden stop in front of her bench. She involuntarily frowned when she saw Chuck Nelson in the driver's seat, though she knew it could not be his car. It must belong to the pale, thin man with dark glasses and dressed all in black who sat in the front passenger seat. Neither man looked very happy to have given a ride to Shari, who was getting out of the backseat.

"Thanks, Chuck. Will you be home for dinner?"

Without answering, in fact without even waiting for the back door to click closed, Chuck sped away. Despite his dark glasses, Laura had the uneasy feeling that the stranger had been staring at her the whole time it took to dislodge Shari. Laura was glad he was wearing the sunglasses, because even shielded, there was something about the stranger's face and manner that gave her chills despite the warmth of the sun.

She was not alone in this discomfort. As Shari came and sat beside her, Laura could almost see the dark clouds hovering over her head. Without saying anything, she reached across and wrapped Shari in a tight hug. When she gently pulled back, Shari had tears in her eyes.

Laura felt her own tears coming and willed herself to be strong. But it was so hard. She thought back to the long sessions they'd spent in her office talking about the pain Shari still felt years after her mom and dad had died in a five-car pileup on the interstate, her dad at the wheel with half a pint of Wild Turkey inside him. How she'd tried to help Shari make sense of it all. Help her work through the anger she felt toward her dad and try to reconnect with the love that had once been there. Help her find a way of giving thanks for everything her mother had been and would always be.

And hardest of all, Laura had tried to give her the strength to reach out to her brother. Chuck had been getting into mischief from the day he could walk, and by the time he was sixteen, the neighbors were no longer taking bets on how long it would be before he found himself in jail. Throughout his troubled adolescence, he'd treated both parents with everything from sullen indifference to outright contempt—and Shari was sure her father's drinking was his way of numbing the hurt, while her mother's heart quietly broke behind her ever-loving smile.

But when Chuck found out that his parents were gone forever, he seemed to go into some kind of shock. As if he suddenly realized there was no chance now of making amends. For a brief period Shari dared to hope that their parents' tragic death would be a kind of terrible wake-up call for him.

Unfortunately, as soon as the shock wore off, Chuck cranked up the bad behavior to an all-new high—drinking, fighting, dealing drugs. It was hard to figure out who he was really trying to punish, his parents or himself, but there was no doubt he was set on a path of self-destruction now and it would be only a matter of time before he achieved his end.

For a sister still dealing with her own grief, seeing Chuck do his best to destroy himself was just too much. So when Judge Johnson handed him some jail time after the police stopped him in a stolen car filled with drugs, it gave Shari some much-needed breathing space. She could sleep at night knowing he wasn't getting into any harm, and maybe her daily prayers for her brother would have a chance to work at last.

But the Chuck who'd turned up on her doorstep was meaner than ever.

And now there was an added concern, this new friend. Laura knew the stranger was the main reason Shari had asked her to lunch.

"I just met him for the first time in the car. I

couldn't even see his face with those creepy dark glasses and his cap pulled down. The way Chuck talks about him it's like he's some sort of godfather. He says he's giving him *important jobs* to do."

"What kind of jobs?"

"He won't say. He just grins like it's some big joke on the rest of us. But whatever they're doing, I don't think it's just stealing cars." She squeezed Laura's hand. "I'm worried. Really worried, Laura. I don't want him getting himself killed."

Laura squeezed back. "Don't worry, Shari. We're not going to let that happen." She didn't have the first idea *how*, but it was important to seem confident and determined. Shari needed to know her friends were strong enough to help her deal with just about anything.

Laura thought for a moment. "If this guy's a criminal, do you think Chuck met him in prison? Maybe we could find out who he is that way."

"I don't think so. Chuck says he met him in town. Said he was having some trouble making a cash withdrawal, and this guy helped him out." She frowned. "But he won't tell me anything else about him."

"Well, that's not much to go on, but why don't I ask Chief Rawley if he can keep an eye out for Chuck and this friend and maybe he can get a better sense of what's going on with the two of them."

"Laura, I don't want to get Chuck angry with me by making him think I'm getting him spied on by the police."

"Oh, Shari, we both know that Chuck is likely to be angry whether you try to help him or not. You're a caring sister, but you can take it only so far. Eventually, he will have to make the decision to help himself."

"I know. I was lucky I had my friend's mother, who started taking me to church for the first time after my parents died. And you and Murph have been so wonderful looking out for me."

"Yes, and speaking of looking out for yourself, how about you, Shari? When was the last time you went out with a friend—a boyfriend?"

"Well, since you brought it up, I had somebody over recently, a transfer student, Paul Wallach, who's in Professor Murphy's class with me."

"Nice. So?"

"So, nothing. I'm just getting to know him. He's got major issues, as in issues with his major, still wrestling with the business course his father forced him into, even though his father died months ago."

"Why don't you tell him to come see me?"

"Oh, I already did, Laura, especially since the course that is really exciting him the most is Professor Murphy's."

"Whew, that's some leap, from the gold mine of business administration to choking on dust, looking for bones in old mines."

"Well, you of all people should know that. I hope you don't mind, I suggested that he should go talk things over with you."

"Mind? That's what I'm here for. Otherwise, I'd have to spend more time in the field with *my* dreamboat archaeologist."

"And isn't that him coming right now?" Murphy

circled his Dodge in front of the bench and stuck his head out of the window.

"Ladies, can I interest either of you in a walk in the North Woods, where I will be winging a few dozen arrows into unsuspecting trees just to keep sharp?"

"I don't think Shari's ever caught your Robin Hood act, but we're going to lunch. Murph, are you skipping off because I asked you to round up the clothes you want to give to the church clothing drive?"

"Busted. I'll do it later." He floored the accelerator before he could hear Laura yelling at him.

Laura shook her head and looked at Shari. "See what I have to deal with? We once figured out that Murphy can say 'later' in twelve languages, most of which are as ancient as his promises to do any chores."

"Oh, I twisted Paul's arm to come to our Wednesday church meeting and told him he should get in the swing of things by helping sort the clothing in the basement."

"Great. But we'd better eat so we can keep our strength up, because if we rely on the men, we'll probably be left doing all the lifting and sorting ourselves."

Talon scowled over at Chuck. "I told you to slow down. I don't want to get stopped in any speed traps down here."

"Okay, okay. It's just that I haven't been behind the wheel for a while. Tell me why we're going all the way up to Raleigh for shopping like yesterday. There's lots of stores closer."

"I don't want anybody to remember what we're buying."

"What did you want to give my sister a lift for? Man, I can tell she doesn't like you."

"Yeah, the feeling's mutual. That's why you can't tell her anything. She'd rat you out to the cops in a heartbeat. So don't tell her anything about what we're doing."

Chuck's bored eyes brightened. "I don't know anything, so what could I tell her? Hey, man, when are you going to tell me what you're planning for? Whatever it is, count me in."

Talon shook his head. "Of course you're in, you fool. Now, just shut up and get us to the mall. We're buying clothes. Lots of clothes."

"Clothes. That's cool. I could use some new duds."

"They're not for you. We're giving them away."

"I don't get it. Why are we buying clothes to give them away? What's the scam?"

"Didn't you listen to your sister natter on in the backseat about that Preston Community Church clothing drive?"

"So? Don't tell me you're making me go to church!" Chuck braked to a stop in the middle of the highway. "What kind of junk are you pulling here, anyway?"

Talon smacked Chuck's head just once, but once was enough. "I told you to shut up and drive. Relax. We're just going to be making a special donation to the church this week."

# THIRTY-SIX

"DESPITE MY GRIEF and shock, I had to come forward to warn the American people." Shane Barrington was speaking in front of dozens of reporters. Though he did not usually make media appearances, he found himself warming to his assignment.

The assignment had been the latest from Talon, to go public with the death of Arthur Barrington, his son. Of course, the story he was now telling was far from the truth. No mention was made of the horrible way in which Talon had murdered his only child. Instead, Barrington had embellished Talon's curt instructions and devised a completely fictitious account of Arthur's death.

Barrington stared into the cameras, calculating whether he should try to manufacture a tear as he told his tale. "Three days ago, my office was contacted with a ransom note informing me that my only son, Arthur, had been kidnapped in broad daylight from the streets of New York. The kidnappers demanded five million dollars for Arthur's safe return—as long as I did not contact any authorities. Like any parent, I was distraught, and my only thought was to do whatever it would take to save my son."

Trying not to distract himself with the true image of how he had actually stood by and watched Talon kill Arthur, Barrington stared straight at the media cameras. "Out of no disrespect to our fine law enforcement officers, in order to do what I felt was necessary to save my son, I instructed my private security team to make contact and arrange the payment of the ransom. Yesterday morning, instead of welcoming my son home alive, my security team uncovered his dead body, horribly mutilated by these heinous criminals."

Even the usually cynical press corps gasped at this terrible revelation by Barrington. "If my son is not safe in this country, your children are not safe either. As I mourn the loss of Arthur, I am setting aside my grief to pledge my personal energies and personal resources to marshal public action for the end to the unchecked and alarming spread of criminal violence in our society. Thank you."

Questions burst forth from the press. "Mr. Barrington." He acknowledged his own network's reporter. "Can you elaborate on what kind of efforts you will mount in your campaign to fight back, as it were, against the violent elements out there?"

Barrington gave a smooth delivery of Talon's answer to the natural question. "There are many actions I plan to lead in the coming months in the fight back by the citizens against the out-of-control violence in our country. Like so many of you, I am fed up with the politicians who do not do enough."

Another question was called out: "Mr. Barrington, are you indicating that you are planning to run for office yourself?"

"To the people of this country"—Barrington fixed his gaze coolly on the cameras—"I will make this pledge: If the politicians do not protect us, then I will set aside my work running Barrington Communications and will lead this country back to citizen safety."

"My colleagues at the Seven are most pleased with our Mr. Barrington." Talon was listening by satellite-link phone to John Bartholomew of the Seven. "You prepped him well, Talon. Over time, we will exploit that gruesome murder of yours into a whole new political power if Barrington can continue to follow orders."

Talon sneered. "If he doesn't, he will meet his own unfortunate, untimely death."

"Now, we have been reviewing your latest update about your Preston progress, Talon. Something you noted in passing actually connected with one of my diabolical colleagues, and it can fit very nicely in this new phase with Barrington."

"What do you want me to do?"

"That young man you mentioned, the Wallach lad who is warming up to Murphy and the sister of your stooge. We have a little change of plan for him."

# THIRTY-SEVEN

ON WEDNESDAY EVENING, Paul Wallach parked in front of the Preston Community Church. In the fading light, its whitewashed clapboard facade gleamed invitingly. His heart skipped a beat and he was not sure if it was because he was about to see Shari or because he was about to *choose* to enter a church for the first time.

The door was open but he didn't go in. He wanted to go right to the basement to show Shari he was sincere about helping out with the clothing sorting. He walked to the side of the building to the steel door that led to the basement. He pushed it open and climbed down the narrow wooden stairs.

As his eyes adjusted to the gloom, Paul could make out a bare concrete floor with neatly stacked piles of wooden planks and some cardboard boxes at the far end. He felt along the wall for a switch, and a single bare bulb flooded the basement with light. He could see more boxes, and piles of clothing spilling out of garbage sacks.

"Hello, I'm here to volunteer," he called. "Where is everybody?"

Over in the corner was what looked like an old boiler and an archway leading to another part of the basement. Ducking under the low ceiling, he stepped in—and nearly fell over a sack of clothes. Except that it wasn't a sack of clothes.

It was a body.

Paul knelt down, and the face of a young man with long blond hair stared sightlessly back up at him, one arm flung out at a strange angle. He did not recognize the man, but Paul instinctively stepped back, bumping his head painfully against the wall, his mouth open in shock. Taking a deep breath, he knelt back down and put a trembling hand to the young man's carotid artery. Nothing. He tried to think what to do next, but his brain wouldn't function. He'd never seen a dead body before. Then a single thought came to him with piercing clarity.

"Shari!"

He stumbled to his feet and looked desperately around the basement. There was a steel table with what looked like a laptop and a tangle of wires, more boxes—and under the table . . .

He ran over. A girl. But not Shari. He felt his throat tighten. The pretty, oval face framed with a mass of auburn hair was familiar. Where had he seen her? On campus? Somewhere in town? What did it matter—*Check for a pulse, you idiot.* It was there, very faint but definitely there. *Okay, remember your CPR.* Breathing first. He put his ear close to her mouth, hoping for a whisper of air.

"Hello, Paul."

He gasped. Chuck Nelson, in a loose-fitting track-suit, was grinning down at him.

"Who's your friend? I thought you had the hots for my little sister. She's going to be real upset when she hears about this." Chuck shook his head. "And in church, too, you dog."

"Chuck, what are you doing here? And where is Shari?"

The grin disappeared. Chuck shrugged. "Who knows? Who cares?"

Paul was torn between making sense of the situation and trying to help the girl. "Look, Shari said to meet her here. Chuck, what's going on?" He put his ear back to the girl's face. "We need help. Have you got a cell phone? We need to call 911."

"Gee, I think I left it at home." Chuck was really enjoying this. "What a shame. Guess it's up to you to wake Sleeping Beauty here. Better hurry. I think she's fading fast."

Paul leaped to his feet and grabbed Chuck by the front of his tracksuit. "Look, this isn't a game. This girl is seriously hurt. Go get help while I try to get her breathing."

Chuck shrugged him off. "She's had all the help she's going to get." He took a step forward, letting something dark slide out of his sleeve and into his palm. "And I'm getting a little tired of your whining."

Paul took a step back, a hand raised defensively in

front of him. At least his brain seemed to be working again. If he could distract Chuck for a second or two, maybe he could make it to the stairs. He half turned, looking for something he could throw in Chuck's face—then there was a flash of movement as something very hard punched him off his feet and his head slammed into the floor.

Then his world went black.

# THIRTY-EIGHT

THE PARKING LOT in front of the church was filling up as Murphy pulled his beat-up Dodge into a spot. He went around to the passenger side to help Laura out, but she waved him away. "Save it, Murph. You don't want to set a bad example for the community."

Standing by the door of the church with a welcoming smile, Reverend Wagoner held his arms out. "Laura, Michael. Good to see you both."

Murphy looked around the almost-full lot. "Likewise, Pastor Bob. Looks like a full house tonight. The free hot dogs seem to be working."

Wagoner laughed. He was dressed in comfortable slacks and a sport jacket over a green polo shirt that showed a hint of a paunch. With his tanned features and thinning white hair, he looked as if he'd just come off the golf course. Which he probably had. "I need something to give me an edge. Actually, I think you two are responsible for the big turnout. Folks are pretty excited about your discovery of this Serpent piece, Murphy."

"As long as you don't want me up at the pulpit, talking about it in front of everybody, Bob. You know I come here for a break from all that. But don't you put me to sleep, okay?"

Laura nudged him in the ribs. "Don't listen to him, Bob. He's just jealous. He knows a really inspirational speaker when he hears one."

"Well, thank you, my dear. Now you're making me nervous."

"Come on, Laura, let's see if we can get a front-row seat. What do the kids call it—the mosh pit?"

Inside, an expectant buzz was already building amid the simple wooden pews. They spotted Shari sitting near the front, looking for someone, and made their way over.

Laura gave her a hug, then noticed her worried look. "What's up?"

"It's Paul. I challenged him to come tonight and said he should come early and help with the sorting for the clothing drive downstairs, but then I got stuck in the library and came right here. His cell phone doesn't seem to be working."

"It looks like we're starting. Let's save a seat for him. If he's like Murphy, he'll probably make a dramatic late entrance, especially if there was work to be done earlier. I'm sure he'll be here any minute."

Shari smiled, but there was still worry in her eyes. "I'll sit with you, but I hope I didn't scare Paul off."

Talon's natural instinct was to slam Chuck's body against the wall to focus his thick-skulled brain on the task at hand. But he had a use for Chuck tonight and not a lot of time. He could not afford to have this slug of a human being curl up and sulk. So he tried a more moderate action. He slapped Chuck's face hard, twice in succession.

"Hey! Ow, what—!"

"Shut up and pay attention. We've dumped your sister's boyfriend here in the church basement, we've spread out all the pamphlets I brought, what's left to do?"

Chuck was breathing hard and rubbing his cheek, paying no attention. Just aching from that head slam, Talon thought. "The backpack, remember? Take it off so I can load it up."

"Okay, okay. It's a little tight over my jacket." Chuck struggled to get the straps of the backpack off but could not get them over his Preston High jacket.

"Then unzip your jacket." Talon rolled his eyes in exasperation.

"I can't. It's stuck. The zipper gets caught a lot."

"How did you ever get out of kindergarten?" Talon grabbed the jacket in both hands and pulled with no success at the zipper. He tried to tear the zipper from its setting. In total exasperation, Talon's right arm flashed up and across the front of Chuck's jacket, cutting it neatly in two halves. He pulled the backpack from Chuck's shoulders.

"Hey, that was the only jacket I have. It's cold tonight."

Talon slashed his sharpened index finger once more, this time across Chuck's throat, nimbly stepping aside to allow the heavy body to fall to the basement floor.

"Not to worry, Chucky. It's warm where you're going."

# THIRTY-NINE

THIS WAS A good night for the Preston Community Church, Reverend Wagoner thought as he stood surveying the faces in the pews. The crowd could be described as hushed and expectant, but what made this such a gratifying event was that almost all of these people could be called a community. He grasped the pulpit firmly and cleared his throat.

"Welcome, friends. It's truly wonderful to see so many of you here this evening. I'd like to give thanks to God for bringing us all together on a day that isn't Sunday. Many of you will have heard about the amazing archaeological find our dear friends Michael and Laura Murphy have brought back from the Holy Land.

"And if you haven't, let me tell you the good news. They've found a piece of Moses' Brazen Serpent. The one King Hezekiah destroyed in Second Kings, Chapter

Eighteen, Verse Four." There were a few gasps. Clearly some people hadn't heard the news. "Now, I'm not going to talk about the archaeological significance of this discovery. I'll leave that to the professionals.

"However, this week, when so much puzzling and disturbing news has been reported at the United Nations and so many shameful things are being said in the media about Christianity, it does make me want to talk a little tonight about some of the significance I think we can still draw from what the Bible tells us about the Brazen Serpent."

Reverend Wagoner paused, and his gaze seemed to fall on each person sitting in the hall.

"You'll recall that the Hebrews who fled out of Egypt in search of the Promised Land didn't have an easy time of it. Sometimes when the going got tough, they began to question, began to doubt God's plan for them. In short, they lost their faith—"

There was a flash, and Murphy had time to wonder why Reverend Wagoner was flying through the air toward them before the thunder of the explosion hit, and then Murphy himself was lifted out of his pew by the blast-wave, his arm instinctively reaching out for Laura as he was flung sideways into the aisle.

After that, everything seemed to happen in slow motion.

The stained-glass windows imploded in a shower of red and gold, and the floor seemed to heave upward, toppling pews and spilling their occupants into the rubble. The chandeliers began swinging violently, the lights flickered once and went out, and then there was just smoke and darkness and the moans of the injured, a faint undertone behind the buzzing in his ears.

Murphy was on his feet and without thinking staggered toward the flames beginning to shoot up from the gaping hole behind the shattered pulpit. For a moment, he felt as if he were looking directly into the depths of hell itself. Then he stopped, and it seemed to take him forever to turn his head back toward the spot where he'd landed. Lungs seared by the acrid smoke pouring into the interior of the church, he felt his way through the debris until he found Laura. He grasped her arm, and he felt her fingers clinging to him and he knew she was alive.

*Out. We have to get out,* he thought, slipping his arms around Laura and hauling her to her feet. Murphy wasn't sure he had the strength to carry her in a fireman's lift, but then he felt her take a step and together they staggered through the haze, over broken pews and huge chunks of plaster, toward the door.

*Air,* he thought. *Air and light.* As they stepped through the doorway, the night air hit them in a wash of blessed relief and they both drew in huge lungfuls. Murphy placed Laura on the ground as gently as he could.

Murphy knelt beside her, blowing bits of wood from around her closed eyes and brushing blackened particles from her cheeks and hair. Laura coughed and opened her eyes, which showed fright and were rimmed by smoky tears.

"I'm okay, Murphy," she said between gasps. "Was it an explosion?"

"It must have been, but I don't think it was the boiler blowing up. Does anything feel broken?"

"My knees are grazed and my elbow hurts a little. . . .
Are you okay?"

"I must look worse than I feel. If you promise to lie
still here and get your breath, I can get back in there and
see if I can help."

"Murph, I'll be fine here, but do you think you
should? We don't know what caused all this. It looks
like there's real damage to the church. You don't know
what could happen still. Please."

"We don't know what happened already, and if anybody's hurt in there I've got to find a way in." He turned
back to the church. Black smoke was billowing out of
the doors. A dozen other people had walked out un-
scathed and were sitting or lying on the grass. That left
how many?

He watched as a petite figure covered in plaster dust
walked unsteadily toward them. Shari.

Murphy went to her, ready to catch her if she fell,
but she shook her head and pushed him away. "Paul,"
she said in a croaky voice. "We have to find Paul."

*She's in shock*, Murphy thought. "It's okay, Shari.
Paul isn't here. He wasn't in the church."

She took his arm in a fierce grip. "His car. It's in the
lot. He must have gotten here early. He's here."

"But where? We would have seen him."

Her eyes went wide. "The basement!"

Murphy gently took her hands and squeezed them
between his. "Okay. Stay here with Laura. Don't worry,
I'll find him."

He pulled out a handkerchief and held it to his nose
and mouth as he stepped back into the inferno. The
smoke was thinning now, and in the dim glow of the

emergency lights he could see people stumbling toward the doors while others tended to the injured. Over the crackle of the flames and the sound of wooden beams splintering like rapid gunshots, he could hear someone moaning.

He saw Wagoner bent over a prostrate figure and clambered over an upturned pew to reach him.

"Bob. Thank God. Are you okay?"

"I think my arm's broken, and my head feels like it's been knocked around a little, but I'm in one piece. I'm not so sure about Jenny," he said, looking down at a middle-aged woman in a tattered white dress streaked with black. Her eyes were closed and she wasn't moving. Murphy put his ear to her mouth while he felt for a pulse.

"I think she's dead."

Wagoner closed his eyes. "Dear God."

Murphy clutched his shoulder. "We need to get help here, Bob."

"I called. They're on their way."

"Good. Can you make it to the door?"

"I'm not going anywhere. There may be other people—"

"The emergency guys will be here any minute. It's not safe. The roof beams could start coming down."

Wagoner got to his feet and started reluctantly for the front of the church. He turned. "What are you doing, Michael?"

Murphy was already heading toward the ruined pulpit. "I'll be right there. Something I've got to do first." And then Wagoner lost him in the smoke.

The explosion had ripped a huge hole in the floor

behind the altar, and through the flames Murphy could see shreds of clothing floating amid a jumble of twisted metal and broken timber. He had no idea how hot it was down there or whether there was any air to breathe, but he could see a spot on the concrete floor that seemed to be clear of debris, so he took a deep breath and jumped.

He landed in a crouch, his hands sinking into a pile of clothing that hadn't yet caught fire, and then he was up, handkerchief to his face, shouting above the roar of collapsing timbers. "Paul! Can you hear me? Paul!"

He thought he heard a noise—something faint but human—coming from the back of the basement, the farthest point from the seat of the blast. Skirting piles of blackened paint tins and upturned filing cabinets, he made his way along the wall until he could see a hand sticking out from under a pile of boxes. He hefted them aside, and there was Paul, curled up with one hand under his chin as if he were asleep. There was no time to examine him properly, to see if any major bones were broken, and he just had to hope there was no damage to his neck or spine. He went down on one knee, got both arms under him, and staggered upright. *Through there,* he thought, turning toward the narrow archway. *Let's just hope there's a way out.*

There was a loud crash behind him, and he felt a rush of heat against the back of his neck. He lurched forward and his knee struck something hard. He almost went down, but he was in the main part of the basement now and he could see the concrete steps. Grimacing with the effort, he shifted his grip to get a better position under Paul's shoulder and put one foot on the bottom step.

"Just one . . ." He put a foot on the next step and pushed upward, straining like a weight lifter. "And . . . uh . . . another," he grunted.

He had his eyes closed and realized he was at the top only when his foot hit the bottom of the door with a clang. Maneuvering around so he could grasp the handle while still keeping hold of Paul, he gave it a firm tug. Nothing. He paused to get a good lungful of air and gave it everything he had. It wouldn't budge. Either it was locked or the explosion had somehow jammed it shut.

He pulled back, mind racing. No point in wasting his last reserves of energy pounding on the door. He'd have to go back the way he'd come and hope the fire hadn't cut them off and they could somehow get through the hole in the floor before the whole structure collapsed on top of them.

He turned to go back down the steps, and suddenly there was a roar of screaming metal, and then a rush of cool air as the door was torn off its hinges and he found he was looking into the face of a young firefighter.

"All right, Mr. Murphy," he said, arms outstretched toward Paul. "Let's get you the heck out of there."

Two paramedics took Paul's weight and carefully laid him down on a stretcher. Murphy's arms suddenly felt as if they were floating upward and all his muscles seemed to relax at once. He sank to his knees, closed his eyes, and was about to give thanks that he'd managed to get Paul out, when the thought struck him like a sudden blow to the temple.

Paul looked like he was dead.

# FORTY

BY THE TIME dawn broke over Preston, the fire trucks and the paramedic vans had gone, leaving only a cluster of police cruisers at the front of the church.

FBI Agent Burton Welsh pulled up the collar of his raincoat against the morning chill and breathed in the sickly smell of wet ashes. The wood-frame structure was still intact, the spire standing proud against the rose-tinted sky, but he guessed it would be a while before the sound of hymns came from the blackened husk.

Because of the unknown nature of the explosion, a bomb was suspected, which led to the FBI's being called in. Hank Baines had been the first agent sent to the scene, making the return trip from Charlotte to Preston. Then, when his preliminary search of the church basement yielded some suspicious material,

Welsh got an emergency summons from his U.N. investigation.

Chief Rawley of the Preston police force was waiting when Welsh arrived. "Your man's down in the basement."

"Body count change in the last hour?"

"Yeah, one more. Don't know who yet, he must have been practically right on top of the blast. Then two more downstairs and two upstairs. Those are the dead. By some miracle, even though there was a pretty good crowd attending church tonight, there were not too many others really badly wounded. Except for the kid they pulled out of the basement, Paul Wallach."

"How's he doing?"

"Last I heard, he still hadn't regained consciousness."

"Well, let's get to it." Welsh followed Rawley down the steps into the basement. They had pumped most of the water out, but the retreating tide had left a scum of sodden ashes under their feet as they made their way to the site of the explosion.

They stopped by the scorched and twisted remains of a steel table that had been blown off its legs. Folding chairs that had fused together in the blast like modernistic sculptures lay around it, along with a scattering of broken power tools.

Welsh leaned closer until his face was just inches from the tabletop. The scorch marks etched deeply into its surface were unmistakable. Baines was studying the marks as well. "Baines. Good work on your phone report."

"Agent Welsh. It's good to see you again, sir.

Quantico seems like a lot of cases ago. What do you think? Was I right?"

The chief wrinkled his brow. "Right about what? Explosive?"

Welsh snorted. "Chief, you don't get these from a gas leak."

Rawley was keen to show he was no hick. "You mean C-four?"

"Ten. Makes these green striations." Welsh started to examine the floor around the table. "Let's see what else we've got here."

He bent down by a paper supermarket bag in the corner and pulled a wire that was hanging over its top. "My, my." He sifted through spools of telephone wire, then held up a pair of detonators. He mimicked pushing the spiked probes into a block of plastic explosive.

Rawley stood with his mouth open as Welsh rummaged some more and came up with a charred circuit board and the half-melted cases of two high-tech cell phones.

He took a plastic evidence bag out of his jacket pocket and slipped the remains of the phones inside. "Baines, get the lab working on these right away. I'm not a technician, but either folks around here leave some very strange items in the pockets of their old suits or this is no ordinary clothing drive."

Rawley looked sickened. "I know what I'm looking at, but I'm telling you, it just can't be."

"Chief, so far every sign I'm seeing down here is pointing one way. Somebody was using the church as a bomb factory. At least for tonight."

"Welsh, that's impossible. These people are my neighbors. They're no more bombers than I am."

Agent Welsh eyed the chief as if to say that was a less than convincing argument. "This was not some penny-ante operation either. They weren't making cherry bombs."

"So, what, you think this C-ten stuff went off accidentally?"

"Sure. Terrorists are always blowing themselves up. Comes with the territory."

"*Terrorists.* I can't believe I'm even saying the word. Not in this place."

"Rawley, terrorists can be anywhere these days. From just a quick look down here, you got yourself a flea market of stuff that can go boom. With a few different kinds of ways to blow people up, it doesn't look like a terrorist bombed this place. Or maybe I should say that some of the neighbors you're swearing by were playing the terrorist home game and blew up the basement by mistake. Happens often enough, especially when you have rank amateurs messing with this stuff."

Agent Welsh picked up a charred flyer from the floor and read out loud. " 'Will you be left behind?!?!' "

"For what it's worth, the reverend of the church says he never saw that flyer before, nor any of these others." Baines pointed to some bundles of now-drenched flyers and brochures on the floor.

"Yeah? I was beginning to think I was the only man in America not on the subscription list for this religious hooey. But it looks like the reverend needed to check down in his basement a little more frequently. Were the dead and wounded all locals?"

"As far as I know. Except for the kid, Paul Wallach. He was from the university, but I don't know where he comes from."

"Chief, does a small-town college like this get a lot of weirdos, freaks, and troublemakers hanging around campus? I mean, you don't know this kid Wallach, I bet. What's to say he's not some out-of-towner down here to shake things up?"

"Well, all I know about him is he's a friend of Shari Nelson, a coed who works for Michael Murphy. She's a great kid, and I couldn't imagine her getting caught up with anything fringe."

"Fringe. That's a quaint term. She a good member of this good church?"

"Yeah. Welsh, you can't be serious that somebody like Shari Nelson or any of these people could actually have been making bombs down here."

"Chief, until we can trace every step of every bit of this stuff and solve this bombing, the only person who's not a suspect is me—and that's only because this is the first church I've set foot in since I was fifteen."

# FORTY-ONE

TALON PREFERRED BEING close in, looking at his victims face-to-face. It was neater, riskier, and always more memorable to look at their fear just before he slashed them. Of course, he also derived extreme pleasure from the deadly precision of the falcons he had trained for so many years.

Explosions were so messy, even with these new thin, ultra-high-powered bombs.

But tonight's was effective. He admired the scene from the shadows of the parking lot. There was enough explosive force in that backpack to bring down half the building, and it had been packed into a plastic sheet that looked like a laminated pocket protector. There were also other explosive materials packed in the bags he and Chuck had planted around the basement, but it would not take the FBI long to determine that those were just window dressing.

It did satisfy him to be perpetrating an act of major mayhem, with a real body count, as opposed to all his work up in New York.

Too bad the oaf Chuck could not have lived to see the results of their setup. Once he had killed Chuck in the basement, he had packed the C-10 explosive sheet into the backpack, since he hadn't wanted Chuck walking around with it, then put the wired backpack back on Chuck and left him in the basement. Talon had checked to make sure that Chuck had left Paul Wallach far from the explosion so that he would survive.

Chaos and fear, those would be the legacies of tonight. Terror coming to a small town, not a big city, and to a church, no less. Making it look like the accidental explosion of a basement bomb factory run by evangelical Christian extremists would not hold up for long under the scrutiny of the FBI. Just like the vapor-thin trail he had left behind with his New York stunt to make it look like extremists were plotting to blow up the U.N.

There would be days of hysterical news reports following the connections of the church members, of Murphy, and of Shari once they found enough of her brother to make an identification, and her connection to her transfer-student friend, Wallach, who would be cast as an out-of-town troublemaker. And that mystery man who had been seen with Chuck. By the time the FBI saw that the bomb factory "evidence" was just window dressing, the media would have moved. In its wake would be a time of noise and confusion, and people would recall mainly a bunch of crazy evangelicals to be afraid of. Not a bad night's work.

Then it hit Talon. Hard. Chuck, that miserable loser, had managed to screw up things even after he was dead! His stupid jacket that he got stuck in, so Talon had to cut him out of it. It had fallen to the floor, and with all he had had to do by himself to finish off the ground-zero site in the church basement, he had forgotten to grab it. And in the pocket were the car keys, which also had Talon's prints, plus he had seen Chuck stuff the last shopping list in his jacket pocket. The chances of the jacket surviving the blast, and of the FBI tracing him from what was left in the pockets, were minute.

But that was enough to make Talon uneasy. He would have to go back, which shouldn't be too hard with all the rescue teams going in and out.

Talon slipped into the church through what had once been the basement door.

As he did so, Laura Murphy circled the side of the building on her way to the Dodge, in which she always had a trunk full of drinks, a first-aid kit, blankets, and other supplies in case she and Murphy decided on a whim to go off exploring. She got a good look at the figure entering the basement, and he did not look like one of the rescue workers, and he certainly was not a church member. Nor did he look like anyone she knew from Preston, but she was positive that she did recognize him as a face that had been hanging around.

The creep who had been hanging around with Shari's brother.

Laura forgot about going for the supplies and decided to follow Chuck's companion and see why he would be going into the bomb site.

*Could it be?* She was horrified at the thought that struck her. Could this stranger and poor, angry, lost Chuck have been involved in this bombing?

She walked down the basement steps, wincing as her wounded knees felt the impact. There was a sound in the darkness ahead, and she limped toward it. The pain in her legs was going to stick with her for a while, it seemed.

But she instantly forgot that pain, because an intense, far greater pain rippled through her as a pair of incredibly strong hands grabbed her arm and throat in the darkness.

"Hello, Mrs. Murphy. It must be bingo night at church, because I've just got the big prize." The voice was hoarse. "I can't do anything to that husband of yours while he's still useful to us. But nobody said anything about needing you. And without you, maybe your husband will have more time to work a little quicker."

Laura did not know what this madman was talking about, but she could not speak, so powerful was the pressure of his hand on her throat. It began crushing her windpipe.

Talon kept pressing, deciding not to use his razor again. The result would be the same.

Laura Murphy looked into the face of Talon, refusing to give him the satisfaction of averting her eyes even though she was shocked by what pure evil could look like.

She started to pray in her silence and she showed him no fear.

# FORTY-TWO

CHIEF RAWLEY USHERED them into the interview room and indicated three chairs on one side of the steel table bolted to the bare floor.

"I'm sorry we couldn't use my office. I don't think I could have fit you all in comfortably. Not with all this..." He indicated the two large cardboard boxes in the center of the table without looking at them. On the other side of the table, Baines stood up and offered his hand with a neutral expression.

"Reverend Wagoner. Professor Murphy." He shook hands solemnly with each of them before sitting down again, and his gaze returned to the boxes.

Rawley seated them like an attentive maître d'. "How's the arm, Bob? You know, folks are saying it's a miracle you're alive."

Wagoner winced as he eased into the chair and

adjusted the cast on his arm. "I can't feel a whole lot, to be honest, Ed. And that goes for my head too." He tapped the bandage around his forehead. "Alma says it just goes to show that the Lord knew what He was doing when He made it out of solid maple."

"And how about you, Murphy?"

"Oh, I'm fine, Ed. Just a few cuts and bruises. I guess I've got some maple in me too."

With a tight smile Rawley went and stood awkwardly to one side of Welsh. He seemed reluctant to occupy the empty chair next to him, as if he wanted to distance himself from what was about to happen.

"We were the lucky ones," said Wagoner. "Four dear friends died, plus one body has yet to be identified in the basement. That poor Wallach boy in a coma . . ." His voice trailed off. "But we're going to start rebuilding just as soon as we can. And then we'll be back in that lovely church, praising the Lord again."

"Don't go do any rebuilding yet, Reverend," Welsh said coldly. "Right now your church is still a crime scene."

"A crime scene? I don't understand."

"That explosion wasn't an accident. That old boiler in the basement is one of the few things that wasn't damaged in the blast."

"Then, what did cause it?"

Welsh looked at him steadily. "I was kind of hoping you could tell me that."

Murphy was on his feet, leaning over the table. "Just what are you suggesting? Bob was nearly killed in there."

Welsh didn't blink. He waited until Murphy sat down again, then lifted the flap of one of the boxes.

"The explosion was caused by a bomb. Plastic explosive. And we found detonators and other equipment for making more bombs. The basement of your church was being used as a bomb factory, Reverend. Your parishioners were making bombs."

He let that sink in, watching as Wagoner went pale.

"That's absurd," Murphy said. "Why would members of this church be making bombs?"

Welsh scratched his chin as if he were asking himself that question for the first time. "How about to blow up the U.N.?"

"The U.N.? What are you talking about?"

"This kid, Paul Wallach, they pulled out of the basement, he wasn't from around here, was he? I know he's a student, supposedly, but my information is that he only recently started attending, is that correct?"

"What are you suggesting? That Paul Wallach was somehow responsible for this explosion? That's crazy. He's just a kid."

Welsh smiled sourly. "In my experience, kids do the funniest things. Especially when they come under the influence of fanatics." He said the last word as if he were spitting out something unpleasant.

Murphy jumped up. "Fanatics? What are you, the Joe McCarthy of G-men, Welsh? Conspiracies everywhere. Fanatics like who?"

"Like the sort of people who believe the U.N. is evil. Evangelical Christians, for instance."

"We don't believe the U.N. is evil," Wagoner interjected. "We believe it does some good work. Peacekeeping in certain third world countries where there is chaos, humanitarian aid, health programs, and so on.

But we are suspicious about their efforts to promote globalism by uniting all religions regardless of their beliefs, and by uniting the world's governments under a single entity. In particular, I'm very concerned about turning the sovereignty of the United States government over to a world court."

"Are you saying you oppose striving for world peace through global unity?"

"Every single attempt to secure a one-world religion or a one-world government in the past has resulted in a totalitarian regime, inevitably causing the deaths of countless numbers of innocent citizens. We must learn from history. Man is incapable of bringing peace to this planet on his own. This world will never enjoy world peace until Christ Himself comes to set up His kingdom. His kingdom will last for a thousand years, and the Bible is very clear regarding this prophecy."

"Then maybe some of your people thought a few bombs might hurry it along."

Wagoner was stunned. "*Our* people? Evangelical Christians don't set off bombs, Agent Welsh."

Welsh jabbed a finger at him. "How about the people who bomb family-planning clinics? Who kill doctors who perform abortions? They're Christians, aren't they?"

"Not in my book," Wagoner said fiercely. "Yes, it's a terrible thing to take the lives of the unborn, but more murder is definitely not the answer. The Christian community universally opposes killing, even to save the unborn from being killed."

Agent Baines had been quiet while Agent Welsh had carried on with his arguments, but he could contain himself no longer. "Sir, I know I'm out of line, but I have to speak up. I certainly don't pretend to know the facts of this bombing, and there is certainly circumstantial evidence that makes it look pretty bad that something crazy was going on in that basement. Except I know these people. Not these people specifically, I don't mean that, I mean I know churchgoing folks in a community like this, because that's who I am. I know their hearts, and they could never be terrorists, bombers, or murderers for any cause, no matter how righteous.

"Look, something terrible has happened here in Preston. People have died, more are in the hospital. And everyone wants to know why. *We* want to know why. Professor Murphy risked his life to save someone. Is that the action of a wanton murderer? Reverend Wagoner was lucky not to be killed himself. These are not the people we should be hunting down. I know that's gut talking, not forensics, sir, but sometimes we have to listen to bigger evidence than what our eyes tell us, don't we?"

Welsh just gave a sour, angry stare to Baines, and never got a chance to answer him, because Laura Murphy stumbled through the doorway looking wild-eyed and in pain.

She stared straight ahead for a moment, as if trying to think of the right word, then Murphy watched in horror as her eyes rolled back in her head and her whole body went limp like a puppet whose strings had suddenly been cut. She put a hand out to steady herself, and the chair crashed to the floor as Murphy caught her in his arms.

"Get an ambulance," he screamed at Baines. "Now!"

# FORTY-THREE

FOR THE SECOND time in a matter of weeks, Stephanie Kovacs thought, the gods of media good fortune were smiling down on her. She had decided to spend the evening in the hotel poring over more of her research before snooping around Preston the next day to get more background about Professor Michael Murphy.

She heard the church bomb ignite from her hotel room and was already beeping her cameraman when the BNN national bureau chief called her. Within an hour of the blast she had gone live with her first report. Even as more reporters swarmed over the site, she stayed ahead of the pack with a combination of her own drive and some additional tips being fed her by the New York and Atlanta bureaus. Now, the day after, she was ready for her next exclusive.

"Stephanie Kovacs, BNN, live from the horrific

bombing of the Preston Community Church in Preston, North Carolina. Even while the search for victims and assessment of the damage continues desperately, there are ugly realities beginning to come to light at the scene.

"Most shocking of all is the report that we are talking not about a terrorist attack upon the innocent churchgoers, but rather a far greater nightmare for the citizens of our country. There is now evidence that, contrary to earlier reports that suggested the church was the *target* of a terrorist bomb, the truth could be something even more deadly and cowardly.

"Sources have revealed to BNN that the cause of the explosion was in fact a bomb *factory* in the basement—a bomb factory that went tragically, horribly wrong for four members of this tightly knit congregation. And these same sources have further suggested that evidence found in the debris here at Preston points to a connection with another recent terrorist attack."

She paused dramatically, as if she needed to compose herself before making her biggest revelation. "Though authorities are making no public statements yet, we are told that there are indications that members of this church terror group were connected to Farley the Fanatic, yes, the suspect who is still at large and wanted for questioning for his role in the recent attack on a United Nations building in New York.

"We're told that there were disturbingly similar materials found at the two investigative scenes, the basement of the Preston Community Church, just a few feet from where I'm standing right now, and the house of Farley the Fanatic, where, you may recall, I was standing reporting to you just a few days ago. I am told these materials include religious publications and pamphlets of the evangelical variety and evidence that the bombing of the U.N. was a very chilling possibility. And still could be, perhaps by surviving members of the terror cell whose plot went so horribly wrong here tonight in this church."

Reluctantly, she broke eye contact with her viewers for a moment and turned to a tall, balding man in a black polo shirt and brown sport jacket.

"I have with me Dr. Archer Fallworth, dean of the School of Arts and Science at Preston University, many of whose students and faculty worship at this church." She smiled sincerely, regretfully. "Thank you so much for taking a few minutes to be with us at this tragic time, Dean Fallworth."

Fallworth looked as if he just managed to stop himself from saying *My pleasure*. He nodded, pursing his lips.

"Dean, I think we're all in a state of shock about these revelations. I mean, members of a church congregation making bombs? And possibly connected to those plotting to commit terrorist attacks in our major cities? Can you throw any kind of light on what's been going on? Can you make any sense of this for us?"

Dean Fallworth looked up with a serious expression. "I'm not sure I *can* explain what appears to have happened here in Preston, Stephanie. I don't know if anyone can. When fanatics maim and kill innocent people, I think we all ... I ..." He shook his head, apparently overcome with emotion.

Stephanie decided to help him out. "When you say

fanatics, Dean Fallworth, what exactly do you mean? Who are these people? What's their agenda?"

Fallworth cleared his throat. "Well, I've been at this university a good number of years, and I have to say I've witnessed some disturbing changes in recent times."

Stephanie's brow was furrowed with concern. "What kind of changes?"

"We've always had a strong evangelical presence here. Nothing wrong with that, of course. But I believe more extreme elements—fundamentalist evangelicals, if you will—are gradually taking control. And I believe these elements may be behind the terrible tragedy we witnessed here yesterday."

"You're obviously well acquainted with this group. What exactly do they believe? And if what we're being told is true—and I'm sure like a lot of our viewers I'm finding it hard to take all this on board—why are they targeting institutions such as the U.N.?"

"Stephanie, I think the most important thing to say is that whatever they believe—whether it's that the end of the world is approaching or the Second Coming or whatever—they just don't accept that you or I might take a different view, that we might have different beliefs—even different *Christian* beliefs."

"So what are they trying to do—bomb us into belief?"

Fallworth gave her a patronizing half smile that would have been familiar to his students. "I think that's very well put, Stephanie. Yes, that's exactly it."

*And I've just written tomorrow's headline,* Stephanie thought.

"Stephanie, the welfare of our students is my topmost priority, and we have to be aware of anybody who may be trying to influence them in a negative or dangerous way."

"Would you say Paul Wallach, who is now in a coma, was influenced in the way you describe?"

He hung his head. "Tragically, I believe so."

"And do you know who is responsible for turning such a promising student into what could be a fanatical killer?"

He flinched a little. Maybe she was laying it on a bit thick. But he couldn't turn back now. *Come on,* she thought, *you know what you have to do. And you really want to do it too.*

"It hurts me deeply to have to say this, but I believe one of our own faculty is the leading voice behind this pernicious movement." He winced to show just how deeply it hurt him.

Stephanie moved the microphone closer, almost as if it were a cattle prod.

"Professor Michael Murphy."

She affected horrified surprise. "And what subject does Professor Murphy teach?"

"Biblical archaeology," he said, making it sound like a disease. "At least that's what he was doing until today." He turned and looked directly into the camera. "In the interest of the students, I will be recommending to the university board that we suspend Professor Murphy until we conduct a proper internal inquiry."

# FORTY-FOUR

MURPHY CROUCHED ON the floor of the ambulance and held Laura's hand while one of the paramedics got an IV into her arm and the other wrapped thermal blankets around her. "She just collapsed?"

The last few hours were a blur. Murphy could hardly think. "Yes. She was in the church when the bomb went off. We both were. But they said she was okay. Just bruises, nothing serious."

As the ambulance sped down Route 147, the paramedic briefed the waiting trauma team. By the time he'd finished, they'd already turned off the highway and onto the main campus roadway leading to the hospital, sirens blaring. Murphy pressed a cold hand to her cheek. "Hang in there, sweetheart."

They stopped with a jolt and the paramedics pulled the gurney out onto the tarmac and started barreling toward the trauma center like a bobsled team trying to gain momentum. The automatic doors slid open and closed like a greedy mouth, and they were in the receiving area, where the waiting trauma team instantly surrounded the gurney, brushed-steel equipment carts at the ready.

More IV needles went in. A vital-signs monitor was hooked up. A nurse started calling out pulse rate and blood pressure. All while the gurney accelerated toward a set of doors marked TRAUMA STAFF ONLY.

Murphy was sucked along in its wake, trying to keep Laura's face in sight as the trauma team worked furiously around her. Then the gurney was bumping through the doors and a hand gently held him back from following.

"I'm sorry. You'll have to wait out here. We'll update you on your wife's condition as soon as we have more information." He mumbled a thank-you and the nurse disappeared after the gurney. He could hear the urgent back-and-forth of the trauma team for a moment, then the doors thumped shut and he was alone.

"Professor Murphy, what's going on? What are you doing here?" Shari's eyes were red-rimmed from crying.

"It's Laura. She just collapsed. They don't know what's wrong with her. I . . ." His voice trailed off.

She slumped in a seat and put her hand to her mouth. "Oh, no. Oh, no. Not Laura too."

Murphy pulled his seat closer and put his arm around her shoulders. He looked toward the double doors. "Paul's through there, too, isn't he?"

She nodded, sobbing quietly. They stayed like that, Shari's head on his shoulder, not knowing what else to do except silently pray. The minutes passed and then Murphy lost all sense of time and he was arguing with Laura about something and then she started laughing and his heart leaped because she was all right and then he realized he must be dreaming and woke up with a start.

Dr. Keller was standing at his elbow. He nodded to Shari. "There's no change in Paul's condition. But we weren't expecting anything just yet." He turned to Murphy. "Laura's stable, but I'm afraid we still don't know why she collapsed. The signs look like someone of enormous strength tried to crush her windpipe.

"We're doing everything possible. And we will continue to do so. But at the moment I have to tell you she's losing ground."

Shari gasped and Murphy instinctively tightened his arm around her shoulders even though he was the one desperately in need of comfort. Then he stood and held a firm hand out to Keller. "Thank you, Doctor. I know you're doing all you can. And we'll do everything we can."

Keller shook his hand and nodded solemnly before walking back through the trauma center doors. Unusually for him, he'd run out of words.

Murphy saw the fatigue drawing dark circles under Shari's eyes. "Come on, I'm sure we could both use some water or a cup of coffee. We've got a lot of praying to do."

# FORTY-FIVE

SEVERAL HOURS LATER, Murphy went to Laura's bed to give her hand a squeeze. Despite the respirator and the IVs and the machines that surrounded her, he thought she looked like a princess from a fairy tale. Her skin was almost porcelain white, her lips impossibly pale. The pill that was making her sleep was a powerful one, but her eyelids fluttered as he watched, showing she was still there, struggling to get out of her prison.

He thought he heard something above the hiss of the respirator—a whimper of protest, as if she were saying, *Please, someone, get me out of here,* but he wasn't sure he could trust his senses anymore.

He bent over and kissed her gently on the forehead. "Hey, baby, I'm here. Don't worry. Everything's going to be okay."

He looked down and was surprised to see he was

clutching something in his hand. Dr. Keller must have given it to him. It was a small Ziploc bag with Laura's personal effects. A thin gold wedding band, wristwatch, pearl earrings, keys. And the little wooden cross on its cord.

He imagined walking out of the hospital still holding the bag, and tears suddenly blurred his vision. "Don't leave me, sweetheart. Please don't leave me." He heard the door open and felt a flash of self-consciousness and then thought, *Don't be so dumb—she's seen it all before.*

But it wasn't the nurse.

Standing by the door, looking past him at Laura with an expression of infinite sadness, was a red-haired woman in a long black coat that looked too big for her. "Mr. Murphy?" she said in a trembling voice. Her accent was lilting and familiar, but for the moment Murphy couldn't place it. "I'm Isis McDonald." She locked eyes briefly with Murphy, then her gaze went back to Laura. "I'm so, so sorry."

He looked perplexed, as if she were a character from a dream and he couldn't understand what she was doing standing there, apparently solid, talking to him like a real person.

"You must forgive me," she said. "I shouldn't have just come like this. I didn't want to intrude on your ... I didn't want to interfere. We don't even know each other. It's just that I ..."

Murphy breathed out and tried to relax his shoulders. He indicated the chair. "I'm sorry. Please, sit down. You've come a long way."

She sat down, clutching a battered-looking briefcase

tightly in her lap. She didn't seem to know what to say or do next.

The awkward silence was broken when the nurse returned with a container of coffee. She took in Isis, nodded hello, and handed the cup to Murphy with a sympathetic smile.

"I don't really want this," he said as the door closed behind her. "Would you like it? No cream or sugar, I'm afraid."

She took the cup, grateful for the distraction. "Thank you. That's fine."

They were silent for what seemed a long time, just looking at Laura and listening to the soft hiss of the respirator.

"Look, it's good of you to be concerned," he said. "But it's not as if you knew Laura. I don't mean to be rude, but what are you doing here?"

Isis put the coffee on the window ledge and settled her hands on top of the briefcase.

"I brought you something." She undid the clasp and pulled a padded manila envelope out of the briefcase. Reaching inside, she tipped the envelope up and something fell out.

The tail of the Serpent lay on the top of the briefcase, gleaming dully.

"I don't understand."

She picked it up and held it out toward him. "I thought you might want it. I thought it might help."

"Help? How is that going to help?"

She couldn't look at him. "Isn't it supposed to . . . Don't you believe it has healing powers?"

Suddenly he understood why she'd come. "No! Absolutely not. It's just a piece of bronze."

She seemed bewildered. "Just a piece of bronze? But you risked your life to get it. I thought it was supposed to have healed the Israelites when they were bitten by poisonous snakes. I thought that's what you believed."

"That is not what I believe. It was God who healed them because of their faith. The power was in their faith, not in the Serpent. When they started worshiping it as if it had magic powers, that's when God told Hezekiah to destroy it."

She still held it out, willing him to take it. "But how do you know? How do you know that it doesn't have any power? How do you know it won't help Laura?"

Murphy cleared his throat. "Because I know that's not how God works. There are no magic tricks."

"What about faith healers? That seems like a magic trick to me."

"No. We don't know why God sometimes heals people. Just like we don't know why . . . why sometimes He lets them get sick." He couldn't help glancing at Laura. "Even good people. Even the best. The very best."

She was standing now, and Murphy thought she was going to press the thing into his hands, like a person desperate to make a sale. "But why not try? Maybe it won't work, but it couldn't do any harm, could it? Isn't it worth trying?"

He put his hands on her thin arms and looked at her, imploring her to understand. "It would be wrong. It would be like saying to God, 'I have more faith in this piece of metal than I do in You.' It would be sinful."

"What does it matter? So what if you commit a sin if it saves Laura's life? You're just being selfish, worrying about the cleanliness of your soul when she could be dead." She flushed again and put a hand to her mouth. "I'm sorry. I shouldn't have said that."

He didn't say anything. Just took the tail of the Serpent and put it back in the envelope and then into the briefcase. He snapped it closed and held it out to her. "Take this back to the museum. Lock it up in the vaults. Then, if you want to say a prayer for Laura..."

She took the briefcase, not looking at him. "Yes. Yes, all right. I'm sorry." He thought she looked like a little girl who'd been caught doing something naughty. "Look, there's something else. I've finished translating the inscription. I know this isn't the right time, but I brought it with me. It's...rather extraordinary. I thought I ought to give it to you as soon as possible."

He looked at her blankly. "I'll call you. When this is...when this is over." She nodded and walked out, gripping the briefcase tightly to her chest.

He took Laura's hand and laid his cheek against it. "I wish you could talk to me, sweetheart. You always know what to do."

Exhaustion finally claimed Murphy, and he slipped into a troubled rest. When he awoke twenty minutes later, it was to the sound of an urgent alarm buzzer from the respirator.

Something in the room had changed. He looked up, confused for a moment, and then he understood what it was. The regular beep-beep-beep of the vital-signs monitor had turned into a single urgent note of alarm. He leaped out of the chair and was halfway to the door when it burst open and Dr. Keller ran in, followed by another doctor and a nurse pushing a trolley.

He watched as they bent over her. The nurse was holding the electric pads in her hands, waiting for Dr. Keller's okay, and then strong hands took hold of him and he closed his eyes.

# FORTY-SIX

THE CRIME SCENE investigators had finally left, the last piece of police tape had been removed, and Preston Community Church was once again what it had always been, a place of worship.

Restoring the physical damage, however, would take longer. Though the structure had been secured with steel props under the weakened floor, a section of scaffolding supporting the east wall, and plastic sheeting covering most of the shattered windows, the charred and smoke-blackened door frame was a reminder that days earlier the interior of the church had been like a vision of hell. Only the steeple, a finger of pristine whiteness pointing to heaven, remained untouched by the blast, and as the church members started to file inside, it was hard not to see it as a symbol of hope and endurance.

Wagoner stood at the entrance, as he had done on the

night of the blast, welcoming the faithful. With one arm still in a sling, he couldn't administer the bear hugs he felt were sometimes needed, but his handshake was as firm and strong as ever. One by one the parishioners filed inside, settling into the dozen or so pews that had remained undamaged and turning their eyes toward the makeshift podium standing in place of the shattered pulpit.

Murphy sat in the front row, Shari at his side, her hand clasped in his. From the east window, now empty of stained glass, a shaft of sunlight angled down, catching the edge of the casket positioned crossways at the foot of the altar, and making the floral arrangements around it blaze with color. Sitting to Murphy's right, Laura's father stared straight ahead, focusing on some distant place that only he could see. His wife clutched his arm, sobbing quietly.

Looking at Laura's face as she lay in the open casket, it was hard to believe she was dead. Her ivory dress seemed luminescent, lending her pale features a vibrant glow that almost matched the flowers framing the coffin and the daisies threaded through her hair. Through the empty window, Murphy could hear birds singing and wondered if they, too, had been fooled by Laura's lifelike appearance. *Someone should tell them,* he thought. *I ought to speak to Pastor Bob.* He started to get up, and felt Shari's hand anchoring him. He settled into the pew again. Perhaps it would be okay to let the birds continue singing for now. They would surely stop when they saw her being put into the ground.

Wagoner slowly climbed the steps to the podium,

keeping his eyes on Laura all the way, then looked out over the congregation.

"This is a very difficult time for all of us," he began. "Sometimes it seems like a lifetime ago, sometimes, I know, it seems like just a few moments, that we were last gathered here. Some of us lost loved ones or family members, all of us lost friends. And all of us bear the scars from that terrible day—and I don't mean the physical scars. I mean the pain of loss that will remain with us forever."

He coughed into his hand, and for a moment it seemed as if the church were full of smoke again. Then he continued, his voice strong, and the air was clear. "If you're like me, some parts of that night will be a little hazy for a while," he said with a wry smile. "But I do remember what I was planning to talk about. I was going to talk about having faith in God's plan for us. About keeping faith even when it might seem as if He's forgotten us." He paused. "And I guess right now might seem like such a time. How could such a terrible thing have happened? And now, adding insult to injury, the very people who have suffered the most in this tragedy are being accused of terrible crimes. On the TV and in the newspapers we are being talked of as murderers and terrorists. How can this be?"

He shifted his arm a little in its sling before continuing. "The truth is, I don't know. God hasn't revealed to me what exactly He has in mind for all of us. But I do know He *has* a plan for us. And I know He's watching to see how we cope with these trials and tribulations." He gripped the edge of the podium with his good hand. "And what does God see when He looks down on us?

Well, I'll tell you what I see. I see people beginning to re-build what's been destroyed. I see people returning to a place that was desecrated by a terrible act of violence and making it holy again with their worship. I see peo-ple keeping the faith. Because ultimately God's plan *will* be revealed to us. It's going to take a lot of hard work—it's going to take all the skills and energy and applica-tion we have to restore this church to what it was. And it's going to take every ounce of our faith in God to get us through the turmoil that now surrounds it. But to-gether, with God's help, we will do it."

He took a deep breath and wiped his brow with a handkerchief. He hoped he'd managed to raise the con-gregation's spirits just a little. They would need all their strength for what was to follow.

All eyes were now on Laura's coffin. The light had moved on, and her face was now in shadow. The flowers had faded to a muted glow.

Wagoner cleared his throat and began. "You don't need me to tell you that Laura Murphy was a beautiful person, inside and out. Anyone who saw her smile, heard her laugh, the way she would make others laugh"—he smiled—"sometimes with a joke at their own expense—and I speak from experience here—will know what a joyful and joy-giving woman she was. She was also a very talented archaeologist who could have had a glittering career—but she chose instead to devote herself to helping others, helping students to achieve the very best that they could. There are a lot of people in this town who owe her a debt of gratitude for setting them on the right path or helping them off the wrong one, and I'm sure there are a few of them here today. If any of you are wondering how such a wonderful person could be struck down when she still had so much to give, I want you to try to think about everything that Laura *has* given us. How many people give so much during their whole lives?"

He heard a few sobs and sniffles from around the church and gave people a moment to collect themselves. Or was it to collect himself? How many times had he done this—dispensing comforting words to the bereaved? And how many times had he secretly needed someone to give him comfort too? But this was the task God had given him, and thankfully He had provided the strength to carry it out.

"Laura loved life and she loved God—and she loved her husband, Michael." He looked down at Murphy, whose eyes were fixed on Laura with a strange half-smile, and he wondered if he really understood that she was gone. "Only those who have lost a loved one know what Michael is feeling today. Our hearts truly go out to him. We pray that God will give him the strength to bear the terrible pain he's feeling."

He drew himself up as straight as he could on the podium. An old leather-bound Bible was open in front of him, but he didn't need to look at it. "Early on in Christianity, when believers died, the living were a bit confused about what would happen to them when Christ returned for them in the rapture. The apostle Paul wrote in First Thessalonians 4:14 to 18 that when Jesus comes from heaven He will descend...with a shout...and the dead in Christ will rise first. Then we who are alive *and* remain shall be caught up in the clouds, to meet the Lord in the air. And we shall always be with the Lord.

"The Bible says that we should comfort one another with these words. And what greater comfort could there be? Laura is now with Jesus. She isn't sad or in pain, as we are. Her body may be broken, but her soul, her perfect soul, is in heaven. And it is God's promise to us that if we believe in His Son's death on the cross for our sins, and that God raised Him from the dead, we shall see her and all fellow believers and 'ever be with the Lord.' No wonder the apostle could say to us in our sorrow, 'Therefore, comfort one another with these words,' for you will see Laura again."

The last words were spoken slowly, and he looked directly at Murphy as he said them.

Then Wagoner picked up his hymnbook. Murphy rose to his feet and soon the sweet sound of voices joined in sorrow and thankfulness rose up from the battered pews.

Murphy walked over to the casket for one final look at Laura. As he looked down, it took him a moment to notice it, and he thought the tears in his eyes were distorting his vision. But as he reached over with his hand, his fingers confirmed the shocking sight. Someone had snuck in and taken the wooden cross Murphy had laid around Laura's neck and partially snapped it so that its three pieces now dangled from the necklace.

# FORTY-SEVEN

MURPHY HEARD THE last shovelful of earth being laid on the top of the grave and finally understood that Laura was gone. The body in the coffin, although it was still beautiful, was not her. She was somewhere else, somewhere he had thought about a good deal over the years but now couldn't quite imagine. He knew she would never grow old there; she would always be as he had seen her last. Perfect.

Laura's parents were clinging to each other by the grave, and he tried to think of something he could do for them, but when he reached inside himself, there was just a huge emptiness and he knew that if he tried to comfort them, the right words wouldn't come.

Shari walked over. "I'm going to take Kurt and Susan back to the hotel. She needs to rest and I can stay there for a while if they want me to." He nodded, grateful for the openheartedness that allowed her to read his mind.

Wagoner was standing by the church door, shaking hands with the departing mourners and offering final words of consolation from his seemingly inexhaustible store. Murphy realized there was nothing more for him to do there.

He got in the car and sat for a moment, then started the engine and drove slowly out of the parking lot. He couldn't go home. Not yet. Her presence there would be too strong, and just seeing a hairbrush or a coffee cup lying where she had left it would paralyze him with grief. He drove aimlessly for a while until he found he was on a road leading to the university. That was no good either. He made a right turn, wishing he could find a place that held no memories, a place Laura had never known and that wouldn't cry out her name as he got near. He decided to keep driving until he was on an unfamiliar road and then he'd keep going until . . . until what? He didn't know. Until something changed, perhaps. He passed a gas station and a row of body shops, and when he saw a sign that said fifty miles to somewhere, he made the turn and put his foot down. The wheel seemed to grow lighter in his hands and the world began to stream behind him. He lost all sense of time.

He heard a horn blaring and wrenched the wheel to the right, narrowly missing a truck coming the other way. He pulled over sharply and rested his head on the wheel, waiting for the hammering in his chest to still.

It was no good. There was no point trying to escape.

He knew where he had to go. He eased into the traffic and headed back the way he'd come.

Half an hour later he came to a halt in front of the church and got out of the car. He was glad to see the parking lot was empty except for Wagoner's old pickup.

He walked back to the grave and stood over it, looking at the pale headstone with its simple inscription. *One day I'll be bringing flowers here and it'll be worn smooth,* he thought. *Moss will be growing in the cracks.*

He looked up and Bob Wagoner was standing on the other side of the grave, hands clasped in front of him. "I thought you'd come back," he said.

Murphy felt something stir inside him and realized that this was what he had come for. "I keep thinking about what you said, about God's plan, and I . . . I just can't accept it. How could He have done this? How could He have let it happen? If I'd been killed in Samaria, or in the fire . . . but Laura. She was such a woman of faith. She didn't have a bad thought in her head. She was . . . like an angel."

Wagoner came and put an arm around his shoulder. "God understands your grief, Michael. He's not offended by your questioning either. Remember, His own Son questioned Him." He noticed Murphy was holding the little wooden cross. He recognized it as the cross Laura had worn around her neck. "You have the answer in the palm of your hand, Michael. When Jesus was dying on the cross, He asked His father, 'Why have you forsaken me?' He felt abandoned, just as you do. But God didn't abandon Him. Just as He hasn't abandoned you. You must trust Him, Michael. It's hard, I know. But it's now, when we're at our lowest ebb, that we need to hold fast to our faith. We'll pray together, Michael, and God will hear us."

"Will He hear us, Bob? Was He listening when we all cried out in pain and terror the night of the bombing, when, it seems clear to me now, whoever blew up our church didn't feel they had done enough evil for one night? So they had to go and attack Laura in the basement and in a way that made sure it would take time for her to die. And they didn't even stop with that."

Murphy held up the wooden cross in his hand. "The final outrage. Whoever was responsible for all this dared to sneak in at some point the day of the funeral and break her cross into three pieces. It's like it's connected to the three pieces of the Serpent search, though I can't begin to think of what the evil connection of all this can be. But most of all, Bob, I cannot see what the point of all this suffering is. I've lost the most important thing in my life. What can God do for me now?"

Pastor Wagoner sighed. "It's natural for you to ask that question at this terrible moment, Michael. All I can tell you is that I have seen it many times before. What God can do for you now is that in the face of the greatest tragedy, the most profound heartache, He gives us what I call coping grace. He gives us the strength we need to get through it. The strength to carry on through our sorrow and fulfill His plans for us."

Murphy snorted. "You think God still has plans for me?"

"I know He does," Wagoner said firmly.

"Well, I'm not too sure I care."

"Look, Michael. Laura was a special person. But so are you. You have a special courage, you're not afraid to go head-to-head with evil. And right now I believe very strongly we need you to do that."

Murphy looked at him quizzically. "What are you talking about?"

"Look around you, Michael. You started to say this yourself. Somebody tried to destroy this church. Literally *and* metaphorically. I'm sure you haven't turned on the TV or read a newspaper since Laura died, but if you had, you would have seen headlines about 'evangelical terrorists' and 'Christian bomb conspiracies.' Someone is trying very hard to discredit us—and so far they're doing a pretty good job, judging by the way the media are jumping on the bandwagon."

Murphy thought for a moment. "But what can I do? I'm just an archaeologist."

"I'm not sure, Michael. But I believe God has a special task for you. And I believe if you let Him, He'll tell you what it is."

"I'll try, Bob. But I think right now I'm too angry about Laura to hear what He has to say."

Wagoner clapped him on the shoulder. "I'm going home now, Michael. But I'll be here tomorrow. There's still plenty of work to do getting the church back into shape. We have to show that evil can't win."

Murphy looked down at the pile of earth in front of them. "Maybe it already has, Bob."

"Nonsense, Michael. Laura is with her Lord in heaven, remember that. Maybe you should go home too. Go home and pray. He'll give you what you need."

Murphy stood by the grave and listened to Wagoner's retreating footsteps. The shadows of the tombstones lengthened on the grass and the sun began to dip behind the trees. After a while a white dove settled on top of Laura's tombstone, seemingly oblivious of his presence, cooing gently as it preened its perfect white wings. He found himself smiling.

"Bless you, sweetheart," Murphy said softly. He put her cross around his neck.

The dove cocked its head to look at him, then suddenly took off and swooped across the tombstones and behind the church.

He looked up to see what had spooked it. High in the branches of a tree a large bird of prey was picking at its talons with a great curved beak. It gave a single piercing shriek, then launched itself lazily into the air, slow wing beats taking it back toward the darkness of the woods. Murphy watched it disappear from sight, then trudged back toward the church. He'd chosen to stay at the church because he knew he'd be alone there, and because he couldn't yet bear to go home. And also because he thought if God wanted to speak to him, communication might be easier in a place of worship. He was tired and confused about so many things. If God wanted him to understand His plan, He'd have to speak loud and clear to get His message across.

# FORTY-EIGHT

HAD IT BEEN a face-to-face conversation, one of the most powerful men in the world would have been lying dead within a minute. Instead, Talon had to listen to the intense screaming of John Bartholomew of the Seven without reacting, except to scrape his sharpened index finger across the motel desk, back and forth, back and forth. If the conversation had lasted longer than two minutes, it is possible the desk might have been cut in half, so vicious were his slashes.

"Talon, I explicity told you nothing was to harm Murphy."

"What are you talking about? I didn't touch him, I killed his wife."

"And if there was any sort of normal gene in your makeup, you would realize that if someone loses a loved one, it can have devastating consequences. We don't care that she's dead, but if it distracts him from getting those last two pieces of the Serpent, you will have failed us. And even you must fear those consequences."

"Look, I made a judgment call. She was in the way and could have exposed me. It was only a matter of time. Besides, I was going stir-crazy just hanging around with only an archaeologist to watch, of all things, and a bombing to plan that had no ... personal satisfaction."

"I am going to trust that we understand each other and that this type of conversation will not need to be had ever again, Talon."

*Try saying this to my face and see how long the next conversation goes,* thought Talon. "That woman from the Parchments for Freedom Foundation visited Murphy in the hospital and I heard her say she got the tail decoded."

"You see, that's all the more reason to get Murphy back on the case. Then that piece can be ours. I do believe that he will snap back quickly. Once he does, you can get back in action. Still not, I repeat not, by harming Murphy. But it is time we claimed that first piece of the Serpent."

"Back in action, that's what I like to hear."

Murphy shot his fiftieth arrow as he had shot each of the previous arrows that afternoon. Aimlessly, just pulling the bowstring taut and launching it into the trees.

Normally, Murphy focused on his archery with precise discipline. Since he was a teenager, he had been a serious bow marksman. He hunted occasionally, but it was target archery that really stimulated Murphy's natural competitive drive.

Even in the distracted fog of his anger, Murphy went through all the motions of a skilled bow shooter. He adjusted the plastic protector around his left forearm before picking an arrow from the quiver hanging at his waist. Slowly, he drew back the bowstring on his laminated carbon-fiber-compound bow. At full draw, the system of cables and eccentric pulleys mounted at the limb tips put an awesome power at Murphy's fingertips. He just needed to breathe out, let go, and his arrow would be speeding toward its target at up to 330 feet per second like a laser-guided missile.

However, this afternoon the tears that streamed from his eyes without warning, the anger that buzzed through his mind, and the residual pain in his shoulder combined to make the arrows speed through the trees in erratic but still deadly fashion.

Murphy did not seem to care. The release from his muscles with each shot of an arrow seemed as natural yet as uncontrolled as his tears.

Unnoticed by Murphy, the man known as Talon had tracked him and was watching from several hundred yards away through binoculars. With the Seven's warnings about Murphy still being off-limits to him, he knew he could not take Murphy that afternoon. Without being able to channel his killing skills into immediate action, Talon was quite surprised to find himself admiring Murphy's clear strength. His physical strength, the arm muscles and coordination needed even to work the bow to shoot wide of any mark, not

Murphy's strength of character, because Talon had zero gift for empathy so he could not appreciate how racked with grief Murphy was.

Talon stirred himself from staring when there was a sound approaching Murphy from the opposite side. In another moment he heard a man's voice but still did not see a figure other than Murphy's. For a second he thought the deeply disturbed Murphy was shouting at himself.

"Ach! You call that shooting, Murphy? I have seen blind men come closer to their targets." Levi Abrams came crashing through the trees on the other side of Murphy.

"Levi, go away. Please."

"I can't. I've been sent by your Smokey the Bear to protect the trees. With all of your anger shooting all these arrows into the trees, you could kill more trees than a forest fire."

"Levi, I'm warning you, I'm in no mood. Leave me alone."

"No can do, Murphy. I'm going to go out on a limb here, while there is actually a limb left on a tree in this entire forest. I will not mince words, Murphy. What happened to Laura was horrible. I can only imagine your pain right now."

Murphy did not stop his automaton-like shooting into the trees. He had only a few arrows left.

"Actually, Murphy, I can do better than imagine what you're going through. When my first wife and daughter were blown up in a bus bombing in Tel Aviv five years ago, I didn't think I could go on. For me it wasn't a bow and arrow. It was two hundred and ten rounds of ammunition on the firing range while I put away a quart of whiskey in record time. That was just the first night. It took me six months to get a grip. And you know what?"

Murphy let loose his last arrow. For the first time all afternoon it landed dead center in the trunk of a tree, the tree closest to where Levi was standing. Murphy threw down his bow and faced Levi with a wild-eyed stare. "What?"

"Those were six wasted months. I was letting those Arab dogs win. I was letting them take in their dirty, bloody murderers' hands the sweet, sweet memories I had of my wife and daughter and twist them into victims. You don't want that for Laura. She was too fine for that. And so are you, my friend."

Murphy turned away. The tears stopped. "Levi, I can't make sense of it."

Levi reached an arm around his friend. "I can't either, Murphy. I am no expert, but I did seek out two people who are experts and I know they can help you get going again, as you must. I spoke to your Pastor Bob. As a Christian, you believe in a resurrection, a life after death, when you will forever be with Laura again. Look forward by faith to that event, and in the meantime, get back to work! You know that is what Laura would want you to do. I don't pretend to understand that part of your faith, but I know you do, and it is time you put it into action.

"Second, Murphy, I spoke to that Isis McDonald. She's ready to go over the translation of your Serpent's tail with you. I've got you a plane to take you to Washington, D.C., this afternoon."

Murphy picked up his bow. He grabbed Levi around the neck. "Levi, thank you, my friend. You would make a good Christian if you ever decide to come on over. You know I'm praying that you will. I will take you up on your plane, but first I've got a stop to make."

Talon watched the two men walk off through the woods. Good, he thought. Now he could also look forward to getting back into action. On to Washington.

# FORTY-NINE

LAURA WOULD HAVE been mortified but not surprised to see the unshaven, dirt-smeared, exhausted
Michael Murphy walk slowly but purposefully up to
the church pulpit.

Reverend Wagoner reached out a hand of welcome.

"Pastor, may I say a few words to the church?"

"Of course, Michael."

"Friends—many of you are my friends, and I guess
that's a concept that becomes more important only
when you're grieving, but I haven't felt much like being
among people since Laura's death.

"I guess because it's clear to me that some sorry excuse for a person, some walking evil, struck her down.

"And I couldn't stop it. Which is why I haven't felt
much like being around myself either.

"And worst of all, I haven't felt much like being

around God, because I've been angry and I've been blaming Him, and I've been just so unable to go on, so let down by Him and confused. But I realize that God has a plan for me, no matter how painful this portion of it has been.

"I guess I started to realize it when a well-meaning colleague of mine brought me the piece of Moses' Brazen Serpent in the hospital. The piece that Laura and I found on our last great adventure together. For a moment I was almost tempted to forsake my God as this colleague suggested and place my faith instead in this false icon.

"I realized this morning that the Serpent is a sign to me not to give up my faith but to renew it. I believe this was what Pastor Bob here was getting ready to talk about the other night when the bomb went off. I was helped to focus on it by, of all people, my Israeli friend, Levi Abrams, which I guess shows us that guidance and inspiration come from all sorts of places if we open ourselves.

"Here, in the face of the greatest pain and most unknowable mystery of my life, the loss of my soul mate, just like Moses with the Serpent, my faith is being tested, but I will not turn away. Just like Moses with the Serpent, I have a responsibility to fulfill, my duties, my service, in the face of all the evil and the fear and the turmoil of the world around me.

"So today, I wish to announce to you, my Christian friends, that I am going to trust our Lord for the future and believe that He still has a plan for my life, even while I am grieving. And with His strength and hope, I can put my life's worst tragedy behind me and get back to work. So, thank you for your prayers and for letting me get this off my chest. Now I'm off to find the other two pieces of the Brazen Serpent. I am confident that is what both God and Laura would want me to do."

# FIFTY

IT WAS A day of wrenching opposite emotions. As Shari kept her vigil with Paul in his unconscious state, he began to stir, and then without any warning opened his eyes. He was very weak, but he was able to speak, and seemed to be showing few effects of his temporary unconsciousness. He even managed to smile at her. The doctors and nurses rushed in and wanted to begin testing Paul, so Shari was asked to step out.

FBI Agent Baines was waiting for her in the hallway of the hospital. His news was horrible, one of her worst nightmares made true, but it brought with it a sense of relief for Shari. Tests had finally revealed the identity of the remaining victim from the church basement. The body had been completely destroyed, so DNA testing had been a challenge. However, they were now convinced that it was her brother, Chuck. And the FBI believed that Chuck had actually been the one to detonate the bomb that had been some form of a pack worn on his back.

Shari had not seen Chuck since the Wednesday morning of the bombing, and, of course, she had worried where he had gone off to, even allowing for the possibility that he could be involved in the bombing in some way, though he was both the most unreligious and unpolitical person she knew. Strangely, she had been rooting for his just having run off on some spree with his new friend.

Now the seeming truth was settled and she felt the hot tears running down her cheeks. What could he possibly want with bombing the church? It had to be his strange friend putting him up to it. Shari braced herself for Agent Baines's likely barrage of questions. To her surprise, he was very kind.

"Miss Nelson, I am sorry for your loss. There are a lot of questions you could help us with about how and why your brother would have bombed the church. But if you need time to deal with this, I understand."

Shari looked at the medical team attending Paul, her happy story, and realized she would probably not get to see him for hours. She turned to Agent Baines. "No, let's deal with Chuck now and start putting this tragedy to rest."

It became clear pretty quickly that Chuck was likely more victim than evil mastermind of the church bombing. Based on his criminal record, the FBI could see he had neither the experience nor the brains to have worked with the explosives, and Shari stressed his complete lack of interest in being part of any religious group, even if there had been a bomb factory of religious zealots in that basement—which the FBI was not inclined to believe once they sifted through the rubble and conducted their interviews.

Agent Baines drove Shari back to the hospital after an hour. "Bizarre as it sounds, I almost wish you all were a bunch of religious fanatics, as the press is making out. This just looks like some nasty attempt to implicate evangelical Christians, as with the U.N. message. To what end, beyond troublemaking, we don't know. But we will figure it out and catch them."

"I hope you do, Agent Baines. We'll all be relieved to be out of this disturbing spotlight someone is shining on our faith, seemingly to hurt innocent people and embarrass us."

When Shari got back to Paul's room at the hospital, she was glad to see that the doctors had left, but he was not alone. A very distinguished-looking man in a handsomely tailored suit was leaning in very close to where Paul lay, talking very seriously.

"Hi, Paul."

Paul smiled as she entered the room. "Oh, Shari, great, you're back. This is Shane Barrington, *the* Shane Barrington. He came here to visit me, can you imagine?"

"How do you do, Miss Nelson. Paul here has been saying what a good friend you have been to him. What a tragedy for a young man to have to struggle with the year he has had, and that was before this."

There was something about Barrington that made Shari stand back and be wary. "Yes, Mr. Barrington. But, forgive me, why would a rich, powerful man like yourself care about what's going on in Paul's life?"

Weak as he was, Shari's question made Paul pale even more. "Shari, there's no reason to be rude to Mr. Barrington."

"Oh, I don't take that as rudeness, Paul. I have recently suffered some terrible violence in my family that took my only son from me. When I heard about this bombing and what happened to Professor Murphy and to you, I felt I wanted to come and offer my support. This is exactly what I talked about in my press conference. I want to help victims and fight criminals of every kind."

Paul smiled. "Well, it sure is good of you to come, sir."

Barrington patted Paul's shoulder. "I'm not here just to be sociable, Paul. My staff looked into your story and it made me think of my son, of the chances he'll never have now, and, I'm sorry to say, of the missed opportunities I had to be there for him when he was growing up and having some problems." He pulled an envelope from his pocket. "So, I have taken the liberty of drawing up a special Barrington Communications scholarship for you to Preston. Now you have no financial worries as long as you stay in school."

Paul's eyes welled up with grateful tears. Shari became even more suspicious of this Mr. Barrington and his sudden interest in Paul. This was turning into quite a day.

# FIFTY-ONE

NEBUCHADNEZZAR STOOD on the highest part of the palace ramparts as a spring breeze from the river gently stirred his robe and filled his nostrils with the smells of new life. How strange are the workings of the mind, he mused. Just a few months earlier he had been tormented by the dream of the great statue, reduced to an impotent wreck by his inability to remember a single detail of it. Then the Hebrew slave, Daniel, had restored it to him, and since that day he had dreamed of the statue every night, intense, almost unbearably vivid reveries that left him not drained and confused as before, but eager and invigorated when he awoke.

Ever since Daniel had explained the dream's meaning, that there would be no greater empire in the history of the world than Babylon, no greater ruler than he, Nebuchadnezzar, king of kings, he had felt a new energy surging in his veins, a heady, intoxicating feeling of almost superhuman power. Surely none could resist him now; surely every tribe, every nation, from the far mountains where the sun rises to the unknown shores where it sinks back into the underworld, must acknowledge his mastery, must bow down before his imperial might and feel his foot upon their necks.

Looking out over the plain, he could already see many of his subject peoples toiling in the spring heat. Hundreds, thousands of men, pulling ropes, lifting great beams, swarming like ants on the arid ground. Even at this distance he could faintly hear the crack of the whips, feel the sting of leather biting into naked flesh as his foremen drove them on beyond the point of exhaustion.

Was it just his imagination, or did he smell the sweat of their labors on the breeze? His wife, Amytis, had filled her gardens with every kind of blossom and shrub to remind her of the lush sanctuaries of her native Persia, and he often walked there, filling his lungs with their rich scents. But even the most exotic of her blooms did not smell as sweet as this, the sweat of men who would die for no other reason than to glorify his name.

As the sun rose higher and the air began to tremble with the coming heat, his eyes lifted from the teeming crowds of workers to the massive object in the center of the plain. It lay like a prostrate giant bound with a massive spider's web of ropes. But the ropes were not to keep it in place. They were there to raise it. And as he heard the shouts of his foremen and the cruel lashing of whips grow in intensity, he knew that the statue was about to take its appointed place at last. That his dream was finally becoming a reality.

For a time the huge figure didn't move, and for one terrible moment he wondered if his engineers had miscalculated, that it was simply impossible to raise such a massive weight from the ground no matter how many slaves you had at your command.

For surely such an ambitious feat had never been tried, never even been imagined before.

But then the groaning of thousands of feet of twisted hemp mingled with the agonized cries of muscles straining beyond endurance gave way to a deeper, wrenching sound as the statue seemed to raise itself out of the dust and started to float upward. The king opened his mouth in awe, unable to shake the conviction that the statue was somehow alive, pushing itself toward him.

Cries of horror and pain suddenly cut through the air as several ropes attached to the statue's huge torso snapped, and dozens of workers were flung to the ground in the vicious recoil. The figure seemed to hesitate; then, as Nebuchadnezzar willed it forward through clenched teeth, it seemed to regain its momentum and with one last mighty effort its great feet thudded into place, sending up a huge cloud of yellow dust.

Nebuchadnezzar didn't hear the sounds of thousands of men crying out either from the pain of torn muscles and snapped tendons or simply relief that their torment was over. All he could hear was the frenzied beating of his heart and the rasping of his breath as he clutched the wall and gulped great lungfuls of air. Slowly, agonizingly slowly, the dust enveloping the statue began to disperse on the wind and his vision gradually shimmered into life before him.

As if someone had touched a flame to a cauldron of oil in a night-dark room, the sun suddenly caught the broad expanse of forehead and at once the great head burst into golden light. Shielding his eyes from the dazzling visage, Nebuchadnezzar heaved great sobs of exaltation as the rest of the statue revealed itself. First the chest and arms of silver, then the belly and thighs of bronze, and finally the legs of iron straddling the heaps of broken scaffolding and bloodied corpses.

Standing fully ninety cubits high, its muscular frame etched in hard, metallic lines, the statue loomed over Babylon like a great, cruel god.

As the king's eyes adjusted to the glare, he could at last make out the features of the golden face. The broad lips were curved downward in a vengeful sneer, the empty eyes blazing with ferocity.

With a roar of laughter that rang out over the plain, he recognized the face as his own.

# FIFTY-TWO

ISIS TOOK A last look at the tail of the Serpent, its bronze scales shimmering under the halogen lights, and dropped it into a nylon bag. She took a card key from around her neck and inserted it into a heavy steel door that swung open with a soft hiss. Inside, the gray metal shelving was mostly empty. Just a strongbox she knew contained a priceless necklace from the site of Troy, and two steel tubes stuffed with papyri from the recently excavated tomb of an Egyptian princess of the Third Dynasty. She placed the bag between the tubes and pushed the door firmly shut.

"This place is like Fort Knox," she said. "I can't imagine how anyone unauthorized could get down here. And if they did get past the alarms and the security guards and what have you, they'd have to get through here." She rapped the door with her knuckles. "Let's just say I sometimes have nightmares about being shut in here by mistake. When they finally opened the door, they'd just find a dried-up old mummy," she said with a shudder.

"I guess that'd be poetic justice, wouldn't it?" said Murphy.

"I'm sorry?"

"You know, to be turned into an ancient artifact."

She sniffed. "If I were an archaeologist, maybe. I think you're the one who needs to be careful." She winced and put her hand to her forehead. "Look, I'm sorry. . . ."

Murphy put a hand on her arm. "Let's get something straight. You don't need to walk on eggshells. You don't need to worry you're going to accidentally mention death and I'll go to pieces. You can even talk about Laura if you want."

She breathed a sigh of relief. "Good. I'd like to. Talk about Laura, I mean."

She walked to a door in the floor-to-ceiling wire-cage wall and opened it with her card key. As it shut automatically behind them, Murphy glanced at the metal plaque, which read: SECURE STORAGE AREA—NO UNAUTHORIZED PERSONNEL BEYOND THIS POINT. He saw Isis disappear around a corner and hurried to keep up. He realized that he would never be able to find his way through this subterranean labyrinth on his own.

"Was this place designed by the same guy who built Annacherib's pyramid?"

"The one with all the dead ends and false corridors? What do they call it—the Maze of Forgetting?" She laughed. "I wouldn't be surprised."

At last she led him up a staircase to a door that, to Murphy's surprise, opened directly onto the employee parking lot. Isis noticed Murphy was looking at the security booth off to one side. "There's one at each entrance," she said. "The security guards are in radio contact with the central security station in the main building. That's where all the electronic surveillance systems are monitored."

He seemed satisfied. "Okay, where are we going?"

"I'm no expert on local restaurants, I'm afraid. I don't eat out an awful lot. Usually I just have a pizza at my desk."

"What about in the evening?"

She looked embarrassed. "Same thing."

"And always pizza?"

"Why not? Pure carbohydrate. Minimal nutrition. It could be the Scottish national dish."

"Pizza it is, then."

She pursed her lips. "I think we can do better than that. How about Scotland's second favorite national dish: curry?"

"Anything hot sounds good."

"You may come to regret that," she said, taking his arm.

A cab took them down the 12th Street Expressway, one of several tunnels that cut through the Mall, the three-mile-long expanse of greenery, monuments, and government buildings at the heart of the city. They emerged onto E Street and were soon headed for Chinatown.

The Star of India, nestled improbably between Yip's Noodle House and the Jade Palace, was dark and virtually empty. Over tea and popadums, they scanned the menu while the latest Hindi show tunes played in the background, Isis settling for a shrimp vindaloo while Murphy acknowledged defeat before the contest had even begun by ordering a chicken bhuna.

"So, tell me about the inscription."

"I thought you'd never ask," she said, clearing a space on the table. She pulled a crumpled piece of paper from her bag and smoothed out the edges. "It took forever. Really quite the trickiest bit of Chaldean I've come across. But after your call, I think I finally cracked it—at least the important bits. I think your theory is right, that the high priest Dakkuri wrote this puzzle with two minds. He wanted the reader to understand how to find the rest of the Serpent, but on the other hand, he's keen that the wrong people not get their hands on it. So he wraps it all up in metaphorical language that's quite tough to penetrate. Like a sort of shell around his message."

"Who are the wrong people?"

"Hard to say. We know that Dakkuri was told by Nebuchadnezzar to get rid of the Serpent, along with all the other idols. Presumably, if someone loyal to the king found where Dakkuri had hidden it, he'd destroy it—and Dakkuri himself wouldn't fare much better."

"That makes sense. So who are the *right* people? Who does Dakkuri want to find the Serpent?"

"Good question." Her finger ran down the lines until she found what she wanted. "Here. There's a formal incantation. It's quite common. You see it on all sorts of inscriptions. Something like 'only the pure of heart shall find what they seek.'"

"Sounds like the good guys."

"I said it was *something like* that. In fact, he substitutes another word for 'pure.' It doesn't quite make sense, but the nearest I can get is 'only the dark of heart' or 'only those with darkness in their hearts.'" She smiled. "So I'm afraid that rather scuppers your chances, doesn't it?"

"You'd be surprised," Murphy said. "There's quite a lot of darkness in my heart right now." She looked at him and bit her lip. He nodded at the paper. "Go on. What else does the man say?"

"Well, there are some more incantations to a few of the lesser-known Babylonian gods—and then we get down to it." She pointed to a paragraph. *"The pieces of the sacred snake are scattered far, yet still are joined. He who is wise enough*—actually 'wily' is probably a better word—*to find the first already holds the second in his hand. Find the third, and the mystery shall return.'* That last bit really had me stumped for a while. I'm still not sure I've got it right. But 'mystery' is the only way I can see of translating it."

"Mystery," Murphy repeated. "Okay. What he's saying is that each piece of the Serpent has an inscription telling you where to find the next one."

"I think so."

He smiled. "So . . . where's the second piece?"

She turned the paper over. "Right at the end. I suppose he assumed that if you'd made it this far, you were definitely his sort of person. Here we are. *'Look to the desert and Erigal's master will take your left hand. . . .'"*

"What does that mean?"

"Well, Erigal is a very minor Babylonian demon.

Some experts don't even include him in the textbooks. But my father was a bit more thorough than most," she said proudly. "I looked him up in one of his old notebooks. Anyway, Erigal's function was doing odd jobs for Shamash, the chief Babylonian god. Like Zeus or Odin. Chief male one, anyway. I couldn't figure out what Dakkuri was on about until I realized Shamash was originally a sun god."

"So?"

"So, Erigal's master—Shamash—taking your hand could mean the sun rising."

"And if he takes your left hand, you'd be facing south."

"Exactly."

"And if you stood near Babylon and looked south, you'd be looking toward . . . Saudi Arabia."

"*The desert.*"

Isis snatched the piece of paper off the table as a waiter in a dazzling white shirt and black bow tie put their plates in front of them. Breathing in the aromatic fumes, Murphy suddenly realized how hungry he was. But he couldn't eat until he had the answer.

"That's a big desert," he said. "Easy to lose an army in there, let alone a foot-long piece of bronze."

"He is a little more specific than that," she said testily, as if Murphy were criticizing her personally. "He goes on to say that '*twenty days hence, the seeker shall slake his thirst. And beneath his feet it shall be found.*'"

Murphy looked at her blankly.

"Don't you see? He must be talking about an oasis. Twenty days south of Babylon." She folded her arms in triumph.

Murphy grinned. "Does this place have a name?"

"Ah," she said, her face falling. "That's the problem. It has a name, all right. And a population of about a million people. If the second piece of the Serpent is under Tar-Qasir, you're going to have to dig through an entire modern city to find it."

# FIFTY-THREE

"LOOK, I'M GRATEFUL for everything you've done." Murphy was sitting in Isis's disaster-area-passing-as-an-office and feeling quite at home. "I wish there were some way I could repay you. But there's no way you're coming to Tar-Qasir. I'm going to leave the Serpent's tail here at the foundation for the time being for safe-keeping, then I'm going to arrange for a trip to the Mideast to find the the rest of it. By myself."

"But what if you do find the second piece in Tar-Qasir?" Isis insisted. "You'll need me to translate whatever's inscribed on it. I'm the only one who can do it." She was aware that her voice was becoming more shrill as her anger flared, but she didn't care.

"You've walked me through the inscription on the tail. I think I've got a feel for it now. I'll call you if I get stuck."

She snorted in derision. "Hah! You wouldn't know where to start. I don't think you'd know this kind of cuneiform from a hole in the ground—which, considering that *you're* an archaeologist and *I'm* a philologist, makes a certain amount of sense, don't you think?"

He sighed. "Look, I don't understand why you're making such a big deal out of this. It's not like you're a field researcher."

Actually, she didn't really understand either. Up until a few days ago, the closest she came to field research was trying to unearth some books or papers from the dusty piles in her office. Now she was volunteering to travel halfway around the world on a bizarre quest for an artifact that, if not actually cursed, certainly seemed to have a distinctly unpleasant aura around it.

She took a deep breath and tried to get a fix on the mix of emotions swirling around inside her. "I'm sure you're trying to be chivalrous and all that nonsense, but I wish you would just admit that if you're serious about finding all the pieces, you're going to need me."

Murphy stayed tight-lipped.

"I know you think I'm just some weak-kneed woman who's spent her life with her head stuck in old books." She caught the beginnings of a smile on Murphy's face. "And maybe you're right. But maybe I've decided it's time to blow away the cobwebs a little. Maybe I've decided it's time to show the world my father wasn't the only Dr. McDonald who was willing to take a few risks to get what he wanted."

Murphy stopped himself from saying *And look what happened to him.* "You're a very stubborn woman, you know that?"

"Yes. Stubborn—and resourceful. I took the liberty of talking with our PFF chairman yesterday. He has agreed that the Parchments of Freedom Foundation will provide their plane and support funding for your expedition—for *our* expedition—in return for being able to exhibit the Serpent here at the PFF Museum. That is, assuming there is a body and head to this Serpent, and we find them, and we can bring them home."

"Isis, you know you were way out of line going for the funding before I agreed you were going." Murphy gave a long sigh. "But thank you, because I don't think I would be getting to Tar-Qasir without the generosity of the foundation."

Isis watched him with nervous anticipation. "All right." Murphy smiled. "*We* go to Tar-Qasir. But if things get out of hand, and I say so, you're on the first plane back. Deal?"

# FIFTY-FOUR

ON THE AFTERNOON of the day Isis McDonald and Michael Murphy flew to the Mideast, the guard in the security booth of the PFF entrance did not notice the pair of peregrines emerging from the roof of a black van in the parking lot. But his job required him to concentrate for long periods with little in the way of stimulation, and it's possible that as dusk fell at the end of a long day, he was beginning to glaze over from the stultifying routine of watching the monitors and checking the hourly logs.

If he had noticed the falcons, he would have seen the slim, dark shapes powering their way skyward in a classic spiral ascent, using the warm updrafts from the sunbeaten asphalt below to augment the regular beats of their muscular wings. Had he been a birder, their elegant silhouettes would have been instantly recognizable and he might well have smiled to himself as he watched, his spirits lifted by the unlooked-for sight.

Peregrines were in some way the epitome of wild, untamed beauty, and it was no surprise that the greed and rapacity of man had driven them from many of their natural habitats. And yet, they were surprisingly well adapted to living in the heart of the most modern and densely populated cities. In the wild, they were happiest nesting on tall cliffs and preying on other birds; in cities, skyscrapers and pigeons provided for their needs in almost supernatural abundance.

Perhaps, had he been of a spiritual turn of mind, the guard might have reflected that a time would come when many cities were abandoned as the world was plunged into conflict and chaos, and the falcons would inherit the empty skyscrapers as if they had belonged to them all along.

What he would not have imagined was that in a matter of minutes, one of the birds was going to kill him.

His colleague, stationed in front of the door from which Murphy and Isis had exited the building, was equally unaware. At the moment the two birds reached their pitch, approximately a thousand feet above the ground, his mind was chewing over a familiar puzzle. His meager salary was not enough to cover his gambling debts, let alone support a wife who seemed to blame him for the way time was ravaging her face and figure and took her revenge out on his credit cards.

And yet here was the guard, literally sitting on a gold mine. A gold mine to which he had the key—or at least some of the many keys—in his hand. Deep down he knew that it would take someone far smarter and more inventive than he would ever be to parlay his security access into hard cash, but in the same way that some people chew tobacco or whittle away at sticks, he found the seemingly pointless process relaxing.

He was very relaxed when the larger of the birds, the female, steadied herself in the air with a flick of her wings and turned her piercing tunnel vision on the tall figure standing in the parking lot a thousand feet below. He was dressed from head to toe in black, and to anyone looking across the lot, he might easily have merged into the lengthening shadows. But to the falcon, he stood out like a beacon. Partly because of her extraordinarily acute vision—and partly because she knew him so well.

She also knew what he expected of her.

The man was holding a falconry glove high over his head. To anyone passing, he would have looked like a man hailing a cab. A strange thing for someone to be doing in the middle of a parking lot, no doubt. But he was in fact doing something much stranger.

He was calling death down from the air.

Talon looked up and saw the speck of black against the delicate pink of the early-evening sky. She seemed to be perched weightlessly in the upper air, and he could almost feel her impatience. She wanted him to cut the invisible thread that held her fast and set her free.

Bringing the glove down sharply to his side, he did just that. Seeing his gesture, she swiveled once to set herself, fixed her eyes on her target, and tucked her wings under her. Gravity did the rest.

A falcon descending from such a height can accelerate to speeds of almost two hundred miles an hour. Too fast for the human eye to follow, the best guide to her progress is the sound of the air being sliced apart by this speeding bullet of muscle, feather, and bone. Talon preferred to watch her target and simply wait for the inevitable.

As his mind wandered through familiar get-rich-quick fantasies, the security guard noticed that a dark-clad man standing between two rows of cars was looking directly at him. Was it his imagination or a trick of the fading light, or was there a look of amused expectation on the man's face? A look that seemed to say *I know something you don't.*

He instinctively turned to his right as a blur of movement registered at the edge of his vision, and then the razors attached to the peregrine's talons tore through his throat with blinding speed. Carotid arteries draining, he staggered a couple of steps, a hand clutched to his shattered larynx, then collapsed in a heap of twitching limbs.

Talon waited until it was over, then walked over and examined the corpse, careful to avoid the spreading pool of blood. Sliding his hand inside the jacket, he removed a set of keys and started feeling for the shape he wanted. Behind him he could hear footsteps coming from the direction of the security booth, slow and deliberate at first, then accelarating into a trot as they came closer. He put the keys in a pocket and waited.

"Okay, buddy. Stand up slowly and turn around. Keep your hands where I can see them."

Talon raised his hands and gave him his best *Who, me?* smile. The guard held him at the end of his revolver and sneaked a look at the body on the ground. Realizing he couldn't help his colleague and keep watch on Talon, he reached for the radio at his belt. Talon let one of his arms drop sharply to his side.

"I said keep your hands—" But the words died in his throat as the second peregrine slammed into the back of his neck, severing his spinal cord with a single punch of its talons. Talon stepped aside as the guard dropped heavily onto the tarmac. Opening a plastic Ziploc bag, he took out a couple of dead mourning doves and held them at arm's length. After a few seconds, both peregrines swooped out of the shadows and settled on his wrists, chewing happily on the unexpected treat as their talons dug into the leather armbands he wore under his jacket.

He walked back to the van and settled the female onto her perch. She hissed angrily as he slipped the hood over her head, then instantly quieted, soothed by the cocoon of darkness that suddenly enveloped her. He held the smaller male by his jesses and turned toward the booth, clucking softly. "You still have work to do, little one." Inside, he quickly found what he was looking for.

The door to the museum at the Parchments of Freedom Foundation opened with a satisfying click, and Talon slipped inside.

It was Saturday, but Fiona Carter had decided to take advantage of Dr. McDonald's absence to try to organize the office. She did treat herself to lunch out at an actual restaurant, something she rarely got to do when she was keeping tabs on Dr. McDonald. Fiona wondered how her boss and Professor Murphy were faring out in the field and wondered which of them was in for the greater shock.

Her mouth dropped open at her own discovery. The bodies of the two security guards were horribly mutilated and tangled together as if they'd been doing a gruesome tango when the killer had struck. Fiona bent down and tried to make sense of their wounds, but could not, and it was all she could do to keep from screaming and fleeing. Instead, she forced herself to enter the building to call 911.

Inside, the corridors were eerily quiet. There was no reason to expect anyone else to be working at this hour on a weekend, but the silence was somehow too thick, as if the whole building had stopped breathing.

Instinct made Fiona head for the secure storage area. Turning the corner, she could see the wire mesh door was open. When she got to the vault, the heavy door was open. Fiona looked inside, knowing what she would find. Or, more accurately, not find.

The tail of the Serpent was gone.

In its place, cut with deep, fresh slashes into the metal shelf of the storage room, was a quickly carved rendering of a snake. The snake was cut into thirds—head, middle, and tail. Next to it was an even more disturbing symbol. She was going to have to page PFF chairman Compton. And then she was going to have to try to track down Professor Murphy and Dr. McDonald. She hoped it was not too late for them to turn back.

# FIFTY-FIVE

THE FIRST LEG of the flight had taken them from Washington to London Heathrow, where the plane was refueled and the crew was changed. Murphy and Isis quickened their pace toward their departure gate. Her slim frame weighed down by a voluminous leather briefcase stuffed with books—rare editions she simply couldn't bear to check—she was struggling to keep up. But repeated offers to carry it for her had met with stiff resistance. "I can manage quite well, thank you. And anyway, you have your own precious cargo to contend with." It was true, the competition bow in its impact-resistant case wasn't exactly heavy, but it was awkward to carry, and she was determined she wasn't going to add to Murphy's burdens.

At least he had stopped arguing about her coming with him. While she thought of herself as a professional equal of Murphy's, and while she could not match his most recent personal loss, when she thought back to the death of her father, she felt she could empathize with him personally as well.

Murphy and Isis didn't talk much during the long journey to Tar-Qasir. Murphy slept for most of the flight to London, unconsciousness unexpectedly settling on him like a blessing almost as soon as he was buckled in. While they waited for their plane to refuel, he paced Heathrow's cavernous corridors and malls in silence, like a man trying out a new pair of shoes. He wasn't thinking about anything. He was just getting used to his new life, his new existence: the one without Laura.

Isis had a sense that she should leave him be, that he needed time to gather his strength for what was to come, and was happy enough to bury herself in her books. Although she wouldn't admit it, she was worried that she was going to slow Murphy down and consequently was determined that at least her linguistic skills would be honed to razor sharpness. If they did manage to find the second piece of the Serpent, she wanted to make sure she could unlock its secrets.

In particular, she was revisiting an old volume that had belonged to her father. Bishop Henry Merton's *Lesser Chaldean Apocrypha.* She had read it before, of course, but not, she was beginning to realize, with quite her full attention. Or perhaps it was simply that Merton's study of some of the more obscure corners of ancient Mesopotamian religious belief had never seemed terribly relevant. Now, however, his exhaustive analyses of Babylonian idol worship seemed tailor-made to her needs.

Of course, he hadn't been "Bishop" Merton when he'd written the book. Just a young country vicar in a half-forgotten parish in Dorset, England's sleepy southwest. That was where her father had first come across him. As he told the story, they had both been reaching for the same first edition of Frazer's *The Golden Bough* in a secondhand bookstore in Dorchester. After a protracted argument, during which they each insisted the other had first claim on the book, her father had finally prevailed (steely Scots self-denial winning out over English politeness), practically herding the young cleric to the counter with his prize.

After that, of course, Merton could do no other than invite his benefactor to tea and scones at the little shop around the corner. It was there, amid the chintz and china, that his interest in the dark rituals of the world's forgotten religions was revealed. An interest, her father recalled, bordering on obsession. Not that there was necessarily anything wrong or even strange about that, given her father's own proclivities—except that Merton was wearing the black shirt and collar of an ordained Church of England vicar. "It just seemed rather odd," he'd recalled, "to listen to this young man, who by rights ought to be spending his time harvesting souls for Jesus, speak with such passionate intensity about the demons inhabiting the gloomier reaches of the Sumerian underworld."

Despite the elder archaeologist's instinctive qualms, a lively correspondence had ensued after they parted. The lure of Merton's vast erudition was simply too much to resist. But after a few months, her father had stopped replying to Merton's letters, and it was clear to the adolescent Isis that something had deeply disturbed him.

She never discovered what it was. But now, as she slowly turned the pages of *Lesser Chaldean Apocrypha*, she remembered that this was the very volume her father had been clutching when they found him.

She shuddered, and her fingers went instinctively to the amulet around her neck. It was the head of the Babylonian goddess Ishtar, a gift from her father, and it was a constant comfort in times of stress.

With a little shake of her head, she returned to the book. Whatever the truth about Bishop Merton, he knew his Chaldean rituals. If anyone was going to provide an insight into the mind of Dakkuri, it was him.

On the flight from London to Riyadh, Murphy hadn't interrupted her reading. It seemed to have the effect of recharging her batteries—something she surely needed after the trauma of the last few days. Certainly by the time they'd made the long taxi ride through the desert to Tar-Qasir itself and settled into a large modern hotel called, appropriately enough, the Oasis, she seemed positively bursting with energy. Murphy had passed out again as soon as he lay down on the cool white sheets before he'd had time to wonder what their next step would be. And now, some hours later, the crisp rat-tat-tat on his door that jolted him out of a dreamless sleep seemed to have all the hallmarks of her restless spirit.

Showered, changed, and newly focused, Murphy met her in the spacious lobby. "I think they should rename this hotel the Empty Quarter," he joked. "Are we the only guests, do you think?"

"Tar-Qasir isn't exactly a tourist destination," she admitted. "But that's not to say it doesn't have its points of interest."

"Such as?"

"I've been doing a little research while you were catching up on your sleep," she said with a twinkle. It sounded as if sleep was something she indulged in only rarely, like the occasional drink. "As we know, it began as an oasis. A convenient crossing point of various trade routes through the desert. Gradually it grew into a proper market town as merchants began to settle here instead of just using it as a watering hole. And by the Middle Ages, it had become a genuine city. Actually, rather a unique and unusual one."

She was clearly enjoying herself, and Murphy was pleased to see it. "Unique *and* unusual? Let me guess, they had ice-cream parlors? No—baseball was invented here!"

She shook her head. "Rather more interesting than that. They had *underground sewers*. You see, the spring that fed the original oasis provided enough water for a remarkably efficient system. Probably the first of its kind."

Murphy scratched his chin. "And it's still in operation?"

"Heavens, no. But the original tunnels may well be intact. They built things to last in those days. If we want to find out what lies beneath the surface of downtown Tar-Qasir, maybe the sewers are the answer."

"That's a lot of maybes," said Murphy. "How do we get in? And how do we find our way around when we're down there?"

Isis hefted her backpack and stood up. She was dressed in combat shorts and hiking boots, but somehow still managed to look like a philologist rather than a mountaineer. "I suggest we pay a visit to Tar-Qasir's municipal library and see if we can find out."

Murphy sighed. A library. Of course. Where else would Isis suggest they go?

Out in the street the heat hit them like a solid wall, and they were relieved when an air-conditioned cab pulled up a minute later. But it was long enough for the sweat to have already soaked though Murphy's shirt. Isis, on the other hand, looked as cool and pale as if they'd been hiking in her native Highlands. *Maybe being an ice maiden does have certain advantages,* Murphy thought.

From the outside, Tar-Qasir's library didn't promise much. The Victorian facade of the modest three-story building boasted more character than the washed-out concrete blocks that seemed to make up most of the downtown area, but its broken windows and dusty entrance hall suggested that its best days were long gone. An impression that was confirmed by the man who appeared to be its only inhabitant.

"We are in need of some refurbishment, it is true," Salim Omar admitted, stroking his trim beard. "Tar-Qasir is a modern city that looks to the future, not the past, and all this"—he gestured to the shelves—or in some cases piles—of books that filled the room—"is considered irrelevant and unworthy of study." He sighed. "It is a shame. For myself, I believe that it is only by looking deeply into the past that we can understand what the future holds for us."

Murphy sipped from his glass of steaming mint tea and nodded. "I'm with you there, Mr. Omar." He felt a surge of fellow feeling for the quiet-spoken librarian who appeared to have been stranded on an outcrop of the past as the tidal wave of modernity swept past him, and would have liked to spend more time drinking tea and learning his story. But Isis was all business.

"Sewers, Mr. Omar. We're interested in sewers."

Omar gave her a quizzical look, and she wasn't sure if he was simply surprised that anyone wanted to know about such things or if he was particularly shocked to hear a woman express an interest. "Dr. McDonald, it is rare enough that anyone comes here seeking a book. Now two people arrive on my doorstep all the way from America and they want to know about sewers. This is most strange, I must say."

"I'm amazed," said Isis with, as far as Murphy could tell, a straight face. "Surely everyone knows about the sewers of Tar-Qasir."

He looked at her as if she were slightly demented. "Perhaps. But very few make the effort to come and see what is left of them."

"And what *is* left of them?" Murphy asked.

Omar spread his hands. "Who can say? No one has been down there for many years."

"What if someone wanted to go down there? Are there any maps, any records of the construction? Any way of navigating?"

Omar glanced at the dust-covered telephone on the desk, and Murphy thought for a moment he was going to call the police to come and arrest these suspicious foreigners with their highly dubious interest in sewers.

He was certainly beginning to look extremely nervous. "It is not good. Tunnels falling down and suchlike. I cannot help you."

Murphy started to get up, but Isis put a pale hand on his arm. "Mr. Omar," she began, giving him her warmest smile. "We would be delighted to make a contribution to assist with the restoration of your fine library if you were able to help us."

He narrowed his eyes. "Some additional shelving would be very welcome. Perhaps some assistance in cataloguing..."

Isis kept smiling. "How much?"

He made a sour face as if to say such things were beneath him. "Shall we say one thousand dollars?"

"Five hundred," Isis shot back.

"Some of the shelves are actually quite dangerous. I had a nasty fall only last week. Eight hundred."

"Six."

"Seven-fifty."

"Agreed."

Before Murphy could adjust to this new assertive Isis he didn't quite recognize, she'd reached into her backpack and counted out a neat stack of bills. Omar flipped through them without comment, then stood up, gesturing for them to follow. Squeezing through a tiny door at the end of the room, they entered a chaotic Aladdin's cave of books and manuscripts piled in drifts against the walls. After several minutes of fruitless burrowing, Omar at last emerged with his prize. He blew the dust off a slim morocco-bound volume before handing it over with a flourish.

"A real treasure. An eighteen forty-four first edition

of Baron de Tocqueville's *A Curious History of Ancient Arabia.* I think you will find it has excellent illustrations of Tar-Qasir's sewerage system as it existed in the nineteenth century."

Murphy watched Isis leafing through the stiff, yellowing pages. She looked as if she were in philologists' heaven. "A first edition," she breathed. "I didn't know there were *any* editions still in existence. My father would have..."

He guided her back toward the door, worried that if they stayed any longer she'd never be able to tear herself away from this treasure-house of books.

"Thank you for all your help, Mr. Omar. And good luck with the restoration."

Omar nodded. "And the very best of luck to you both," he said solemnly.

After the heavy front door had closed behind them, he sat down at his desk, poured himself another cup of tea, and sipped it thoughtfully. After a while a young man dressed in a white djellaba slid silently out from behind a stack of books. He began riffling through the notes on Omar's desk. "You let them go?"

Omar shrugged. "What could I do? They seemed very determined."

"The woman was beautiful. I have never seen such pale skin. Do you think we will see them again?"

Omar put down his tea. "Are you serious? Knowing what is down there?"

The young man sighed. "What a shame. She really was very pretty."

# FIFTY-SIX

TALON PASSED THROUGH the ornately carved archway that led into the great hall and wondered if he was about to die. He had been summoned to the castle rarely during the two years he had been employed by the council, and each time he had been taken to the subterranean vault, his employers sat behind a huge obsidian table, seven anonymous black silhouettes that for all he knew were distorted further to conceal their identities.

Now, for the first time, a sightless footman, who seemed to navigate his way through the castle by some extra sense, was pointing to a seat at the end of a long oak table where the Seven sat in clear daylight, their features unmasked. If they no longer cared that he could identify them, it could mean only one of two things: Either they trusted him completely or they weren't intending to let him leave the castle alive. If it was the latter, he knew there was no point in trying to formulate an escape plan. But he did wonder how they would do it.

He suspected it would be efficient but also a little theatrical. They definitely seemed to enjoy a spectacle. And they had a keen sense of history too. Something medieval, in keeping with the castle's setting? Perhaps a man-at-arms in chain mail was standing behind his seat at this very moment, ready to decapitate him with a razor-sharp halberd. Or something with more of a religious feel to it, perhaps. Could it be he was about to be flayed alive like St. Bartholomew, or broken on a spiked wheel like St. Catherine? That would certainly be spectacular. In fact, in a curious way, he almost looked forward to it.

At the other end of the long table, a gray-haired man with hard eyes and a nose like a hatchet was smiling at him as if he could read his thoughts. "Welcome, Talon." He spoke quietly, but his voice had enough power to fill the hall. "No doubt you are wondering why you are here. Or, more specifically, why you are being allowed to see us without the benefit of . . . technological trickery. Let me assure you, it is not because we have decided to dispense with your services. Quite the opposite. You have proved yourself most efficient and reliable. Indispensable, even." Nods from around the table. "In tune with our objectives of global governance. All done in the name of world peace, of course. If all goes according to plan, there will be much for you to do in the future—a future I doubt you can even begin to imagine. But I promise you will find it extremely fulfilling."

Talon said nothing. He didn't even change expression

from the neutral mask he habitually wore. He didn't want them to think he'd cared about dying. And neither did he want them to see his excitement at the prospect of more killing. Though they were prepared to reveal themselves to him, he wasn't sure he was ready to return the favor quite yet.

He noticed a plump, bespectacled man to the speaker's left, who seemed to be in some agitation. "I think now it might be time to see what Mr. Talon has brought us, don't you think?" he said.

The gray-haired man nodded and the sightless footman was suddenly at Talon's elbow. Talon pulled a cotton bag from inside his jacket and handed it over. Holding it out in front of him as if it were made of glass, the footman slowly walked to the other end of the table and laid it down.

There was a moment's silence as all eyes fixed on the bag, and Talon took the time to scrutinize each member of the council. Nearest to him, to his left, an Asian man in a tailored gray suit sat ramrod-straight, his neutral gaze unfathomable. Next to him was a woman, fleshy, Germanic-looking, with her blond hair pulled tightly back from her forehead. She, too, seemed only mildly interested in what Talon had brought. But the next member of the council, a Hispanic man in an electric-blue jacket, with a neatly trimmed mustache, was leaning back and grinning. At the head of the table, the gray-haired man maintained his cold stare in Talon's direction.

Judging by outward appearances, nothing seemed to unite these seven starkly different people. And yet Talon knew from experience the strength of their common purpose. Something had brought them together. Something that required huge resources but also cast-iron secrecy. Something that was worth shedding a good deal of blood for. Something that reached back into the Biblical past and made evangelical Christians their mortal enemies.

As he turned it over in his mind, searching for the elusive link, Talon wondered if he should be looking inside himself. After all, they seemed to think he was almost one of them now. So what did he see when he looked inside his heart? He allowed himself a thin smile. The same as always. Just blood and horror and darkness. Talon was driven by a fascination with evil and ruthless acts. His only interest in the Seven's global plans was that they could provide him the means and unlimited resources to fulfill his twisted desires.

Then an angular woman in a striking emerald dress and with a shock of wild red hair put her hand on the moon-faced man's arm and hissed, "Let's see it. We've waited long enough."

Slowly Sir William Merton reached forward and pulled the foot-long piece of bronze from the bag. As he held it up to the light, Talon could see his plump hand was shaking. Then a curious thing happened. The air seemed to thicken, there was an audible crackle of electricity, and Merton's hand steadied. It must have been a trick of the light, Talon thought, but his eyes seemed to change color, from gray to a deep midnight blue. And when he spoke, the English accent was gone, replaced by something deeper and harder to place.

"Soon you shall again be one. As it was in the first days. And sacrifice shall be yours once more." Then he closed his eyes and let out a long breath, and he seemed to deflate, becoming physically smaller. When he opened his eyes, he looked once again like a portly English cleric.

Talon had had plenty of time to examine the tail of the Serpent, but he looked at it now with a new curiosity. If this was what one piece could do, what were they expecting to happen when they had all three?

Merton had taken off his glasses now, and was peering intently at the Serpent's belly. Around the table, a hush of expectation was building. "Yes, yes," Merton said at last. "Yes, I see. Beautiful, beautiful." He set the tail down and folded his hands over his belly with a satisfied smile.

"Well?" John Bartholomew said.

"Murphy is still working with Isis—Dr. McDonald?"

Bartholomew nodded. "They were last seen on their way to Riyadh."

"The Desert Kingdom. Of course, of course. Well, if she's her father's daughter, she should have no trouble deciphering Dakkuri's little puzzle. Perhaps Murphy even has the second piece in his hands as we speak," Merton chuckled.

General Li turned his head a fraction toward Merton. "Then, should we not be taking it out of his hands, *as we speak*?"

Merton seemed unfazed by the general's tone. "No indeed. I think not. She must have time to translate the next part of the riddle. As you know, the second piece leads to the third, and the third leads . . . well, I don't need to tell you what that leads to." The looks of ravenous expectation around the table confirmed he didn't.

"We must be patient. When Murphy has the last piece in his grasp"—he nodded in Talon's direction—"that is the time to strike. And perhaps then," he added with a leer, "Dr. McDonald and I might have an opportunity to reminisce a little."

# FIFTY-SEVEN

MURPHY GRIPPED THE iron ring in both hands, braced himself against the wall of the narrow alley, and heaved. He felt the beads of sweat begin to trickle down his forehead as his arms started to shake with the effort, but the stone slab remained firmly in place, exactly where it had been for what he estimated to be several centuries.

"You're sure this is our best way in?" he grunted.

"Definitely. This will take us directly into the main sewer."

"Assuming it still exists."

"Have a little faith, Murphy. Come on, are you sure you're really trying your absolute hardest?"

Out of the corner of his eye Murphy watched her as she leaned beside him in the moonlight, mouth pursed in concentration. If a bullwhip had been handy, he had no doubt she'd have used it on him. He was about to tell her to try lending a hand when he felt the great slab shift fractionally. He took a deep breath without relaxing his grip and gritted his teeth. The stone slab started to loosen, and he finally managed to drag it aside. Falling to his knees, he peered into the dark, airless hole.

"Give me the flashlight."

She handed it over and he leaned farther in.

"What can you see?"

The darkness sucked the beam greedily into the depths.

"Nothing much. The brickwork seems pretty much intact near the top, but farther down . . . I don't know. I guess there's only one way to find out."

She was beginning to look a little nervous now. "How do we . . . ?"

"When in doubt, just jump right in. That's my philosophy."

Her enthusiasm was definitely fading. "You can't be serious. It could be a hundred feet to the bottom."

He swung his legs into the hole and gripped the sides. "I seem to recall this was your idea. Come on." He saw the look of panic on her face and relented. "Okay, they built little handholds into the sides. Just take it slow and follow me."

It wasn't quite a hundred feet, and, remarkably, the ceramic rungs were mostly intact. Apart from the few times Isis lost her footing and a boot came thudding into Murphy's shoulder, they descended without incident. They landed at a junction of four tunnels, and Murphy gave Isis a moment to regain her composure.

"So, where to now?"

Her flashlight beam made her pale face float in the darkness like an apparition as she flipped through the pages of de Tocqueville. "Well, the likeliest spot is at the source of the original well. That's what Dakkuri would have been talking about."

Murphy grabbed a handful of dust and let it trickle through his fingers. "How do we find that? It's dry as a bone down here."

Her frown made her look even more ghostly. "We just need to figure out the direction of flow, then work backward."

Murphy crouched down and played the beam over the floor. "Okay, when the water finally dried up, it should have left some striations in the mud, and with a little luck they could have been preserved, like fossils." He shuffled forward a few steps and focused the beam on what looked like a long, flat stone. "Here. Unless I'm very much mistaken, we need to go this way."

She followed him into the dark, guided by his flashlight as it swept from side to side along the walls. Inching slowly through the narrow brick passage, drawing the dead, centuries-old air into her lungs, she was beginning to remember why she had never wanted to be an archaeologist. The clean, modern hotel somewhere above their heads seemed a hundred miles and a thousand years away.

She bumped into Murphy's back. "Dead end," he said.

They retraced their steps to the junction and examined the floor for more traces of the water's passage. Murphy pointed down another tunnel.

"Are you sure?" Isis asked.

"I don't know about you, but this is my first time in a medieval sewer. To be honest, I'm just following my nose."

"Sounds like a plan," Isis said. "In a sewer, I mean."

They started down the tunnel with less confidence now, hoping for a sign that would tell them they were on the right track. After several minutes of slow trudging, Murphy stopped. He pointed at the ground with his flashlight.

"What do you think that is?"

It didn't look like anything. Just a shadow. Then she gasped. "A footprint."

"Yeah, that's what I thought. And it looks new. I guess that means we're going the right way."

To Isis it didn't mean anything of the sort. It meant someone else was down there. Perhaps Omar had sent someone after them to get the rest of their money. She wanted desperately to retrace their steps as quickly as possible and get back to light and people and the twenty-first century. But she wasn't going to try it on her own. She gave her amulet a nervous tug, and hurried after Murphy's retreating back.

After a few minutes they saw another footprint. Then another. The footprints were coming in clusters now, blurring together, like the tracks of a herd of animals. She tugged Murphy's sleeve. "Should we really be following, do you think? There seem to be rather a lot of them."

"You got a better idea?"

"Apart from going back, you mean?"

Murphy turned to face her. "Look, this may be a

wild-goose chase, but it's the only wild-goose chase in town right now. At least we know we're not heading down another blind alley. These tracks must go *some-where*." He waved the flashlight in the direction they'd come, and as it passed across her face he saw raw fear etched on her elfin features. "Look, I'm not going to force you to carry on. Do you really want to go back?"

A wave of relief went through her, followed by a curious hollow feeling, as if in that instant her life had suddenly become meaningless. She took a deep breath, then turned him around and gave him a gentle push forward. "No, no. I just felt a little light-headed for a moment. The dust, probably. I'm fine now."

He grunted, and they set off again. She kept the beam of her flashlight pointed straight ahead, not wanting to see any more traces of their invisible companions.

When they came to another junction, with tunnels branching off to the left and right, she kept her eyes closed and concentrated on keeping her breathing steady.

"It's going to get narrower," Murphy said over his shoulder. "You okay?"

"I'm not claustrophobic, you know," she said with as much indignation as she could summon. It was true, she'd never been frightened of confined spaces. Once, when Miss McTavish had locked her in a storage cupboard for a whole afternoon, she'd felt nothing but a blessed sense of relief to be out of the clutches of her schoolmates for a few hours and able to let her mind wander free among the gods and creatures of mythology who were already thronging her imagination.

But this was different. Not only were they in a catacomb of dark and increasingly airless tunnels, they were not alone. According to Omar, no one had been down here for generations. So whom did the footprints belong to? Her anxiety was heightened by Murphy's own lack of concern. Clearly his philosophy really was simply to charge blindly forward, trusting some higher power would keep him from falling down a deep, dark hole. Not to mention her.

She had steeled herself for the plunge into the next tunnel, but Murphy was still rooted to the spot. "Do you hear something?"

She cocked her head to one side. "Like what?"

"I don't know. Wind, maybe?"

She held a hand in front of her face and shook her head. "Not a breath. No, it sounds like ... water."

He nodded. "And the footprints go in the same direction. Look."

He set off down the left-hand tunnel, crouching so he didn't bump his head against the roof. Isis clung to his arm, no longer caring what he thought. As they went farther, the rushing sound got louder, until she was sure she could actually smell the water above the scent of dust and decay.

When they started to hear another sound, they stopped instinctively. This time they both knew what it was. It came in waves, louder, then fainter, then louder again. Isis put a trembling hand to her amulet and waited for Murphy to say something.

"Can you make out what language that is? It doesn't sound like Arabic."

She forced herself to listen. It had an odd singsong quality, a definite rhythm, as if they were chanting. "I ...

I don't know. There's a hint of Aramaic, perhaps. It could be my imagination. What are we going to do?"

"We're going to be careful," Murphy said, pulling her forward.

As she stumbled after him, a crazy mix of thoughts swirled around in her head. Had she locked her filing cabinet, the one where she kept her private diary? Had she remembered to return her copy of Gilroy's commentary on the *Epic of Gilgamesh* to Professor Hitashi? Had she removed *all* the mousetraps Fiona had insisted on putting down in her office?

With a start she realized she wasn't expecting to return to Washington. She had convinced herself she was going to die. Well, if she had to go now, at least she wasn't leaving any family behind. A thought that led her to speculate on who would attend her funeral. Not many, she supposed. But of course they'd never find her body. So there wouldn't be a funeral. She would just be missing, forever. Like a lost soul ...

Murphy was touching her on the shoulder and pointing up ahead. There was a distinct rushing sound like water moving swiftly over stone, and the chanting now sounded ominously close. And there was light, too, a ghostly flickering against the tunnel walls.

They inched forward, and Isis felt her toe connect with something hard. The floor of the tunnel was littered with bricks. She looked up and saw a ragged hole in the tunnel wall. Her legs carried her toward it, independent of her will. She no longer felt fear. Her mind seemed to have shut down, just a primitive core remaining—enough to keep her body moving. The last thought she had was that this was what it must feel like to be a zombie.

Murphy was shaking her, jolting her back into full consciousness. In the uncertain light, he was looking at her with a stern expression, a finger to his lips. She nodded and slowly turned her head to look through the hole in the tunnel wall. Her eyes seemed to have closed of their own accord, and she forced them open.

The skulls were the first thing she saw. There were seven of them arranged in a rough semicircle like Halloween pumpkins, eye sockets ablaze with an oily light that spilled greedily over the body arranged on the dirt floor. The body was stiff, but she was clearly a girl who could not have been older than ten. A ragged cotton blanket covered most of her body, and her narrow face looked waxy, but you could see hints of the beauty she would grow to be.

If she wasn't already dead, that is.

The three men were naked to the waist, swaying back and forth, propelled by the rhythmic chanting that filled the shadowy space. Isis gasped as she saw the long butcher's knife each clutched in his lap, and Murphy clapped a hand over her mouth.

She took a deep breath and he slowly took his hand away, then pointed beyond the skulls.

On the end of a pole stuck in the dirt was a thick S-shape of gleaming metal.

*The middle section of the Brazen Serpent!*

As she realized what it was, she felt herself being sucked down through the centuries into a world of primitive darkness. It was like being in Miss McTavish's cupboard, but this time with real gods and demons and no hope of ever being let out. A whimper rose in her throat and she barely managed to choke it off.

Then Murphy was pulling her back into the tunnel and she felt her whole body relax. They were going back. They were going to survive.

# FIFTY-EIGHT

MURPHY GRIPPED ISIS by the shoulders and tried to gauge her expression. In the gloom of the tunnel all he could see were her eyes, and they seemed to be pleading silently. "Can you do it?" he asked.

A whisper escaped her throat. Was that a yes? He gripped harder, almost shaking her, and she nodded. That would have to do. There was no time to go through it with her again. He crawled back to the hole in the wall and she watched as he waited for his moment, then slid into the flickering shadows.

Shuffling after him, she crouched at the entrance, a hand clamped to her mouth to stop herself from crying. She could hardly bear to watch him. But she couldn't tear her eyes away. If she lost sight of him she'd be truly alone. She gripped the flashlight as a drowning man might clutch a life preserver.

Murphy chanced a glance back in her direction as he belly-crawled his way through the bricks and loose rocks on the other side of the tunnel wall. He could feel her eyes on him, but otherwise she was just another shadow blending into the dark.

He was confident the soft dust covering the floor would muffle his approach, but when his knee struck a brick and sent it skittering into the dark, his whole body tensed. He buried his face in the dirt, not daring to look up, hardly daring to breathe. But the chanting of the three executioners maintained its dirgelike rhythm. They seemed to be in some sort of trance, maybe high on something, but he knew at some point the chanting would stop and those vicious-looking knives would come into play.

He blamed himself for leaving his competition bow back at the hotel. Who knew he'd find himself interrupting a human sacrifice in a medieval sewer, but by now he should have learned to expect the unexpected. He flashed back to the initial phone call with Methusaleh. If he'd known where it would lead, would he have told the old man what he could do with his artifact, Daniel or no Daniel? The killings, the bombing at the church, Laura—it all seemed to have started somehow with that phone call. But he knew there was no point thinking about it. He was sure now that God had set him on a certain path and there was nothing he could do but follow it to the end.

Whatever the cost.

The image of the girl lying just moments from being a human sacrifice came back to him, his courage rising, and he wondered if Isis would be able to follow through.

She'd seemed taut as a bowstring when he'd first met her. Now, having been catapulted out of her academic cocoon, he was afraid she was on the edge of a total emotional collapse.

He prayed her nerve would hold.

He started to move again, keeping as far away from the three swaying bodies as he could. Was it his imagination, or was the rushing sound getting louder? He didn't want to end up as a bonus sacrificial victim, but he didn't want to disappear into an underground stream either. If they turned their heads to the right, he was in their line of sight now. He couldn't rely on their drugged-up state to keep them oblivious of his presence much longer. He turned his wrist, and the luminous dial of his watch told him there was another minute to wait. Too long. He was suddenly convinced the three executioners would finish their prayers any second and then it would be too late.

*Keep going, fellas. Just a few more verses.* He concentrated on the haunting sound and felt his focus slipping. He willed the hands of his watch to move faster. Then, just as his head began to throb and his grip on the real world began to loosen, he heard a clatter of dust and rocks and craned his neck to look behind him.

What he saw made his heart jam in his throat.

Framed in the hole in the tunnel wall where he had last seen Isis, a ghastly apparition now appeared, as if the heathen chanting had summoned up a demoness. Lit from below by the flashlight, her corpse-white face seemed to be emitting an unnatural glow of its own as it floated unsupported in the darkness.

For a crazy moment he wasn't sure if it really was

Isis, then reality took hold again and he sprang forward. As he'd hoped, the three men were now on their feet, gesturing toward Isis in horrified silence. They didn't seem to notice as he stumbled past them toward the pole and the glowing Serpent, but who knew how long they'd buy Isis's circus act? He bent down to grasp the shoulder of the unconscious girl.

She was not restrained in any way and she was as stiff as a stone angel. *Let's hope she's not already playing that role*, Murphy thought. If she was still alive, then they must have drugged her into this unconscious state, and it could be a mistake to try to bring her awake suddenly, but whatever the consequences, Murphy figured they would be better than being slaughtered by the Serpent worshipers.

After two firm shakes of her shoulders, the girl's eyes shot open and she started to scream at the sight of Murphy. He was counting on Isis keeping the men completely distracted, but to be certain he covered her mouth with one hand while he put his other to his own to try to mime *quiet*. The girl's eyes were nearly popping out of her head with fear, with no sign of any drug aftereffects, but she managed to nod that she understood Murphy's gesture for silence.

He rose and turned toward the pole holding the Serpent's body. Its fiery glow in the reflection of the blazing torches was mesmerizing. He reached up and with trembling fingers began untying the hemp cords securing the bronze segment to the pole. Murphy held it in his hands and marveled at the weight of it, which seemed to perfectly match the feel of the tail.

His study was cut short abruptly as a shout arose behind him from the three sacrificers. Their attention had been torn from Isis by the sight of the girl running toward the hole in the wall. They stopped gesturing toward the escaping sacrifice when one of them spied Murphy holding their icon. They dropped their interest in either female and turned toward him with the full fury of their spoiled evening about to explode upon him.

They advanced on Murphy, grunting with rage, knife blades raised, and showing none of the signs of their trancelike sluggishness of a moment before.

Murphy was out of ideas. He couldn't run. That would leave Isis at their mercy. And there was no way he could take on three knife-wielding maniacs and hope to win. He had done his best; there was nothing else he could do. He hoped Isis would have the presence of mind to run back the way they'd come while they were butchering him.

He tried to suppress his fear and began to pray. In a few minutes he would be seeing Laura again.

He was shaken out of his reverie as the chanting started again. But it was different now. Higher-pitched. A woman's voice. He looked over the shoulders of his attackers and realized it was Isis. She was pointing an imperious hand in his direction and pouring out a stream of gibberish in a strangely commanding voice. At least it sounded like gibberish to him. The three men had stopped in their tracks and were looking back in her direction, mouths gaping, as if they couldn't believe what they were hearing.

While their attention was diverted, Murphy made his move, but as he rushed past them a hand lashed out and he felt a stabbing pain in his side. He fell to one knee, expecting the next blow to slice through his throat. Then a sound halfway between a scream and a growl cut through the darkness and he heard the three men fall to the ground.

Isis was revving it up now, barking furiously and waving her thin arms in wide circles. Whatever she was saying, they seemed to have gotten the message. Throwing caution to the wind, Murphy scrambled past her and into the tunnel. He grabbed her arm and she turned a furious look on him as if she were outraged that a mere mortal had dared to manhandle a goddess.

"Come on, goddess, snap out of it," he whispered. "We've got to get out of here before your fan club realizes they've been had."

Isis laughed contemptuously but allowed him to steer her back the way they'd come. "I don't think they'll be going anywhere for a while. Not unless they want to end up as food for the scorpion men."

"I thought you didn't speak their lingo," Murphy said as he hustled her down the tunnel.

"It came to me eventually. A dialect of Terammasic. Dead for a thousand years supposedly."

"And you just happen to speak it?"

"I learned it at the university. Just for fun. It's such an oddity, I thought somebody ought to keep it alive."

"And what were you yelling at them? It got their attention all right."

They'd passed the fork and were rapidly approaching the junction where they'd entered the tunnels. Murphy couldn't hear any signs of pursuit.

"I just reminded them they owed their miserable existences to the creation goddess, and if they touched my familiar dog-spirit they'd be sorry."

Murphy boosted her onto the first rung. "Your dog-spirit? That's the best you could think of for me was your dog-spirit?"

"I was going to call you my snake-spirit, but I didn't think you look believably evil."

"Thanks, I think."

"Murphy, I can go back and tell them you're a Biblical archaeologist if you'd prefer."

"On second thought, dog-spirit is just fine," Murphy grunted.

She slithered over the top and took the belly of the Serpent from him as he scrambled after her. Together they heaved the stone slab back into place and sat back against the wall, the bizarre world they had just left now banished like a terrifying dream.

"What do you think happened to that poor girl?" Isis said after a while.

Murphy held up a scrap of cloth. "It looks like she made it out. This is a bit of the dress she was wearing that was caught on a jagged edge of the handholds." He stared at Isis. With her eyes closed, her face still looked ghostly in the moonlight. "Nice work down there, Dr. McDonald. Quite a cabaret act you pulled off."

She bolted to her feet and started brushing the dust off her pants. "It was nothing. My father always said I was a reincarnation of some goddess or other. I guess it comes naturally to me." She seemed embarrassed now, as if Murphy had seen her naked and they could never just be friends again in the same way as before. "Come on, let's get back to the hotel," she said. "I don't know about you, but I could do with a large glass of scotch."

Murphy didn't reply, and Isis wondered if he disapproved. She was about to tell him that she would drink a whole bottle if she felt like it, thank you very much, after what he'd put her through, when she noticed that his eyes were closed. Then, as she watched, he slid slowly down the wall until his head was resting in the dirt.

It was only then that she noticed the blood.

# FIFTY-NINE

"MISS KOVACS IS here, sir."

Shane Barrington had been looking forward to her arrival at his office. "Send her in. And I do not wish to be disturbed."

The woman who stood in the doorway seemed subtly different from the Stephanie Kovacs who'd first walked into his office a month earlier. She still dressed in that provocative-but-don't-mess-with-me way, stilettos and a short skirt offset by her buttoned-up jacket and black turtleneck, and her carefully disordered hair and subtly applied makeup reinforced the image of an attractive woman who had more important things to do than look good. Her stride was still confident, assertive, stopping just short of aggressive as she walked to the single chair in front of his desk and sat down.

But her eyes told him she had undergone a dramatic

change since they had last met. Instead of shining with that morally superior glow her viewers had come to love, they were dull and vacant, as if something behind them had died. They were the eyes of someone who'd sold her soul.

"Stephanie. Thanks for dropping by. I wanted to thank you personally for the work you've been doing."

She looked at him warily. "I'm sorry the church-bombing story didn't pan out. The FBI were hot for it at first, but now they've gotten all cautious. And Dean Fallworth is just a blowhard. Nothing he gave me was enough to nail Murphy the way you wanted. Believe me, I—"

Barrington waved a hand dismissively. "It's okay, Stephanie. You did well. We just wanted to free up some of Professor Murphy's time, plant some seeds in the public's mind. You'll be uncovering more revelations about our evangelical friends in time."

Stephanie regarded him with the weary indifference of someone who's already lost the most important thing she has. "You said 'we.' I've been wondering who's really behind all this. You don't strike me as the type who gets hot under the collar about religion, Mr. Barrington."

He smiled. "Ever the fearless investigative reporter. I guess that bloodhound's nose of yours never stops sniffing. Even when I've got you chained and muzzled," he added, enjoying the sudden blush that colored her cheeks.

He got up and went to a smoked-glass cabinet. "Let me get you a drink."

She shook her head. "Not while I'm working."

He laughed. "Come on." He took out a dark bottle

and began untwisting the wire holding the cork in place. "A glass of champagne."

"Champagne? Are we celebrating something?"

"I hope so, Stephanie. I very much hope so."

He eased the cork into a napkin with a muffled pop and poured two glasses. She accepted hers expressionlessly.

"So what's the toast?"

He raised his glass toward her with a dark smile. "To marketplace domination, of course."

They clinked glasses. "I'll always drink to that," she said wryly.

He put his glass down and leaned against the desk. She was uncomfortably aware of his closeness.

"It could soon be a reality, Stephanie. Barrington Communications is the most powerful communications business on the planet, as you know. But that's just the beginning. Soon there could be so much more."

She looked at him skeptically. "What are you going to do, run for president?"

"I'm talking about *real* power, Stephanie. The sort you can only dream about."

She took a sip of her champagne. "Well, here's to you, Mr. Barrington. But I don't understand what this has got to do with me."

"Please, call me Shane." He stood and walked to the window. "Power and wealth can bring you many things, Stephanie. But I'll be honest, it can be lonely at the top. There have been women, of course, since my divorce, but when you have as much money as I do, it's hard to find someone you can really trust. Someone you can really

share with. Do you understand what I'm talking
about?"

She was beginning to think she understood completely. He'd bought her soul, and now he wanted the
rest of her. Her first instinct was to panic, but then she
started to think about it. Maybe it wouldn't be such a
bad deal. If she was going to sell out, she might as well
get the best price. Barrington seemed to think he was
going to be king of the world. She could do worse than
be his queen.

She walked over to him and together they looked
down over the city. After a while an image from her recent bout of Bible study came into her mind. Satan and
Jesus on the mountaintop. Hadn't he offered Him the
kingdoms of the world if He would just bow down and
worship him?

She leaned her head on Barrington's shoulder. Well,
she was smarter than that. Mr. Barrington . . . Shane . . .
wouldn't even have to ask her twice.

# SIXTY

ISIS WATCHED DR. AZIZ disappear into the elevator, bulging black bag tucked under his arm, and closed the door behind her. At the last count she spoke a dozen varieties of Arabic as well as another ten distinct Near and Middle Eastern languages, adding up to who knew how many millions of words. But she was beginning to realize that only one really mattered.

*Baksheesh.*

For a few dollars, the young man at the front desk had been happy to call Dr. Aziz, assuring them he was "very discreet." And the doctor himself, for another reasonable consideration, had been delighted to patch Murphy up. As she ushered him out, he'd given Isis an old roué's gold-toothed grin. "No police, no police!" he said, putting a finger to his lips.

Whether she could trust either of them not to play

both ends of the street and bring the cops running, she didn't know. If it came to it, she and Murphy hadn't done anything illegal, had they? As far as she knew, they hadn't killed anybody, and as for taking the belly of the Serpent, it was hard to say whom it really belonged to. She was beginning to think Hezekiah had had the right idea: It would be better if no one had it.

She leaned back against the door, her body suddenly heavy. "You'll live, apparently. He's given me some nasty-looking painkillers which I think are probably for horses, but seeing as you're stubborn as a mule... Murphy?"

His eyes were closed and he looked very pale, but she thought she could see the slow rise and fall of his breathing. She approached the bed and felt an impulse to touch him. *Just to make sure he's really alive,* she told herself.

His skin was cool but she could definitely feel the blood pulsing just above his collarbone. "Good night, Murphy," she whispered. "Pleasant dreams."

Returning to her own room, she lay on the bed and closed her eyes for a few minutes, letting the confusing rush of emotions swirl around her head. Eventually she took a long breath, blew it out slowly, and sat upright. Work. That was the only way to regain her equilibrium.

She poured herself a glass of Famous Grouse, arranged a dozen sharpened pencils next to a stack of yellow legal pads, then placed the belly of the Serpent in the pool of light cast by the desk lamp. It was going to be a long night.

She awoke to the sound of glass breaking. Yellow pages blew around the room in gusts as the wind poured in through the open window. The bedclothes had been blown aside, leaving her shivering. The lamp lay on the floor, flickering on and off with the fizz of frayed circuits.

Someone was hammering on the door and she instinctively reached down to cover herself. Her hand felt the soft cotton of her nightgown. Confused, she reached for the bedside light.

Everything was in its place. The lamp was on the desk. The pages in a neat pile, with the Serpent on top. The window was closed. Apart from her ragged breathing, all was silent.

Laughing with relief, she went to the desk and read what she'd written on the top sheet. At least she hadn't dreamed that. She read it through one more time, trying to fix it in her mind, then climbed between the sheets. She was asleep before she could recite it to herself.

The next morning Murphy showed no signs of his ordeal. As she joined him at the only occupied table in the cavernous restaurant, he was happily feasting on rolls and coffee.

"You seem very chipper," she said.

He winked. "Sleep of the just."

"Well, take it easy. Dr. Aziz said you should stay in bed for a couple of days at least."

Murphy snorted. "He was just hustling you for a few more bucks, making it look like it was life-and-death. It's just a scratch. Anyhow, we have work to do."

She reached into her bag with a look of triumph. "Relax. All done."

He took the wrinkled piece of paper and read it

through. "I'm beginning to think your father was right about you. Didn't you sleep at all?"

She studied the tablecloth. "It didn't take long."

"And you're sure you've got it right?"

She tried to snatch the sheet of paper back, but he whisked it out of reach. "Just kidding." He read it through again. "*In the land of the flood, it rests with a queen.* 'The land of the flood.' That could be the Biblical Flood."

She nodded. "Plenty of references to that in Babylonian literature. The question is, where exactly is it?"

"A lot of people think the Ark came to rest on Mount Ararat. Maybe Anatolia, then. Any queens we know of in that neighborhood?"

"Not in the right time frame. Too far north."

"Okay, maybe he didn't mean *the* Flood, just a place where it floods regularly."

She poured herself a cup of tea and stirred in some milk. "Like where?"

"How about Egypt? The Nile floods every year like clockwork. Without it there would have been no Egyptian civilization. No Sphinx, no pyramids."

"Makes sense. Read the next bit."

"*Entombed by stone, it floats in the air.*" Murphy shook his head. "Beats me."

She put down her cup. "Hold on. If you're right and Dakkuri's talking about Egypt, then entombed by stone, resting with a queen, that must mean it's in a pyramid, right?"

"Right."

"Come on, you're the archaeologist. How many pyramids are there?"

"More than you'd think."

"But this is no ordinary pyramid."

He slapped his hand on the table and a waiter scurried out of the kitchen to see what was wrong. Isis waved him back with a frown.

"Ever heard of the Pyramid of the Winds?"

"Can't say that I have. Are you sure you haven't just made it up?"

He grinned. "It exists all right. On the Giza plateau just west of Cairo, all by its lonesome. Not close enough to the big three—Khufu, Khafre, and Menkure—to get onto the postcards, so no one pays it much attention."

"So how come the fancy name?"

"According to legend, there's supposed to be some sort of updraft in the center of the pyramid, so powerful it could keep a man suspended above the ground forever."

"A man...or the head of a bronze Serpent," she said.

"Why not. If I remember correctly, it's also the last resting place of Queen Hephrat the Second."

"Bingo! *Entombed by stone but floating in air.* So what do we do now?"

"We take a look inside, of course. Come on."

Back in Murphy's room, she watched over his shoulder as he fired up his laptop and logged into a database in the Preston University mainframe. After a few seconds, a complex diagrammatic of the Pyramid of the Winds unfolded across the computer screen, revealing the interior in three dimensions.

Isis pointed at the series of square holes ringing the base of the pyramid. "What are those?"

"Air shafts. Air is drawn into the great chamber—that's the big empty space at the center of the pyramid, above Hephrat's burial chamber—and it comes out here, these smaller holes two-thirds of the way up."

"That's very impressive. Trust the ancient Egyptians to invent air-conditioning three thousand years before the fact."

"Only for royalty," Murphy said. "And even they had to be dead first. Maybe that kind of logic explains why Egyptian civilization didn't last."

Isis gave him a wry smile. "So where does the legend about things floating in midair come from?"

"I barely remember my high school physics, but here's my theory. The air is drawn in through the shafts at the bottom. Inside the great chamber it heats up, rises, and gets compressed as the pyramid narrows. That increases its velocity and sends it rushing out of the shafts at the top, at the same time sucking in more air from below. Kind of an endless cycle."

"So you think the head of the Serpent is going to be floating in midair in the great chamber?"

"I doubt that. My bet is it's either in the burial chamber or more likely one of the air shafts."

Isis studied the screen with a skeptical expression. "You know I said I wasn't claustrophobic, but those air shafts look rather narrow to me. How are we going to . . . ?"

Murphy tapped some more keys and the Pyramid of the Winds disappeared. In its place a rotating graphic of what looked like some kind of high-tech vacuum cleaner filled the screen.

"Behold the Pyramid Crawler. A remote-controlled robot specifically designed for navigating the air shafts of pyramids."

"You're joking. Somebody actually makes these things?"

"Sure. I don't know if it's the iRobot Corporation's biggest seller, but right now it's just what we need. What color paintwork do you want? I think the choices are dark gray or a slightly darker gray."

Isis was reading the product specifications: a computer-controlled, quadra-tracked vehicle with two sets of tank treads arranged one on top of the other, so one set was pushed against the floor of the shaft and the other against the ceiling, providing stone-gripping traction. An array of sensors, lights, and miniature TV cameras completed the picture.

"Let's say you can get hold of one of these things. I still don't see how we're going to get access to the pyramid. I know you're not a stickler for red tape, but you can't just hire a camel or two and start digging, you know."

He looked offended. "You think I don't have connections? Ever heard of Dr. Boutrous Hawass, the director of the pyramids? Well, my best buddy at grad school was a man called Jassim Amram. Now he's a professor of archaeology at the American University in Cairo and just happens to be Hawass's right-hand guy. If I know Jassim, he's already got one of these Pyramid Crawlers trained to mix a decent martini and bring it to him in front of the TV."

"All right," Isis said, opening the door. "You fix things up with your friend Professor Amram and I'll track down our pilot and tell him to get us ready to depart for Cairo."

Murphy had closed the laptop and was already throwing clothes into his backpack. "Sounds good."

The phone rang. It was a secretary's voice. "Oh, thank God, Dr. McDonald. Please hold for Chairman Compton of the Parchments of Freedom Foundation."

"Isis." Harvey Compton sounded rather tense, Isis thought. He was probably worried that she had scuffed up the interior of his airplane. She rushed to assure him he was getting his money's worth. "Harvey, we've got the second piece and have our eyes set on the head of the Serpent."

"Yes, well, never mind that. I've been trying to reach you. Two people have been murdered here and the tail of the Serpent has been stolen. Isis, you and Professor Murphy must abandon your trip and come home immediately."

# SIXTY-ONE

STRANGE. STRANGE AND horrible. The murders of the two guards had occurred literally a world away, yet, because they were the real lives of men she had worked with, she was devastated.

"Isis, I'm sorry I got you and the foundation into this." Murphy knew it was no consolation. "Chairman Compton is right, of course, we must head back."

Isis sat staring at the wall. "Murphy, we're not going back. Not now. Especially not now. Whoever, whatever force is trying to take over the Serpent must be stopped."

"Isis, you're in shock. You are in greater danger than we even knew here in Tar-Qasir, and that was no kindergarten outing. Pack up."

"No, Murphy. We're staying the course. Chairman Compton is too far away to shut us down now. Besides, there is something I haven't told you about the scene at the foundation."

"What?"

"Murphy, whoever took the Serpent's tail was pretty brazen himself. He took the time to leave what could only be a taunting message for you. He carved the symbol of a snake into the metal shelf on which the tail had been kept. It was a snake broken into three pieces."

Murphy walked to the window. After a few moments' reflection, he turned and said, "Well, whoever came after the Serpent's tail is well aware of our quest. Of the few people whom we have confided in about the details of what we're seeking, none of them are murderers or thieves."

"At least up to now, you mean. There's obviously something about this Serpent that over the centuries has made lots of people do lots of strange things."

"Yes, you would have to think that it's not some rival archaeologist who would murder and steal for that tail. So, we can assume that whoever is onto us is working the decidedly dark side of the street."

Isis had a worried look in her eyes as she reached for Murphy's hand before she added the final news. "Murphy, there's something else I have to tell you about the scene at the foundation. Remember what you told me about the cross necklace you gave Laura, and how someone had broken it at the funeral when you took your last look into her casket? Well, carved right next to the snake on the PFF shelf, the same maniac carved a cross broken into three pieces."

Murphy sat in shocked silence. Then he walked over to the wall and banged his fist as hard as he could three times. "Worst suspicions confirmed. It's all starting to make a bizarre kind of sense. All of the signs are pointing to one mysterious connecting element to so many of the events we've been going through. The stranger coming to Preston and teaming up with Chuck Nelson for trouble, the bombing at the church, the theft of the tail—" His voice cracked as he thought about the final link.

Isis finished the thought. "The fact that Laura wasn't killed as a result of some debris falling on her. That she was definitely murdered."

"Isis, this is beyond archaeology, or even faith and validating the Bible now. It's personal. We're going to find the head of that Serpent if it kills us. And by keeping up our search, it's only a matter of time before we confront this evil stranger face-to-face."

# SIXTY-TWO

"SO AFTER WE find the head of the Serpent, what then?"

Murphy was concentrating on the buzzing, dusty, glaring chaos that was Cairo as their taxi inched its way laboriously through the cars, bicycles, pedestrians, and occasional ox thronging the narrow streets. The question caught him off guard.

"I mean," Isis continued, "it's not as if you can put it back together. The man who broke into the foundation has got the tail now. I mean, I understand about authenticating the Biblical account. You could still do that with two pieces. But that's not why we're here, is it?"

She'd caught a little bit of sun since they'd been in the Middle East, and it suited her. She looked more confident, less like a creature of the dark ready to scurry back into her hole at the foundation at the slightest sign the outside world was getting too close. But he wasn't sure he wanted to deal with her new assertiveness just then.

"Proving the Bible is true is what I do. I can't think of anything more important."

She considered him skeptically, then reached for the door handle as the driver swerved to avoid an old man on a swaying bicycle. Regaining her equilibrium, she said, "No? What about prophecy? Biblical prophecy."

"That's part of it. If we can demonstrate that the Old Testament prophets were writing at the time they say they were, then that proves they were genuine."

"I don't follow."

Reluctantly, he turned his gaze away from the buzzing confusion of the streets. "Some of what they predicted has happened. Skeptics say that's because they were actually writing after the event, so they were looking backward, not forward. If we can show they were writing at the time they claimed, then that proves they really could see history in advance."

"And why is that so important?"

"Because of the predictions that *haven't* come true yet. So people can be sure they *will* happen."

She nodded as if he'd confirmed something she already knew. "Then tell me about the part of the Book of Daniel that hasn't come true yet."

"Daniel? I thought you were more interested in Marduk and Ereshkigal and all that crowd."

She looked at him with an intensity he hadn't seen before, and he realized he was being too harsh with her.

For the first time, he noticed she wasn't wearing her amulet.

"I'm sorry. Yes, I'll tell you about Daniel if you like. But why now?"

"You told me your search for the Brazen Serpent began with a mysterious message about Daniel. I think that's what this is all about. That's what we're risking our lives for. So I thought I might as well find out what I'm getting into."

She was trying for a flippant tone, but he didn't quite buy it.

"All right. Through Daniel, God was telling Nebuchadnezzar that throughout history there would be four world empires: his own, the Babylonian, represented by the Golden Head of his statue; then the empire of the Medes and Persians; then the Greeks; and finally the Romans. Each one gets progressively weaker, until with the Romans it actually splits in half—like the two legs of the statue."

"Rome and Byzantium."

"Right. So, four world empires. Just four. No one since the Romans—not Napoleon, not Hitler—has managed to set up a fifth."

She looked puzzled. "So what's the prediction that hasn't come true yet?"

"There's one part of Nebuchadnezzar's statue left. The ten toes. Prophecy experts believe the toes—made of clay and iron—represent an unstable form of government that will take over from today's nation-states in the near future. Probably ten kings or rulers of some kind, paving the way for the Antichrist."

She looked away, taking a moment to try to absorb what he was saying. They were cruising comfortably now as they took the Corniche al-Nil, the main thoroughfare that paralleled the east bank of the Nile, and the opulent mansions of the embassy district streamed past the window in a stately procession.

"And you think the secret, the mystery, Dakkuri was talking about might have something to do with that?"

He shrugged. "My gut tells me it has something to do with Daniel's predictions, yes. Something was nagging away at the back of my mind, and it took me a while to figure out what it was. The word you just used: *mystery*. In the Book of Revelation, that means Babylon. Dakkuri said the mystery would return."

"I don't understand. Babylon's going to return?"

He nodded. "The power of Babylon, yes. When the Antichrist sets up his one-world government."

She ran her hands through her hair. "Now you've lost me. Let's go back to the Serpent for a moment. If what we saw in the sewers was anything to go by, people have been worshiping it—or at least the middle piece of it—in secret for years, possibly thousands of years. Heaven knows how many innocents have been sacrificed along the way."

"I know. It's incredible. Horrifying."

"But has this cult got anything to do with what you were talking about—the return of Babylon?"

He scratched his jaw. "Let's just say there's a strong underlying connection. The forces of darkness. Evil. In the end it's all the same."

"And you and I are heading straight into the jaws of the dragon, aren't we?"

He struggled for something to say, some way of reassuring her, but at that moment the taxi pulled up at the main building of the American University, and a tall, white-suited man with a broad, brilliant smile was opening the door, ushering them into the blast-furnace heat.

"Murphy, you old dog! Welcome back to Cairo." Ten minutes later Jassim was sitting back in an uncomfortable-looking steel-backed chair that somehow seemed to perfectly accommodate his gangly frame. He sipped appreciatively from his martini glass.

"You're sure you won't?"

"Are you kidding? I know what you put in that stuff. The alcohol is the least of it."

Jassim laughed his rich, mellifluous laugh. "Same old Murphy."

"Same old Jassim." Murphy raised his glass of lemonade.

"Yes, sadly, I am a very bad Muslim."

"I don't know about that, but you're still a very good man in my book. Your letter after Laura died really helped."

Jassim's ebullient expression sobered. "I'm sure it didn't, but I had to tell you what was in my heart."

They drank in silence for a while, lost in memories of Laura.

Eventually Jassim said, "Dr. McDonald is okay? She was very pleasant, but perhaps a little distracted." Isis had made her excuses and gone straight to the lodging Jassim had arranged for them both in the campus complex for visiting professors and their families.

"She's got a lot on her mind," Murphy said.

Jassim didn't pursue it. "Well, I hope she is fit and well tomorrow. We have a big day ahead of us." He shifted in his chair, beaming like a kid on Christmas Eve.

"So, Professor Hawass went for it?"

"In a big way. When they X-rayed the tomb of Queen Hephrat back in the sixties, it was totally empty. The tomb robbers had beaten us once again."

"By a couple of thousand years, probably," said Murphy.

Jassim laughed. "All that was left was a deep, dark, empty hole at the bottom of the pyramid. So the notion that there is something still in there, something the robbers may have missed—something a Chaldean priest from the time of Nebuchadnezzar may have hidden there—the head of Moses' Brazen Serpent, no less! That would be quite an amazing story. Professor Hawass was delighted to put all of our humble resources at your service."

"Could we start by storing the middle section of the Serpent here? Given what happened at Washington, I would understand if you said no."

Jassim waved his hand. "We do not scare easily here. We will guard the piece with honor and discretion."

Murphy clapped his old friend on the shoulder. "Great. That's a relief. So you got a Pyramid Crawler for me?"

"Oh, yes. And I am very much looking forward to seeing it in action. The tomb robbers sometimes used young children or even midgets to get into these narrow passages." He shook his head. "Sadly, those unfortunates were often unable to get out again. Hopefully with the Pyramid Crawler we will be able to penetrate our pyramid's deepest secrets without any loss of life!"

"I hope so, Jassim, old friend," said Murphy, his face darkening. "I very much hope so."

# SIXTY-THREE

WHEN THEY MET up early the next morning, ready to drive out to the pyramid in Jassim's equipment-laden Land Rover, Murphy got a sense that Isis had settled something in her mind. She didn't say much, but the measured, businesslike way she went about checking that they had everything they needed suggested an inner calm he had never seen in her.

As they took the Rodah Island bridge across the Nile and into the Shar'a al-Haram, running straight through the Giza district to the desert's edge, he wondered why he didn't feel the same way. After a few fretful hours tossing and turning in the grip of feverish dreams, he had given up on sleep and had spent the rest of the night pacing the garden at the back of their lodging.

Murphy had been hoping for something—a sign, perhaps, that he was doing the right thing, that it was part of God's plan for him to be there. But dawn had broken leaving him unrested and no wiser than before.

He looked at the Sphinx-like smile on Isis's face as she listened to Jassim's ridiculous stories of mummies' curses and haunted scarabs, and wondered if God had chosen to give her the sign, not him. Perhaps, like the prodigal son, she was the one God had favored. Not that he begrudged her. As long as *someone* knew they were on the right road.

Pyramid Road. He remembered that's what they called the approach to the desert. And when he had first driven along it in an old tin can of a Citroën with Laura, there had still been traces of the lush acacia, tamarind, and eucalyptus groves that had now totally disappeared beneath a tidal wave of urban sprawl.

As the concrete apartment buildings finally gave way and the three Giza pyramids appeared on the horizon, bringing a gasp of amazement from Isis and an accompanying chuckle from Jassim, Murphy wondered if the remarkable juxtaposition of ancient and modern was perhaps the sign he had been waiting for.

Here in Cairo, people rushed headlong into the future while the monuments of mankind's deepest past looked on, unchanging, as if to say, *If you want to know what really lies ahead, look behind you.*

The road climbed to the top of the square-mile plateau and curved around the Sphinx, with its thousand-year stare, and then the three awesome pyramids were there before them, housing respectively a royal father, son, and grandson. Clustered around the Big Three, the much smaller pyramids of queens and princesses only added to the sense of majestic scale. As the Land Rover continued on, circling to the northeastern edge of the plateau, the great pyramids started to shrink into the distance again. Isis craned her neck, trying to fix every fleeting detail of the extraordinary panorama in her mind, until Jassim tapped her on the shoulder and pointed dead ahead.

Standing aloof in this empty corner of the plateau, the Pyramid of the Winds could have been built yesterday, so perfect was its ancient geometry. Smaller than its more famous cousins, it was in its way just as impressive, its sheer walls of smoothly fitting stone blocks a testament to the timeless genius of its creators.

"It's amazing," Isis said, scrambling out of the Land Rover and squinting through the fierce haze.

"One of the world's great feats of engineering," Jassim agreed.

"It helps if you have thousands of slaves to drag the stone blocks into place," added Murphy.

"Of course. That is why our modern buildings are so puny in comparison," Jassim laughed. "You just cannot get the slaves these days."

Isis unrolled the three-dimensional map of the pyramid's interior while Jassim and Murphy checked that the Crawler's systems were in working order. "Perfect," Jassim pronounced finally as a crystal-clear image of the pyramid appeared on the screen of the laptop balanced on his knees. "And she seems to be responding correctly to all my commands." He patted the Crawler like a faithful dog and pointed toward the pyramid. "Go, fetch," he said sternly.

Tucking the Crawler under his arm, Murphy started clambering over the huge limestone blocks toward the entrance of the first air shaft. "The prevailing wind is from the south," Isis explained to Jassim, "so this shaft is likely to have the strongest inflow. It seemed like the most logical place to start."

Jassim nodded. "Let us hope the wind has not blown it full of sand."

Murphy jogged back over the sand and Jassim started the Crawler on its journey up the shaft. Over his shoulder, Murphy and Isis watched the grainy images slowly fill the screen.

"It seems to be clear. The Crawler's moving without any problem. I estimate it should reach the end of the shaft in about three minutes. So far there don't seem to be any objects in its path."

Three minutes seemed like thirty as they huddled in the Land Rover's air-conditioned interior, trying to interpret the shadowy pictures the Crawler was transmitting from its miniature cameras. Finally Jassim pressed a key and brought it to a halt. "Far enough, I think. It must be near the lip of the shaft. We don't want to lose her. If there was anything in the shaft, we'd have seen it by now."

Murphy wondered when the Crawler had become a *her*. "Just let her go a few more feet, Jassim." He peered intently at the screen. "What's that? I can see something moving."

Jassim reluctantly moved the Crawler forward. "It could be a small animal, a rat perhaps, though I doubt there is much worth nibbling inside the tomb now."

"Okay, stop. There it is again. There's definitely something moving at the end of the shaft."

Jassim adjusted the focus of the twin cameras. "Let me see, is that any better?"

Murphy nodded. "It must be something beyond the air shaft. Something inside the great chamber."

"Like the head of a bronze Serpent floating in midair?" Jassim laughed.

Murphy gave him a steady look. "Only one way to find out."

While Jassim maneuvered the Crawler back down the shaft, muttering under his breath, Murphy checked that he had everything he needed. Rope, flashlight, utility knife. And his bow.

Jassim looked at him as if he'd gone mad. "What on earth do you need that for?"

"The last time I went down a hole looking for a piece of the Serpent, I could have used it. I'm not making that mistake again."

Isis didn't say anything as they walked over to the base of the pyramid, but as he prepared to climb to the entrance of the shaft, she put a hand on his arm. "Be careful."

He looked into her eyes. "I always *try* to be careful." But the devil-may-care grin he tried for wouldn't come.

"I mean it," she said.

With the bow strapped tightly to his body, and knees, shoulders, and elbows all wedged tightly against the walls, Murphy was beginning to understand why the tomb robbers had left it to children and midgets to negotiate the pyramid's air shafts. But a summer of caving in Mexico had taught him that even an average-sized man could worm his way through a surprisingly tight space if he could control his nerves. More often than not it was panic that made you stuck, not the physical dimensions of the hole you were squeezing through. He took a moment to slow his breathing, tried to relax his muscles, and inched forward, feeling the warm air being sucked past him. *I may never make it out of here, but at least I'm not going to suffocate,* he thought.

After ten minutes his knees and elbows were scraped raw and he was starting to wonder if taking the cumbersome bow with him had been a mistake. Without it, he'd have reached the lip of the shaft by now. He closed his eyes, knowing from experience that total darkness would paradoxically lessen his sense of claustrophobia, and slid forward again.

A few minutes later his fingers closed over the edge of the shaft and he opened his eyes. Pulling himself forward, he looked down at the abyss below. Somewhere in the darkness was the tomb of Queen Hephrat, but the incline of the pyramid's walls ensured that scaling them would be an impossible feat. He couldn't imagine how the orginal tomb robbers had managed it.

He squeezed out and rolled onto a narrow ledge. When he was sure he could stand safely without toppling into the dark, he raised his eyes. The winds were swirling all around him, seemingly from all directions. The power of the winds was not strong enough to blow him from his perch on the landing, but his hair and clothes began to whip every which way in the shifting air currents.

As he began to get used to the winds, he noticed that he was not standing in total darkness. A thin stream of light from one of the air shafts at the top of the pyramid shone straight down into the abyss. That light seemed to have been designed purposefully to produce the incredible spectacle that Murphy now found himself watching.

Probably no more than one hundred feet across the shaft from where he stood, high over his head, there was an object tumbling about miraculously in the void. The stream of light brought out a dull shine on what appeared to be a fist-sized lump of metal rolling about in midair. Just the right size, Murphy guessed, to be the head of the Brazen Serpent.

Murphy didn't know how long he just stood there, transfixed by the sight of the Serpent's head, watching it dancing in air as it had been, unobserved, for thousands of years, but it seemed impossible to tear his gaze away. He knew he would never see anything so extraordinary as long as he lived.

As if his mind were being read, a voice shattered his reverie.

"A magnificent sight, Murphy. But you must ask yourself: Will it be your last?"

# SIXTY-FOUR

MURPHY LOOKED PAST the floating Serpent's head through the surrounding gloom to see where the voice had come from. On the opposite ledge he could barely see the outline of a human figure.

"Who are you?"

"My name is Talon. I told it to your wife, but I guess she never got to share it with you."

Finally the evil that struck down Laura had a name and a face. Every fiber of Murphy's being was screaming for revenge, and if anger alone could have powered him, he would have leaped the void in one bound and gone for this Talon's throat. Instead, he tried to control his rage to focus on the standoff before him.

"You monster. So, I was right. You are the same man who is responsible for all of the horrors of the recent weeks."

"Yes, who would have thought an archaeologist would see this much action. You cover a lot of ground, Murphy, I'll give you that, but with enough money and power against you, there are no secrets, yours or the ancients', that can't be revealed."

"What do you want with the Serpent? How can it be worth murdering for?"

"I don't have to reveal *my* secrets to you, Murphy. All you need to know is that thanks to you, I will have the Serpent's head and then circle back to the American University, where you've locked up the middle piece."

"You are an awfully confident monster, Talon, I see that. But it doesn't look like you're any closer to grabbing the Serpent's head than I am over here. All the modern money and power you brag about doesn't look like it's any match for a clever ancient mind and a little wind."

Talon laughed. "That, Professor, is where you are wrong. It looks like you're the one who has no way to get out in the middle to grab the head, whereas I have a solution that is almost older than the pyramid itself."

Murphy saw a dark flutter of movement, and for a moment it was as if two objects were being tossed in the air in the center of the shaft. One was the head of the Serpent, the other was actually moving on its own, fighting the wind.

*A bird*, he thought. *Of course. A falcon.* Despite himself, Murphy had to concede that Talon had come up with an ingenious method for plucking the Serpent's head from out of the vortex.

Even in the uncertain light of the pyramid's interior, Murphy could see what a magnificent creature the falcon was. He could see the chestnut sheen of its wings, the dappled cream of its breast. A kestrel. Its ancient name, the windhover, came into his mind as he watched it miraculously keeping in place a few feet from the vortex's grip. *She is used to riding updrafts and crosscurrents,* Murphy thought, *but nothing like this. She must feel as if she's been caught in a blizzard. But she's learning fast. A couple of more passes and she'll have it.*

Without thinking, he slid his bow out of its case and notched an arrow.

He zeroed in on the falcon, which was now only a few feet from the floating head. Feeling his willpower drain, Murphy shifted his bow toward the target he could not resist. Talon. He drew the string back until every molecule of the bow was begging for release. With just a loosening of his fingers an arrow would streak across the space between them and through Talon's black heart.

*Vengeance is mine.*

Laura's killer just stood there. Was it Murphy's imagination, or was Talon smiling? *He knows I've got him in my sights,* Murphy thought. *Does he think I won't do it?* He felt his whole body quiver with the effort of keeping the arrow from loosing itself as if it had a mind of its own.

Time seemed to stop as he waited to see what his mind would do. The chamber suddenly echoed to the sound of Talon clapping his hands.

"Come on, Murphy. Do it! What's holding you back? It's just the two of us now. Your precious God can't see you! Do it!"

Murphy felt his bow finger trembling. He couldn't hold it much longer.

He swung the bow up and to his left and fired.

Despite the winds, the arrow hit its target. The falcon. Murphy could not take another man's life. Even the monster who had killed Laura. He also realized in the final second that Talon had been baiting him to distract his attention from the bird, who had grabbed hold of the Serpent's head.

And he could not let the monster Talon get the Serpent's head.

The kestrel plunged into the solid stream of air, talons extended. She gripped the head by the thin curve of bronze that would connect it to the middle piece and beat her wings furiously to turn toward Talon.

Murphy's arrow caught the falcon on the very edge of its left wing. With a horrible screech that echoed throughout the shaft, the Serpent's head was knocked out of the bird's grip. It seemed to hang in the air for a moment, as if it had forever renounced the pull of gravity, then plummeted down into the dark. Somehow, having left the particular pull of its centuries-old rotations, the head was now free to plummet into the void. The wounded kestrel was falling almost as quickly.

Murphy watched it fall. It had almost been close enough for him to reach out and touch it. Now the Serpent could never be made whole again.

He wheeled back in Talon's direction, but the shadows had swallowed him.

Then he felt a sharp pain dig into the back of his neck and heard an even louder bloodcurdling squawk. It was a second bird. Murphy was able to recover in time to knock it away, and then it seemed distracted by the falling of the first falcon and flew off, perhaps to help it.

Murphy watched it fly away clutching in its claw Laura's cross, which it had ripped from around his neck.

# SIXTY-FIVE

THE CLIMB BACK through the air shaft had the quality of a nightmare. Every inch seemed to take forever as Murphy imagined Isis and Jassim being butchered by the killer he had had in his sights. The thought tormented him as he forced his bruised and bleeding body through the shaft: *I could have stopped him. I could have stopped him.*

When he finally scrambled out and tumbled onto the sand, he couldn't see anything—the sunlight had temporarily blinded him. Then he felt arms around him, pulling him to his feet, and he could hear their excited voices. They were okay.

Back in the Land Rover, in between gulps from a bottle of mineral water, Murphy told them what had happened inside the pyramid.

"It is a good thing I know you are a man of limited

imagination," said Jassim, rolling his eyes, "or I would be sure you had made it all up. A bird, you say, trained to snatch the head out of the air where it had been spinning for eons! Even now I am not sure I believe it."

"Just keep your eye out for another vehicle," Murphy said. "He must have approached the pyramid from the other side."

"How did he know we were here? That's what I don't understand," said Isis.

Murphy shook his head. "Beats me." He closed his eyes, suddenly exhausted. "I failed," he said more to himself than anyone else. "I thought that's what God wanted me to do. Find the Serpent. That was my task."

Isis was smiling her Sphinx smile. "What makes you think you failed?"

Murphy pounded his fist against the window. "I lost the head of the Serpent. It's at the bottom of the pyramid by now. No one will ever find it there."

"Maybe that's for the best," Isis said. "I think the Serpent—every bit of it—was nothing but evil. If God had a task for you, perhaps it was just to find the inscription. Dakkuri's final message."

"Well, guess what, that's at the bottom of the pyramid, too, in case you hadn't figured it out."

Isis ignored his sarcastic tone. "Not necessarily."

"What are you talking about?"

"The Crawler's camera was focused on the head for two or three minutes. The images may not be crystal clear, but the way it was moving in space, we'll certainly have it from every angle. If Jassim's lab has half the equipment he claims, we can reconstruct and enhance each frame. Perhaps we'll be able to put together a composite image—enough to read the cuneiforms anyway."

"Of course," agreed Jassim. "It is quite possible."

Murphy spent the trip back to the American University replaying the sequence of events inside the pyramid. He'd been about to kill Talon. He had no recollection of changing his mind. He didn't even remember aiming at the falcon—it just happened, as if the bow were aiming him, not the other way around.

That was always how a perfect shot felt. As if it were divinely inspired. *Well, maybe it was*, he thought.

Jassim was as impatient as Isis to see what the Crawler's tapes would reveal and kept the accelerator to the floor, even when the morning rush-hour traffic started congealing around them. Isis kept her hands pressed together in her lap and her eyes closed. When they finally arrived in front of the elegant stucco building that housed Jassim's lab, he insisted on making everything ready while they showered and, in Murphy's case, changed the dressing on his knife wound as well as applying Band-Aids to his various cuts and scrapes.

Half an hour later they were hunched over a computer screen as Jassim's long fingers flew over the keys. After a few moments a grainy image of the Serpent's head appeared, glinting faintly in the murky light as it revolved on its own axis. "To think it had been there for two and a half thousand years"—he made a clucking sound—"and now—*poof*—gone."

"We got the snapshots to show the folks back home, that's what counts," Murphy said.

"But they don't show anything. Not yet," Isis chided. "Move it forward—slowly."

Jassim advanced the film frame by digital frame until the underside of the head started to come into view. "Stop it there!" Isis commanded, and Murphy couldn't help remembering the effect she'd had on the idol worshipers in the sewers. "Give me as much magnification as you can."

Slowly the image grew until it filled the screen. Then, as Jassim magnified it still further, the outline was lost and all they could see was a scarred and pitted landscape of bronze, like the surface of a distant yellow moon.

Jassim shook his head. "That's about as much as—"

"There!" Isis shrieked.

Murphy leaned closer. She was right. What had seemed moments before like the random scratches and fissures of any weather-beaten piece of metal suddenly took on the orderly form of written characters: the distinctive cuneiform etchings of Dakkuri.

Jassim prepared to print the image. "I expect it is something else I will find impossible to believe," he said, "but perhaps now is the time to tell me what this is all about."

Murphy put a hand on his friend's shoulder. "Wait until Isis has figured out what it means. Then I promise I'll tell you everything."

Jassim nodded as Isis practically tore the printout from the machine. None of them moved. However long it took, they weren't going anywhere.

"At least it's short," she said after a while. "I suppose he thought if the reader had made it this far, there was no point playing games anymore."

Her eyes darted back and forth across the piece of

paper, and Murphy felt he could almost hear her brain working. Her lips moved silently, mouthing the words over and over until they made sense. Then she placed the sheet carefully down on the desk.

"Well?" Jassim seemed even more agitated than Murphy, who had stopped breathing.

She took a moment to compose herself, and began. "It starts with a ritual exhortation, as usual: *The servants of the snake have kept this secret. Honor to them and power hereafter.*"

She coughed. "Then comes the important bit.

> "*Babylon's great towers are dust, the wind blows them where it pleases.*
> "*But find the head and the body shall rise after, casting its shadow again over all the earth.*
> "*It is of gold and marks a king, the most powerful.*
> "*In Marduk's dwelling shall you find it.*
> "*O faithful servant of the dark, be commanded to raise it up.*
> "*From the dust Babylon shall be raised up also to rule again.*"

The silence dragged on, and Isis said, "That's it."

"It's enough," said Murphy quietly.

"But what does it mean?" asked Jassim.

"It means Babylon will rise again. At least, it will if the wrong people get hold of the Golden Head."

Isis looked at him thoughtfully, but Jassim was out of his chair, wringing his hands in frustration. "You're talking in riddles, Murphy. How can Babylon rise again? What is this *Golden* Head? I thought you were looking for—and just lost—the head of the *bronze* Serpent."

"I'm sorry, Jassim. Let me try to explain. According to Daniel's interpretation of Nebuchadnezzar's dream, the Babylonian empire was the most powerful the world would ever know. That power was symbolized by the Golden Head of the statue in the dream—the one he then had built. When Nebuchadnezzar saw the error of his ways, he had the statue destroyed. But I'm betting that the head was buried somewhere by the people who worshiped the Brazen Serpent."

"But why? If they didn't want to destroy it, why not melt it down? The gold must have been worth an unbelievable fortune."

"I'm pretty sure because they believed that if they preserved the head, then one day the right person would find it, and Babylon would rise up again."

Jassim rubbed his eyes as if he were checking he wasn't dreaming. "And what does this mean: *Babylon will rise up*? The old city will be rebuilt?"

"Not just that," Murphy said. "It means the power of Babylon will be rebuilt too. This time, as an evil power dominating the world."

Jassim turned to Isis. "I would like to know what you think of all this, Dr. McDonald. You are a sensible person, like myself, I think. Do you really believe that an evil cult hid Nebuchadnezzar's Golden Head for two and a half thousand years, waiting for their chance to take over the world?"

Isis took her time to answer. "I'm not sure. My view of what's possible, what's real and what isn't, has changed recently. You see, I think I've seen evil at work now—genuine pure evil. Innocent people killed for a piece of brass." Her eyes caught Murphy's for a second. "I don't know what to believe about the Golden Head, the return of Babylon, all that. All I know is I'm afraid. More afraid than I've ever been in my life."

Jassim nodded solemnly, then turned to Murphy. "I am like Dr. McDonald. I do not know what to believe. But just to be on the safe side, I think it might be a good idea to find this Golden Head before anyone else does."

"I'll second that," Murphy said.

"So, where do you suppose Marduk's dwelling is?"

"That's an easy one," Isis said. "The temple of Marduk was in Babylon."

"So you're saying..."

Murphy nodded. "Exactly. For this one, I'm going to have to call in everybody: the Parchments of Freedom Foundation, the American University, and my friend Levi, to pull every string in the region. We've got to get into Iraq."

# SIXTY-SIX

"THE HANGING GARDENS of Babylon," Isis said dreamily, stirring her iced tea. "I can't think of five more mysterious and seductive words. They sound so familiar—but nobody actually knows what they looked like."

Murphy watched her catlike sips. "Are you sure about that? You don't have a memory of walking through them two and a half thousand years ago?"

Isis took out a piece of ice and threw it at him. "Stop that."

Jassim frowned. He had chosen the restaurant because it was quiet and it was possible to find a table in an alcove where you could talk without being overheard. He was in no mood for games. "So that is where the temple of Marduk is located? In the Hanging Gardens?"

"Or above them. We won't really know until we get there," Murphy said.

"You make it sound so simple. Surely it is not possible to turn up at the site and just start digging. So many of Iraq's antiquities have already been looted."

"That's the point, Jassim. The best place for Iraq's ancient treasures right now is a museum someplace far away. When law and order have been restored, and Iraq's own museums are up and running again, then everything can be returned and the Iraqi people will be able to appreciate their ancient heritage without worrying that some hoodlum is going to take it and put it on the open market."

Jassim looked skeptical. "It is hard to believe that something so big—What did you tell me? Fifteen feet tall, six or seven in diameter?—could have evaded the looters. Either the ones who came after the war *or* the ones who were running the country for thirty years. I think perhaps it was melted down and turned into gold faucets for Saddam's bathrooms a long time ago."

"That's a lot of faucets," Murphy said.

"He had a lot of bathrooms."

Murphy sipped his water thoughtfully. "Dakkuri has proved to be pretty smart so far. He managed to hide a Biblical artifact so no one would find it until . . . the time was right. I'm betting he hid the head pretty well too."

"And now the time is right to find it?"

"I'm not sure there will ever be a right time to find a thing like that. But anytime is the right time to stop the wrong people from getting their hands on it."

Isis checked her watch and picked her backpack up from the floor. "Then, let's get a move on. Our plane leaves in two hours."

Jassim put a hand on her arm. "Wait just a minute, please, Dr. McDonald."

"Isis. Please." It was odd, but now that her goddesses no longer seemed so real to her, she felt more comfortable with her name. "What is it, Jassim?"

He looked uncomfortable. "You, Murphy, are a brave man. Or perhaps just foolhardy—but no matter. Perhaps it is all the same. And you, Isis, you have endured some truly terrifying experiences with an extraordinary fortitude. I, on the other hand, am no kind of hero. The people who want to get hold of the Golden Head are clearly very powerful and utterly ruthless. It is not a combination I like."

"I hear what you're saying, Jassim," Murphy said. "And if you don't feel comfortable coming with us to Iraq, I wouldn't blame you. I'll admit it would make our job harder not having you around to help with the logistics. But we could manage. However, two things make me think we won't be coming up against the likes of our birdman again. First, he never got to see the inscription on the Serpent's head, and you destroyed the film and deleted everything on the computer. We're the only three people who know where the Golden Head is."

"I wish I shared your confidence." Jassim looked nervously around the restaurant. "This terrible man, this Talon, seems to have been a step behind you every inch of the way, if you don't mind my saying so. How can we be sure he isn't somehow listening in to our conversation at this very moment?"

"Maybe he is," Murphy admitted. "But here's the second thing. We're not going to be on our own when we get to the temple of Marduk. Right now, a unit of U.S. Marines is securing the site."

Jassim stroked his chin. "Well, I hope they have orders to shoot on sight any suspicious characters—and any suspicious birds of prey, for that matter."

"I'm sure they do, Jassim. So, are you in?"

"I believe I am making a very foolish decision," he sighed. "But I think if you did find the head and I was not there to share the greatest archaeological discovery of modern times, I would have to kill myself anyway. So, yes, I am in."

# SIXTY-SEVEN

AS THE LAND CRUISER bumped its way slowly through the scattered ruins of the ancient city, Isis had to pinch herself to check that she wasn't dreaming. Since the loving presence of her father had departed, she'd lived her life in hiding. Her academic studies had been a way of avoiding all the things in life that scared her, and her little office buried at the Foundation was really a kind of bunker from which she had successfully kept the outside world at bay.

Until Michael Murphy had turned up in her life, that is.

Now, in the space of a few short days, she'd been exposed to danger, to fear, and to death. She'd ventured quite literally into the unknown. She'd journeyed through the dark underground heart of a medieval city.

She'd seen the inside of a pyramid. And now she was about to walk on the ground of Babylon itself.

On the walls flanking the famed Ishtar Gate, fierce dragons met her wide-eyed gaze, survivors of three thousand years of rain, wind, and sandstorms. But her heart didn't quite leap the way she'd expected. Perhaps after a lifetime of studying the multifarious gods and goddesses that men had worshiped through the ages, she had finally caught a glimpse of something greater.

"There they are." Murphy was pointing to a nearby hillside, where crumbling walls still rose from the stepped terraces of Queen Amytis's original design. At the top, the temple of Marduk was marked by a lonely pinnacle of sandstone.

As Jassim had predicted, the site looked as if the jackals had long ago picked it clean. Whole sections of the hillside had collapsed, covering what had once been the remains of ancient doorways and staircases with earth and rubble. Any remaining segments of stone with any sort of engraving or design had been taken, from hand-sized fragments to actual pillars.

Murphy was surveying the devastation when a tanned marine officer in aviator shades trotted up the hillside to introduce himself. "Colonel Davis, U.S. Marines. You must be Professor Murphy."

Murphy submitted to a bone-crunching handshake. "It's good to see you, Colonel." For the first time, he noticed the handful of soldiers in desert camouflage forming a loose perimeter around the hillside. "And your men."

"Our pleasure. Anything we can do, just holler."

"I don't know where to start," Murphy admitted.

"We need to see what's under the rubble. We're looking for some sort of underground chamber."

The colonel grinned. "Figured you might be. So I did a little digging around when we got here. Seems the fellas who cleaned this place out left a couple of items they couldn't find a use for on the black market."

Murphy brightened. "Such as?"

"How would a sonar sled suit you?"

Murphy broke out laughing. "That would suit me just fine, Colonel."

Half an hour later Murphy and Jassim were dragging the sled—a lightweight plastic oblong the size of a child's mattress—slowly across the rockslide while Isis watched the images forming on Murphy's laptop computer screen a few yards away.

So far all she'd seen were the shadowy outlines of collapsed chambers and empty vaults. Then her attention was taken by the remarkable symmetry of a pair of dark parallel lines on the screen. "Hold on! Can you back it up a little?"

Murphy and Jassim steered the sled in a crisscross pattern over the rocks. There was no mistaking them now. Some sort of man-made object was down there, perhaps a dozen feet beneath the surface. And it wasn't small.

Murphy and Jassim walked over and looked at the screen. Jassim nodded. "A set of doors, perhaps? An entrance of some kind, anyway."

"But how are we going to get to it?" Isis asked.

Colonel Davis had been standing to one side, observing her at work. "Pardon me, ma'am, but would a bulldozer help?"

Without waiting for an answer, he marched off, and a few minutes later they heard the groaning of the bulldozer's engine as it crested the hill. It pulled up a few feet from where Murphy and Jassim had been working the sled. Murphy gave the thumbs-up and the bulldozer started to heave the rubble aside. Its first pass just seemed to skim the surface, but the fresh-faced marine perched in the bulldozer's cab soon warmed to his work and after twenty minutes Murphy gave the signal to stop.

He walked over to the area of newly excavated earth, then turned to Colonel Davis. "Now all we need is a few shovels."

Davis saluted smartly. "Coming right up. And I've got twenty men with plenty of experience digging holes, if you need 'em."

By the time they'd dug down to a depth of about ten feet, Murphy and Jassim were getting dizzy with the effort, but the half-dozen marines alongside them hadn't even broken a sweat. "Whoa, that sounded like metal," one of them said as his shovel bounced off something hard. On their hands and knees they brushed the last of the loose earth away and then stood aside.

Joined by Isis, Murphy and Jassim looked down on a huge set of bronze doors. Encrusted with mineral deposits and a patina of discoloring sediment, the sculpted panels still had the power to astonish, as images of Nebuchadnezzar's many conquests came into focus after an interval of three thousand years. And there, towering above even the great Nebuchadnezzar, was the image of Marduk, the warrior-god.

For moments, nobody spoke. Then Jassim said, "I'd

say we were in the place where Marduk dwells, all right. Shall we go in?"

The nearly horizontal doors looked as if they had been sealed for all time, and even if the combined manpower of all present could pry them apart, they had no way of knowing whether there was anything more than earth behind them. The whole structure had long ago shifted from the vertical, perhaps in one of the frequent earthquakes the region was subject to, and it was possible the doors opened onto nothing.

Under Murphy's direction, three marines stood on one of the doors and attempted to lever the other one open with their shovels. Soon even they were sweating, and Murphy began to suspect the doors had been cunningly designed to suggest a chamber beyond that didn't in fact exist.

Then suddenly there was a wrenching sound and a shovel flew out of one of the soldier's hands as a crack appeared and a rush of stale air escaped from below. Grabbing hold of the door's edge, they heaved, and it slowly swung upward with a groaning of ancient hinges.

Holding on to one of the doors, Murphy eased himself down into the blackness, his legs hanging free in the empty space. So, the doors did open onto *something*. The fetid air was almost unbearable now, an acrid stench of decay more powerful than anything he'd ever experienced. He felt a wave of nausea and then his chest started heaving as his lungs convulsed. He heard Isis scream as his fingers slipped off the edge of the door, and then he was tumbling downward.

The moment seemed to stretch out, and Murphy thought of drowning men whose whole lives flash past them in a split second. Then a jarring impact sent a lightning pulse of pain shuddering through his legs. Before he could cry out, his head smashed against something hard and unyielding, and a black cloud ballooned inside his head, blotting everything out.

When he came to, he could hear voices from above. For a moment it was just noise, then the sounds turned back into words again and he understood it was Isis and Jassim asking if he was all right. He heard the second door being hauled back.

"I'm okay," he managed to say, hauling himself onto his hands and knees. Another wave of coughing seized him as more of the black air forced itself into his heaving lungs and he felt his eyes stinging with tears. He waited until the fit had passed, then wiped his face with the back of his hand. His head was ringing, but the pain in his legs had subsided to a steady throbbing. He opened his eyes.

Then closed them again as his head filled with an agonizing brightness. *The blow on the head,* he thought. *I've blinded myself.* Fighting down a wave of panic, he steadied his breathing and squinted through half-open lids. The golden light was still overwhelming, but he forced himself to keep his eyes open and gradually the fierce haze that filled his field of vision resolved itself into a solid object.

He was looking into the iris of a huge golden eye.

Still on his hands and knees, he shuffled backward in the dirt until the rest of the object came into focus. At first the powerful ridges and curving lines of sculpted metal didn't make any sense—like the jumbled features of a giant Picasso. Then his perspective adjusted to its horizontal position and the face of Nebuchadnezzar glared at him across a chasm of two and a half thousand years.

Murphy shuffled back farther until he leaned against the wall of earth and looked into the face of the king. How faithfully the sculptor had managed to capture the king's features he had no way of knowing, but the sculpture definitely had an unnerving realism. The great eyes seemed to bore straight through Murphy like lasers, and the sneer of command etched into the huge mouth seemed to be saying, *Raise me up, you dog! I have lain in the dust long enough!*

He didn't know how long he had been crouching there, mesmerized by the imperious stare of the long-dead king, before he heard the thud of boots alongside him and the sound of excited voices raised in wonder and awe. Then strong hands hauled him upright and he closed his eyes again, grateful not to have to look anymore into the face of evil.

# SIXTY-EIGHT

SHARI TUGGED AT Paul's hand. It was still weak
from his long hospital stay.

"Hey," he protested, "the plaster came off only yesterday. You're going to pull it out of its socket."

"Stop fussing," she said. "Dr. Keller said too much
sympathy wouldn't be good for you. It would impede
the healing process. Look—there he is!"

He had let her drag him all the way to Washington,
D.C., to wait at the airstrip where the Parchments of
Freedom Foundation had arranged for the cargo plane to
land. They had not arranged for the vast array of cameras
and reporters, but it was hard to keep the arrival of such a
spectacular artifact from the press.

When the plane touched down, Shari started waving
frantically before Michael Murphy came bounding
down the steps. "Professor Murphy!"

He turned with a quizzical expression, then walked over, beaming. "It's okay, Officer. You can let these two through. They've earned it."

The guard grudgingly stepped aside and Murphy and Shari hugged. Paul could feel the wordless communication passing between them.

They pulled apart and Shari said, "I can't believe you did it. I can't believe it's really here. In the States!"

Murphy grinned. "It wasn't easy. We had to persuade a lot of people it was the right thing to do. I couldn't have done it without my friends here"—he indicated a petite redhead with elfin features and an elegant, dark-complexioned man in a cream suit who were talking animatedly to the trucking crew—"putting the weight of the Parchments of Freedom Foundation and the American University of Cairo behind it. You know me, I'm not very good at playing nice with bureaucrats."

"But you did it!" Shari said again.

"I even got some behind-the-scenes help from a very special place, from someone who had already helped us tremendously." Murphy pulled a copy of a letter from the pocket of his jacket. "Wait till you read this, guys. As momentous as the arrival of the Golden Head is today, this is even greater reason for celebration. This letter was waiting for me when I got to the plane. Listen.

"My dear Professor Murphy—

"Thank you for honoring my home with your visit, and for allowing me to help you with your search for what I now know was the Brazen Serpent, which has in turn led you to the Golden Head of Nebuchadnez-.

zar. I am doubly honored to have played some small part in arranging for the exit for its temporary home in your charge.

"But most of all, thank you for taking the time to explain to me so clearly the real reason why Christianity is the one true path to God.

"After you went to bed that night, I sat alone in my room contemplating what you had told me about the nature of God. For the first time, I understood that Jesus Christ had died for my sins and for the sins of the world. He then rose from the dead.

"That night, I received Him by faith, as you had urged, and I invited Him into my life.

"If I do not see you again in this life, I certainly will see you in the next, in heaven.

"Sincerely,
"Sheikh Umar al-Khaliq"

Shari broke out into a wide smile. "Oh, Professor Murphy, that has got to be such a great feeling, to know that you helped this sheikh in his search."

Murphy hugged her and noticed Paul again. He gripped his hand. "Hey, it's good to see you, Paul. You're looking well. And I understand you have a new scholarship from the Barrington folks. I trust that will allow you to really bear down and find some course of study that excites you more than business."

"Yes, sir. Shari here would not have let me agree to it otherwise. She's been a great help." He blushed, and Shari poked him hard in the ribs.

"Go easy on him, Shari," Murphy said. "He's still a

young man. It will take a while before he realizes he's got to turn most of his life decisions over to God and a good woman, in that order."

She wagged a finger. "Professor Murphy!"

The lanky figure of Dean Fallworth sidled out of the hangar and blocked Murphy's path. Before he could react, Dean Fallworth grabbed his hand and started pumping it enthusiastically.

"Murphy—great to have you back. The faculty board and I, we're all tremendously proud of what you've achieved for the university. This is a proud day indeed for Preston, with one of our finest in the news." A sheepish look briefly supplanted his huckster's grin, and he lowered his voice so only Murphy could hear. "I hope we can put our little misunderstanding behind us. My comments on that TV interview were taken totally out of context, you know. In fact, I'm considering a formal complaint against BNN and that awful reporter. She practically put the words into my mouth."

Murphy really couldn't think of anything to say. He would settle his account with Fallworth when the time came. Right now he was simply relieved that his position at the university was secure. When all the fuss and publicity died down, he'd be able to get back to his real job of inspiring his students. He knew that was what Laura would have wanted him to do.

He gave Fallworth a look to let him know he wasn't going to pick a fight now, but he wasn't necessarily letting him off the hook either. "Later, Dean." He brushed past him, leaving Fallworth standing, his fixed smile holding him in place.

"Isis, Jassim. I want you to meet some good friends and students of mine, Shari Nelson and Paul Wallach."

Jassim held his hand out while Isis delivered some last-minute instructions to one of the crew preparing to open the crate. "The pleasure is all mine," he said. "I have heard many good things about you both. Preston University is truly fortunate to have such outstanding students of archaeology—especially considering the, shall we say, *unconventional* habits of your professor." He indicated Murphy with a wink.

Isis joined them. "Take no notice of Jassim. He's just making the most of being in the limelight. He thinks maybe some bigwig from the Discovery Channel is going to give him a series on the secrets of the pyramids."

"And why not?" said Jassim, doing his best to look offended. "I am an excellent communicator, I think, and I have the sort of face the camera likes. Miss Nelson, what do you say?"

"I'd tune in," she said, laughing. "After everything you two have done to help Murphy find the Golden Head, it's the least I could do."

Murphy coughed. "Speaking of which, let's start unloading."

It took the best part of an hour to unload the crate from the cargo bay and set it on a huge flatbed truck. Now the crate stood alone in the center of the truck like an enormous piece of modern art.

Murphy gave the signal, and the loading crew, evenly spaced around the crate, pulled at the ropes securing the panels on each of its four sides. The wooden panels crashed to the ground simultaneously. A team from the PFF raced over to cut the protective coats of fabric and plastic that had been fashioned around the head. As the last layer of wadding fell away, Murphy stepped up to the microphone set up alongside the head.

"Ladies and gentlemen of the world, there is much to tell about this great find, how we came to discover it, to reclaim it, and understand its significance. That will all have to wait until we have it safely in place in its temporary home, the Parchments of Freedom Foundation, which has generously put up the funds for this great artifact to be studied thoroughly and expeditiously. I want to thank God for His strength and guidance throughout the entire process. We look forward to sharing its wonders and secrets with you soon. Thank you."

In this moment of great professional triumph, Murphy was saddened by his thoughts of Laura and the guards at the PFF, and all the other terrible events that had led to this wondrous achievement. As if by reflex, he also shuddered when he thought about the man who was responsible for so much of that suffering, Talon, who was still at large, and would presumably be as keen to possess the Golden Head of Nebuchadnezzar as he was the Brazen Serpent.

Maybe even more so, because Murphy had thwarted his chances to put the Serpent back together. And if this mystery man Talon truly did have an interest in these icons for the dark powers many believed they still possessed, Murphy was beginning to have a feeling that as eventful as the last few weeks had been, the days ahead would present even greater challenges.

With God's help and protection, he would be ready.

# SIXTY-NINE

THE SLAVES PULLED in unison on the ropes, straining with all their might. Finally, the massive piece of gold came crashing to the ground. The idol that had brought the king and his people so much torment now lay in ruins in the swirling dust, its disembodied head staring with betrayal at the man whose image it had been fashioned after. King Nebuchadnezzar then ordered that the pieces be gathered up and delivered to Dakkuri, the chief Chaldean priest, back in the city. The gold would be reused for sacred vessels, or so the king had been led to believe.

The king was mad, of that Dakkuri had no doubt. For seven years Nebuchadnezzar had groveled in the dirt, living like a beast in the shadow of his own palace, his wits scattered to the four corners of an empire that hung by a thread while jealous neighbors plotted its overthrow. And yet, now that the king's sanity had been restored, now that he spoke and thought and acted like a man once more, Dakkuri had a strange sense that he was madder than ever.

What else could explain his decree that all the idols should be destroyed? Somehow, Daniel and his God had the king under their spell.

Dakkuri shivered, and it was not just because of the damp air in his chamber. If the worship of idols was ended, who would the people turn to in times of danger and uncertainty, when plague and pestilence struck, when the crops failed or the rivers overflowed their banks? From whom would they receive the strength to destroy their enemies, to raze their cities and enslave their sons? Who would give them the power to rule the world?

More to the point, where would Dakkuri's own power and prestige come from? When he looked into the sacred fire, it was he—and he alone—who could interpret the shifting shapes of light. When Nergal, the fierce god of the underworld, was angry, only Dakkuri could interpret the signs. If Nergal's wrath could be stemmed only by human sacrifices, it was Dakkuri who chose the victims. When demons entered the city, only he could decide who was possessed and who was not—who must be stoned to death and who spared. Sometimes, he flattered himself, the common people feared him more than their cruel king.

And the rewards were in keeping with his status. Robes woven with gold thread that glittered like the sun. The rarest sweetmeats, the richest wines, whenever he desired. And naturally he could take his pick of the temple dancing girls.

But in a world without idols, all that would be gone.

He lifted his eyes. Against the bare stone wall the lamplight flickered. And there, glinting in the shadows, was the Serpent.

He no longer remembered what impulse had led him to weld the broken pieces together again, to raise the Serpent up and give *it an honored place among Babylon's many deities. But seeing it whole again, he had felt a dark power filling his body—like a goblet being filled to the brim with strong wine. His head had filled with light; a delicious, unbearable fire had bubbled through his veins. He felt like a giant. He could do anything. A knife blade struck at his heart would have been melted by the energy that glowed through him. He was a god.*

*And from that moment on he was the Serpent's slave.*

*Breathing deeply and slowly, he focused on the sinuous bronze form before him. It seemed huge in the half-light, its shadow writhing on the wall like a living thing. He opened his mind, felt his will draining away like water from a broken pitcher.*

*As the familiar ecstasy crept into him, he smiled through closed lids. "Tell me what it is I must do," he whispered.*

As far as Nebuchadnezzar was concerned, Dakkuri could be trusted. He had served many faithful years as a priest in the vicinity of the king's palace. But Dakkuri had a secret. He had become a devotee of the former angel of light who had rebelled against the Creator. Dakkuri, the Chaldean, belonged to, and was a servant of, the dark angel Lucifer.

Standing in the basement of the temple, Dakkuri addressed three of his most trusted disciples. The broken pieces of Nebuchadnezzar's image now lay alongside other sacred and profane vessels of worship in the dark and foreboding storage area. Most of these priceless items had been captured by Nebuchadnezzar's army during the raid on Jerusalem many years before.

Dakkuri spoke with quiet passion to his three Luciferian disciples. Each disciple had sworn an oath to carry out the task that *was about to be assigned. It was a plan that would forever change the course of human history.*

*"Fellow servants of Lucifer, hear me. The Golden Head of Nebuchadnezzar must be hidden from the world until the time of the end."*

*Dakkuri picked up the beautifully formed Brazen Serpent, a fitting symbol indeed.*

*"I have inscribed on this Serpent the words to lead to the precise area where the head of gold is to be buried."*

*Dakkuri placed the Serpent on the vessel worktable and proceeded to break it into three pieces with a large hammer. He then handed one piece to each of the three disciples.*

*"Each of you is to travel to your predetermined areas and bury your portion of the Serpent as instructed. Each of the Serpent pieces will of course be useless without the other two."*

*One of the disciples stood and asked, "Master, why must the Golden Head remain hidden?"*

*"The world has no need for the head of gold at this time. But there is coming a time when the world's leader will have need of the Luciferian power that this Golden Head represents. That time is yet future. It is the time spoken of by Daniel the prophet in his interpretation of the king's dream. . . ."*

*Dakkuri paused to reflect on the implication of his words.*

*"It is the time when Babylon will rise a second time and rule the entire world."*

# SEVENTY

THE SEVEN SAT in their chamber deep within the castle. The man called Talon sat before them. Far from showing any fear at not having met their goals, he was showing annoyance at having to answer their questions.

"Murphy got lucky. He had the help of the U.S. Marines, and remember, you instructed me not to kill him or do any further harm to his circle."

"Yes." The British voice was doing the debriefing. "This has been a disappointment. We will never know what powers the Brazen Serpent might have had. A shame, but whatever powers it had, we do not need them in order to move forward."

"Well, it served its purpose," Talon replied offhandedly, seeming to be concentrating more on the object he toyed with in his hand, poking it with his sharpened fingertip, than on his words. "It led Murphy to your precious Golden Head."

"Indeed. It led Murphy there. Not you. Now we must adjust our strategy. Now that the Golden Head is known around the world because of his discovery. That will require some careful rethinking and planning. But the good news, Talon, which is why you are still in our good graces, is that with all this notoriety, when we do take control of it—and we will—it will be a symbol of even greater power and glory."

Talon rose. "Good. You let me know how to proceed. You can have the power and glory." He turned to leave, swinging the object he had been preoccupied with as he walked away. It was a leather strip holding a cross, one he had once broken into three pieces, but which was now glued together.

"I've got a personal interest in this now."

# AFTERWORD

I hope you have enjoyed *Babylon Rising*. As noted in my introductory message, I am having a great time creating this adventure, and I can't wait for you to read the next book in the series. I'm in the middle of writing it now and I'm having even more exciting times working on the second book than I had on this first one. And that's saying something.

Look for the second novel in the Babylon Rising series in hardcover in fall 2004.

In the meantime, please share your thoughts with me about this first book and look for additional information and news updates from me at my website:

www.timlahaye.com

I also invite you to visit www.babylonrisingbook.com, the official website of the series. Bantam Books and I have tried to make this website an enhancement of your reading experience. In the coming months on this site, you will find additional background information about the series, the characters, and the revelations in the novels. You can sign up for the Babylon Rising newsletter, read excerpts of forthcoming titles, post comments, keep in touch with the Babylon Rising team, and send a Babylon Rising electronic postcard with your own custom message.

Again, thank you for reading *Babylon Rising*.

# ACKNOWLEDGMENTS

No man is an island unto himself! That is certainly true of authors. If the truth be known, we have all been influenced by scores of people who helped develop our skills and knowledge so that we have something interesting and meaningful to share with millions of potential readers.

I particularly want to thank Joel Gotler, my agent, whose vision, faith, and contacts put me in touch with Irwyn Applebaum of Bantam, the most can-do, driven publisher I have ever met. Many thanks as well to my editor, Bill Massey, and the great professional skills and experience that he applied to this book.

I am also grateful to my agent for putting me together with Greg Dinallo, a great fiction writer who caught my vision for merging informative and challenging prophecy with exciting action. It was a pleasure to work with him.

Finally, I wish to express my profound appreciation and thanks to David Minasian, my personal research assistant, who shares my love for God's Word and has provided much invaluable help in researching, editing, and suggesting material throughout this book project.

# ABOUT THE AUTHOR

Dr. Tim LaHaye is the creator and co-author of the Left Behind® series and is also a noted scholar of Biblical prophecy, the author of more than forty nonfiction books, a minister, and an educator. He is the founder and president of Tim LaHaye Ministries. Dr. LaHaye and his wife, Beverly, live in southern California. Greg Dinallo is a veteran suspense novelist. He lives with his wife, Gloria, in New York City.

The adventure continues with

# BABYLON RISING: THE SECRET ON ARARAT

by

## Tim LaHaye

and

## Bob Phillips

Read on for an exciting excerpt from the next book in the Babylon Rising series coming from Bantam Books in September 2004

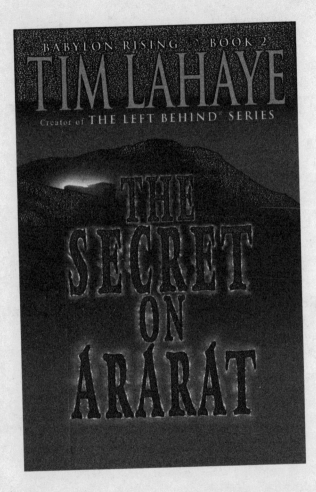

BABYLON RISING · BOOK 2

# TIM LAHAYE

Creator of THE LEFT BEHIND® SERIES

# THE SECRET ON ARARAT

# BABYLON RISING:
# THE SECRET ON ARARAT

## On sale September 2004

*Breathe.* He desperately needed to breathe. But he knew instinctively that if he opened his mouth to try and suck in a breath, he would die.

Gritting his teeth fiercely, Murphy opened his eyes instead. And a pair of yellow, animal eyes stared back. Then a wildly gaping jaw came into focus through the greenish gloom, pointed teeth bared in a silent snarl. Murphy reached out, but the dog-face had disappeared, sucked back into the watery darkness.

It was no good. He had to get some air into his lungs before they burst. He turned his face upward, toward the feeble light, and after an agonizing few seconds, during which he had the horrifying sense that he was sinking, not rising, his head broke the surface.

He sucked in a huge, spluttering breath, simultaneously grabbing on to the narrow stone ledge that projected from the side of the pit. Resting his head against the jagged rock, he could feel something warm mingling with the freezing water. Blood. As the pain suddenly hit him, a wild carousel of thoughts started racing round his brain.

*Laura. He would never see her again. She wouldn't even know he had died here, in this remote, godforsaken place. She would never know his last thoughts had been about her.*

Then he remembered. Laura was dead. She died in his arms.

And now he was about to join her. With that thought, his body seemed to relax, accepting its fate, and he felt himself slipping back into the surging torrent.

No! He couldn't give up. He couldn't let the crazy old man win at last. He had to find a way out.

But first he had to find those puppies.


As he let himself slip back under the freezing water, he wondered—not for the first time—how he managed to get himself into these messes.

The answer was simple. One word: *Methusaleh.*

Murphy had been making his way carefully through the cave, fanning his flashlight across the dank, black walls, when he had found himself standing not on loose shale but what felt like solid, wooden planks. Ever alert to tricks and traps, Murphy instinctively reacted as if he'd just stepped onto a tray of burning coals—but before he could leap aside, the trapdoor sprang open. As he felt himself plunging into the void, a familiar cackling laugh shattered the silence, echoing crazily off the rock walls.

"Welcome to the game, Murphy! Get out of this one if you can!"

Cartwheeling through space, Murphy's brain was still trying to come up with a suitable response. But all that came out was a grunt as he slammed into the ground like a bag of cement and the air was punched out of his lungs, before the impact flung him sideways and his head connected with a boulder. For a moment all was black, buzzing darkness. Then he raised himself up on his hands and knees and his senses returned one by one: He could feel the damp grit between his fingers; he could taste it in his mouth; he could smell stagnant water; he could dimly make out the shadowy walls of the pit he'd fallen into.

And he could hear the fretful whining of what sounded like two very scared dogs.

He turned toward the sound and there they were, shivering together on a narrow ledge. A pair of German shepherd puppies. Murphy shook his head: He always tried to prepare himself for *anything* where Methusaleh was concerned, but what were a couple of puppies doing in the middle of an underground cave complex miles from anywhere?

They were part of the game.

Fighting his natural instinct to gather the bedraggled pups tightly in his arms, he approached the ledge cautiously. They looked so helpless. But that didn't mean harmless. Nothing in Methusaleh's games was harmless.

Just then the steady dripping sound that had been nagging away at the back of Murphy's consciousness since he had landed in the pit started to get louder. He turned in the direction of the noise and suddenly it became a roar, as a huge wave of water surged through a narrow gap in the rocks. In a second a frothing tide was tugging at his ankles, pulling him off-balance. Forgetting Methusaleh's mind games, he pushed himself back toward the ledge, scooped up the puppies, and stuffed them under his jacket. His eyes darted round the walls of the pit, looking for anything that would help him find a way out, as the rising water swirled around his chest. The puppies were just a diversion, he thought bitterly, fighting to keep his footing. Then the torrent lifted him off his feet and the panicking dogs squirmed out of his jacket. Fighting to keep his head above the surface, he grabbed for them but his fingers closed on icy water and then he too was engulfed, spinning out of control.

He closed his eyes and even as his lungs started hungrily demanding air, he tried to find a calm place in his mind, where he could think. The water would soon reach the level of the trapdoor, which was no doubt secured against escape. So, search for another way out under the water or look for the puppies again before they drowned?

But there was no way he could figure it out while his lungs were screaming, and his thought processes were beginning to go fuzzy due to lack of oxygen.

Get some air. Then go after those puppies. If he was still alive after that, maybe God would give him some inspiration.

When Murphy walked into the lab, he was greeted by the sight of a young woman bent over a work desk, her jet-black hair tied back in a ponytail, making a stark contrast with her crisp, white lab coat as she scrutinized a sheet of parchment. Shari Nelson was one of the top students in his Biblical archaeology class at Preston University, and for almost two years she had been his part-time research assistant. In that time he'd come to appreciate her passion for the subject, her limitless capacity for hard work, and her sharp intelligence. But most of all, he valued her warm and generous spirit.

"So what's up, Shari?"

"Something arrived for you." She gestured toward a large white envelope with the orange lettering of Federal Express.

"Strange," he mused. "No return address. Just *Babylon*. Doesn't look like it went through the usal FedEx mailing process." He heard Shari gasp. *Babylon*, she knew all too well, could only mean one thing: a whole heap of trouble.

Murphy carefully opened the envelope and shook the contents out onto the workbench. A smaller envelope with the words *Professor Murphy* printed in heavy marker and a xeroxed page from a map. He glanced at the map, then opened the second envelope. Inside was an index card with three words typed on it.

CHEMAR. ZEPHETH. KOPHER.

He handed it to Shari while he examined the map. A route had been marked in pink felt-tip from Raleigh, moving west across the border into Tennessee. Where the snaking line stopped there was an X and four barely legible words written in a spidery scrawl.

"*Cave of the waters.* Mean anything to you, Shari?"

"It sounds like somewhere you definitely don't want to go," she replied firmly.

He winced. Exactly what Laura would have said. Same tone of voice, even.

"It's coming back to me. I've heard of this place. It's in the Great Smoky Mountains . . . past Asheville, somewhere between Waynesville and Bryson City." If he remembered it right, the cave was discovered in the early

900s, but had never been fully explored because of the high water table in the area, which caused the chambers to flood periodically. It was supposed to contain a vast labyrinth of passageways, but no one knew how far they extended. Caving expeditions had been offically discouraged after three cavers were lost without a trace in the early seventies.

"Now what about the message on the card? What do you make of it, Shari?"

She repeated the words: "Chemar. Zepheth. Kopher. It's Hebrew. No problem there. But beyond that it's got me stumped. Does it have something to do with Babylon? And there's no signature. No return address. Who could have sent this?"

Murphy gave a half smile. "Come on, Shari. A mysterious message in an ancient langauge? A set of directions to a remote spot? *Babylon?* He didn't really need to sign it, did he?"

Shari sighed. "I guess not. I was just hoping . . . you know, that it might be something else. Not one of these crazy games where you—"

She could tell Murphy wasn't listening anymore. He was studying the map intently, already halfway there. Her heart sank as she realized there was nothing she could do to stop him.

All she could do now was pray.


It had been a beautiful drive from Winston-Salem, past Lake Hickory. He'd left before sunup and covered the 280 miles in good time. Now the bright sunshine at his back was giving way to a sharp chill as he made his way farther into the mountains. He stopped to check the map again and turned down a dirt road that bumped along for a hundred yards or so before he reached a fork. He stopped again. This time the map didn't help. Frowning, he laid it on the dash and stepped out onto the sun-baked dirt. Both roads snaked into the trees in similar fashion.

Then something caught his eye in the thick weeds at the side of the road. He knelt down and cleared away the foliage from a rusting sign. The yellow paint had almost gone, but he could just make out the words: CAVE OF THE WATERS. Then something else, in red paint this time: DANGER.

He carefully raised the sign and stuck it firmly back in the ground. It seemed to be pointing left. "I haven't even got there yet, and already you're playing games, old man," he muttered, slamming the car door shut. He revved the engine and turned up the narrow track.

It took another half hour to arrive at the cave entrance. At first, as the dirt track came to an abrupt stop in front of a huge oak, Murphy suspected another of Methusaleh's tricks. Beyond the oak, the mountainside rose steeply, covered with dense undergrowth. There was no sign to tell him he was at the right place. Searching for a sign to indicate where he was supposed to go, he felt his scalp begin to prickle as the reality of the situation struck him. He was alone. Unarmed. Miles from the nearest habitation. At the invitation of a madman who had tried to kill him on several previous occasions, and who was probably watching him from some hideaway on the mountain at this very moment. He could almost feel the crosshairs moving over his heart.

When you put it like that, it didn't sound good.

But he'd come too far now to think of turning back,

nd he trusted in God that he was doing the right thing. After all, this might be a game, but the stakes were high.

He scanned the mountainside, looking for any irregularity that would indicate the entrance to the cave, and his eyes caught a glint of metal amidst the rocks and scrawny bushes. He squinted into the glare and tried to focus on the spot. Whether it was the cave was another matter, but what choice did he have? He hefted his backpack and started up the slope.

Twenty minutes later he was standing on a horizontal outcrop, wiping the sweat from his eyes and trying to catch his breath. In front of him was a tangle of wire—what had clearly once been a chain-link fence designed to seal off the gaping hole in the rock. He crouched down and gingerly eased himself through the wire, stepping into the mouth of the cave.

He pulled his flashlight out of his backpack and switched it on. The two cardinal rules of cave exploration came unbidden into his mind. Never cave alone, and never cave without three sources of light. *And I guess you could add: Never enter a cave when you know there's a psycho lurking in there somewhere*, he thought.

Although the cave entrance was relatively wide, it quickly narrowed, and Murphy soon had to crawl on his hands and knees over the floor of loose stones and grit. After a few minutes of gentle twists and turns, the only light he could see was the beam of his torch, and the familiar thrill, a unique mix of anxiety and excitement that all speleologists experience on entering a new cave system, took over. He could feel the humidity increasing as the temperature in the cave plummeted. Drops of water from stalactites on the ceiling started falling onto the back of his head and over his face, and he wiped them away with his sleeve. He pushed himself on, despite the soreness in his knees and elbows, hoping the cave wasn't narrowing further. After another ten minutes, he decided to take a breather, easing himself onto his back. Energy conservation was a key element of survival in this kind of unfamiliar environment.

And he needed to keep his wits sharp. He wasn't just dealing with an unmapped cave system, which at any moment could narrow into a stone vise from which he'd never be able to extricate himself or a sheer cliff from which he might plunge into fathomless space. At every step he had to remember why he was here. Methusaleh had planned it all. And that meant there was some artifact of great value for an archaeologist—but especially a Biblical archaeologist—waiting for him at the end of his journey. But Methusaleh wouldn't be content to see him rack up a few scrapes and bruises in search of his prize. For his own insane reasons, Methusaleh required Murphy to risk his life. That was how you played the game.

Taking a deep, calming breath, he rolled back onto his hands and knees and crawled forward. Soon the cave walls started to get higher, and the floor flattened and broadened out. After a few minutes he could walk easily without ducking his head, and then a sudden turn brought him to a large chamber. Playing his flashlight over the walls, he looked for some sign that someone had been here before him. Something out of place, anything that didn't look natural. But all he could see was water glistening on sheer, black walls and a cluster of stalactites hugging the roof over his head.

"No booby traps that I can see," he muttered to himself. "Nothing here that God didn't create, unless I'm much mistaken." So why was his scalp beginning to itch? Why was his unconscious mind telling him something wasn't right?

Then it hit him. It wasn't what he could see. It was what he could hear. Just on the very edge of audibility. A muffled keening, almost a whining sound. Like an animal—maybe more than one animal—in distress. But how could that be? No animal could survive down here—except possibly for bats, and this was too deep even for them, surely.

He moved slowly toward the sound, hefting his flashlight like a weapon, every sense alert for danger. And that was when his feet first touched the wooden planks.


His lungs full of air, Murphy had difficulty pushing himself down into the icy depths of the flooded pit, but after a few powerful strokes, he managed to grab on to a rock projecting off the bottom and took a moment to get his bearings. He could feel the rush of water at his back as it continued to power its way into the cave. He figured that must be where the light, which turned what would have been pitch-black into a ghostly, greenish gloom, was coming from. And the puppies must have been swept in the opposite direction. Then suddenly he felt, rather than saw, the two little bodies sweeping past him. But something about the way the puppies seemed to be pulled through the water gave him hope. It was almost as if they were in a giant bath, and the puppies were being sucked down the plug hole. In which case water was going out of the pit as well as coming in.

Maybe there was a way out after all.

He followed in the direction the puppies had taken, and after a few strokes he could see them, their little bodies churning in the water as dirt and debris streamed toward a narrow gap in the rock wall. He thought of going back to the surface for another breath, then realized that this was his only shot. Either they managed to push their way out now, or they were done for.

Scooping the puppies up and stuffing them back into the front of his jacket, he could feel them squirming in utter panic as the last molecules of oxygen disappeared from their lungs. Finding a handhold on the wall, he braced himself, then kicked his legs forward until his feet disappeared into the crevice. Every instinct told him to get himself back out, to get back to the surface, knowing that he was probably doing no more than wedging himself into a fissure from which there would be no escape, but he grimly forced himself farther in, his feet now above his head, feeling the water pushing past him through the crack.

With a twist of his hips, he corkscrewed farther in, the jagged sides of the opening scraping deep lacerations into his thighs. But he hardly felt the pain. He was a machine now, with just one purpose: to get through to the other side.

As his head entered the fissure, he could feel his lungs about to give out. With his last scrap of willpower he kicked forward, and a giant hand suddenly seemed to be pulling him through from the other side. With a violent wrench, his head bumping roughly against the rock, he was spewed out onto the floor of another chamber, and as the waters still surged over him, he managed at last to take a huge gulp of air—along with a large mouthful of water—into his lungs.

Choking violently, he raised himself onto his hands and knees, and for the first time in what seemed an eternity, his head was fully out of the water, caressed by an icy blast of precious air. And then it was being caressed by two eager pink tongues, as the puppies struggled out of his jacket, yelping with joy as they filled their little lungs, and Murphy found he was gasping, laughing, and crying for joy all at the same time.

Once he had managed to steady his breathing and regain his composure, he tried to take stock of his surroundings. Behind, he could hear the water still pouring through the gap in the rock, but this chamber was thankfully not filling up like the other one. The flood tide remained just a few inches deep and seemed to be draining away through a sinkhole at the other end. For now, at least, they were safe, and Murphy gave silent thanks for their delivery.

That was when he noticed he was shivering uncontrollably. Hypothermia. The chief cause of death among cave explorers. And the subject of a class on wilderness survival he himself had taught. He remembered the young man at the back who had raised his hand at the end of the lecture.

"How long does it take for a person to die of hypothermia?" he asked.

"That depends," Murphy replied, "on how fast your core temperature drops. When it drops to ninety-six degrees, you begin intense shivering. Between ninety-five and ninety-one degrees, the ability to think is reduced. Your speech starts to slur and you become disoriented. As the core temperature drops between ninety and eighty-six, muscle rigidity and amnesia kick in. Pulse and respiration slow, and you get a glassy stare.

Between eighty-five and seventy-seven degrees, death will occur."

That had seemed to impress the questioner. And it impressed Murphy now that he could remember it word for word. So, amnesia hadn't kicked in yet. But it was nothing to get complacent about. The next stage would be when you couldn't think straight anymore, and thinking straight was what he needed to do right now.

He gently pushed one of the pups away as it started gnawing at his wristwatch. How could he think straight when— Of course! "You've got more sense than I have, you clever little pooch," he said happily, touching the button on the side of the Special Forces watch. A small blue light lit up the chamber for a few feet around him. He switched it off again to conserve the battery and tried to think. The water was draining out of the chamber through one exit, but he'd had enough of water for one day. He certainly wasn't going to risk diving into the sinkhole in the hope that he'd emerge into another air pocket. But something else gave him a sliver of hope. The right side of his body was a little colder than the left, and that meant the air must be moving slightly. There was a breeze coming from somewhere, and therefore maybe a route to the surface.

He switched the light on again and swung his wrist in a slow arc around his body. His eye was caught by a narrow pillar of rock in the middle of the cave. Something oddly shaped was perched on the top. He crawled over to it cautiously, herding the puppies in front of him. Reaching up, he ran a hand over the object. It felt like a chunk of some kind of very dense wood, the sort of sea-worn fragment you might find washed up on a beach. Had Methusaleh put this here? Was this what he had come for? Was his prize for risking his life a worthless piece of flotsam?

There was no point speculating about it now. If Methusaleh had finally cracked, that wasn't such a big surprise, and if this was the booby prize, then maybe Murphy deserved it for agreeing to play a madman's game by a madman's rules. He slipped the piece of wood into a pocket in his combat trousers and turned his face back in the direction of the gentle breeze.

"Come on, you guys. Unless you've got a better idea, I think it's time to follow our noses and see if we can get back home."

*Could this piece of wood that Michael Murphy has retrieved lead him to the discovery of one of the greatest artifacts from the Book of Genesis: Noah's Ark?*
*And can Murphy uncover the true secrets behind the deadly evils planned by The Seven?*
*Find out in the next adventure,*
**BABYLON RISING Book 2:**
**THE SECRET ON ARARAT,**
*on sale September 2004,*
*wherever hardcover books are sold.*